PRAISE FOR
ERIC WILSON'S NOVELS

Jerusalem #2

"... easily one of the best and most powerful novels I've read in years."

—TheChristianManifesto.com review of *Field of Blood*

"*Haunt of Jackals* is not just a good novel; it's a crazy, bloody, vampire butt-kicking romp through history, legend, and Wilson's remarkable imagination. What a story! Do yourself a favor and don't miss a single volume of the keep-you-up-all-night Jerusalem's Undead Trilogy."

—Claudia Mair Burney, author of *Deadly Charm*
and *Wounded: A Love Story*

HAUNT

OF

JERUSALEM'S UNDEAD TRILOGY

HAUNT
OF

ERIC WILSON

THOMAS NELSON
Since 1798

NASHVILLE   DALLAS   MEXICO CITY   RIO DE JANEIRO   BEIJING

Published in Nashville, Tennessee, by Thomas Nelson. Thomas Nelson is a registered trademark of Thomas Nelson, Inc.

Page design by Mandi Cofer.

Thomas Nelson, Inc., titles may be purchased in bulk for educational, business, fund-raising, or sales promotional use. For information, please e-mail SpecialMarkets@ThomasNelson.com.

Scriptures are taken from the *Holy Bible*, New Living Translation. © 1996, 2004. Used by permission of Tyndale House Publishers, Inc., Wheaton, Illinois 60189. All rights reserved.

Publisher's Note: This novel is a work of fiction. Names, characters, places, and incidents are either products of the author's imagination or used fictitiously. All characters are fictional, and any similarity to people living or dead is purely coincidental.

Library of Congress Cataloging-in-Publication Data

Wilson, Eric (Eric P.)
  Haunt of jackals / Eric Wilson.
    p. cm. -- (The Jerusalem's undead trilogy ; bk. 2)
  ISBN 1-59554-459-3 (pbk.)
  1. Vampires--Fiction. 2. Jerusalem--Fiction. I. Title.
  PS3623.I583H38 2009
  813'.6--dc22

Printed in the United States of America

09 10 11 12 13 RRD 7 6 5 4 3 2 1

A NOTE FROM
THE AUTHOR

Instead of buying a car during my college years, I used my summers and limited income to explore the world. Many of my stories have grown from my subsequent travels, and the deepest concepts for the Jerusalem's Undead Trilogy came to me while visiting the Holy Land two years ago. Before that, however, ideas were already percolating as I crisscrossed Romania in trains, cars, and buses.

Romania first grabbed hold of my heart in 1972. I was six years old. I later wrote of those experiences in my first published article, "The Robber's Dance." It recounted lessons I'd learned at the hands of local gypsies.

On a subsequent trip in '85, I was comforted by vistas of rugged, snow-dusted mountains as I mourned the death of a close uncle.

My most recent visit occurred in late 2005.

What started as a dream come true—a writers' tour of this beautiful land—soon turned into a nightmare. Treacherous sorts whose motives I still question sapped money, time, and energy as efficiently as any creature I could concoct. A number of my companions and I felt trapped.

One midnight in Bucharest, a decision was made.

It was dark. The streets were empty. A writer friend, Joe, and I had no particular destination in mind, only the knowledge that we had to *get outta there*.

Hefting our belongings, we fled our "captors" on foot, but it wasn't until reaching Elvis's Villa Hostel that we shared a sense of escape.

Such frustrations were offset by the heartwarming friendships I made. In the city of Arad, for example, a former communist official welcomed me for a few nights as a guest in his home. Like many Romanians, he was wary of the vampire stereotypes generated by Bram Stoker's *Dracula*, and told me of the more pertinent issues that sap life from his people.

"In the time of communism," he said, "we were chickens in a coop. After the '89 Revolution tore away our constraints, we weren't sure what to do. We had wings, but we had been trapped so long that we'd forgotten we could fly."

Another man, a worker at an HIV center, let me spend time among the orphans there. Many had been discarded, shut up in closets, shunned by relatives. Pity would do them no good. They needed social skills, work ethics, and genuine friendships.

I played chess with one boy who'd been in trouble with the police. Though his handshake was soft and he would hardly look me in the eye, he seemed to sit up taller with each move. By the end we were laughing like old buddies.

So what is it about the country I love so much?

I can't put a finger on it.

Maybe it's the good food and drink, the traditional costumes and tales, or this generation's fumbling attempts to stay in step with pop culture. There's classic beauty in the architecture. The castles range from resplendent to plain spooky, and the painted monasteries are famous across Europe. From the shores of the Black Sea to the majestic peaks of Transylvania, Romania has so much to offer.

I suppose, though, that the country's primary appeal is found in its constant struggle for survival. It has withstood hordes of invaders and more recent abuses under President Ceausescu. These are hearty folks, resilient, able to weep with those who weep and rejoice with those who rejoice.

My kind of people.

Hopefully you've already met Gina Lazarescu and Cal Nichols and read of their struggle against the Collectors. Their journey's not over yet, and it's my job to guide them along the next portion of the trail.

But don't let me misrepresent myself. I'm often uncertain where a story will take me, and it's been no different with this series.

I sit. I type. It's an act of faith that requires one step, one page, at a time. As a reader you become a partner in the process, allowing the story to come alive in your own heart and mind.

Are you ready, then? Let's do this.

—Eric Wilson, December 2008

To the Intensive Care Team at St. Elizabeth Hospital (Neuwied, Germany):

Your generous hearts and loving hands were a blessing beyond words, and I am so glad to have had some good last days with my mother as a result of your dedication. I'll never forget your hard work, and my door is always open to you.

And to Linda Wilson (mother):

So much of this series came from my talks and travels with you. You were an incredible mom, and I will miss you on this earth.

WHAT CAME BEFORE

The story of Regina Lazarescu, Cal Nichols, and the opposing sets of Jerusalem's Undead began in *Field of Blood*. Those events were dredged from the memories in four separate drops of blood and recorded by an anonymous journaler. *Haunt of Jackals* reveals more of the events captured in those droplets, with the conclusion to come in book three, *Valley of Bones*.

Since days of yore, clusters of Collectors have roamed the earth. They have been called Those Who Hunt by some. Due to their Master's rebellion against the Almighty, they have been Separated from their use of the physical senses, disembodied spirits looking for mortal hosts to both inhabit and infest. They hope to usher in their own brand of Final Vengeance, at which time they will sustain themselves on mankind's torment and blood.

A unique breed of Collectors emerged in 1989 from ancient burial caves beneath the *Akeldama*. This was the very field in which Judas Iscariot took his own life after his betrayal of the Nazarene nearly two thousand years earlier. Filled with enmity, Judas' blood seeped down through the dirt and stained the bones of two households below. Finding unnatural life in their now-polluted corpses, they rose, the Houses of Ariston and Eros, to form the Akeldama Cluster. Undead and immortal, they are able to see things that are dark to mortal eyes, including the letter *Tav* that marks the foreheads of the *Nistarim*.

According to Judaic tradition, the Nistarim are the Concealed Ones, humble souls who shoulder humanity's sorrow and corruption. If even one of them should stumble, another righteous man must step in to take his place or the entire world will collapse. Collectors, particularly those of the Akeldama Cluster, believe Final Vengeance can best be triggered by tearing down these Concealed Ones, either by death or by simply adding to the weight of mankind's iniquity.

Handsome Cal Nichols is one of the original Nistarim. There were thirty-six of them, saints raised from their tombs during the Nazarene's death and resurrection (as recorded in the twenty-seventh chapter of the Gospel of Matthew). For eons they have lived and walked among us. Commissioned to neither give nor take in marriage, they bear sorrows and protect humanity. They also seek to recruit Those Who Resist, men and women who find life in the Nazarene Blood while opposing the Master Collector and his legions.

Although Cal retained his immortality, he lost the distinguishing mark on his forehead after turning his back for one night on centuries of servitude. In 1965, in his desire for physical intimacy, he joined himself with a beautiful woman named Nikki Lazarescu. Twins were conceived. Cal now spends his days hoping to alleviate his guilt by raising up future Concealed Ones, regular mortals capable of taking the place of any Nistarim who falls—even as he did.

Cal's daughter, Gina Lazarescu, is unaware of their genetic connection. Due to her heritage, though, she ages at half the usual rate. She is immune to death, so long as she is brought back from that abyss within three days by a drop of Nazarene Blood.

Steeped in fear and superstition, Nikki kept most of this information from her daughter and even tried to bleed out her childhood memories.

Gina knows only that Cal Nichols is a friend of the family and that Collectors have been stalking her in an effort to destroy any who play a role among the Concealed Ones. Though she's been told she has a destiny, her experiences have involved mostly anguish—from early abuse to her son's death to the reluctant separation from her husband, Jed Turney.

At the conclusion of *Field of Blood*, Gina found herself in a secluded Romanian cave, captive to Lord Ariston, leader of the Akeldama Cluster. In a final desperate maneuver, she wrenched her arm free from entwining vines and used their thorns to sever her bonds. She then destroyed Ariston with her dagger "of ancient origin."

She does not know why this weapon succeeded where others might've failed. She does not know what happened to Cal and orphan-boy Dov Amit, who were last seen confronting a bear in the village down the slopes.

She knows only that she is weak and bleeding, yet more determined than ever to protect the helpless from the evil that crouches at their doorsteps.

Thorns will overrun its palaces;
nettles and thistles will grow in its forts.
The ruins will become a haunt for jackals . . .

—ISAIAH 34:13

PROLOGUE

July 1944 —Pisa, Italy

One corpse was all he wanted.

Here in Galileo's birthplace, a stone's throw from the renowned Leaning Tower, marble walkways covered hundreds of skeletons in their tombs. Gothic traceries graced the moon-splashed cloister, and vast frescoes peered through open arches at an inner lawn.

The Collector hovered over the courtyard as he had countless nights before. Even now, the remains he desired lay trapped deep beneath the soil of *el camposanto*.

Campo Santo: the Holy Field.

Seven centuries earlier, Knights Templar had carted shiploads of earth here from Jerusalem, inadvertently transporting bones from the first century AD as well. The mixture of lime and clay was said to disintegrate dead bodies quickly, and in fact the Templars had built a structure in Jerusalem for just that purpose. The ruins of their charnel house still clung to the slopes of the Akeldama, the Field of Blood. Site of Judas Iscariot's death.

So it was, from one field to another, the fabled dirt had come. And Pisan dignitaries paid exorbitant sums to be buried in the Campo Santo, trusting the imported soil to hasten their steps through the pearly gates.

Only death could reveal the validity of those hopes.

A low drone now disrupted the courtyard's stillness, and the Collector came to attention. Was this it, at last? For ages he'd waited, a mere vapor, cut off from the eighteen others in his cluster. Like Collectors everywhere, he had been stripped of his physical senses by the Separation, a punishment triggered by the defiance of the Master Collector.

Master, may you ever walk free of blame.

He knew, though, that a host—whether man or beast—could provide him access to eyes, ears, mouth, nose, and skin; and in the past he'd found willing vessels for his carnal pursuits. It was through their senses he had familiarized himself with Pisa and this Tuscan countryside.

Of course, none of them could equal his current host of choice.

Natira, son of Lord Ariston. A warrior.

His bones, drenched in Judas' profane blood, were those unwittingly barreled and shipped to these distant shores.

Again the Collector detected vibrations in the atmosphere. This time he could not mistake the rumble of approaching Allied planes. He'd most recently inhabited Nazi Doktor Ubelhaar and through the man's eyes marveled at such airborne contraptions. This instant, however, his Separated state allowed him to see only shadows passing across the moon, then objects dropping, erupting across the city in earth-shaking concussions.

Even as flashes of light strafed his monochromatic vision, he filled in the blanks from memory: red-yellow bursts of flame, scorching heat, and bodies split apart like rotten tree stumps.

Yes, these flying machines had been turned into instruments of war. Surely Collectors of Souls had inspired such banality.

To feed, breed, persuade, and possess . . . These were the Collectors' goals, wherever they roamed, and tonight there would be feedings across this land, sustenance gained by unnatural means.

Another machine droned overhead. More droppings.

Wrapped around an arch's mullions, the lone Collector waited. He was powerless to manipulate the physical world, forced to rely on the whims of mankind to unearth the corpse deep beneath this Holy Field.

Please, let this be the night.

His wish was granted with the third wave of bombers.

The explosion tore across the Campo Santo and sent him reeling through the ether. A blaze galloped along the cloister roof and turned its surface to molten lead. Artwork bubbled and seethed on the arcade walls. Considered by many to be the world's most beautiful cemetery, the place became a funeral pyre.

As swirling winds lowered him back to ground level, he had little time to savor the irony that a gruesome fresco, *The Triumph of Death,* had been devastated in only minutes. No, his focus was on the courtyard.

On the dark chasm in the dirt.

On bones that seemed to glow in this Italian firelight.

The Collector slithered toward the raw wound in the Campo Santo's lawn. He settled over Natira's exposed remains, conjuring forces locked in the dormant bloodstains.

Was there anything here? Anyone?

Ah, yes.

A feather of malice tickled the femur, stirring a reaction. A hip bone tumbled over clods of dirt, joined moments later by a pelvis. The Collector seeped into the gathering frame. Sipped of its marrow. Began drawing from the recollections of his soon-to-be-undead habitation.

Not long and he would rise again, stitched together with skin and tissue, infused with the nature of his progenitor.

Master, may the same spirit that cursed the Nazarene dwell in me.

❦

Activated by the Collector within, Natira stumbled past the Romanesque cathedral toward the Arno River. This was a strange new world, and the rush of details disoriented him. Where was his family? Had they already inhabited Jerusalemite hosts, or was he the only one to have risen from that tainted dirt?

First he needed something to wet his parched throat, and then he would join the Nazis in fleeing this attack. All around, others scurried through the bombardment's aftermath, and a wheeled vehicle, a U.S. Army jeep, raced into the square through the Porta di Santa Maria.

These observations passed effortlessly between Collector and host. An excellent sign. Already they were beginning to work as one.

A fleeing BMW motorcycle squealed around a corner, its sidecar painted with the symbol of the German *Wehrmacht*. Perhaps, his Collector realized, Natira could catch a ride and find a way back to the pliable Nazi doctor.

He stepped around a crater in the road and found his senses overwhelmed: strewn bodies and the odors of smoke and burnt flesh.

Mmm. Yes.

His tongue swelled with hunger.

A hand touched his naked shoulder and he pivoted toward a woman in a white outfit. Was that a red cross on her cap? Why wear such a symbol? For Natira it triggered images of Roman torture and crucifixion.

"Dear heart," the woman said, "you need help."

Aided by the Collector, he managed to grasp her meaning, yet his mouth was too dry to respond. He needed a drink. Just one.

"Can you hear me?" she said.

He stared at the throbbing vein in her neck.

"Oh, I bet you were near the blast, weren't you? And look at you, without any clothes." Her hand moved down his arm. "I think you're in shock. Do you feel pain in your ribs, dear? Were you caught beneath the rubble?"

Natira studied his chest and noted a long diagonal scar as well as an odd sunken area, results of old battle wounds. And what was this? His right hand was a giant pincer, bearing only a pinkie finger and thumb. Apparently, some of his bones had gone missing between the Akeldama and Campo Santo. No wonder his breathing felt irregular—if, indeed, breathing was what this was called. More like the fanning of air over stale bones.

"Please," the nurse said. "Come along, and let me help you."

Natira stiffened with desire.

"But we can't dally. You're not the only one who needs taking care of."

Natira felt certain he could take care of himself. His lips curled back, making room for crooked incisors that jutted from tender gums. She was right. He should not delay this any longer.

Driven by thirst, he drew her into an embrace and drained her dry.

THE FIRST TASTE:
EX CRUCIO

*One of white's pieces is in check! . . . it becomes easier
to conquer if the forces are split and in confusion.*

—STEPHEN KING, *'SALEM'S LOT*

These people are the ones who are creating divisions among you.

—JUDE 1:19

Journal Entry

July 6, 2010—Lummi Island

Instinct tells me to stay hidden, but I feel helpless and alone here on this island. Am I supposed to just sit around waiting to die?

I've decided that on my way to the ferry crossing I'm going to hide something in the church graveyard. At least that way, in case I don't make it far, the police'll find proof I was here. I'm convinced Those Who Hunt are after me. But if I decide to just hide, to do nothing, won't that be the same as joining in their schemes?

Looking east across Puget Sound, I see the snowy peaks of Washington State, but also signs of civilization. I smell salt water and dead fish in the air. Is that a bad omen?

My troubles started a couple weeks ago when an old Hebrew map showed up in the mail. It was stained with blood. Four droplets. Out of curiosity, I tasted each one and found memories stored there, belonging to Ariston, Erota, Megiste, and . . . Gina? Could she be who she seems? How could that even be possible?

Now, with the ferry ride ahead of me, I can't help wondering where this'll lead. How'll people react when they see me? Am I being lured from safety? I've got the map here in my pocket, and I'm tempted to search for more clues—you know, let my saliva seep back down into these crusty stains.

Last time I tried this, it stirred all sorts of images. Maybe this time around I'll find deeper secrets and answers to my questions.

Here goes nothing. Guess it's time to find out.

CHAPTER ONE

April 2000—Zalmoxis Cave, Romania

She was free, for now. The first step . . .

With dagger in hand, Gina Lazarescu faced the cave opening where the sounds of scuffing feet seemed to mark the presence of another. A Collector? One of Jerusalem's Undead?

Bleeding, she stood still and waited.

Drip, drip . . .

White-hot pain was the price of her freedom. Her spring dress displayed splotches of red, while the skin of her left arm hung in ribbons where she'd wrenched loose from razor-edged thorns and reached for her weapon. Moments later she'd sliced through the restraints on her right wrist, then cut the tangle from her throat. A slave no longer to her mother's brand of bitterness.

Or so she wanted to believe.

Either way, she was a Lazarescu—born to work her fingers to the bone, raised to accept life's burdens without complaint.

Drippp . . . drippp . . .

She felt numb, probably going into shock, but there was nothing more the Collectors could do to her. Already they'd stolen the life of her newborn son with a pipe bomb full of nails, and only hours ago they'd desecrated Good Friday by impaling young Petre Podran against the charter bus.

She blinked against that memory. Let the Collectors tear at her neck, her arms. It would be an escape from the images seared into her skull.

When nothing but the wind moaned through the mouth of the cave, she decided she should get going. To stay would be to risk another confrontation.

As Gina moved forward, her vampire captor gasped. She had thrust this blade into his chest and felt it pierce that malignant heart, dropping him where he stood. *"It has its own symbolic power,"* she'd been assured.

Apparently so.

Ariston's last breath now blew like desert heat over desiccated flesh. The contrast to the high-mountain chill caused Gina to shiver, and her earrings trembled against her neck.

"You took it all," she hissed at him. "Isn't that what you wanted?"

She thought of the whisk broom from her childhood chores in the village of Cuvin, and wished she could sweep away these Collectors once and for all. She kicked at the creature, determined to keep him from ever rising again.

A metallic sound rang out.

An old coin.

Kneeling, she ignored crimson drops that pooled at her feet and took hold of the object that had rolled from Ariston's clothes. Words ran along the circumference, encircling a Maltese cross. She'd seen the cross in history books, embroidered on Knights Templar vestments. It was similar to the letter Tav.

She'd once borne that symbol on her own forehead while carrying her son in the womb. She'd been told that in Hebrew it signified salvation, that it marked her child's purpose. And then . . .

Well, then everything had come undone.

Stay on task here, Gina scolded herself. *Pull it together.*

She suspected Cal Nichols could tell her more about the coin's place of origin, but he wasn't here. He'd agreed to meet her in Bucharest when this was over, and that now became her goal. She would proceed on the belief that Cal and young Dov had survived the bear attack at the Sinaia train depot. It was the only thing keeping her upright.

She slipped the coin into the breast pocket of her dress. This time, she was certain she heard footsteps in the musty space.

"Lord Ariston?"

Gina recognized the female voice. Shalom: the sharp-fanged entity who had first carted her up the slope to this spot. The Jewish name borrowed from her human host had nothing to do with peace.

"Father?" Shalom called. "Are you there?"

Gina raised her blade to meet this returning threat, but teetered before a wave of blackness. She braced herself, then eased around a bend in the cavern, stilling her breath and lifting her left arm over her head. She hoped to slow the flow from her wounds, yet the drops kept spilling, warm and sticky, into her hair.

Faint . . . feeling faint. Eyesight blurring.

She had to hold herself together, had to get out of here.

Pebbles scraped along the dirt, and she figured Shalom must've found her father by now. In confirmation, an anguished keening echoed through the subterranean chambers, indication of the Collector's conflict between her own rapacious nature and the familial concerns of her host.

Gina pressed further back and bumped into a pair of makeshift coffins. Dust quavered along the lids, and the smell of rot rose from fissures in the wood. From what she understood, these Akeldama Collectors had no fear of the sun, no need for Dracula-styled naps in felt-lined caskets. So what was this? Their vampiric burial site?

Murky light from the cave opening revealed names carved into each lid.

Sol and *Eros*.

She'd heard from Cal that the Akeldama Cluster was a union between the Houses of Ariston and Eros. Though unsure of Sol's identity, she knew Ariston lay lifeless only feet away, and here beside her was Eros. Both leaders, fallen. So, then, was this the end of the cluster?

It couldn't be that easy. Nothing ever was.

In Cal's words, she knew she'd fulfilled part of her "destiny," but soon enough a new leader would step in to rechannel the Collectors' hostility.

From around the bend, Shalom's warbling cries turned Gina's knees to water. Her strength was ebbing. She doubted her own ability to put up much of a fight. Not yet. Not with vitality still seeping from her thorn-scoured arm.

If, however, she stayed quiet, maybe the Collector would leave.

Drip, drip . . .

She looked down, and even in the dim light she couldn't miss the trail of red-black circles that betrayed her location.

"Gina?" A low-pitched snarl gave way to a voice of caution. "I know you're there. Come out so we can talk."

"There's nothing to say."

"My father's been banished," Shalom said. "How'd you manage that?"

"C'mon back here and I'll show you." Gina knew that in seconds she would be cornered anyway, and in her present condition she was sure to lose a hand-to-hand battle. Perhaps, if she kept her wounds out of sight, she could ward off her foe with a fearless display.

"I'm not fooled," the she-vampire said. "You're hurt."

"Then c'mon."

"You're trapped. There's no way out but through the front of this cave."

"Why don't you just come end it now? Or are you afraid to fight one-handed. I bet that's it, huh? I saw what happened at the station." A quick image: Shalom sprinting forward, then howling, as one of Cal's metal tent pegs took off her hand at the wrist. "See," Gina said, "that's the problem with relying on a host. You want the full use of the senses, but with it comes a whole world of pain."

"I like pain."

"Must run in the family. Your dad, he just kept begging for more."
Shalom snapped her teeth.

"Maybe Cal could sew your hand back on for you," Gina goaded.
"He only did it because you were trying to kill the kids. Can you blame the
man?"

"Where is he now, do you think?"

"How should I know, since you dragged me off before I could say
proper good-byes? Either way, I'm sure he and the bus of orphans are long
gone."

"He's gone, yes," Shalom said. "Erota destroyed him."

The possibility there was any truth in those words shoved Gina back
against the stone wall. She'd seen Erota attack in the form of a predatory
bear. She could still picture those massive claws and yellowed teeth.

Without Cal, who would there be to guide her through this new para-
digm of bloodthirsty beasts and half-truths? Yes, he'd failed her back in
Chattanooga, but at least he'd tried to warn her. And even though she
questioned his hands-off approach through most of her childhood, none
of it negated her need for him.

"I don't buy it. He's still alive."

"He gave himself up," Shalom said. "We told him we'd kill you
otherwise."

"Is that a fact?" Gina envisioned Cal's waves of wheat-colored hair,
his broad shoulders, the gentle strength in his gold-flecked gaze. Were his
feelings for her personal? He'd seemed to imply as much. Or was he simply
carrying out a duty, an obligation to her?

"And what about Dov?" she added.

"A victim too," Shalom said.

As a Romanian Jew, Gina Lazarescu had grown up with tales of the
Nistarim, the Concealed Ones. They were thirty-six souls, cloaked in humility, who bore the weight of humanity's woes. At age thirteen, a man by
Jewish standards, Dov Amit had been marked with the letter Tav as one of
them.

"You're lying, Shalom. If even one of the Concealed Ones falls without a replacement, the entire world crumbles. Isn't that how the legend goes?"

"Silly stories."

"Then why do you want him so bad? Nope. Dov's still out there."

A raspy snarl.

"I bet he's escaped, hasn't he?"

"Tomorrow's Hope," Shalom said, shifting the focus. "What a ridiculous name for your orphanage. There is no hope for the fatherless. In 1989 we infected many of them with the virus, and—"

"They're just *children*."

"Correct. And already thousands have succumbed."

Gina clenched her jaw. It was true that a unique strain of HIV had ravaged her homeland, taking down the helpless and the weak. "But not Dov," she said.

"We're not done with our infestations."

"Your dear old dad is."

Another snarl, but this time Gina heard rocks shifting. Was the Collector using the growls to disguise a soft-footed approach? Gina flexed her fingers around the dagger's hilt and willed strength into her muscles. She scooted behind the wooden boxes, using the creature's next growl to cover her movements.

"Have you ever tried Nazarene Blood?" she asked.

"What?"

"I hear it's good stuff," she said, trying to buy herself time. Her ruby-orb earrings, a gift from Cal, were said to contain drops of that sacred blood, but she wasn't yet ready to place her trust in such improbabilities.

Shalom sniffed twice. "I don't smell it in you."

Of course not. Gina bore the scars of her mother's religious lunacies, and she'd cut herself loose from that only minutes ago. Doing this on her own terms, thank you very much.

"Well, then." She dropped behind the coffins. "What're you waiting for?"

The Collector rounded the outcropping, eyes glowing like back-lit emeralds. Her undead habitation was unable to regenerate skin and bone, and a cauterized stump was all that remained of her right hand. Her other, however, wielded long, serrated fingernails.

"I won't hurt you," Shalom said. "Not yet. I'd first like to know how you vanquished Lord Ariston. It seems you've thrown our house into disarray."

"Not really my problem."

"I detect an acid tone. We've both lost loved ones, have we not?"

"Life goes on."

"I've heard of the cuttings you endured from your own mother. Let me soothe you. Let me show you the warmth of a woman's touch."

Gina slumped to the ground, pulse fluttering in her temples, vision darkening. Despite her aversion to this enemy, she found herself lulled, beguiled, by the invitation. Warmth. Touch. Could there be anything wrong in that? Emerald eyes, gazing into hers . . . Lean limbs, holding her . . . Elongated nails, tracing her skin and cupping her face as they tilted her head back and . . .

"No!"

She flailed with her blade. Scrambled to a knee. With her spine pressed against the cave wall, she kicked against the nearest coffin and saw splinters fly.

Shalom snickered. "My, you're a feisty one."

Another flurry of kicks compromised the box. Wood cracked, nails pinged against stone, and the casket rolled across loose gravel as though placed on oiled casters. The front end caught Shalom at the knees. She buckled over the lid, face slamming into crude planks, eyes fixing upon the name of the deceased.

"Sol?"

Shalom's nostrils flared as grit from the coffin swirled. Tears welled, then oozed in pale green lines down her cheeks. Her sneer twisted into a frown.

"It's so dry," Shalom gasped. "So . . . so restless."

Gina clambered into a standing position, but the vampire showed no interest. According to Cal, the Restless Desert was a place of banishment, and it seemed Shalom was either grieving Sol's demise or anticipating her own doom. She was still bent over, tips of sable hair brushing the etched wood. Drool spilled from her fangs and sizzled like skillet grease.

Well, Gina figured, let the revenant mourn her comrades. Technically, weren't they all undead anyway?

She made a move toward the Collector, hoping to take off the head at the neck, but her arms hung like lumps of lead at her sides. At her throat, the thorn's root swelled, constricting her breath. Hadn't she cut that away? Apparently, she'd failed to get the last bits of it, and she now felt weakened by it. Her grip on the dagger was tenuous, and another futile stab at the creature might only break the spell and provoke a counterattack.

Knowing her legs were her best allies now, Gina chose flight over fight.

Cal and Dov, please hold on.

She brushed through the cave opening, past a veil of moss and foliage. No doubt, Shalom would come storming after her soon enough. With the coin in her pocket and the weapon back in its sheath on her thigh, she lurched down the slope while a pink-tinged dawn bled through soaring evergreens.

CHAPTER
TWO

Sinaia

For hours, Cal and Dov had battled the bristling monster.

In the shadows of the Bucegi Mastiff, this resort town bordered on one of the richest wildlife regions in Europe. Wealthy Germans with boardroom bellies came to these Carpathian Mountains to hunt tusked and clawed carnivores, while Spanish aristocrats chased down trophies for their Castilian palaces.

Scavenging brown bears, despite their size, preferred easy meals to confrontation, and attacks here on humans were rare.

But this bear was different.

Late last night, Erota had taken up temporary residence in this four-legged beast and charged Cal and Dov from the trees along the train station. She was not just any Collector. Even now, her bones resonated with Judas' blood and her Master's loathing. Whereas most Collectors relied on mere mortal vessels, she and her cluster had gained access to ossuaries beneath Jerusalem's soil.

Nineteen graves . . . emptied.

Nineteen hosts . . . unhallowed and immortal.

Only eighteen revenants had broken free of those burial caves in 1989, but Cal's own memory provided the identity of the nineteenth—a powerful vampire named Natira. How and when he had escaped the Akeldama, Cal was unsure, yet there was no denying the warrior's same spectral qualities.

And hadn't Cal faced off with Natira in the ashes of the Third Reich? Hadn't they collided again years later and halfway around the globe?

Cal's heart twisted with grief.

Don't, he told himself. *Don't let them use sorrow to drag you down.*

He narrowed his eyes. The pavement shook as Erota dropped to all fours and took a swipe at Dov. The teen darted away.

Through the night, Cal and Dov had hurtled their metal tent pegs and watched them career off this bear's thick hide. Now they each had only one MTP left. They held them like knives, hoping to skewer that gargantuan skull. Sisera, a commander from biblical times, had fallen victim in such a manner, and those connected to the Collectors had shown susceptibility to this weapon ever since.

A tent peg. A rustic spike through the temple. So simple, yet Cal knew the meaning went deeper than that.

Working as a team, he and Dov angled in from separate sides for a death blow, while the brute kept them at bay with scimitar-like claws. Cal had already suffered a strike to his thigh. Now Dov caught a cuff to the shoulder that sent him sprawling across the parking lot, and the bear moved to finish him.

Cal stepped into its path. "Don't even think about it."

The beast rose on hind legs, a mountain of muscle and rippling fur. Cal swung his lone MTP, caught an outstretched paw, and watched blood spray the air. He ducked a retaliatory blow, darted ahead, then stabbed at the exposed belly. Felt the spike pierce through.

Erota bellowed. Staggered. In her descent, she bludgeoned Cal to the pavement. She roared in agony and clamped her snout around his head.

The force was incredible. Cal thought his skull would crack, and his scalp seemed to peel away in bands of fire-roasted flesh. He knew, though, that Erota's Collector risked ingesting his blood and its potent properties from the Nazarene. If she did so, she would drink judgment unto herself, and to survive another day she would need to keep it from flushing down her gullet.

Cal heard Dov's footsteps.

"Take that!" the kid shouted.

Another roar. And was that the screech of a blackbird?

Though Cal's head was still caught in the jaws, they eased off. The monster's tongue twitched, then lay still along his bloodied hairline.

"Cal." Dov's hands pried at the massive jaws. "Are you okay?"

He grunted in response.

"We have to go. Look, I think a police car's coming down the hill."

Cal rolled free from the bear, pulled himself up on one knee. He didn't have time for explaining this mess to stern-faced officials. He needed to get back to the other orphans, needed to find Gina and implement a plan he had growing in his mind. There was still so much to tell her.

"We can't outrun them," he muttered.

"What about the river?" Dov said.

Cal's head pounded at each point where the teeth had been. Had the pressure done something to his vision? The parking lot seemed not only convex, but tinged in pink. Or maybe that was dawn breaking across the Prahova Valley.

"Do you need me to carry you?"

He waved off Dov's suggestion with a wry chuckle and looked back at the animal on the ground. An MTP was planted in the skull, a silver stalk rising from the soil of a lifeless eye. "You think you got her?"

"She's dead."

"I mean Erota. Think she might've switched hosts?"

Cal had seen it happen before. When a temporary host died, the Collector was left floating, a vapor at the mercy of the wind, unless able to first slip from one vessel to another via eye contact.

"There was a blackbird," Dov said.

"Yeah, I heard it a minute ago." Cal rose to his feet, scanned the sky for feathered possibilities. Erota would want to get back to her permanent human shell, but Cal had no clue where that lay hidden. Probably up there between the wooded slopes and crags.

He gestured at the bear. "Well, Erota's not in *there*, I'll tell you that much. She'll be back soon, hoping for some other way to get to you."

"If the police don't beat her to it."

Sirens wailed and rooftop lights whipped at the trees.

"The river?" Dov said again.

A steep embankment led to white-capped torrents. Not only would they find a quick ride out of here, but a thorough covering of their tracks.

"Yep," Cal said. "That looks like our best bet."

Rapids sucked Cal Nichols down the Prahova River and crashed around his face. He held his breath in the troughs, gasped for air on the crests. His thigh bore claw marks, and his skull still pounded from the immense force exerted by the bear's jaws. At least this spring runoff provided some relief.

Well, lookie here. He'd made it another day. All around, dawn was tinting the valley in hues of gold and dusty rose.

He cast a glance back upstream and saw Dov riding the current on his back, eyes pointed ahead to assess logjams or undercut rocks.

Good deal. The kid was putting his training to use.

Early last year, Cal had worked with this pupil in the remote heart of the Carpathians. Their time had been cut short, but he'd done his best to provide book knowledge, survival skills, and weapons instruction. He'd demanded discipline. Tested endurance. All while easing the pain of his own mistakes.

For centuries, Cal had walked this world alone, shifting identities, nationalities, occupations, and appearances. He and the other Concealed Ones had been raised immortal at the time of Yeshua's resurrection—doubly alive to counter the doubly dead. Strengthened by Nazarene Blood, he'd still let the strain of battle pull at him, dragging him from his purpose toward physical intimacy.

He had fallen. Failed.

Surrendered to the comfort in Nikki Lazarescu's kiss.

The river now gave him a brisk slap to the face, then swept him through a gap in the rocks. He didn't fear for his own life. Though he'd strayed, he remained impervious to the sting of death, and when the time came he would be carted to heaven by otherworldly means, just as Enoch and Elijah.

Dov was another matter. If he died, who would take his place?

Already, with the misery of the world increasing exponentially, other Nistarim stumbled beneath the weight. And as Final Vengeance neared, the attrition rate grew. Cal spent his days seeking out and mentoring those who might fill the Nistarim's shoes. With Jewish ancestry passed through the mother, these male children could be just about anywhere—Marrakech, New York City, or St. Petersburg.

As it stood, Cal believed he knew of another one, humble in spirit, who could step in to fill Dov's shoes, but that particular child was not yet old enough.

And none of it changed Cal's concern for Dov.

Frothy water indicated a submerged boulder ahead. Cal used flexed legs to bounce away from the threat and wondered where this current would lead. If they made it out of here alive, how long till they could reunite with the orphans? In the midst of the battle with Erota, Cal had ordered the orphanage workers, the *muncitors*, to take the bus and children to Bucharest.

As for Gina? She, too, knew to rendezvous in the capital, but would she be able to locate them in a city of two million people?

He had no guarantee she was even alive.

Cal had damaged her trust, and there was so much he wanted to share with her. Nikki, her mother, had insisted that he keep the connections between them secret, wanting not only to hide her shame but to keep her daughter safe. Didn't he deserve some say in the matter, though?

Yes. The next time he saw Gina—if, indeed, the chance ever came—he would tell her everything.

Well, almost everything.

Another slab of granite rose before him. Water flowed through branches gathered there, but he saw he would be trapped by the debris, crushed by the deluge.

He rolled onto his stomach, pulling himself toward the bank with cupped hands and vigorous kicks. Once into a smoother section, he got his feet beneath him. Guessing they'd traveled four or five kilometers from the station, he doubted the authorities would search this far downriver.

"Dov." He looked back. "You've got to get out of that current."

The kid had already flipped over, trying to break free.

"You can do it," Cal yelled.

Despite valiant efforts, the teenager made little progress.

Cal's heart shoved at his ribs, knotted again by a personal grief less than thirty years old. How could he ever forget finding a loved one's body caught in a mid-river entanglement? He'd touched the puckered bite marks that ringed the throat. Seen the wounds, the bruises. The lifeless eyes.

Sure, Cal had struck down numerous Collectors in his day, but he'd never faced a foe like the one that night, the one responsible for his loss.

Natira . . .

A ghoulish abomination.

In 1989, along the Dead Sea's shores, Cal Nichols had discovered another corpse ravaged by similar violence. And yet another, outside Jerusalem's walls, torn open by eighteen distinct bite patterns. He knew then that Natira was not the only one of his kind. Counterfeit life pulsed through these Akeldama Collectors, and Natira was simply the first to have escaped his burial plot.

Of course, this knowledge couldn't blunt Cal's loss.

I'm not going to lose Dov too. Not like this.

He splashed through the shallows, thighs churning up water on his way toward his pupil. The distance was too great, though. Too late to intervene. At this point, only one option remained, something they'd discussed in training yet never practiced due to the risks.

Cal could only pray that Dov remembered. And quickly.

CHAPTER THREE

Gravity pulled Gina down the slope toward the village of Sinaia. Her legs wobbled as she came to a stop beside a knee-deep stream. Sinew and muscle tissue glistened, each laceration burning like lava on her arm.

She scooped handfuls of water to her mouth, shivering in these alpine heights, then rinsed her injuries until bronze skin turned milky blue. Next she cut strips from the hem of her dress, deciding to bind her wounds or risk leaving a bright, red-dotted trail for Shalom to follow. Not to mention that any additional blood loss might prove disastrous all on its own.

Should she sit down to do this? Rest would do her good, right? She fought the overwhelming temptation to curl up on a bed of leaves for a long nap.

Nope. Don't do it.

She knew she might never rise again.

Braced against a fir tree, Gina wrapped her left arm from wrist to bicep. She tied the cloth's corners around a twig, held her breath, then twisted the tourniquet until she could bear it no longer. She had to staunch the flow.

From now on, each throb of pain beneath this wrapping would remind her of the dangers still faced by those she cared about.

If she made it down alive, would she find any other survivors?

Last night, two Collectors had been slain at the train depot. What would authorities deduce from pierced skulls, a severed hand, and globules of crimson and green? It wasn't every day you came across defiled blood and the tears of the undead.

And what about the children of Tomorrow's Hope? Were they still huddled in the bus, or had they been driven to safety?

Oh, God, please don't let anything happen to the kids.

Though Gina had never been a praying woman, the barest glimmer of belief still glowed beneath her cynicism. She reached with her uninjured arm and touched one of her earrings. She thought of Cal's assertion that these innocuous bits of jewelry contained blood from Yeshua, the Nazarene.

Years ago, she had been revived by a drop from the vial that hung around Cal's neck, and he'd told her that deeper cleansing would come if she ever decided to ingest it of her own free will.

A complete transfusion. Renewal. Who wouldn't want that?

Of course, it meant buying into a mentality Gina found disturbing in others. Drinking blood? Identifying with death? These Christian themes seemed outdated. Here in her homeland, superstitions still haunted the minds of the uneducated, while TV personalities and pulpit-pounders in America used newer forms of fear to manipulate the weak.

"One drop is all it takes."

Despite her intellectual objections, that phrase struck a spark of hope somewhere deep in her chest. She had the sense that her heart was a torch waiting to be ignited, and if she would only subject it to the flame, it could illuminate the dark path ahead.

Or it could burn her alive. Reduce her to ashes.

Much easier to trust herself, thank you, than to make a move toward something so cryptic.

She touched the tree trunk at her back, comforted by the feel of rough bark. In her arm, the throbbing was tangible, undeniable. These physical realities would propel her onward.

Finding her balance, she pushed away. She plucked blackberries from a nearby bush and relished the bittersweet flavor as they burst in her mouth. Rather than crossing to the path on the other side of the stream, she veered off into dense woods. Let Shalom assume her tracks had been lost in the water; meanwhile, Gina would widen the gap between them.

The hunter might be slowed for only minutes, though at this point the quarry would take any advantage she could get.

Dov was probably out of earshot amidst the thundering rapids, but that didn't stop Cal from cupping both hands to his mouth and yelling: "Catapult!"

Seconds from impact.

Thrashing water.

"Just do it, Dov! The way we talked about."

The kid turned toward the fast-approaching obstacle. Was he giving up the fight? Accepting his fate? If so, his head would smash into the boulder.

Myriad thoughts flashed through Cal's head. What would happen if Dov were to submerge and never resurface? He bore the Letter. He had stepped in as one of the Concealed Ones. He was mortal, though, despite his divine calling.

Cal's mind flipped back to Gina's run-in with a delivery van, four years ago in Chattanooga. Yes, she'd survived that fatal collision, but then again she was unique, wasn't she? She had a combination of his genes and Nikki's.

Regina Lazarescu . . . *Queen of the Resurrected.*

Being half-immortal, Gina had a three-day window in which to be brought back before the earth would grip her to its bosom.

Dov didn't have that luxury. If he drowned in this river, that was it.

"Hey!" Waist-deep near the shore, Cal waved his arms. "Get *outta* there."

The kid showed no signs of hearing. He was driving his head toward branches and stone, moments from being turned to pulp.

Catapult . . .

Oh, no. Was he actually going to try it?

"Go into it feet first," Cal called across the water. "Push off with your legs."

Old images tugged at his heart—vacant eyes, limp arms, and bloodless lips. He couldn't believe this was happening again, after almost thirty years. He couldn't lose another on his watch.

Doubting the teen could accomplish the untested maneuver, he tried to wave him away from danger. Instead Dov swam forward as though bent on destruction.

No. Please don't . . .

In one fluid motion, Cal's pupil caught a trapped tree limb with his left hand, placed his right on the boulder, and used the river's momentum and his own propulsion to vault clear of the white-speckled waves. He performed a complete flip, coming down with legs spread, arms flailing, on the other side of the granite hurdle. His body plunged beneath the surface, bobbed up for air, dipped again, and came up sputtering.

Dov had made it, actually pulled it off.

The Prahova River wasn't done with him, though, and towed him away.

If Cal had learned anything as a fan of Tolkien's writings, it was this: "fellowship" did not exist when only one person was involved. Strength came in numbers, where two or more joined together. And here in the real world, there was no such thing as He Who Resists or She Who Resists.

It was *They.* Plural. All for one, and one for all.

Okay, kid. Here I come.

Cal Nichols squared his shoulders, drew in a deep breath, and threw himself back into the icy river.

CHAPTER
FOUR

The blackbird was an excitable creature. She'd started her morning early, woken by the chirps of sparrows and thrushes. Not one to lose out on a meal, she had ridden the river breeze in search of mice and carrion, then worked her way up the bank toward the Sinaia train station.

There, she'd seen an awful sight, very upsetting—a bear's bulky form darkening the asphalt.

Careful now, careful.

She'd swept closer and found her gaze drawn to the dying light in the predator's eyes. A startling message, a visual invitation, passed between beast and bird in that second.

Oh, the possibilities. Oh, the dangers, the enticement.

Unblinking, the blackbird opened herself and felt an inky presence rise from the perishing bear into her own flapping frame. She thought briefly, fearfully, that she would plummet from the sky, and then a surge of energy crackled from her pointed beak down to her talons.

My, oh my, wasn't she one of the more intelligent birds around? Very smart, indeed, inhabited now with the essence of Erota's Collector.

Erota? Why, there was a pretty name for a blackbird.

Circling the depot, she noted the carnage and a wafting coppery scent. And what were those shiny pools that sparkled in the dawn? Time to investigate.

No, not now. Cut toward the timberline.

The bird screeched at this conflicting thought. It was not her custom to leave such things unexplored, but here was this presence, this invader within, already making demands.

Don't you see the girl moving through the shadows? That's Gina.

Indeed, there was a chestnut-haired woman coming down the path.

Strengthened by berries, warmed by daybreak, Gina descended the mountain and skirted the town's gabled chalets and grand old hotels. On this sleepy Saturday morning, not many people were up and about. Though she'd seen no signs of Shalom, she suspected the she-vampire was not far behind.

Blue markers pointed to the train depot, guiding Gina through a wooded park and down flights of stone stairs, to the edge of E60, the main road between Bucharest and Brasov.

Her skin tingled. Only hours ago, the Collectors had come through this same stretch of trees for the ambush at the station. A pair of police vehicles now guarded the macabre scene.

Dark smears.

A hand.

A pair of Collector's corpses . . . *Good luck identifying those centuries-old hosts*, she thought.

And a mammoth, ruddy carcass.

The metal protuberance in the brown bear's head told her what she needed to know. Cal and Dov had been victorious. Two against one. Rational humans versus a Collector in an instinct-driven carnivore.

Did this mean Erota was gone for good?

According to Cal, Collectors could be forever undone by MTPs, Gina's dagger, and Nazarene Blood. Nothing else. Was it possible, though, that Erota had transferred from the bear to another host before coming to such an end?

Gina retreated beneath the tree line. Best to be careful. She also wanted to avoid the attention of the officers pacing the pavement.

A blackbird squawked from a nearby pine, then flew off. A Collector, already pinpointing her location?

Despite her many questions and concerns, she sighed in momentary relief. Her men had made it. Strange that she should think of them that way, but it seemed to fit. She had watched over Dov Amit since finding him in one of Arad's city parks last year, and she'd bartered with her own weekly allowance for him to have a spot at the orphanage. As for Cal, he'd been part of her life since her and Nikki's exodus from Cuvin.

Or did their ties go back even further?

She'd always questioned the source of her chess knowledge, and Cal claimed to be the one who'd taught her. Was it true? Had he been there earlier than she remembered, fostering her sense of honor, duty, and combat?

Cal . . . In Romanian: *knight.*

Gina pushed aside thoughts of fairy-tale romance and damsels in distress. That was not her. She was independent, a survivor.

She was also married to Jed Turney, whom she still loved despite the child's loss that had torn them apart. Last she'd heard from him, he was in Oregon with his uncle, Sergeant Turney.

And what about Teodor, her childhood sweetheart? She touched her mouth, where his goat's-milk scented lips had melted into hers on her twelfth birthday.

Cal, Dov, Jed, Teo . . .

Although she would never expect them to understand, she treasured feelings for each one. She was a woman, after all. Her heart had rooms and antechambers, corridors, and closets—some that led nowhere, and others that opened upon other lifetimes, other worlds of possibility. There was no disloyalty or betrayal in that, only the frank realization that certain doors must forever remain locked.

In this moment, however, she had no doubt. Cal and Dov were her priority, and they were still out here somewhere, alive.

For their safety, she knew what she must do.

Obeying orders like a good girl, the blackbird zipped through the treetops and followed the rise of the Bucegi slopes. She passed over cottages, gardens, the steeples of Sinaia Monastery, and a winding walkway that led to Peles Castle. These were some of her favorite feeding places, particularly when tourists flocked, but Erota's Collector drove her on.

There: another woman, hurrying down the mountain path.

It's my companion, Shalom. Go to her.

Very well.

Tell her to keep tracking the girl we saw down near the station.

The blackbird lighted on the dirt, where Shalom started to kick at her, then hesitated. Their eyes locked.

"Erota?" Shalom said.

The bird bobbed her head.

"Have you spotted Gina?"

Answer her, birdbrain, said the Collector. *Show her what you know.*

Limited as this feathered host might be, she was not above a bit of playacting. She hobbled along on her oh-so-shiny talons and dragged a wing across the ground. She hoped she was communicating.

"So Gina made it into town? I suppose she went to the depot, then." Another head bob.

"I'll find her, you can be sure," said Shalom. "She must pay for having destroyed Lord Ariston. Erota, will you join me in the hunt?"

Shake your head like a good bird, then flap your wings.

The blackbird did so.

"I'll assume you're going after Cal and Dov. Very well. Don't fret over me. I'll make certain this time that Gina does not escape."

The bird bowed and twittered in agreement, then rose into the air, propelled by the determination of Erota's Collector. Yes, oh yes, an adventure was underway. How very exciting. So where would they be off to next?

Time to find the man and the boy, the Collector ordered.

A village road wound its way from the center of Sinaia, then dipped through a stand of spruce trees to merge with E60. From a shaded bend, Gina flagged down a white Volvo. She told the driver she was headed to Busteni, the city just up the highway. As she settled into the passenger seat, she spotted a bird in the sideview mirror.

"Busteni? This is no problem. I live there," the woman said. She wore stylish lipstick and blue eye shadow. "But look at you. What has happened to your arm?"

"I fell."

"The fall must've been dramatic, *da?*"

"Yeah, I was . . . I was climbing last night and didn't see a drop-off."

The driver shifted into gear. "Most painful, I should think."

Gina nodded and looked back through the rear window, but the bird had disappeared. Had it flown off to sound the alarm? She hoped so, if it meant leading the Collectors away from her men.

"Are you running from someone?" the driver asked.

"Running? No, I'm . . . I just need some help for my arm."

The woman upshifted. "Let me take you to the clinic."

"Actually, you can just drop me off at Hotel Silva." Gina knew of the place because the orphans had been booked to stay there, along with a scheduled cable car ride and trail hike. "I'm sure the staff doctor can take a look at it."

"What is his name?"

"I . . . I don't know. But I'm sure—"

"*Nu*, not him. I wish to know who did this to you."

"I fell," Gina repeated. "That's all."

"Please." A click of the tongue. "I am Roxana. You must trust me."

"I'm Regina." Gina rolled the *r* of her given Romanian name.

"Regina and Roxana. We could be sisters, da?"

Gina bit her lip and stared off through the window, worried that Roxana's kindness might draw out the whole story, further subjecting the woman to danger. Already she questioned involving this stranger in her troubles.

"I think you were not climbing last night, were you? Even in summer time," Roxana pointed out, "we do not hike these mountains in thin dresses."

"But I—"

"Please, sister. What is the man's name?"

"Whose?"

Roxana tugged on the sleeve of her sweater, uncovering bruises. "I, too, have such problems. Serban is not always a happy husband, particularly when he drinks."

"Your husband did that to you?"

"Phaw. The old mindset is still in place, and neighbors think it none of their business if a man is displeased."

"He shouldn't get away with that."

"It's my fault, they say. I must be stubborn or even unfaithful." Roxana put on a brave grin. "I am punished for something I do not do."

Gina felt indignant. She knew this was not uncommon in her homeland, but that didn't mean it should remain status quo.

"I do not complain," Roxana said, "I have a roof over my head, a car to use."

"That's not the point."

"We know this, you and I. We are women. I speak openly so that you will leave your own man before it's too late. Do not stay trapped as I am."

"You can find help."

"From whom? Government officials, they do not care. Neighbors, they look away." The woman steered left into Busteni, a gateway to alpine meadows and gray-white cliffs. "Regina, you are certain you do not want to go to the clinic?"

"I . . . No, I'll be okay."

"Then you must open the glove box there. Please, take my aspirin with you and let it dull the pain. This I know from experience."

"*Multumesc.*"

To reject Roxana's kindness would've been an insult. Gina rattled a handful of pills into her hand, put two in her mouth and the rest into her pocket, where they clinked against the old coin from the cave.

The Volvo pointed up the road, then circled around to the front of Hotel Silva. Nearby, a line of cable cars rose into low-lying clouds. Gina half hoped to see the orphanage bus in the hotel lot, proof that the past twelve hours had been a terrible nightmare. Such was not the case, though.

"You be safe, Regina."

"You too." Gina opened the passenger door, then turned to meet the driver's eyes. "And don't let Serban hurt you again."

"Serban will do what Serban does."

"But you're not his doormat, you know."

"I do not know *who* I am anymore."

Gina placed a hand on her arm. "You are my sister."

The woman's eyes brimmed with moisture, and she gave a curt nod. "Here," she said, reaching into the backseat. "You should take this also."

"Your coat, Roxana? But I—"

"It's good for this region, very thick. You'll be kept warm."

"Don't you need it?"

"Perhaps you will also find something helpful in the pockets. *Ciao.*"

"Ciao," Gina echoed in farewell.

She watched the brake lights flash, then the Volvo completed its turn down the hill and vanished from sight. She eased into the newly acquired ski jacket, blue with cream accents, and surveyed the road, waiting—for what, she was not sure.

Sable-haired Shalom? A secondary animal host?

Shivering, she warmed her hands in the jacket pockets. There she found a small purse, from which she counted out the equivalent of ninety U.S. dollars.

"Roxana." Gina's whisper turned husky. "I'll find a way to pay you back."

She turned to study the Bucegis' lofty outcroppings. Having already survived face-to-face encounters with Ariston and Shalom, a night in a cave, and the shredding of her own skin, she braced herself for what lay ahead.

Curse Judas, the Man from Kerioth. Curse the place of his birth. Wouldn't it be better if he'd never been born? It was his blood, his betrayal, that had invigorated these relentless foes.

Gina sensed things might get worse before the day was done.

CHAPTER
FIVE

Ruins of Kerioth-Hezron, Israel

"Don't worry," Barabbas said. "I won't kill you."

"Urrh-uhhh."

"But I will tear out your tongue if you don't keep quiet."

A gurgle of fear, followed by silence.

"Todah," Barabbas thanked his captive in Hebrew.

Earlier, outside a village to the south, he had caught this fellow injecting a needle into his arm. Drugging methods had evolved over the centuries but the intentions remained the same, and Barabbas felt no sympathy. Instead, he sank jagged teeth into the man's flesh, using the prior needle marks to introduce a poison of his own. Seeds of evil already existed in the bloodstream, but this venom would cause those thorns to grow and proliferate.

Now, with one hand, he dragged his prey along the dry streambed of a *wadi*. The man still lived, barely, the feeble kicks of his heels leaving crimson smears coagulating in the Judean Desert.

For thousands of years, this region had played host to camels, horned ibex, and carrion birds. Hadn't the Nazarene wandered this wilderness, tempted by the Master Collector himself? Barabbas had stood side by side with the alleged messiah, before being released in exchange for the man's crucifixion.

"May his blood be upon our hands," the crowd had shouted.

The burly henchman shook off that memory like a gnat. Muscles bulged beneath his tan shirt as he lugged his victim forward, and a jackal's witchy cries propelled him along until he reached a barren valley.

While the state of Israel, *Ersetz Yisrael*, flourished, this pocket of land continued to wilt. Sand spat against these ruins of former winepresses, houses, and temples. Here was nothing but desolation.

Kerioth-Hezron . . . Birthplace to the Man from Kerioth.

Another eerie cry.

Barabbas knew the scent of blood drew scavengers, but tourists posed an even greater concern. Although few blundered this way, the ones who did were often adventurers more likely to investigate the terrain's inconsistencies.

"Domna," he ordered, "go back and clean up after me."

Standing guard, the female Collector started to say something, then thought better of it. She nodded and trotted off.

Barabbas hauled his morning catch toward a cleft in the rock. There, Megiste met him with auburn hair coiled about her alabaster face. The former priestess had taken over the House of Eros and led them back to this Israeli wasteland. They were Akeldama Collectors, a splinter group answering to no one, with their energies now centered on the Nistarim's imminent downfall. Bit by bloody bit, they did their part.

She smiled. "My dear, you look truly *delicious* in this heat."

"It's not even summer yet."

"An unseasonably warm day, and for that I am thankful." She took hold of the captive's hair, looked the man over, then let him thud to the ground. The sound of skull hitting stone was the same as knuckles knocking cantaloupe at the local *souk*. "Of course, tapping this fellow's veins should thaw my chilly bones."

"I knew you'd be pleased. He matched at least two of your conditions."

"Mine? No, the list is the Almighty's, straight from His own vile book: 'six . . . no, seven things the Lord detests.' And He cannot deny His own words, can He? Why, Barabbas, that's what makes them so unblessedly potent."

"How many more bodies will it take?"

"For our masterpiece? Oh, my dear, do not grow weary in hell's doing. Wherever the Concealed Ones may be, they cannot hide from the misery we wreak." Megiste worked fingers under his shirt, prodding divots where bullets had once punched past his ribs. "And you *know* the pain I can inflict."

A strange fire ignited in his loins, stoked by his imagination.

"I'm sorry," she said, "but you'll have to wait." She pushed away, kneeling beside the body in the dirt. "For today, *this* fellow should be just what I need."

Nearby, jackals echoed her desire with yelps and fierce howls.

CHAPTER
SIX

Comarnic

Cal's clothes were waterlogged, his wounds wrinkled, and his heart hammered against his ribs. On their backs, he and Dov had braved the turbulence a few more kilometers, until just ahead he saw a bridge carrying a horse-drawn cart. By his guess, they were nearing the town of Comarnic.

"Here," he said. "Let's get out here."

Nowadays, Cal realized, people paid for thrills such as shooting these rapids. He himself had tried some of the more popular extreme sports— bungee jumping and skydiving, for starters—but in his immortal state they seemed self-indulgent. Hadn't he already experienced his share of hair-raising, history-shaping events?

The Concealed Tales . . .

Man, he could fill volumes with the things he had seen.

As the river curved, Cal and Dov flipped onto their stomachs and swam toward the shallows beneath the bridge. They scaled the bank, water eddying about their waists. Their teeth chattered.

Dov pulled damp black hair from his eyes. The letter Tav glowed pale blue on his brow. "You okay, Nickel?"

"All in one piece."

Cal's nickname helped pinpoint his latest alias. He'd used many during his earthly sojourn, and although he remained the same underneath, he found it disorienting to be German in one persona, Russian in another, American in the next. He wore dyed brown hair and a mustache as part of his present identity.

"What about you, kid? You did good back there."

"Tried to do what you taught me."

"Well, that catapult was a thing of beauty, but I've got to take off points for you not keeping your toes pointed."

Dov tried to hide his grin.

"I'll cut you some slack," Cal said, "since you kept my head from getting turned to grits."

"Grits?"

"Like oatmeal, only . . . grittier. Hey, you hungry?"

"I can keep going."

"Nah, we've been up all night. No use working on empty stomachs."

"But I thought you didn't need food."

"I don't." Cal peeled off wet clothes and gestured for Dov to do the same. "Let me tell you, though, even the Nazarene enjoyed some broiled fish after coming out of the grave. You really think once you've kicked the bucket, you're done eating and drinking, enjoying all your God-given senses?"

"What about the Separation?"

Cal wrung moisture from his shirt. In his role as a mentor, he never bypassed an opportunity to pass along knowledge. "For the Collectors, it means being cut off from the physical domain—unless they can find a host. As for humans, we just never get the full effect. Our senses and spirits are dulled."

"Is that why we're never satisfied?"

"You've noticed that, huh?" Cal pulled his shirt back on, careful to avoid his injuries. "We're all looking through a glass darkly at a whole other realm."

"Sometimes I can feel that darkness."

"Because you're helping hold it at bay."

"Why me, Nickel? I'm nobody. How come the Nazarene doesn't step in?"

"Hey now, He conquered the greatest darkness of all."

Cal watched Dov Amit tug his sock over a foot missing a big toe. He was no pampered fifteen-year-old. Two years ago in Lipova, Dov had struck down his mother's killer and fled his father's into the foothills. He'd survived with a tent and sleeping bag, a stack of family photos, an iron will, and zero emotion. During his exile, he'd lost the toe in a wolf attack, but the wolf had paid an even higher price.

"Listen," Cal said. "One day it'll all be over. The Almighty'll bring about Final Vengeance—on His own terms, not the Collectors'—and justice will be served. Physical and spiritual will reunite, the way they were created to be."

"So food will taste better?"

"Even grits."

"And things'll look brighter?"

"We're talking out of this world. An entire truckload of Day-Glo colors."

"Hmm." Dov stepped from beneath the ramparts and lifted his face into the sunlight cutting over a nearby ridge. "I hope that day comes soon."

"Yeah, well, there's still work to do. Seen any sign of that blackbird yet? Last thing we need is Erota tracking us to Bucharest."

"I've been watching. Nothing's shown us much interest."

"Still doesn't mean we're free and clear." Cal pulled Dov behind thick bushes that hugged the bridge's ramparts. From this position, approaching birds would be visible through the branches. "We'll hide for now, and the next cart that comes along, we'll scoot up the bank and sneak a ride."

"Then what?"

"You tell me. What would you do if you were on your own?"

Dov shrugged. "Find a warm place to sleep. A barn, maybe. And I'd get something to drink."

"There's a river right here. What're you waiting for? Perrier?"

"There could be bacteria," Dov said. His face was a map of green shadows and stippled light. "Plus, I peed in it on my way down."

"Ah-ha. I wondered why the water got warmer."

"Did what I had to do. Isn't that what you taught me, Nickel?"

"Sure." Cal lifted an eyebrow. "If you say so. Hey, since you're so smart, you got any suggestions for dealing with these teeth marks in my scalp?"

Erota's Collector wrestled with annoyance over the blackbird's flighty behavior. She would've preferred her primary host, but her human shell lay high up in the rocks.

Had Cal or Dov seen her exit the bear for the bird? She'd fled the scene before either could identify her latest nesting place. Now she swooped back down upon the station parking lot, over the heads of two police officers. Time to relocate her targets.

Cal Nichols, the fallen.

And Dov Amit, the Nistarim's newest addition.

She'd been so close to destroying the kid, to tearing away one of the pillars of righteousness upon which this world depended. What did the Almighty see in these measly human beings anyhow?

Using the bird's sharp eyes, she followed scuff marks to the river and figured this was where they'd made their getaway. Typical men. Putting their own skins first, abandoning Ms. Lazarescu to another day all by herself—and with Shalom hot on her trail.

Ah, poor Gina.

The Collector combed the area from the air, eyes probing shrubs and trees, shores and shallows. She moved with resolve from the east side of the concourse to the west. Back and forth. Sweeping, sweeping.

The blackbird protested this thoroughness.

Keep looking, the Collector said. *They're along here somewhere. We've disposed of Jacob and Petre, and it's time to add Dov to the list.*

A pair of cars rumbled across the bridge and rained down flecks of gravel.

Huddled beneath the bushes, Cal watched Dov pluck a handful of dandelions and snap the stems, revealing beads of milky salve.

"Here, Nickel. Rub it on your cuts."

"Weeds?"

"They help sanitize."

With eyes pointed upriver, Cal pressed the verdant foliage to his head, felt its moisture cool his wounds. "Feels good."

"My father taught it to me."

Benyamin Amit . . . He'd been patrolling the Dead Sea when a bite-ravaged corpse washed up on the shores at Ein Bokek. It was his report that had triggered Cal's summons to the scene and his conflict with Jerusalem's Undead.

"I liked your dad," Cal said. "Of course, with him being trained by the Israeli police, I'd expect that he knew all sorts of good stuff."

Dov's eyes turned dark, unreadable. Was he thinking about that fateful night at Totorcea Vineyards, when he'd lost both parents. As far as Cal knew, Dov had yet to shed a tear for his family.

"You know," Cal said, "your dad would be proud to see you like this."

"Like what?"

"Refusing to give in to your enemies."

"He should've never brought our family to Romania."

"Probably not."

"Then none of this would've happened. He would still be here."

"Hard to say, isn't it?"

Years earlier, Megiste had overseen the infestation that led to Benyamin's untimely demise. Recently, she'd bent the House of Eros to her will and driven them south again, using Barabbas as her enforcer. And, for a moment, Cal thought of going back to the Dead Sea to search for their hideaway. Had they settled in Jerusalem? In Israeli Arad? As former priestess, Megiste no doubt spent her time concocting new outlets for her household's depravity.

"Thanks for the herbal advice," Cal said to Dov. He edged down soggy pants to apply the salve to abrasions on his thigh. "Feeling better already."

"Will you get scars?"

"With my being immortal, you mean? I'm no Superman." He let the dandelions slip away, then refastened his pants. "I still bleed, feel pain. The Nazarene beat the grave, but His scars didn't go away, did they? He even told Thomas to touch them, just to prove He wasn't some sort of ghost."

Furrows cut across Dov's brow. "I don't like that."

"Like what?"

"We shouldn't have to see them in heaven."

"We might not," Cal conceded. "Maybe scars'll look different to us there—like beauty marks, or the very best sort of tattoos. Maybe each one'll be a symbol for sadnesses we endured here or a reminder of lessons we learned."

"I don't want to see what happened, Nickel. I don't care."

"Is this about your parents?"

Dov hunkered down against the ramparts.

Staring out over the river, Cal pulled his pupil closer to consolidate their body warmth. "Listen," he said. "I used to be a Concealed One. I know what it's like to be alone, to feel the pain of everyone around you. We both saw what happened to Petre last night. You did all you could, you protected Gina, but you'll never forget his loss. It hurts. You think if you even let out a breath, the entire world'll come crashing in on your chest."

Silence.

"It's not easy, is it?"

"Mm-mmm."

"Believe me, I still feel the weight sometimes. I think humans every-where share some of that load. As for Those Who Resist, it's part of our duty to carry one another's burdens. You, though? You're in a special position, Dov. You bear it every minute, every second. You endure."

"I don't *feel* special."

Cal cupped a reassuring hand on Dov's neck. "That's okay."

Through the bushes, a blast of wind clawed at their wet clothing, skeleton fingers imbued with the malice that had long ravaged this region.

"You *are* special, Dov." He pulled the kid closer. "Doesn't matter if you feel anything or not. Emotions? They're just like these dandelions you gave me." He toed the plant stems at their feet. "They'll sprout up all over the place, out of control, and the best thing you can do is pluck them and let them work *for* you."

"It's a flimsy weed."

"Or so I thought, until you showed me otherwise. Here . . ." He fished a braided necklace from under his shirt and gestured for Dov to do the same. "Let's drink. Let's do this in remembrance."

The attached vials contained Nazarene Blood, and precious as the substance was, it never seemed to run dry.

In unison, Cal and Dov partook.

Cal still remembered the first time, two thousand years earlier, that he'd experienced this sensation of vitality and warmth. The Nazarene had not only conquered death, He'd gathered Cal and thirty-five others from their Jerusalemite tombs, asking if they were willing to share the "*wine of My suffering*." When they each gave consent, He told them to "*drink from this cup*," then squeezed blood from nail-scarred hands, one by one upon their tongues.

The life was in the blood, as stated by Mosaic Law . . . life everlasting. And Yeshua's peace came without fear.

"Nickel."

The sound of Cal's nickname tapped at his thoughts.

"Nickel. Do you hear that?"

Cal shook off the swirling recollections. Over the river's din, the clop of horse hooves drifted from the bridge. This was their opportunity.

He scrambled up the embankment with Dov right behind him, and from the cover of a low stone wall they watched a cart draw near. Felled tree limbs and piled brush weighed down the rubber tires. At the front, an old farmer in a felt cap sat hunched with elbows on knees, reins dangling from dirt-caked hands.

"We'll wait till he goes by," Cal said. "Best if he never sees us."

"If we don't go now, *she's* going to see us."

Cal followed Dov's jutting chin and saw a black-feathered wraith rounding the distant bend, growing larger by the second.

Cloppp-clop, cloppp-clop . . .

"Now?"

"Hold on." Cal waited till the bird swooped to investigate a pile of boulders upriver. With her interest diverted, he whispered, "Now. Go, go, *go.*"

CHAPTER
SEVEN

Busteni

Gina strolled into Hotel Silva, past the lobby, day bar, and salon, and found a shop for tourists and guests. More thankful than ever for inexpensive eastern European fashions, she selected the cheapest pair of jeans, hard-soled hiking shoes, and a bargain T-shirt.

She washed up in the lobby restroom. On her lower back, tattooed angel wings spread, stained red by blood that'd dripped down through her garments.

She took another aspirin and redressed her wounds. Then changed clothes, pushing the old ones deep into the wastebasket. Strapped to her shin beneath the jeans, her dagger sat in a leather sheath crafted by Jed. He'd given this gift to her before their exchange of civil vows in '97, the birth of Jacob Lazarescu Turney later that year, and the explosion that had destroyed a section of Erlanger East Medical Clinic.

They'd been so young, in love. Why had they let grief drive a wedge between them?

She longed to have Jed here at her side now. He'd always known how to make her smile, even while leaving socks, cans of Pabst Blue Ribbon, and soggy bowls of Count Chocula cereal scattered about their apartment.

Oh, to have back the harmless vampires, the grocery-store kind.

One little bat, ah-ah-ahhh . . .

The loss of blood must be making her loopy. Risking a peek at herself in the restroom mirror, she saw sallow cheeks and puffy eyes. What a mess.

She pushed fingers through straggles of shoulder-length hair, holding it back so that her earrings pulsed ruby-red in the light. Her neck was still swollen and tinged bluish-green where she had cut away the thorns. Until last night she'd been unaware of—or refused to acknowledge?—their presence beneath her skin, and now they in turn refused to be ignored. Nasty little things.

She scratched the itchy wound, telling herself she was now free.

The sentiment felt forced.

Flipping up the collar of Roxana's jacket to cover the sore, she pasted on a smile and headed for the registration desk.

"Buna dimineata," the hotel clerk greeted her.

"Good morning. I'm here with Tomorrow's Hope Orphanage, and I'm just hoping to check in a little early. Everything should've been paid in advance."

"You are alone?" the clerk said.

Gina couldn't bring herself to answer yes. She simply nodded.

The woman had her sign in before handing over the room key. "Will there be anything else?"

"Yes, I'd like to go up the mountain before the, uh . . . all the children arrive. Do you have our tickets, or should I pick mine up at the cable car?"

"We're holding them here. It was part of the package."

"Great." Gina started to turn away.

"Would you like yours now?"

"Oh. That'd be good." She took the ticket. "I appreciate the help."

She nibbled on fresh fruit and chips from the gift shop while riding the elevator to the fourth floor. The shaded room smelled of smoke and floral deodorizer. She locked the door, then lumped pillows beneath the bedspread until it looked as though a person was resting there. It'd be nice to lie down under those covers herself, but sleep would have to come later.

In her mind's eye, she played all this out like the moves of a chess game. Such vision came naturally to her—attacks, feints, and counterattacks.

Today, she decided, she would attempt a diversion by hiking through the Bucegis. For it to succeed, though, she'd need someone waiting at the other end. Even on the miniature battlefield, the chess pieces—in her native tongue, *piese de sah*—could not work alone. Without help, even the formidable queen was powerless to force an opponent into checkmate.

She peeked through the curtains at the World War I memorial cross, unflinching atop the cliffs. Built in the late 1920s, it had been a gift from Queen Marie to her people. That's what queens did; they served those relying upon them.

Gina felt alone like never before. Cal and Dov faced their own troubles. Her mother lived halfway around the world, untouchable as ever. And Jed, her husband still on paper, was too far away to be of any help.

She had one she could still think of, one she might to turn to.

On the edge of the bed in the dark room, she sat and dialed the phone. "Teodor? This is Gina. Did I wake you up?"

"I was just leaving for the office." He lived in Arad on the country's western edge, but the time zone was the same. "Are you okay?"

"I'm . . ."

"What's wrong? Talk to me."

At the sound of his heartfelt concern, she choked up. "You have work to do. I shouldn't bug you."

"No, Gina. Tell me what's going on. I thought you were supposed to be on a trip with Tomorrow's Hope."

"Yeah, I'm . . . I'm in Busteni now."

"Where are the kids?"

"I don't know."

"A whole busload of orphans, and you don't know? What about Dov?"

She questioned this sudden interest on Teo's part. Was that annoyance in his voice? Gasping as pain coiled around her arm, she closed her eyes and rested her forehead against the wall. "Listen, Teo."

"I'm listening," he said. Then, in a rush: "Should I call the police?"

"I don't think they can help. Not now."

Gina wondered whether she should pull him into this. She still remembered Teo as a kid in Cuvin, cowering in his uncle's presence, yet always showing her kindness. For years he'd watched after her pet, a three-legged dog named Treia.

Although she hated to take advantage of anyone, especially a friend, she could think of no one else who might come to her aid.

"What is it?" Teo pressed.

"Do you have money for a full tank of gas? Maybe two?"

"Is that all you need? You had me scared, Gina. Sure, I'll wire it today."

"Actually, I had something else in mind. Have you ever been to Bran Castle?" She pronounced *bran* so that it sounded like *brawn*.

"Dracula's Castle?"

"Or so they say."

"A tourist trap. There's no proof Vlad ever stayed there more than a night or two. Teutonic Knights first built the place, and it wasn't till years later that Romanians and Hungarians restored it."

"That's not what I asked."

"Forgive me," he said. "I grow tired of foreigners distorting our legends."

Thinking of her mother, Gina said, "Some of our very own people make a good living off such things."

Her head spun with fragmented memories—her sins bled at knife-point, her mother swatting away mosquitoes so that they wouldn't suck dry her daughter's soul. Even now, Nikki gave quasi-spiritual seminars across America, her head wrapped in a gypsy scarf while she spouted her latest slogan: *Let Bygones Be Bye, Gone . . . A session with N. K. Lazarescu.*

"I interrupted you," Teo said. "What did you need?"

"I was hoping . . . Do you think you could you meet me there?"

Even as Gina said it, she imagined steady Teodor—the castle, the rook—sliding across the board's black-and-white squares. In chess terminology: *doubled rooks*, a formation for attack or defense.

"At Bran?" he inquired. "When?"

"Tonight before closing. Unless you're afraid Vlad'll come after you."

"Don't even joke."

"I thought you said you didn't believe in all—"

"What about you?" he said. "How're you going to get there?"

"Over the trails."

"From Busteni? Even for you, that's a good day's hike. Why the rush? Will you be on your own, or do you think you'll have found Dov by then?"

"I . . . I don't know. Please, Teo, just tell me you'll be there."

Comarnic

"Pull your feet in."

"What?"

"Your feet," Cal urged.

They'd eased their weight onto the back of the wagon, taking advantage of the soft rubber tires so as not to draw the elderly farmer's attention. Cal crawled on his belly, leading his pupil deep beneath brush, limbs, and kindling.

"He can't see us back here," Dov said.

"It's the bird I'm worried about, not the ol' coot."

Dov pulled his knees toward his chest. "You're older than he is."

"By millennia or two, which gives me the right to call him an ol' coot."

The cart rattled on. Pine needles and sap grabbed at their still-damp clothing while spiders scurried through the entanglement, roused by these brash upstarts.

"Arachnids." Cal shivered. "Man, I hate them with a passion."

"They can't hurt *you*, of all people."

"Can't kill me, true. But they *can* hurt me. Not to mention they give me the heebie-jeebies."

"Didn't you teach me that most insects, even some spiders, are edible?"

"Only if things get desperate. Crickets and ants? Not bad. Fat chance, though, that you'll find me popping anything with eight legs into my mouth."

"In Cambodia, they eat fried tarantulas for snacks."

"Where'd you hear that?"

"On the Internet, Nickel. You should be more computer savvy."

"Yeah? Well, I like kickin' it old-school."

"Real old-school."

The cart shuddered, jarring loose bark, dust, and twigs. Cal shielded his eyes and held his breath until things settled. He winced as a branch wrenched across his scalp wounds. They traveled on, shaken to and fro by the wagon bed.

The blackbird was thrilled with this new game. Erota's Collector was a bit of a dictator—*oh, bossy, bossy*—but this beat searching for lukewarm roadkill.

She'd started by cruising the riverbanks, darting this way and that in an evasive manner she'd mastered in this hunter's paradise of Prahova Valley, after being shot at and losing a few tail feathers.

Her talons were still so shiny, though. Look at them, just look.

Stop preening. We need to find the man and the boy.

The winged host cawed, then lowered her head, accelerating toward the bridge that was her usual boundary marker. Beyond this point, she often found herself pestered by a cantankerous hawk. She was about to spiral back when she noticed wide wet spots on the rocks.

Take us closer, the Collector commanded.

Flexing her talons, the blackbird followed disrupted vegetation up the embankment. The humans had come this way, but their footprints ended here.

She hopped about. Flexed her neck left, then right.

Ah, there. Grooves cut through the dirt toward sloped pastures and a distant ridge, and she once again took flight.

Cal spotted the approaching blackbird through tangled limbs. "Okay, Dov," he said in a hushed voice, "you're going to have to stay still."

"What?"

"I don't think we'll pass a close inspection. Not here."

"She's on to us again?"

"Least a bird's better than a bear, right?"

"Either way, we're out of MTPs."

"I've got more back on the bus, but they're just symbols of something greater. You should know that. We've gone over this before."

"I still feel unarmed."

"You do make a point, symbolically speaking. Sit still and cover your eyes." Cal scooped organic debris over the teen's head while the feathered stalker loomed large, beak glistening, talons at the ready.

"Does she see us?"

"Don't look up. Animals can sense when they're being watched. Now give me a few seconds, and I'll be back around."

"What? You can't leave me. Where're you going?"

"Sorry, kid. No time to explain."

Even as Cal uttered the words, boughs and branches shifted over the area where his body had been and collapsed like a net over Dov's youthful frame.

The bird bore down on the traditional horse-drawn wagon. She circled once and took note of the farmer bent, almost asleep, over the reins. With keen eyes, she picked through the layers of piled wood, initially finding nothing of interest.

And then: a lumpy shape in the darkness.

A stump? A mound of leaves?

Put that beak of yours down in there and start tearing.

Tearing? That was a maneuver saved for dead meat. On occasion, the blackbird had nibbled at small forest animals that lay paralyzed yet still breathing and found the meat to be unspoiled, a true delicacy. But she'd never considered preying upon humans before.

Get down there! Drive your beak through the kid's eyes into his brain.

Spurred by indignation, the bird folded back her wings and dive-bombed the cart. With a mandible designed for stripping sinew and flesh, she pecked and heard a groan. The human squirmed, only worsening his predicament.

"Nickel," the kid cried out. "I'm trapped."

Where had the larger man gone? What sort of mammal abandoned its young to an attack?

Another peck. Harder this time. Well, why not? Hawks feasted on whatever they liked. Why should she be the flighty, fearful one? Her beak's tip snared the kid's waving forearm, peeling open the skin as he tried to yank loose.

Make sure not to swallow the blood, the Collector cautioned. *But feed, feed, feed! Tear into the whiny whelp.*

"Nickel!"

CHAPTER EIGHT

Though Cal heard his pupil calling out, the words sounded flattened. Prolonged. Far away. To Cal, time and space were now dimensions without boundaries. He was liquid gel, a shapeless substance, melted down to his base elements, surrendered and malleable.

The faded whisper of his name curled about him, floated through him.

"N-i-c-k-e-l . . ."

It came apart letter by letter, as though each one contained a world of meaning only fathomable at a subatomic level.

"N . . . i . . . c . . . k . . . e . . . l . . ."

And then, in an instant that filled his head with the sounds of booming surf and mallets striking iron, his joints and bones and muscle, inner thoughts and outward clothing, came rushing back together in painless precision. Time reasserted itself as the tightrope upon which he walked, and space was once again a box in which he lived and breathed.

Less than a second had passed.

Dirt. He was on . . .

Furrowed earth received his body beneath the horse-drawn cart. As planned, he'd melted through the planks and rematerialized flat on his back, watching wagon axles pass overhead while sunlight bladed across his vision.

He had done it. He'd bridged the gap between seen and unseen.

For too long, the Separation intended for Collectors and their inflexible Master had also soured this planet's intended delights. Humanity had made its choices, played the accomplice. And only the Unfallen, those heavenly beings who stood faithful at the Almighty's side, functioned fully immune to the accursed divide.

The Nazarene, however, had crossed that chasm. With arms outstretched and fingers clenched in agony, He had drawn the two sides back to center.

He'd risen from His tomb.

Broken bread, eaten meals, and allowed His scars to be examined.

He also walked through walls and defied laws of gravity, free to maneuver between realms of spirit and flesh. In so doing, He granted immortality to the original Nistarim; and, as heirs to such, they had inherited similar abilities.

But bridging did not come naturally.

The first time Cal tried the wall trick, he nearly broke his nose. It was, he learned, more about letting go than about grasping hold of a technique. Even during his mortal days, the same principle had been in place, with enjoyment being a combination of spiritual and physical, most fully appreciated on that edge between control and abandon.

"Nickel, I'm trapped!"

From the hard turf, Cal was now stirred by Dov's pleas. Mere seconds had passed. He also heard flapping wings, tearing skin, and an angry squawk.

He snapped to his feet, took three steps, and leaped onto the tail end of the rolling cart. With her back to him, the bird had fallen into a maniacal frenzy, tearing at the wood to get at Dov underneath.

Cal grabbed a stout birch bough.

Hauled back, took a swing.

Erota's Collector was livid. She could smell the Nazarene Blood in this youth, diluted yet potent, and she found herself mesmerized by the thought of tapping Dov's carotid artery. She might find memories in that gushing liquid, or clues as to the man-child's destination.

But, no. Such a taste would be a ticket to the Restless Desert.

In her human shell, she would've been able to wring the life from his throat with merciless hands; instead, hampered by aviary limitations, she could only hope to drive a beak through his eye socket into the brain.

Maybe it would work. The kid was still trapped and alone.

From the back of the cart, a blow came thundering toward her and knocked her over the edge.

Cawww!

"You okay?" she heard Cal asking the boy.

"Where were you?" Dov fired at him.

"Told you I'd be back. I was just setting a little trap."

The blackbird cawed again, ruffling her feathers. On bruised pinions, she rose to meet Cal and his confounded branch.

From within, Erota's Collector evaluated this scenario. She could read eyes with the same intensity and accuracy of a scholar pouring over ancient texts. She knew when a beast was available to her, when it was open to corruption, but here in Cal Nichols' stare she ran headlong into impenetrable stone.

The bird dodged his wide-arcing swing, felt the hiss of air just over her head, and went in for the injured boy once more. In the moment that Dov tried clambering to his feet, the farmer brought the wagon to a sharp halt. Dov toppled over the buckboard, and the blackbird brushed by, again missing her target.

"Be gone," the farmer barked, swatting his hat at bird and boy. "Gone!"

His words were impotent, though. His felt hat a joke. It was Cal's blow that ended things.

The Collector expected it, but in the commotion—and perhaps in her greed for one morsel from the man-child—the blackbird darted into the club's descending path. Skull-shattering pain exploded through her small body, and then her world ebbed from black into dismal, irreversible gray.

"Get off my cart," the crusty farmer fumed. "Both of you."

"*Te rog,*" Dov pleaded in Romanian. "Please, we only wanted a ride."

"Off!"

"We didn't mean any harm."

From his position in the back, Cal tuned out their exchange and brought down his club once more on their assailant's skull. The air shimmered with bone, feathers, and blood.

He hated killing anything, particularly a forest creature. Sure, even animals manifested varying degrees of ill will, but he wondered if this bird had understood the dangers of welcoming a Collector. For the Nistarim, such questions were too weighty to ignore. Striking without reason, or destroying without soul searching, were sensitive matters for even the most callous of men, and anything less erased the line between Those Who Hunt and Those Who Resist.

A beautiful bird, gone forever . . .

Cal gasped aloud at the sheer waste—and in the midst of that gasp, the falling droplets sprayed his mustache and open lips.

He nearly vomited over the cart's side. His eyes burned at the corners. He never willfully drank the life of any living thing, and he had avoided a vegetarian lifestyle only because of the many customs and cultures he blended in with.

However, these few dribbles did provide information: memories, shards of thought, and illicit motives.

Erota's Collector. Yes, she'd been the one at the helm.

Expelled by the bird's demise, Erota was once again without physical form and unable to initiate visual contact with alternate hosts. She would be forced to maneuver the day's winds in hopes of returning to her permanent vessel . . . tucked away near a ridge not far, according to the info in this blood.

Once there, she would rise and come hunting them again.

They had to get moving, had to find the bus of orphans. For Dov and Gina, of course, there would be no return to the orphanage. They'd been exposed and nothing would ever be the same.

"Off, you hear?" The farmer was still ranting. "Or I will call the *politie*."

"We were cold," Dov said. "See my clothes? They're still damp."

"I don't need your gypsy excuses."

"Gypsy? I'm Jewish."

"I don't care if you're the late Queen Marie's grandson." The farmer slapped at the kid with his hat. "Off you go." *Slap.* "Off."

"We can work for you."

The farmer halted his next blow. "You? You're small."

"I'm strong." Dov glanced at Cal. "Like my father was."

"Even stronger," Cal said. "But I don't know if we have time right now."

"There is work to do. I think you two owe me," the farmer said.

"We have our friends to get back to. They need us."

"These friends, are they in town?" The farmer rubbed his chin as sun wrinkles spread from his eyes. "I am going that way. First, you come to my house, unload this wagon, and then I take you. It will be much quicker."

"You've got a point, I guess."

"And food, *te rog*?" said Dov. "My friend might not need it, but I do."

"Soup? Da. Potatoes? Okay. First, you work."

Dov settled in beside the farmer and looked to Cal for confirmation.

"I suppose we do owe you," Cal told the elderly man. He glanced up the road, where a thatch-roofed cottage crouched in the shadows of a cliff and billowed smoke from a stone chimney. "Is that your place?"

"Ours. It belongs to me and my wife of thirty-five years."

"Congratulations."

Cal made himself as comfortable as possible in the back of the cart. He crushed a spider beneath his heel, then let his thoughts drift.

Thirty-five years . . .

The same time frame since his fall into Nikki's arms and the resulting birth of twins, a baby boy and girl. That girl was Gina, with half-immortal genes woven through her deep-brown eyes and chestnut hair. Aging at half the rate of others, she now appeared seventeen or eighteen; based on her completed school years, she believed herself to be in her early twenties.

His daughter. His blood. His mistake. And, paradoxically, part of his investment in this world's survival.

Assuming she was still alive.

The farmer drew the cart to a halt. "Here we are."

CHAPTER NINE

Bucegi Mountains

Gina sat in one of the red cable cars that lurched its way up the slope. Behind her, a locked hotel room and soft bed ridiculed her decision to leave, but she had a goal. Not only did she intend to mislead the Collectors, she had a rendezvous with Teo at Bran Castle.

What would be her next step from there? Were there doors in her heart still to be opened, feelings to be explored?

Despite Cal's good intentions, she had only narrowly survived these past twenty-four hours, while others had lost their lives. There was no denying the Collectors' gruesome existence, and that made any talk of her own destiny seem like a sick joke.

Mother to the Motherless? Queen of the Resurrected?

Try telling that to the ones I've failed.

For ten minutes now, Gina and a pair of day hikers had been trapped in this compartment, suspended from a wire no thicker than her arm—the injured one, at that. At least it felt better now that it was dried and cleansed. Her natural endorphins, too, seemed to be kicking in.

Through the window, the breathtaking panorama unfolded—soaring granite formations, splashes of bright spring flowers, and pulled-cotton clouds. Far below, shale and boulders coaxed a thin stream between stands of towering conifers. Her focus, though, lay elsewhere.

Was she still being followed? Had the Collectors swallowed the bait?

She pressed against the glass, hoping to be noticed. Any birds of prey looking this way? A sharp-eyed lynx among the trees? Somewhere there must be a creature tuned in to her movements.

Facing her fellow travelers, she heard them discussing an early lunch at the mountaintop *cabana*. Originally built for hunters, such huts now offered food and local drink to tourists and nature lovers.

"First," the man said, "we can hike out to the memorial cross."

"It's too cold."

"Which means . . ." Puffing out his chest, he eyed his blonde escort with a lecherous smirk. "We should be all alone."

That earned him a playful slap. "You never quit, do you, Serban?"

Gina jolted at the name.

"Now let's be nice," he said. "This is our one chance to be together."

Gina bristled at his words. She thought of tender-eyed Roxana and her bruised forearm, of this husband who trusted his culture to excuse his abuse.

"Serban will do what Serban does."

Not today. Not if she could help it.

"Oh, it is you." Gina reached out and touched Serban's wrist. "Didn't we meet at one of Roxana's get-togethers? Perhaps it was Easter of last year."

"What?"

"Roxana. Your wife."

"I know who she is," the man snapped.

"Not that I expect you to remember, but perhaps you recognize this." Gina lifted a sleeve of the ski jacket. "She let me borrow it."

"Is that so? And now you've come to spy on me, no doubt."

"A spy?" The blonde woman turned on Gina. "Is that what you are? Look, we're grown adults, so I suggest keeping your nose out of our affairs."

"Nice choice of words," Gina said.

Serban gripped his escort's shoulder with a hairy hand and lifted the other in Gina's face. Veins snaked along the knuckles, pushing at scabbed sores. "Go on back and tell Roxana what you like. She has no say in how I spend my spare time." He ran his eyes from Gina's full lips to her thighs. "Or, if you'd like, you're more than welcome to come along with us. Really, we don't bite."

His companion started to counter but stayed silent in his grip.

"Tempting," Gina said. "But I've heard about your condition, Serban."

The blonde shot him a glare. He gave a dismissive chuckle, but the anxious flexing of his fist squeezed speckles of pus from beneath his scabs.

"And you're contagious too," Gina said. "Isn't that right?"

"What?"

"That can't be fun. Then again, even school children are warned about being promiscuous."

"What's she talking about, Serban?" the blonde demanded. "Is it in other places, as well? You said it was a rash and nothing more."

"But how . . ." Stammering, he moved toward Gina. "Who told you?"

The carriage bobbed to a halt at the top of the slope and the door opened upon a blustery plateau.

"You just did," she said.

Masquerading as a Tomorrow's Hope muncitor, Shalom had visited the hotel desk and discovered Gina's departure only minutes earlier. Now alone in her own cable car, Shalom stared past jagged rock and spotted her quarry exiting a few cars ahead, followed by two other humans.

Was one of them Serban? Not much of a surprise, actually.

Shalom had made a habit of plundering the local villages, infecting those who flaunted weakness. In the same way that the House of Ariston tended grape trellises at Totorcea Vineyards—plucking, squeezing, crushing—she harvested the veins of those in her personal Collection.

And Serban had been part of their most recent vintage. Was it any wonder the vineyards' wines were growing in popularity, flavored as they were with the blood of the damned?

The idea of again tapping the man thrilled Shalom. With the fluids lost from her severed wrist she could use a warming elixir, even one as thin as his.

More desirous by far, of course, was Gina Lazarescu.

As the cable car swayed the last few meters, Shalom watched Serban shove his escort toward the cabana. Gina was out of sight, a minute or two ahead, but Shalom would soon catch up.

Imbeciles, that's all these two-leggers were. Carbon-based cretins marring their Maker's reflection.

Not that it kept the Almighty from fawning over them. It seemed He was ever extending His kindness, if only so that He could wring blind devotion from them later. Turn them into gutless slaves. Ask them to die to themselves, even as He'd demanded of His own Son.

If true mercy were to be shown, the All-so-wonderful would go ahead and put them out of their misery.

And since He won't, we have to do it for Him.

Coming to a stop, the cable car released Shalom to her task.

⟡

Comarnic

Barnyard smells cut through Cal's ruminations. Alongside the cart, chickens strutted and clucked, while a pair of goats chewed at the grass by the fence. The farmer dropped to the ground and slapped the wagon with his felt hat.

"Get to work, men," he said. "Start unloading."

Cal and Dov followed directions, shouldering kindling and stacking it beneath the cottage's lean-to while the old man ducked indoors to make meal arrangements with the missus.

"Nickel, I saw you swallow that bird's blood," Dov said. "That means you know where Erota's headed, don't you?"

"She's not our concern right now. We're Bucharest-bound."

"We could stop her once and for all." Dov studied the wound on his wrist, then lifted another bundle. "All we have to do is beat her to her human shell."

"There's more where she came from, clusters of Collectors spread out through every city, every nation. Worse than maggots on old meat."

"She's different, though. Part of the Akeldama Cluster."

"Exactly. With her immortal eyes, she can see that Letter on your forehead." Cal wagged a finger at the iridescent mark. "If we go looking for her now, I'd be walking you right into a trap."

"You don't think I'm ready, do you?"

"Don't be ridiculous. I just watched you kill a bear and ride the rapids. You performed a stinkin' catapult, of all things."

"You see?" Dov dumped his armload. "I'm not just a kid anymore."

"I still can't risk losing you."

"Because you can't risk failing again?"

"You know," Cal said, pointing a branch, "for someone who's supposed to be humble, you can be a real pain in the backside."

Dov was undaunted. "If we destroy Erota, we'll have that much less to worry about. How many are still left?"

"From the Akeldama?"

"Mm-hmm."

"Well," Cal said, "their number's been cut to . . . let's see . . ."

He flipped mentally through the list of those who'd emerged from the Field of Blood. In modern terms, he considered himself an intel broker, pooling information so that he might assist Those Who Resist. This particular data he had received from a brave Israel Antiquities Authority woman who'd crawled through burial caves, cataloguing the names engraved upon the ossuaries.

Three chambers. Two households. Nineteen vacated boxes.

House of Ariston

Ariston—Cluster leader, household leader, husband, and father (last seen in these mountains, deceased?)

Shelamzion—Ariston's first wife, mother of Sol, Shalom, and Salome (housed in Lipova, widowed?)

Sol—Ariston and Shelamzion's adult son (deceased)

Natira—Ariston and Helene's adult son (whereabouts unknown)

Shalom—Ariston and Shelamzion's teen daughter (last seen taking Gina hostage in these mountains)

Salome—Ariston and Shelamzion's youngest daughter (deceased?)

Helene—Ariston's second wife, mother of Natira, sister of Dorotheus (housed in Lipova, widowed?)

Auge—Sol's wife, Kyria's mother, daughter of Dorotheus (deceased)

Kyria—Sol and Auge's young daughter (housed in Lipova, orphaned)

Nehemiah—Ariston's brother, Shabtai's father (deceased)

Shabtai—Nehemiah's teen son (housed in Lipova, orphaned)

Matrona—Nehemiah's young daughter (housed in Lipova, orphaned)

House of Eros

Eros—household leader, father of Erota and Domna (deceased)

Hermione—Eros's sister (returned to Israel)

Dorotheus—mother of Eros, Hermione, and Auge, sister of Helene (returned to Israel)

Megiste—Eros's former mistress, household priestess, new household leader (returned to Israel)

Domna—Eros's youngest teen daughter (returned to Israel)

Erota—Eros's oldest teen daughter (here in these mountains)

Barabbas—Ariston's former attendant, new attendant to Megiste (returned to Israel)

Cal gathered more wood. "By my count, we still have twelve to deal with."

"Including Ariston?"

"I'm marking him as a victim to Gina's dagger." Though Cal knew this was presumptive, he had to believe his daughter had survived her encounter with Shalom and Ariston. Any other outcome would be more than he could accept.

"But that only brings it down to fourteen, not twelve."

"Way to stay sharp. As you know, the cluster came this way in '89, with the House of Eros migrating to Ukraine and the House of Ariston setting up camp here in Romania at Totorcea Vineyards. I've linked all the Collectors with names and dimensions from their graves, but it leaves two who never made it this far."

"Who?" Dov asked.

"Ariston's daughter, Salome, for starters. Don't know what happened to her, but I suspect she was banished soon after their rise from the Akeldama."

"And the other?"

"Natira."

"Hmm. It's a pretty name."

"Don't tell *him* that. Judging by his ossuary, he was the biggest of the bunch—a fact I've verified in person. He's scary strong. Imagine the deformed monsters from your dreams and you'll start to have an idea."

"Why would he leave the others? Wasn't Ariston his father?"

"Maybe he got dug up from the Field of Blood, released by accident." Cal led Dov into the sunlight and brushed leaves from his shoulders and hair. "All I know is that he starting hunting me decades ago, stalking my steps. Little by little, he wore me down."

"Natira's the reason you fell?"

"I'm the reason I fell. No excuses. But he destroyed many of those around me, and yes, that left me feeling lonely, like I needed to prove my manhood again. After I got Nikki pregnant, he came to pay me one last visit."

"Where is he now, then?"

"Been trying to figure that out for nearly thirty years. If Ariston's gone, it'll be even more important to find his son, because that puts him in position to lead the cluster."

"He could be dead."

"Undead. Remember, we're not fighting against flesh and blood."

"Sure feels like it sometimes."

"Believe me, the consequences are real. That's why I need to locate him. Even though Natira knows he has a role to play, he can't do so while certain people stand in his path. And if he ever finds out about Gina, he'll tear her apart."

"He doesn't know you have a daughter?"

"Not yet. And I'd rather we keep it that way."

"Well, she's smart. She's a survivor. At the orphanage, she beat me and the other boys at chess with her eyes closed."

"Take no prisoners. That's the way I taught her to play."

Dov brightened. "Which is why we need to go deal with Erota."

"Sorry, not today."

The teen's countenance dropped. "You're afraid."

Cal filled his lungs with the cold air sweeping down the cliffs. His body was young and fit; he loved this planet and its people; yet behind these eyes he was thousands of years old. Some days, he wanted nothing more than to sink into an armchair and drift off to a place without sorrow or pain.

Until then, there was still work to be done. Risk and sacrifice.

In fact, now that he thought about it, maybe there were some benefits in Dov's suggestion. Hmm . . . A little goat's milk. A confrontation. Yep, this might be the opportunity he needed to gather a few clues regarding Natira's whereabouts.

"Listen." He cupped his pupil's neck. "We'll go in and eat, then hitch a ride back across the river. From there, we should be able to find her . . . Okay, okay, don't give me that look. Yes, I'm talking about Erota."

"Really?"

"Really."

"I knew it. I knew you weren't afraid."

"Hold on now. I thought you said that—"

"*I'm* the one." Dov rubbed at the Letter on his brow and shrugged. "Sometimes, I just get worried that I'll . . . that I'm not qualified, not strong enough. Who else do I have, Nickel? If you don't lead, I'm not sure where to go."

"Strength in numbers, kid. Even I need direction."

"So, let's get ready to go collect a Collector."

CHAPTER
TEN

Ruins of Kerioth-Hezron

Like biblical Esau, Barabbas boasted ruddy hair and a wiry beard. Some rabbis believed that Esau had possessed vampiric traits and that his embrace of his brother Jacob had actually been a bite upon the neck, deflected at the last second as the Almighty turned Jacob's skin to marble.

Barabbas found such tales amusing. Given the chance, he'd punch his huge teeth through such a barrier. He stood guard now at the fissure in the rock, half naked in khaki pants, deflecting the spring winds with his broad chest.

"May I go in?" Domna asked.

"She's working alone today," Barabbas said. Tortured screams issued from the earthen chamber, evidence of Megiste's handiwork, and he suspected that even now far-flung Concealed Ones doubled over in parallel pain.

"You wouldn't deny me a little fun, would you?"

"I have my orders."

"Please." The brunette Collector nudged closer on tan legs, her features almost identical to her sister Erota's. As former temple prostitutes, both women had served under Megiste and become well versed in the foibles of men.

"No, Domna."

"You can be such a spoilsport. Are you afraid Megiste will withdraw her intimacies? You know, don't you, that there are younger females for the taking?"

He squared his jaw and stared out over the valley as another scream tore from the cave. Long ago, after his release from Roman chains, he'd been taken in by the House of Ariston as henchman for its less savory errands. Although he stayed true to his household, he'd often noticed Erota and Domna—what male wouldn't?—and here now was an opportunity to do more than stare.

No! For all the salt in Sodom, not today.

With the personal favors he already enjoyed from Megiste, why risk her wrath for a moment of fleeting seduction?

"Domna, you should go," he said.

"You're a strange one," she said.

"It's best that you return to your dwelling."

"Since when does any one Collector stay true to another?"

"It's a question your sister might ask of you."

Domna's backhand raked his bicep. "Erota is no concern of yours. If you remember, she ran off and married an American. She tried striking at the Nistarim without even involving us. I say let her rot, along with Ariston and his entire vineyard. We're better off here with Megiste."

"Which is why I'm asking you to leave."

"Okay then, I guess it's back to my cave I go." She turned and sauntered off, hips swaying. "But at least you know where to find me."

Barabbas couldn't deny his rising desire—he was a Collector in a man's body, after all—but he felt no sympathy for the seventeen-year-old. Despite her pouting tone, Domna's "cave" was more elaborate than the word implied.

Beneath these arid slopes, time and torrential floods had carved out a labyrinth of tunnels and grottos. He and the household's women had fashioned for themselves dwellings adorned with tapestries, carpeted with plush animal skins, and illuminated by tapered beeswax in tall candelabra. They feasted on the flesh and blood of local wildlife and found little need for the electronic luxuries of this modern age. With Megiste at the helm, they imagined themselves bohemians, subsisting off the land as a means of honing artistic focus.

Their canvas: the human condition.

Their palate: the hues of sorrow and sin.

Barabbas and the priestess shared the most extravagant of the caverns, and she provided pleasure in exchange for his strong-armed servitude.

Truly, this was there they belonged—on unholy ground. Hadn't the Man from Kerioth been weaned here? Yes, among these very ruins Judas, that squirmy little pup, had first dreamed of playing a part in something big, and he'd done just that with his kiss of betrayal.

The Nazarene's response?

"Woe to that man . . . better for him if he had not been born."

In days of yore, this place had also been called Hazor—not to be confused with Tel Hazor near Galilee—and Jeremiah declared it would become a *"haunt of jackals, a desolate place forever . . . and no man shall live there."*

Not to worry. Such words failed to account for the undead.

From above, a pebble tumbled past Barabbas' head. He blinked away images of Domna's hips and swiveled to survey the hillside. Only a scurrying lizard, he told himself. And then he spotted shimmers of . . .

Of what?

Capable of seeing beyond the mortal realm, he couldn't shake the sense there was something out there, something that skirted the edges of natural life and took measure of him in silence.

"Megiste," he called through the fissure.

Fading whimpers told him she was ending her session of pain, and he realized how foolish his concerns would sound.

"Barabbas? Did you call? I'm very nearly done."

"I thought I saw something lurking across the slopes."

"Such as?"

"Well, it was . . . it was more a hint of something."

"A hint?" Long ringlets swayed as Megiste poked her head into the open. "What're you saying? It wasn't *him*, was it?"

The henchman shook his head, though he wasn't so sure.

"Because you know what he'll do if he finds us, don't you? He'll try wresting control from our hands, taking credit for all our efforts. Can you imagine the nerve?"

"But he is the rightful heir, the—"

"Yes, yes, the son of Ariston. Natira the brave. All so *dreary*, don't you think? He abandons us in Jerusalem, goes off to chart his own path—more power to him—and in so doing disqualifies himself from any influence within our cluster."

As Ariston's progeny, Natira did indeed have authority over the Houses of Ariston and Eros in accordance with the Collector Procedure Manual. Barabbas, however, took this opportunity to explore another angle. "What if he was never released? He might still be trapped somewhere, unable to break loose."

"Possibly. It's happened to even the most powerful of Collectors."

"You mean the—"

"Don't *even* say it, dear. Don't."

Unspoken was their cluster's one-time entrapment in a herd of swine, with their resulting stampede of humiliation off a nearby cliff. The Nazarene had been the one responsible, casting them with away a word. Could anything be more degrading, more villifying? Particularly before a bunch of kosher-minded Jews?

"The point," Megiste said, "is that, yes, Natira may be out there. If you remember, Ariston had planned to track him, starting with the old coin he found by Natira's ossuary. He was to be assisted by Erota, and I don't believe she'll let go of the matter, considering her personal feelings for Natira during their earthly existences."

Barabbas fought off the genetic holdovers of his own jealousy.

"So we'll stay vigilant, and we'll be on the lookout for Erota as well."

"I can do that," he said.

"Of that I have *nooo* doubt." The priestess touched his cheek. "Come, even among other Collectors, it's been months without a whisper of our long-lost warrior. We'll worry about him tomorrow. For now, won't you join me as I finish up today's work with that perfectly delectable man you brought me?"

"But it's my job to protect the household."

"And you do it fabulously, my dear. *Fabulously.*" Her scarlet-tinged lips brushed his, then let out an airy laugh. "Stop your jabbering and give me a hand, would you? With our list of Six, No, Seven Things, a harvest of desolation is only a matter of time."

It was her velvety voice that undid him.

The bearded henchman squeezed his bare chest through the gap in the rock and stepped into the cavernous chamber where the household's masterwork grew larger by the day. He drew in a breath of repugnance.

But by Sodom's salt, it was beautiful.

Before him spread the collage, seven separate panels, each monstrous in its own way and reeking of human entrails.

CHAPTER
ELEVEN

Bucegi Mountains

The mastiff's top was flat, nearly devoid of vegetation, with trails meandering through sections of rock and snow. Despite the morning chill, sunlight cut in from the east and chased shadows down the valley of this horseshoe-shaped range.

A yellow-and-black sign pointed Gina in the direction of Bran Castle, former toll castle for wayfarers such as herself.

Centuries ago Vlad Tepes had ruled this region, punishing local criminals and crushing foreign invaders with the vengeance of one violated in his youth. He'd butchered some. Beheaded others. Or, for his own dining entertainment, impaled captives on whittled Transylvanian trees.

Vlad the Impaler. Known to some as Dracula.

Although he'd never actually supped from human throats, the prince had used tales of bloodlust to ward off the marauders of his day.

Gina zipped her jacket around her neck and aimed up the gradual incline. Her wound rubbed against the collar, and she longed to be back indoors, warm and safe. By coming out here, she'd advanced a piece

upon her mental chessboard and now wondered whether it was the correct move.

Touch move: once you let go of a piece, you can't take it back.

Okay, then. She'd stick with her plan.

Bucharest had once been known as *Micul Paris*, little Paris, and it was
her rendezvous point with Cal Nichols. At present, she headed in the
opposite direction. There was no way she could risk leading Shalom and
her kin into the city to feed on those Gina loved.

She'd die first, die gladly.

And if possible, take Collectors along with her.

Ahead, the cabana offered shelter. Behind, Serban's and Blondie's voices
carried, still angry and loud.

Although disrupting Serban's licentious ways was paltry compensation
for Roxana's kindness, it was the best Gina could manage under the circumstances. As for Roxana, she would soon have some hard choices to make.

From the cabana a college-aged trio emerged and hefted their packs
before setting off toward the memorial cross. Further on, a family explored
the *Sphinx* and *Babele* formations—*babele* meaning "old ladies," which fit
the sandstone's pockmarked appearance.

It also matched the way Gina felt. Nearing her twenty-third birthday,
she shouldn't feel this tired, should she? This weary of the world?

She ventured a glance back at the arguing couple, and that's when she
spotted the head of sable hair cresting the slope from the cable system.

Shalom!

Drawing her dagger in a flash of silver and brass, Gina dove and
rolled behind a boulder. In her hand, the blade bore nicks and nocks from
ancient battles, a humble object, certainly nothing sleek Kate Beckinsale
would carry for her brand of Hollywood vampire films.

Regina, the Vampire-Huntress . . .

Great. Is that what I've been reduced to?

Gina rose into a crouch, her fingers flexed around the weapon, while
her eyes peeked past tall blades of grass. The she-vampire was gaining
ground.

Comarnic

"Had enough to eat yet, Dov?

In response to Cal's question, Dov grunted and shook his chin from side to side, crumbs spilling as he mopped more bread through egg yolk on his plate.

Despite Gina's work on his manners at the orphanage, he still lacked certain social skills and sat hunched over the table with black hair dangling in his eyes. Earlier he'd dried out his river-damp clothes by the fireplace while the farmer's wife cleansed and wrapped his injured wrist.

The skin was torn . . . In Hebrew: *traife.*

The Torah warned against the eating of torn flesh, and Talmudic wisdom forbade hunting, particularly for sport. Which, Cal figured, pretty much condemned Collectors everywhere. They were called Those Who Hunt for a reason, and their actions led to the detriment of all concerned.

"We should hurry," Cal said. "If we're going to stick to our plan."

"Almost done."

"You would like some more?" the farmer's wife asked Cal.

Cal knew Dov needed sustenance, but food was no longer a necessity for himself. Instead, he savored his sips and bites with sublime abandon. Items avoided during his natural life, such as salts and sugars, now simply dissolved on their way down. With spirit and flesh working in harmony, food and drink had become servants of his will rather than rulers of it.

He patted his stomach. "I'm good."

"And you, Dov?"

"I'll take whatever you want to give."

She beamed. "You're a growing child," she said, dolloping out another helping. With arms thick as her husband's waist, she looked to be a mix of German and Romanian stock. "You need all the food you can get."

"I'll be sixteen soon," Dov said.

"Da." The farmer clapped him on the back. "And with this appetite, I think a man like you will owe us more work."

"He'd love to stay and help," Cal said. "But we need to get moving."

"Bah. It's always hurry, hurry, hurry with you young people."

Cal had to smile at that. If they only knew, if only.

At last Dov pushed away from the table. "*Multumesc pentru tot*," he told the lady of the house. *Thank you for everything.*

"*Cu placere.*" Her eyes glowed above weathered cheeks. *You're welcome.*

The men gathered in the yard. With the cart unloaded, Cal had plenty of leg room in the back. Once across the river, he figured he and Dov would head into the woods to ferret out Erota's human form and hope she didn't get there first. His earlier peek into her memories would guide them.

The farmer crawled into his seat and took the reins.

"Wait, Nickel," Dov said. "You had the hard seat before, so you should take my place up front."

"It's fine. Lookie here, I think you've made a friend for life."

The farmer's wife had puttered from the cottage, her spine bowed from years of manual labor. She bestowed upon Dov a prized can of Coca-Cola, plus homemade sweet rolls wrapped in colorful Romanian cloth. When he tried to decline, she waved in mock annoyance.

She turned next to Cal, handing him a bottle of fresh milk from one of her goats. When she'd offered goodies for the road, this had been his request. Not exactly his favorite, but it would serve a specific purpose—if all went as planned.

"Multumesc," Dov said to her. "You remind me of my mother."

"Is that so? And you remind me of my son."

At this, the farmer adjusted his felt cap and fixed his gaze ahead.

"Son?" Dov said. "Where is he?"

She patted a hand at her heart, and Cal watched Dov's face soften with the compassion of the Nistarim. He thought of butting in, but let the interaction unfold on its own.

"I think he must've loved you very much," Dov said to the woman.

"He was unhappy."

This brought a reproving look from the farmer.

"But it's true," she said. "He died in Constanta. An overdose, according to the politie."

"We don't know that," the farmer said. "He was alone when it happened."

"He was lonely."

"Did we tell him to leave? Nu, he could've been here with us."

"We should've gone looking for him."

"I bet you two were good parents to him," Dov interjected. "Sometimes people don't want to be found."

The farmer studied wisps of clouds to the southeast, mumbling something about inclement weather. His face remained hidden from the others.

Blinking, the wife took Dov's hand in her own wrinkled paw and squeezed. She said, "You come back to see us, da? I will feed you anytime."

"I'd like that."

"We must go now," the farmer said. "Time to be off."

He snapped the reins, and the horse circled onto the road. At the cottage door, the stout woman raised one hand, the other clutched to her bosom.

Cal cushioned the milk jug in his lap against the cart's rough ride. He questioned if he'd made the right decision, aimed back toward the forested ridges. Wouldn't it be wiser to consolidate forces in Bucharest?

No. He steeled his gaze. Time to seize the initiative.

From Anderssen and Alekhine to Fischer and Kasparov, the world's greatest chess players had shown boldness in the face of aggression, putting it all on the line to achieve victory. Up there among the stands of evergreens, a female Collector lay waiting, and he knew he'd have to deal with this queen and her cohorts if he ever hoped to defeat the black king.

Bucegi Mountains

Shalom's legs carried her up the hill, while undead eyes scanned each quadrant of terrain. Though Gina was nowhere to be seen, she couldn't have gone far. Even at a dead run, the girl would be no match for the one now hunting her.

As if to undermine Shalom's smug confidence, hammers began pounding again in her temples, strafing her vision with orange sparks. These blasted headaches, they were symptoms of having occupied a human host. Even more insistent was the pain in her severed wrist, but for this she had a temporary cure.

Still walking, she withdrew her arm from the pocket of her overcoat. She stared at the stump of tendons, epidermis, and bone.

Then plunged fangs into the glistening mass.

Agony exploded up to her shoulder, but she held grimacing lips against the raw meat and worked her cuspids even deeper. Would it be so horrible to devour her own flesh inch by inch? To mix pleasure and pain in one dish?

Like all Collectors, her saliva contained anesthetizing properties meant to shut down a victim's defenses, and after a few moments it accomplished its purpose. A warm sensation oozed from the punctures and through her limb, suppressing neurological responses.

She unlatched her jaws and moved forward with new resolve. She still needed warmth, needed nourishment.

Serban came into view. How serendipitous.

At a standstill on the trail, he sneered as he faced his blonde friend's ire. Veins and sinews popped along his neck, fed by his fury. Shalom had tapped him before, indulging in the domestic violence that was not so uncommon in these parts—all part of the local Collectors' schemes.

"Who are you to complain?" he was saying to the attractive blonde. "I feed you, give you flowers. Even pleasure you."

"Is that what you call it?"

"You've never complained."

"You told me you'd leave her, Serban. Do I look like a woman who's used to sharing?"

"She's my wife. What am I to do?"

"You lied to me, then, is that what you're saying?"

"I'll leave her. I will." He stood taller, scabbed knuckles cracking as he curled his fingers. "All I need is a just little more convincing."

"Convincing?" She slapped him so hard that welts rose on his cheeks.

His leer spread into a greasy smile, then with one hairy fist, he punched her in the face, whipping her jaw back and tumbling her to the dirt. His scabs tore free in the assault. Dry, spiky tendrils spooled from beds of pus, snaked around his clenched hand and slithered up his forearm, with individual thorns hooking into his skin.

The blonde blinked in shock. "That woman was right. You *are* infected."

Serban stared down at the thorns, his eyes first widening with horror then narrowing in grim bemusement. Shalom even heard him chuckle.

These two-leggers, they would never learn.

Caught up in their own drama, the couple ignored Shalom's approach. The Collector marveled that these piteous humans seemed blind to their own sicknesses while so ready to point them out in others. Did the blonde not recognize the vines even now coiling through her oh-so-glorious hair?

Mortal need overrode Shalom's larger goal of destroying Gina. She snatched the tether around Serban's arm and jerked him to his knees. One bite into his neck sedated him; later, when he awakened, his short-term memory would be hazy at best.

Before his escort could escape, she, too, felt the prick of ice-cold incisors.

Sustenance—*ahhh*. And heat—*ah, yes.*

Serban tried to pull free from his captor. "We don't want to . . . be disturbed," he muttered, as though trying to turn a salesman from his door.

"Oh?" Shalom grinned. "I'd say you're quite disturbed."

She dodged the wild swing of his left fist. Already she crouched on his doorstep, so to speak, ready to devour. One quick yank, and his eyes rolled back as he collapsed beside his female companion.

Shalom tugged the brambles through his ruptured knuckles, snapping off their triangular tips one by one. His life force quivered in these thorn-cups, and it filled her with a sense of warmth as it pumped through her fraudulent heart.

Snap, sipppp . . . Snap, sipppp.

Temples throbbed as Shalom tapped the last of his juices. She felt stronger already, and she knew the pesky Ms. Lazarescu was not far ahead. She stood, plotting her best mode of attack.

Back in the cave this morning, she'd caught nightmarish glimpses of the Restless Desert, and she had no desire to follow her father there.

So, then—how to go about this?

Gone was the element of surprise, since Gina may have spotted her. Gone was the hope of direct attack, considering the weapon in Gina's possession. Here, though, was the Collector's advantage: the disguise of a temporary host, thus making an ambush possible.

Run, my little church mouse. Run!

CHAPTER
TWELVE

She'd chickened out, plain and simple.

Gina had seen Shalom's attack near the cabana, but chose not to go to Serban and Blondie's rescue. While the revenant drank her fill, Gina widened the distance between quarry and hunter. Self-preservation kicked into high gear now. She had to reach her Transylvanian destination alive.

Transylvania . . . In Romanian, it meant "across the woods."

Nothing spooky about that.

Regardless, Gina could not deny that real danger existed in this region, just as in the Pacific Northwest that Jed now called home. Collectors ranged far and wide, body thieves set on breeding despair; and at this moment, Shalom hunted somewhere close, chasing her across this mastiff's stony backbone.

Gina's hiking shoes chafed at her ankles, but she could not stop. Her legs churned along the trail's switchbacks, the thunking of her steps stirring thoughts from yesterday.

Yesterday? It seemed a lifetime ago.

On the bus's passage through these mountains, she'd heard villagers hammering on wooden planks—*thunk-thunk, thunk-thunk*—as part of a Good Friday tradition meant to chase off evil spirits. Tomorrow was Easter, and church bells would ring this midnight to celebrate new life and resurrection.

So where did she stand on such matters? If Shalom were to track her down and tear out her throat, what would become of her soul?

In Gina's youth, communists had told the schoolchildren to put faith in reason, in science. Lenin famously called electricity the new god, and teachers professed that such advances would usher in an era free from famine and war. Of course, no such thing had transpired, and she thought it sad how some grew drunk on knowledge while others peddled the "opiate of the people." Hadn't her own mother used religious rituals to subjugate and control?

Gina ignored the throbbing at her neck and kept walking.

Thunk-thunk . . .

She touched her dangling red earrings, filled with Nazarene Blood. For the Collectors, it was death. Whereas for her, it was life.

Three years ago, outside Rembrandt's Coffee House, her mangled body had tasted one drop from Cal's vial, then experienced a revitalizing jolt, the shifting of bones, and the jump-starting of her heart. She'd lifted herself from the pavement and stumbled home.

A miracle by all counts. But what did that really mean?

Cal's explanation was that she was immortal, so long as she stayed connected to the Blood.

Even after her own encounters with it, it all sounded farfetched. What did immortality really matter if she kept losing those close to her? Was it worth spending a hundred lifetimes alone? Better to risk it all than to have Shalom pursuing the men Gina loved.

She ignored the dull ache in her left arm and slid her right hand to the dagger's outline on her shin. Yes. Something tangible. She pivoted and shouted. "Shalom, are you out there?"

Her voice carried across the tundra, bouncing between boulders before dropping over a sun-spangled cliff.

"Shalom!"

A twin-horned chamois eyed Gina from the cliffs, and she thought for a moment it was her foe in disguise. Would the thing bound down and gouge her?

"C'mon!" she called. "Forget the wild goose chase and let's finish this."

She stood ready, weapon in hand. Considering its age, the dagger showed remarkable resistance to oxidation and rust. She touched it to her neck, and her skin writhed beneath the metal.

Impossible. Were these briars edging out from the wound?

With their location now unmasked, the thorns appeared to grow in persistence, and she gritted her teeth as she dug out the latest segment. Like a small bird's nest tinged with blood, it dropped to the ground, and she wondered if its rancidness could be detected in the wind.

Still no sign of Shalom, though.

In the valley below, bushes quivered then fell still, and Gina watched them with a weary eye. When no threat appeared, she blamed it on the wind and faced her westward route. With temperatures dropping here in the lee of Omu Peak, she sheathed her dagger, eased hands into her pockets, and pressed onward.

The farmer dropped off Cal and Dov at the E60 junction, where Easter weekend traffic sped by and tourists snapped photos of Prahova River from a nearby vantage point.

The race was on.

Somewhere among these mountains, Erota's inert human form lay hidden, her Collector probably closing in even now, riding capricious air currents in an effort to get back.

Shading his eyes, Cal scanned the rocky parapets. Again he debated if Bucharest would be the wiser move here. In chess, hadn't he often warned that overextending one's forces could lead to brutal counterattack?

"We can cross after this truck," said Dov.

In that nonchalant statement, the decision was made.

Cal led the dash to the road's other side, then edged through rhododendrons into the woods. He had the bottle of fresh milk as his age-old recipe for interrogation, and before this afternoon was over he hoped to know the whereabouts of his nemesis.

"It's about to get steep," Cal said. "You ready to bust a move?"

"Bust a . . . ?" Dov frowned. "I don't think anyone over thirty should be trying to sound cool."

"Hey, someday you'll be older than me."

"Depends on how you're counting."

"Yeah, well, what can be cooler than eternal youth?" Following the earlier clues from the blackbird's blood, Cal angled through the underbrush in what he believed was the correct direction. "I knew what cool was before most people on this planet were alive."

"That was called the Ice Age, I think."

"Ohh. You think you're stinkin' hilarious, don't you?"

Dov tried to hide his grin. His attempts at humor being rare, he seemed embarrassed by them. "Nickel," he said, "I bet you've never even played a computer game."

"Don't plan on it either. Why stare at a screen when there's real-time adventure all around? I've faced off with vampires and werewolves, run surveillance on Rasputin, helped smuggle Jews out of Nazi prison camps. And that's just for starters. I ever tell you about my escapades near the Pyramids?"

"The actual ones? In Egypt?"

"A very long time ago."

Farther up the slope, foliage and large rocks huddled beneath evergreens. Cal began the arduous climb, expecting his pupil to follow along, and within minutes the stillness of boreal ridges and woods swallowed them.

"I don't think you understand," Dov said, catching up with his mentor. "Games are a training tool."

"Please tell me you're kidding."

"You're the one who tells me to envision myself doing things. 'Without a vision, people perish.' Isn't that how you put it?"

"Doomed without a dream."

"Right." Dov ducked beneath a pine branch. "Take that catapult I did in the river, for example."

"Totally righteous."

Dov groaned.

"A *splendid* bit of water sport," Cal added in his cheesiest British accent.

"You're not listening," Dov said. "What I'm telling you is I used to lie in my tent visualizing that move. When it came to the real thing, in the middle of all that water, I wasn't worried. I knew what to do."

"Which just proves my point. You've got to do it in real time."

"It proves *my* point. Playing computer games is one way some kids keep their dreams alive—being heroic, courageous, all that stuff you talk about."

"You know, Mr. Amit, you have a nasty stubborn streak."

"My mom said every Jewish boy needs a backbone to survive."

"Well, I'm not arguing with Mom. A backbone's a good thing."

"Do you think I'm right, though?" Dov huffed. "About gaming?"

"You're a teenager. Of course you're right."

"I'm serious."

Cal paused beside a boulder. As soon as Dov drew alongside, he locked him in the crook of his arm and mussed his hair. "Yes, you made your point. Guess I never thought about it before, but I suppose it could have some value as a training tool."

"Does that mean you'll try playing one?"

"Don't you remember? No one over thirty should even try being cool. But I will keep what you said in mind. Now"—he released his hold—"no more slacking, okay?"

"Nickel?"

"Yeah?"

"Did you mean what you said, about me being stubborn?"

"Sometimes."

"I'm not trying to be."

"No problem, kid. Now envision keeping up with me."

"You won't do that disappearing trick again, will you?"

"Bridging the Separation? Nah, that wouldn't be fair."

"Unless you wanted to teach it to me."

"Nope." Cal shrugged. "Like I told you, it's not something that can be done in a fully mortal frame—save rare exceptions when the Almighty allows it. Even for me, it can be draining to bridge more than an arm's length or two."

"So that's why you're not bridging ahead?"

"Why would I do that when these ol' legs can beat you up the mountain all by themselves?"

CHAPTER
THIRTEEN

The rock badger was dead. They found the ill-fated thing beneath a limestone overhang, a dribble of dried blood leading back to fang marks on the neck. Even with the day's chill inhibiting decay, a stench wafted from the furry carcass.

"Erota," Cal said. "She must've fed on it last night, before she found that bear to serve her will."

"We're on the right track then. Her host must be hidden up this way."

"Let's keep moving."

"One minute."

Dov breathed through his mouth, his nostrils pinched against the odor. He gathered an armful of leaves and pine needles to cover the animal. It would hold off the eaters of the dead only so long, but it was a show of respect Cal found encouraging from his young ward.

"Okay, let's go," Cal said at last.

The teen stared at the mound, then pulled his eyes away and led the march between fallen, moss-draped logs and treacherous landslides. He pressed on for ten minutes without a word.

Cal found himself admiring this boy who'd lost so much and had so much to give. Dov thought nothing of himself, only of his responsibility. As one of the Nistarim, his days were punctuated by moans and winces, and sometimes he buckled beneath unwitnessed horrors that swelled the veins along his otherwise smooth brow. He never complained. Kept pressing on.

Guess I've done my job, Cal thought. *Not much longer, and I'll need to leave him to his task. There are others to evaluate and mentor.*

From just ahead, Dov's voice was soft. "Why did they kill him?"

"It was a badger, kid. You can't let it—"

"No, that's not what I mean."

"Then what?" Cal came alongside. "What is it?"

Dov breathed through his nose, his lips forming a rigid line as he struggled with something much deeper.

"Your dad?" Cal said at last.

Dov's chest heaved but he said nothing.

This was a subject Cal had tried broaching before, always butting into silence. Even during last year's training, the kid had stayed resolute. Now, the tragedy of a simple forest creature had cracked open the door.

"That's it, isn't it?" Cal breathed. "You're thinking about what happened."

"Why, Nickel? Why him?"

"They're Collectors and Benyamin was in their way. Simple as that."

"But they're the ones who made him come here."

"To Romania, you mean?"

"He told us it was time to relocate. Even though Mom didn't want to leave Israel, he made us move here to this country's city of Arad. Did he want to? No, I think they dragged him here against his will."

"Not exactly."

"But I saw his thorns." Dov's tone dripped acid. "One night after drinking he passed out on the couch, and there they were—thick and crusty, curling out from his heel. There was nothing he could do."

"We all have the Power of Choice, Dov. Even those from the Akeldama can't take that from us."

"They took it from my father."

"This particular cluster seems to be playing by its own rules, doesn't it? A stinkin' mosquito bite, that's all it took to plant the infection in your dad, but it spread through his dependence on alcohol." Cal tried to match Dov's hurried steps. "He had the choice to deal with it. He ignored it."

"Maybe he didn't know."

"I wish that were the case. You know how guys hate going to the doctor? Well, that was your dad. He didn't want help, didn't think he needed it."

"How do you know all this?"

"I was trying to recruit him as one of Those Who Resist. We even met at a café." Cal remembered sitting with Benyamin Amit over iced coffee. Benyamin had remained complacent, even flippant. At last, Cal had reached into his daypack and resorted to the blowing of the *shofar*, the ram's horn, a Hebrew instrument for calling soldiers to battle and sinners to repentance.

"And?" Dov looked up through overhanging leaves.

"He walked out on me. Said he was done playing games."

"Maybe he had it handled."

"You think any of us can fight off infection on our own? Sure, we're blessed with some natural antibodies—an act of grace, as far as I'm concerned—but if we don't deal with Collectors' bites as they come, we're done for. Easy meals. Wilting away and breeding despair like there's no tomorrow."

"So we give up?" Dov balled his hands near his chest, drilled his gaze into his mentor. "Then what's the purpose of even being one of Those Who Resist?"

"Oh, we have to resist. Believe me. We just can't do it alone."

"Yeah, you should know."

"What?"

"Isn't that why *you* fell, Nickel? You were lonely."

Cal swallowed.

"Where were the other Nistarim, I wonder? The Thirty-Six, the Lamed Vov—and you couldn't work with any of them?" Dov was a bull-dog, jaws locked on. "Or maybe you were too stubborn to trust anyone but yourself."

Cal knew his pupil's grief masqueraded as anger, yet he couldn't brush away the accusation. This was an issue Cal had long avoided. How could a man bearing the Letter, resurrected by the Nazarene, lose sight of his own commission? With fellow sojourners at his side and the life force of Yeshua at his disposal, why had he drifted into desperate solitude?

Natira's granite-chiseled face floated into view, those obsidian eyes, and his wide jaws locked onto—

"Listen, Dov. It's not that simple."

"Why do adults always try to complicate things?"

He reached out a hand, which Dov shrugged off. "I guess as you get older the infection spreads. You start believing things that aren't true and doubting things you once would've died for."

"See," Dov seethed. "I think you're still being stubborn."

"But that's not what made me keep to myself."

"What was it then?"

"Fear."

Dov waited for more.

"I was afraid," Cal said, "of letting the other Nistarim down, of being let down. Even with immortal blood, I let this earth start seeping into me again, pulling me apart."

"So then you shouldn't be pointing fingers at my father. Maybe *you* failed, but he could've fought that infection on his own. He was strong."

"Not strong enough, kid. That's my point. If he had been, he—"

Dov's fists shot forward like small battering rams. From his precarious position on the steep grade, he pummeled Cal's ribs, as short cries and grunts burst from his own lungs. Without comment, Cal absorbed the blows. Each was deserved, each a lashing for his own disloyalty in Nikki's arms. Regardless, they wouldn't reinstate the Letter on his forehead or end his self-appointed task of mentoring the next Nistarim. No, he wouldn't get off that easy.

The strikes did, however, bond him with his pupil in shared grief.

As they lost velocity, Cal slipped his arms over Dov's shoulders and pulled him to his chest. For over two years, this teen had been yoked to the world's suffering, bent beneath every injustice and violent act, every hateful word, and the anguish of his parents' loss.

Family . . . That vital cord of fellowship.

Wasn't this the thing both Cal and Dov longed for? Both lacked?

Sobs wracked the young man's body. His hot tears seeped into Cal's shirt while Cal ran a hand through his black hair and whispered soothing words and wished that he had not disqualified himself from sharing in the Nistarim's load.

At the theater, such a moment would've had closure as the final credits rolled; at a restaurant, meals often ended with dessert or a calming beverage. Here, however, life neglected to extend such a luxury. Even as Cal tried to provide comfort, an oily smudge appeared in the trees overhead.

Dov saw it too. "Look," he said, standing straight again, swiping at his face. "I bet that's Erota's Collector, trying to beat us to the punch."

Gina stepped around loose shale and churned down a dip in the path. She still had her afternoon meeting with Teo at Bran Castle, and that meant no delays. A sudden gust pricked the corners of her eyes, and when tears appeared she swiped them away with her right coat sleeve.

Who had time for self-pity? Since when had that been her thing?

As a teenager in Chattanooga, she'd been around for the grunge music of Kurt Cobain and other wrinkled-shirt, middle-class moaners. Her classmates had cranked Discmans to the smells of "teen spirit" and visions of "black-hole sun" while she and Jed shook their heads and played ABBA albums in a more profound show of defiance.

Later, Jed tacked up a Cobain poster in their apartment as a reminder that even riches and fame were no match for self-indulgent gloom.

Yet gloom had become her undeniable foe, while Gina carried her son in the womb. As a rising Concealed One, Jacob shared each spike of his torment with her, and their world became an unstable place.

Through it all, Jed Turney stood beside her: artist, dreamer, boyfriend . . . estranged husband. She remembered sitting together in their High Street apartment, city lights winking through the window while she beat the poor guy at chess—as always—and he'd accepted defeat with grace.

That evening, though, with black-rimmed glasses removed from deep-blue eyes, he conquered her in his own loving way, and she believed in her heart, with that intuition a woman can neither define nor defend, that precious Jacob had been conceived in those moments.

Even now, she could hear Jed's voice, husky in the darkness . . .

"Sweetheart?"

"Yeah?"

"You still awake?"

"Me?" She laughed. "Usually you're the one who falls asleep afterwards."

"I can't."

"This is your way of begging, isn't it?"

"You wish." He gave her a nudge. "No, I keep thinking about this dude that came into the Chamber of Commerce today. He had a dark-gray mark on his forehead, two lines like a cross. He said they were ashes, part of—"

"Ash Wednesday."

"Right. A symbol of repentance, he said."

Gina rolled away onto her hip, arms wrapped around her pillow. "Sounds like something Nikki would be into."

"Yeah, but this guy didn't seem pushy about it."

"What? As in, 'Here, I have some ashes to sell you. Cheap, dirt cheap.'"

"Listen, Gina." Jed's fingers brushed through her hair and lighted on her bare shoulder. "I know the way your mom's screwed with your head, but I can't help thinking this man was onto something. I mean, he seemed okay, looked me in the eye, even thanked me for the work I'd done. Just a regular dude."

"Walking around in public with ashes on his head?"

"Okay, not your average citizen. But he had purpose. Don't you ever wonder about that, if there's something greater we're supposed to be doing?"

She sniffed. She nuzzled against him, taking in his musky sweat mixed with CK One cologne, and hoped he would let the subject go.

At the time she'd known very little about the Nistarim. Invisible to most everyone but her, the letter Tav on her brow hinted at her own greater purpose—for good or evil, she wasn't sure. Her later research had unveiled accounts of such markings, everything from the mark of the beast to the Hindu *tilak* circle to the promise in the book of Revelation that God would mark the foreheads of His faithful ones.

Who, at their core, didn't want to believe they were someone special? But such responsibility raised questions and came at a cost.

For Gina, the cost had been the life of her newborn son.

And later, her marriage.

She promised herself now, high up on this mastiff, that if she survived the day, she would go to see Jed. She'd scrape the money together, book a flight to Portland, Oregon, and hitchhike if necessary—anything to reach him at his uncle's place in the Willamette Valley. It sounded so peaceful. So far from this present turmoil. She imagined a reunion of warm hugs and tearful kisses. Jed would trace the inevitable scars on her arm and call them road maps to better places. He would—

Stop it, Gina. Don't even start.

It was idiocy to dream of such things. She was in her twenties, not some starry-eyed schoolgirl, and they'd been split for nearly a year already.

From the scrub brush to her right came sounds of rolling pebbles and a snapping branch. To her left, a cliff fell away into a ravine.

She turned toward the potential threat, and this time heard a wet guttural sound followed by a snort.

A snort?

The wild boar smashed into Gina's thigh with cannonball force. She'd seen stuffed and mounted specimens in this region, often in excess of two hundred pounds, but she weighed a mere one-twenty. With the hard crown of its head, the muscular thing rammed her to the turf and drove her toward the adjacent ledge.

Pain radiated from her hip. She grabbed at a rock anchored into the soil, felt the boar tumble over her in a rush of foul-smelling fur and sharp hooves. No tusks. Only that long ugly snout with rows of jagged teeth.

Shalom?

It had to be.

Gina pushed herself up on her wrapped arm, triggering a fusillade of agony.

She reached along her right leg for the dagger, aware that the sow had braked and whipped back around. Coming at her, the beast was a blur amid red-black bursts of pain, and Gina fumbled with a pant cuff that had caught on the metal eyelets of her boot.

CHAPTER
FOURTEEN

"Are you certain, Nickel?"

"This is the place. It's gotta be. That cleft in the rock, and all this moss here—I'm sure it's the same ravine that I extracted from her memory."

"So where's Erota?"

Cal scooped a handful of leaves into the air and watched them zip down through this chasm on the Carpathians' eastern fringe. He scoured the rocks, bushes, trees, saw no sign of the inky smear that would indicate Erota's return. Since their first glimpse nearly two hours ago, they'd lost track of her.

At least she was Separated from the senses, meaning she would be coming in blind to Dov and Cal, an airplane in a snowstorm.

"I don't buy that she beat us here," Cal said, "not while fighting that wind. I mean, it could take her all day to work her way up to this spot."

"Well, we did pause for a break."

The kid was right. They'd dipped into the refreshments from the farmer's wife, and Cal still carried three-quarters of a bottle of goat's milk, whereas Dov had polished off his Coke and burped twice to show his pleasure.

"Know what *aura* means in Latin?" Cal asked. "Means 'breeze.' The aura of Erota's host is what's drawing her back this way, and that's exactly what she's at the mercy of—whatever breeze happens to blow her along."

A cold gust ran through Dov's hair.

"Relax," Cal said, chuckling at his wide-eyed expression. "If she makes it this far, I'm sure she'll prefer her own head of hair."

"Is she pretty?"

"Just keep searching, Dov. We're missing something."

"She could be hiding, watching us as we speak."

"Nah, I'd sense those eyes on me. After a couple of centuries you learn to recognize that feeling."

"But I won't get hundreds of years to learn, will I?"

"Hey. Enough of that."

"I'm not afraid to die."

"Let's just make sure you get all the time you're supposed to." Cal ran a hand over his mustache, then set down his glass bottle and picked up a bare branch. He poked it at the foliage. "Don't stop looking. She would've made sure she was well hidden, almost comatose, while away in any temporary hosts."

Dov rolled a fallen log with his shoe. "What's Erota look like? I've never seen her in the flesh."

"All you need to know is that you're looking for a human body."

"Is she wearing clothes?"

Spinning, Cal jabbed his stick at Dov's chest. "Don't even talk like that."

"What?"

"Sure, all of us are drawn to the Collectors' poison in one form or another, same way an addict thinks he can handle his final overdose. But it's sick is what it is. Sickness at its . . . sickest."

"I just wanted to know—"

"Famous last words." Cal jabbed again. "The knowledge of good and evil, that's how this all got started. The Separation divides spirit from flesh"—*jab*—"by tempting you to use either one"—*jab*—"for your own"—*jab*—"selfish needs."

Dov's eyes fell, his arms dangling at his sides.

"You listening to me?"

The teen nodded.

Cal realized that by lashing out from his own regrets he'd probably only intensified Dov's curiosity. He cleared his throat. "You want to know what she looks like? I'll tell you. She's got olive skin, long legs, and almond eyes as seductive as hell. She looks good. Real good. Is that what you wanted to hear?"

Dov swallowed once. "Maybe I was a bit curious."

"You think?"

"How do you know what's going through my head?"

"You're fifteen. No big brainteaser."

"I'm sorry, Nickel."

"It's not like you're the only one. Similar thoughts are what brought me to my knees. I had a commission, straight from the Nazarene—and what'd I do? I squandered it for one night of intimacy."

"The Torah says it's not good for a man to be alone."

"God's very own words."

"But then why couldn't you . . . ?"

"Be with a woman?"

"Mm-hmm."

"I could, while living in old Jerusalem." Cal was still sweeping knee-high bushes, leading Dov forward on their search. "You know I was married then, before I went into the grave."

"Really?"

"You're allowed to do the same, Dov. Being mortal, you're not bound to remain single forever. In fact, most men are stronger with a woman at their side."

Tentative hope sparked in Dov's eyes.

"The lovey-dovey feelings, they get you over the hump," Cal said, "but it's commitment that keeps you there. As for me, I was first spared from judgment during those days of Ezekiel. My wife died, though, and I kicked the bucket a few years later. From there it was a long, long wait for the Nazarene."

"What was her name?"

"Please. No, those're tales for another day. The point is that the Nazarene's resurrection freed me from my grave. He wanted to know if I would serve Him, and how could I say no? I wanted to do whatever He asked, no matter how long it took or what suffering I'd have to endure."

"And you became one of the Concealed Ones."

"Just like you." Cal arched an eyebrow. "Except I was among the originals, doubly alive. The only stipulation: that I remain celibate in my task of guarding Those Who Resist."

"But then Nikki came along."

"And Gina. Despite our failures, the Creator finds ways to bring new life from the midst of death."

"I like Gina."

"Well, don't go getting any ideas. She's about twice as old as you think."

"She's like a big sister to me."

"Good way of looking at it, kid."

Cal planted the branch's tip into the dirt and leaned forward, feeling like an old man with his cane. "You know, I still remember her as a little girl, darling dimples and big brown eyes. She doesn't even know how much I love her."

"Then tell her."

"I did. Once. There's so much more I should say, but her mom's been against it. Going on record right now, that's going to change."

"We'll find her, Nickel. I know we will."

"She's supposed to meet me in Bucharest. We never did hammer out the details, so I can only hope we make the connection."

"You'll think of something. You're Cal, right? The knight."

"Yeah." Cal tapped two fingers against his cheek. "Yeah, that gives me an idea. For now, though, our priority is bagging one of Jerusalem's Undead."

Together, mentor and pupil performed another check of the gully. Dov stopped. Pointed up the flank of the nearest outcropping. From this angle, a mound of collapsed shale and limestone hinted at the belly of a cave.

"Do you think she could be in there?"

Cal stared, wondering how he could've missed it. Now that he was facing that direction, he could hear something restless and diabolical calling to him, kindling doubts he thought he'd put to rest.

"Time to go wake the dead," he said. "And please, no goofy puns."

"Not on your life."

"I'm ignoring that, Dov. Let's go."

Gina fumbled for her dagger.

Although it was possible she'd stirred the rancor of a wild sow, getting too close to its young, she figured a seasoned mother would not have brought offspring so close to known human pathways. She was facing Shalom's Collector. She was sure of it.

The animal grunted. For Gina, the porcine behavior hearkened back to the biblical account of demons tossed into swine. Funny that Shalom would choose, on her own, to inhabit a squinty-eyed boar.

The shame of it, the ignominy.

*Pig*nominy.

Such irreverent thoughts were nothing but a coping mechanism, and Gina's fingers at last found the hilt of her weapon. She rolled to avoid the boar's second charge and drove her hand upward.

The blade impaled the space vacated by the Collector, and then the creature was back upon her. Colliding with the arm Gina had raised in self-defense, coarse bristles that ran from ears to coiled tail drove like splinters through her coat sleeve. She cried out, hating herself for this show of weakness, and heard the weapon clatter from her hand to the ground.

Disoriented, she kicked out with both feet and her heels found their mark in the sow's underbelly. Windmilling her legs, the sow tried to right herself and almost skewed sideways into the void. She rose and shook herself off before launching yet another assault.

Gina was on her knees, still without her weapon. Three times the creature rushed forward, and each time Gina dodged the razored teeth.

"Shalom?"

From within, the Collector's rage blazed green in those close-set eyes. The boar snuffled. Froth lined the dark lips. Moisture shone in both snout holes.

"C'mon, you slobbery hog. What're you waiting for?"

The next charge edged Gina closer to the precipice. She scrabbled in the stubble above the cliff's lip, and one more swipe of that head would send her spiraling down the face of these crags. Unarmed, she had no means of gaining back ground, and the only thing sparing her at the moment was the animal's caution this close to the drop-off. If she came too quickly, the sow would find herself pawing at thin air.

Gina needed her dagger.

The sow also seemed cognizant of the dropped weapon. Between her onslaughts, she angled her body between Gina and the glimmering metal.

Gina positioned herself to parry the next attack. She waited till the boar had fully committed with mouth open and head driving upward, then spun herself away to the left and landed on her good arm. Her enemy's rear hooves drove down into her extended shins and she groaned, but that was immaterial.

Forget the pain.

There was the dagger, only inches from her fingertips.

"You think her human shell's in there?" Dov said.

"I know it. I can feel it."

Cal and Dov groaned in an effort to shift a rock the size of a man.

They'd reached the entrance to the cave only to find themselves blocked by this avalanche of stone. While Cal could defy the Separation, he could not undo the physical properties of other objects, and he estimated it would be hours before he and his pupil could create an adequate crawl hole.

"Maybe this was the bear's cave," Dov said.

"Not a bad guess."

"So it must've had some other way to get out of there. That means Erota might know another way in."

"Makes sense to me. Start looking." Even as the words ran off Cal's tongue, he detected movement from down the slope. He pointed into a stand of birch trees. "You see that?"

"Where?"

"To the left of that overhang. See her fighting the wind?"

A specter moved over the treetops, so faint it could've been mistaken for the gloom of a passing cloud. Though a good distance off, it was coming closer.

"She's almost caught up with us."

Cal turned back to the wall of stone. "I'll have to bridge my way in."

"What if you aim wrong? You'll be stuck in the mountain and it could be hours before you have enough energy to return."

"Are you questioning my driving skills?"

"I'd be left on my own. What if she finds her host and comes after me?"

"You resist. It's what we do."

"What? I couldn't just leave you in there."

"I appreciate that, but someday, Dov, we will have to part ways." Cal glided fingers over a boulder, gauging his next move. "When that happens, Collectors far and wide'll try making you feel isolated. They'll tell you it's about you and only you."

"Divide and conquer."

"Exactly. Worst-case scenario, you fall back on the contingency plans we've talked about."

"Go into hiding. Lay low."

"Bingo. I mean, how else're you gonna live up to your name? Then, after things calm down, you make contact with the other Concealed Ones." Cal cupped Dov's neck. "They're good guys, every one of them, so don't try running off on your own the way I did. You carry one another's burdens, you hear me?"

"Yes, Nickel."

"Good." Cal tousled the kid's shaggy bangs, his hand tinged blue by the Letter's luminescence. "You're never alone. Just remember that."

"But I don't want you to—"

"Say it."

"I'm never alone."

"That's right. Day by day, no matter what happens, you keep drawing your life from the Blood." He tapped the vial hanging next to Dov's heart. "Never alone. Now," he said, waggling his bottle of milk, "sit tight and keep an eye peeled."

"Peeled?"

"It's an American expression. Ciao for now. I'm going in."

CHAPTER
FIFTEEN

The boar righted herself and turned in Gina's direction. If Gina continued reaching for the nearby knife, she'd be exposed to a rib-cracking assault. Instead she clambered to her knees and ventured a glance to her left.

The chasm waited there, hungry for a morsel.

She saw the boar's ears stiffen and hooves poise for action. Gina dug her own feet into the earth and determined what she must do. It would require a stable position as well as a denial of pain, because even the slightest wavering would leave her plummeting to her own demise.

If that were to happen, would she be found in time? What if Cal had been captured already, or disposed of in some way, leaving her corpse to rot past the three-day time frame?

Gina locked eyes with her foe while her left arm reached upward. They faced off, parallel to the cliff's edge, and this gave the sow an opening.

With a grunt, she came at full speed. Her thick neck quivered, while strands of drool stretched back from open jaws. Teeth flashed. Black eyes burned. The snout aimed for Gina's throat.

Gina's arm was still lifting, lifting. Touching her collar, then her neck. Her fingers were deadened, her muscles slow to respond, and everything in her screamed to abandon the plan and dive for cover.

She'd committed now, though. No going back.

The boar rocketed off the dirt. In that same instant, the earring came loose in Gina's fingers.

Clutched in her fist, the orb rested warm and round against her skin. She chose to protect her good arm and stabbed the earring forward with her mangled and useless left.

This was going to hurt.

Midair, the sow found herself swallowing half a limb. Gina rolled back with the impact, felt shoulders grind against small stones. A shadow loomed as the creature soared past, teeth still clamped into the meat at her elbow. Roots, carrion, and small mammals made up a normal sow's diet, and Gina could only hope this one would accept this newest addition to her menu.

C'mon, you pig. Take what I give you.

The torque yanked Gina's arm backward, dislocating it from its socket as the beast thudded onto compact earth. White bursts blinded Gina to the sky overhead. Red confetti swirled through her vision, shot through with streaks of black and sputtering silver. The puncture points from embedded teeth fired off messages to her brain, each one demanding that she do something to free herself, though that was impossible.

In light of her predicament, her mind offered another option. She could just drift, drift away. Let everything fade to black.

Gina's arm twisted again as the boar tried to clamber to her feet. The sandpaper tongue scraped along her elbow, jolting her back from the abyss of unconsciousness.

She told herself there was a purpose to all this. A plan.

The earring . . .

In the lee of the ridge, the breeze vanished, mollified by late afternoon sun. Cal knew that wherever Erota's Collector was, she must be caught in that quandary between no wind at all and wind headed in the wrong direction.

He edged closer to the limestone boulder, making a slight adjustment.

When it came to bridging, it was best to get it right, and he was a compass dialing in his declination so as to advance with maximum efficiency.

Finally certain of his aim, he pressed himself against the rock, on that line between control and abandon, and eased free of his constraints. He saw his left hand and his bottle-cupping right reach forward through solid rock, then lost sight of them as time slowed to a   c . . . r . . . a . . . w . . . l.

Space was

      rendered irrelevant here,

               the

                        boundaries

       b l u r r e d

between

                    material objects.

He was the sum of his parts, yet even at levels beyond the measurement of man-made instruments he remained wholly individual. He was more than a mishmash of molecules; he was a distinctive being, knitted together in the image of his Maker.

All around, the boulder became porous as a sponge, its particles leaving plenty of room for his passage through and around.

Then he was coming back together. Piece by piece.

He experienced a rush of acceleration as his physical being found restored unity on the inside wall of the cave, whole once again. In working order.

His eyes blinked and his fingers flexed. His toes curled in his shoes, detecting solid ground underneath. Pale light illuminated the chamber through narrow cracks in the barricade behind him.

Sprawled before him, Erota's female form exuded undeniable sensuality. Even in jeans that made most adult women appear preadolescent, her hips were curvy, her legs long. Ray-Ban sunglasses hid the almond shape of her eyes, while a fitted blouse accentuated other feminine attributes.

Trouble, all right.

Cal gripped the milk bottle like a hand grenade. He knew well his own male predilections, not to mention the sexual misdeeds perpetrated through the ages in the names of nobles, priests, and kings. Erota, as a nineteen-year-old, had played temple prostitute to Greek and Roman supplicants, and here she was centuries later, once again stirring the hormones of men—a few women, as well—as she added to the Collection of Souls.

But Cal had the Power of Choice. So long as he walked upon this earth, immortal or otherwise, his will was his own to direct.

He edged toward the woman, scanning the darkness for any sign of her Collector's approach. If Erota began to rise again, he could wrestle her down. Physically, he was the larger and stronger of the two, and both of them were subject to their human forms. The main thing was to keep her from switching hosts yet again.

Man, she looked good. That silky hair and—

No! Get a grip here.

Cal knew that the sin was in the dwelling upon the possibilities, and there would be none of that from him. No way, no how. He would not be swayed.

He set down the bottle, took a sip from the vial around his neck.

Felt his mind begin to clear.

He tore both sleeves from his shirt and divided them into strips, soaked one in the vial's flow of Nazarene Blood, then stuffed it into the she-vampire's mouth. The gag he knotted around her head would keep her from spitting out her little goody.

Next, he tied her hands behind her back. He clambered about in the semi-blackness, found a stray branch, and shoved it through the crooks of her elbows so as to maintain tension between her bound arms and spine.

One last thing . . .

He removed Erota's Ray-Bans and stepped back. As soon as her Collector arrived, as soon as those eyes glowed with their reprobate fire, he would blindfold her, cutting off any visual escape. If she tried to swallow, she'd find herself drinking unworthily of the Blood, taking the fast route to the Restless Desert.

He grinned at his work.

Talk about taking every thought captive.

The earring . . .

With her fist wedged at the back of the predator's throat, Gina summoned her strength and squeezed. The ruby orb burst in her palm, nothing more dramatic than the pop of a small red grape as it released its piquant juice.

Liquid oozed between her fingers. Drop by drop.

The wild sow worked against the encumbrance in her mouth, grunts mixing with vexed squeals as she tried to find her feet and wrench away.

Agony tore once more along Gina's skin, from fingertips to shoulder blade. Tears pooled in her eyes, uninvited. What to do, though? Sometimes such things couldn't be helped. She felt delirium sweep through her body, narrowing the range of her thoughts while battening down pain receptors against this excruciating scene.

Interesting word. With her Romanian background, Gina was well aware of its Latin source.

Ex crucio: "out of pain."

Same root as "crucifixion."

In her palm, Nazarene Blood still dribbled from the earring. It spilled around her fingers. It ran in rivulets. The sow shuddered and fought against this arm shoved down her gullet, and still the crushed emblem that should've been empty by this point poured forth unabated.

The creature stiffened, fell silent. Could it be over as easy as that?

Eyelids fluttering, Gina started to rise.

A nerve-jangling squeal welled up from the boar's innards, followed by a convulsion so violent it could only have come from Shalom's Collector within. On her side, the mortal beast started flopping, feet pawing the air. Her jaws locked down on Gina's arm, holding her captive during these final moments.

And still, that ceaseless flow from the crushed orb . . .

CHAPTER
SIXTEEN

"I think I see something moving," Dov called from the other side of the barrier, his voice distant-sounding but clear. "Looks like she's slipping through the gap and coming your way."

Cal whipped around. He'd left Erota's eyes uncovered to facilitate the Collector's return, but after doing so she might hop visually from this dwelling into yet another temporary one—a bat, mosquito, or fox—and thus evade him.

On the ground, the feminine form was still constrained with arms caught beneath her spine. Whatever allure she'd projected moments earlier now seemed unladylike, even crass.

"Dov, you're sure you saw something?" he said.

"I'm sure."

Cal paused, noting that Erota's eyes were now closed. "They were open before," he muttered.

As if in response to his statement, the she-vampire's eyelids lifted to reveal irises infused with emerald fire. She turned toward the sound of the Concealed One only steps away, on the cave's exterior. She wanted Dov. Her back curled, snapping her forward into a sitting position, and she kicked out a leg at Cal. Then her heel froze, still hovering off the ground as her mouth closed around the gag.

"You like that?" he said.

She blinked.

"Oh, yeah," he said. "Nazarene Blood. You know you want it."

Her eyes widened, cauldrons of desire and dread.

"Go ahead and take a sip, Erota. Let it slide down and see just how rich and satisfying it really is."

A purring sound rattled in her throat. Cal knew this revenant had never tasted sustenance such as this, free of contaminants and not once thinned by unwholesome diet or addiction. Despite its allure, she could not swallow. She knew the curse of these drops within her unholy frame.

"Well, you've gotta be thirsty," he said. "Am I right?"

The revenant's foot settled to the dirt and she lowered her chin, perhaps trying to keep those sacred drops from slipping down her throat.

"Now you're tracking with me," Cal said.

He lowered the bottle to the cave floor and cinched a strip from his sleeve around Erota's eyes. She seethed, her canine teeth punching through pink gums, tapered and ready to pass on infection.

He swung his leg and kicked her back to a prone position, where her jaw worked against the gag and its wet material.

"Is everything okay, Nickel?"

"Fine, Dov. Stay quiet and out of sight."

"What? I can't even see you in there."

"She's in here now so just stay back. No unnecessary risks."

The wind moaning through the gap was all the response Cal received. Trusting that Dov's safety had been addressed, he calmed his nerves and took hold of his weapon. Innocuous as it seemed, there was a precedent for goat milk's success against Collectors and their kind.

"I know you're thirsty," Cal told Erota. "And I have a drink for you."

Long ago, a giant of a man named Sisera had commanded the hosts of Hazor and oppressed the people of Israel. He was a *"thorn in their side,"* as predicted years earlier by one of the Unfallen. Sisera, by his sheer size and cruel demeanor, was suspected of an affiliation with the *Nephilim*, figures of sinister origin whose kinship was intertwined with the Collectors.

Yet Sisera was no match for the Almighty. The commander fought the stars of the heavens and lost, his defeat coming through the hands of a woman. On the run, he asked her for a place to hide in her tent. And could he please have a drink of water?

Instead she gave him a cup of the local *lebben*, or curdled goat's milk. Known for its soothing properties, it pacified the commander and dropped him to the earth, asleep. The woman seized the opportunity, took a mallet in hand, and drove a metal tent peg through her enemy's temple.

Okay, but Cal had used his current supply of MTPs at the train station and the rest were in his daypack on the orphanage bus. He did, however, have this home-brewed lebben to offer, soured after a day outdoors.

He said, "You can have a drink if you want, Erota, a little brew to satisfy your human host. You'll have to lie still, though, while I remove the gag. Either that or I ram a bellyful of Nazarene richness down that pretty throat of yours."

The purring started up again.

Cal lifted the glass bottle, removed the cap, and positioned the rim over the vampire's lips. He yanked away her gag with his free hand, instructing her to spit out the wadded cloth.

Erota hesitated, still at war with her own bloodlust, then complied. A turn of his wrist sent lebben cascading over her lips. Blindfolded and bound, she lapped at the milk as it sloshed down her neck. Off-white dribbles pooled upon the rock. Her shoulders began to sag.

"On its own, lebben is powerless," Cal had explained earlier to Dov. "Symbols gain a hold over us based only on our perceptions and our willingness to give them rein. You see a swastika and what do you think of? The *Shoah*, right? The Holocaust. With all those negative connotations, nobody's going to campaign for president with a swastika on their arm. And what about a man who looks at a woman with a wedding ring? That symbol tells him she's off-limits—or should be, anyway. That piece of metal then takes on a certain power."

The power of symbols had long affected Collectors, reminding them of prior defeats. Now with Erota at his feet, Cal noticed the lebben taking hold as her chest rose and fell, as her eye-catching legs went limp.

He was all alone with her, and—

Forget it, Cal! Stay on task.

As an intel broker, he had information to gather. That's why he was here. Once he'd pulled from her what he needed, he would use Nazarene droplets to put an end to her once and for all.

"So." Cal prodded her shoulder with his shoe. "Feeling a little drowsy?"

She groaned.

He crouched beside her. "Ready for a little chitchat?" In times past, he'd found that Collectors' guards went down while under the lebben's influence, prompting them to reveal things they might not otherwise.

Her lips, still frothy, formed a soundless circle.

"You and I are both searching for someone we'd like to destroy. Me for Natira. You for Dov."

The circle became an oval. Erota's tongue slipped between curved fangs and performed a sensuous lick.

In cauda venenum, Cal reminded himself. *"In the tail is the poison."*

The reference was to a scorpion and to the fact it could still inject a fatal sting while having its head crushed beneath one's foot. Here he was, ready to extract information before destroying her, and it was no time to grow lax.

"That's right," he said. "You've been trying to get your grimy little paws on Dov ever since his father was infected back in Arad."

From the cave floor, Erota gasped out the word: "Arad . . ."

Cal wiped a milky dribble from his forearm. "What about it?"

The Collector lay motionless, save her human's instinctual filling and emptying of lungs. A brackish smell wafted about her.

"Tell me about Arad," he prodded.

"Megiste . . . Barabbas . . ."

"Yes?"

"They took the House of Eros." Her face contorted. "And my sister."

"To Israel, I know. Is that the Arad you're talking about?"

She nodded. "The haunt of jackals."

Cal reeled back from that. He had prayed, hoped to God, he would never again have to face the evil associated with that place. The very phrase clamped itself around his innards and squeezed, exerting the sort of bladder-emptying pressure he'd seen implemented in torture chambers of the Dark Ages.

He had to be sure. "The ruins of Kerioth-Hezron, north of town? Is that where you mean?"

Erota was silent.

"The birthplace of Judas?"

A simpering grin appeared beneath her blindfold.

"Is that where Natira is?"

"Natira . . ." She stretched the syllables into a passionate sigh.

"Is he at Kerioth-Hezron?"

"He's gone . . . gone . . ."

"I know he escaped the Akeldama before the rest of your cluster, but have you seen him since? Has he tried to contact you?"

Her lips turned down into a pout, the look of a jilted teenage girl. Although this was nothing more than the residue of her human emotion, it was something worth exploiting.

"You liked him, didn't you?" Cal said. "I can find him, if you'll just give me a few clues to work with."

"Find him?"

"That's right. I'll make sure you both get to be together again." *In hell*, he thought of adding, but kept that to himself.

Erota's right foot twitched.

"Talk to me," Cal said, sensing that her strength was beginning to combat the lebben's effects. "Where should I start looking? Has he tried contacting you?"

She shook her head. A twitch of the left foot this time.

"So he's cut off all ties with you and the cluster?"

"Yes." Erota giggled. "He's wrapped himself in knotsies."

Cal was not amused and demanded to know where Natira had gone.

"He went to prepare a gift," Erota said. "He's a gift to the world."
She then broke into laughter that sprayed the air with white flecks. Her
undead glee intensified, shifting from cackles to piercing shrieks that
bounced between this fissure's confines.

Cal resisted the urge to cover his ears. What was this creature up to?

"Dov," he called out. "Get back a little farther."

No response.

"Talk to me, Dov. Where are you?"

Shalom, by entering into symbiotic relationship with an animal host, had
made herself vulnerable to the boar's needs and indulgences. Unless she
managed a swift visual escape to another vessel, the hot droplets funneling
down the esophagus would destroy her.

Gina rolled onto her belly. The movement caused her left shoulder to
pop back into place, and she screamed before pulling herself toward the
convulsing sow. The swallowed arm was immobile, but with her right hand
she reached out to cover the creature's eyes.

There would be no escape. Not today.

One last bellow, nasal and hot, burst from the sow's mouth before she
twitched twice and lay still. An entity rose from her snout, an ethereal
smudge.

Gina dragged her arm from slack jaws and watched the vapor writhe
like a vulgar flame. It separated into smaller blurs, then smaller, until
nothing remained but salty whiffs that dissipated in the mountain air.

Shalom's Collector?

Gone.

On the ground, the wild sow was no longer a threat. She seemed ravaged by the Collector's exit, the breath torn permanently from her lungs.

Gina lifted on a knee. She touched the orb that still hung from her other ear. What was keeping her from embracing its life-sustaining power? Why not drink, and drink deeply? Just one drop. Just one.

At her neck, the vine squirmed and veins bulged beneath her skin.

One drop? It might tear her apart, might turn her inside out and leave her gasping for oxygen. She'd just seen what it could do. While filled with her own corrosion, she couldn't risk ingesting something so pure. First she'd have to cut away this root so that she could cleanse herself of—

Listen to her. Like mother, like daughter.

For Gina, the irony was evident. In her desperation to be free last night, she'd lacerated her own skin and nearly bled herself dry. By rejecting the droplets in her earrings, she'd copied her mother's methods.

Gina wobbled to her feet, found her brass-handled dagger and returned it to its sheath. She untied the ski jacket from her waist and pulled it back on, wincing as it enclosed her wounds in a downy cocoon.

Chalk one up for the vampire hunter. She had singlehandedly diverted and destroyed another Akeldama Collector.

Well, not singlehandedly.

She had to admit that her actions alone, her suffering, would've failed to subdue this foe. There was more to this victory than that.

Ex crucio . . .

She'd protected those she loved, out of pain. She'd preserved her own life, out of pain. Whose pain, though?

Her palm was still wet from that warm crimson flow.

CHAPTER
SEVENTEEN

In the cave's overhead space, a cloud of winged insects began congregating—drawn by Erota's high-pitched shrieks? Where was Dov?

Cal swatted at the bugs and surveyed for the first time this chamber's far reaches. Dusky light came into focus, and he squinted to determine its distance. From the other direction, bats swooped in like an oily wave, drawn by the night and the promise of sustenance.

The Collector, in her sleepy delirium, began laughing it up again. Her sulfuric odor was growing thicker and it made Cal feel sick to his stomach. He ducked from a bat, then took a step toward the light in hopes of fresh air.

"Nickel? You in there?"

Cal heard the voice in front of him, rather than from behind the stone wall. Is that where Dov had disappeared to, searching for the cave's other opening?

From the shadows, the teen's form took shape.

"Dov?"

"Nickel, watch out!"

Cal snapped back toward the she-vampire, who was now clambering to her knees. Her hands were behind her back, the branch still shoved between her arms and spine but slanted upward. With the tip, she'd snagged her blindfold and pried it over her brow. Her eyes flamed.

Dov charged into the chamber, ready to act, and Cal realized how far off course this whole scenario had veered.

"No," he growled. "Don't go near her."

Another bat darted past their heads.

"Get that thing out of here," Cal said. "I'll take care of Erota."

Dov hefted the empty glass bottle, while Cal blocked the way from the cavern with his wide stance. Even if Erota managed a visual switch, he would be sure to gain custody of her permanent host until she returned.

She locked eyes with him. He glared back, standing firm.

Her gaze went to the bat as it flitted about with its echo-location as a guide. It seemed to pause before the fiery-eyed Collector, then it shot off again and Erota's shell crumpled to the earth like a human stripped from its skeleton. Had she made visual contact? Switched hosts?

"The bat," Cal shouted. "Dov, kill that thing!"

On his second swing of the bottle, Dov nicked the bloodsucker's wing and it dodged up a natural rock chimney.

"Make sure that you don't let it get by—"

Cal's last word was bludgeoned from his mouth by a blow to the front of the neck. He gasped. His Adam's apple felt like used gum, sticking to back of his throat. Anticipating a second blow, he ducked low and felt a whoosh of air, while peripheral vision showed him what he'd already deduced.

In her fake fall, Erota had jarred the stick from between her elbows and pulled tied wrists up under her heels. She now gripped the wood like a javelin and headed for Dov.

Though Cal knew Dov was a capable defender, it didn't negate his own need to join the fight. He launched himself from bent knees, interposing himself between Those Who Hunt and the hunted. Erota's crude weapon pierced his lower back in midair, punching through cloth and skin, grazing his spine. Pain flared, then burned to the tips of his hands and feet before gathering again in his belly's furnace. Freed from the Separation, his spirit and flesh would work in tandem to regenerate, but that didn't stop the signals that now tore through his nervous system to the brain.

He landed on top of Dov and rolled, snapping off the wooden stake. Regained his footing. Stretched for the broken bit of wood.

Erota was a rabid beast, her claws scything the air at Dov's face.

The kid feinted once, twice. The vampire's fangs dripped glowing globules, ready to bring down the Nistarim—and humanity—in one fatal blow.

Cal swung for that pretty head. The tip of the tree limb, the one still dripping with his own fluids, raked through her hair and left her with a bald spot.

She whipped her jaw toward him, spraying spittle.

He lowered his head and plowed forward with the stake, hoping to catch her in a mammoth tackle. Beating him to it, a bottle exploded against the bridge of her nose, shooting blood and the last drops of lebben into the air. The center of Erota's face was a mess of red and white and tan-colored skin.

"She's getting away," Dov yelled.

Cal turned to cut off her exit, but she slipped past.

He and Dov pursued her to the end of the tunnel, where they emerged upon an expanse of frosty shale and limestone. This must be the spot Erota had exited yesterday in her bristling brown bear host.

Far off to their left, Erota crested a ridge and dropped from view. Mentor and pupil went after her, skirting the shale and cutting through low brush. They halted beside a gnarled tree at the edge of the cliff, then combed the terrain below with their eyes. There were no telltale signs of the Collector. She had vanished.

"Dov, you okay?"

"I'm all right," came the reply.

"Nice aim with the bottle."

"What about your back?"

"Hurts."

"Here, Nickel." Dov lifted the vial from around his neck. "See if this helps."

Cal subjected himself to his young pupil's ministrations, chiding himself for being careless, even cavalier—something he'd been accused of before—in his search for information. But at least he now knew the location of the House of Eros, entrenched at Kerioth-Hezron near Israeli Arad.

And there was something else.

Erota, despite her devious nature, had provided a few clues about Natira, and Cal sensed he was zeroing in on his enemy. The next time they met, Cal would not go alone.

➤

Gina watched hawks wheel overhead in the Saturday afternoon sun. In another hour or two, she'd reach Bran Castle, where Teo would pick her up and drive her to Bucharest. She'd dispatched her pursuers and there was no longer any fear of betraying Cal and Dov's destination.

One thing was clear, though . . . Her reprieve from the grief in Chattanooga and her return to the place of her childhood were over. Whereas many state-run facilities were ill-kempt and dirty, Tomorrow's Hope in Arad provided the children a nice place to study, play, and rest, and she'd served the last nine months as a muncitor there, bonding with the orphans.

"And now I can't go back."

She said the words aloud, and this realization nearly dropped her to her knees. Even as a girl, she had dreamed of serving the abandoned, diseased, and abused. She'd loved her three-legged dog all the more for what he lacked.

Now that earliest of dreams was in jeopardy.

She ran her tongue along the backs of her teeth, counting, thinking of something to be thankful for. Anything.

Cal, Dov, Jed . . . and Teo.

She heeled her boots into the earth and marched up the path on exhausted legs. A survivor, that's what her mother called her, and it was true that Gina would die a thousand deaths before giving up.

"The answer dies within."

Those were Cal's words. He'd told her she shouldn't reject the Nazarene's truth because of Nikki's lies. He said life with the Blood was a gift, but it would involve dying daily to her own will, sharing in Yeshua's sufferings on the path to unshakable peace.

Suffering? Well, what was new?

Right now Gina's path led toward a medieval fortress. She paused to draw in full draughts of air, then quickened her gait.

At her neck, the remaining earring flicked back and forth, catching the sunlight and casting crimson halos across patches of pure white snow.

Bran Castle

Gina arrived on stiff legs. She thought she would feel a rush of emotion upon seeing the castle, but instead she let out a sigh and pressed on toward turrets tinted coral by the waning sun. This was a way-station in her journey, and the larger questions still loomed:

Would she and Cal Nichols ever work together again?

Where would she go when this was all over?

What about Dov?

Ahead a cliff grew like a tooth into one of the citadel walls. Historians debated the details, but most conceded Vlad Tepes had been held here a few nights as a prisoner in the late 1400s. That was enough to create dark intrigue, and tourists came from around the world to take photos at Dracula's Castle.

Adding to the mystery, the bulwarks contained secret stairways and passages, some still hidden from the public. There were those who believed that mementos of Vlad's violent past were locked within these walls.

All Gina wanted was a meal, a drink, and a view of Teo's face.

Twenty minutes till the tourist gates closed, and still no sign of her friend. Was it so hard to get here on time? She'd shared her first kiss with him, after all.

After paying the entrance fee with the remaining lei from Roxana's purse, she wandered through a market square, where plastic fangs—were those supposed to be scary after all she'd gone through?—and blood-red wine were sold alongside carvings and gypsy tapestries. Russian tourists jostled by and she felt the crush of bodies against her wounds.

She was climbing steps toward the fortress when her ears caught the carefree speech of a broad-shouldered American in a Texas Longhorns jacket. He met her eye and ran a hand through his wheat-colored hair.

Gina wanted to slap him for his self-absorbed manner. Then wanted desperately to hug him and not let go.

Cal, wherever you are, don't give up on me. I'm still alive.

She continued her climb, tourist brochure in hand. The castle had been built and added onto over the ages, incorporating an asymmetrical floor plan replete with lofty lookouts, an inner courtyard, and a deep stone well. A garrison of archers had once lived here, and later, customs officials and local rulers took advantage of its elevated location.

In the early twentieth century, Queen Marie, a relative of the Russian czar, received the castle as a gift after marrying into Romanian royalty. She considered it her favorite residence and, despite travels throughout Europe and America, found these mountains appealing to her free-spirited, mystical nature.

Queen Marie was now dead, her heart buried on the premises. Yet rumors persisted that other treasures were hidden here as well: Orthodox icons, Fabergé jewels, relics, and reliquaries.

Many had been smuggled to surviving relatives after the 1918 assassination of the Imperial czars, and it was well documented that numerous such items made up the queen's personal collection—some still on display within this fortress, others donated to Maryhill Museum in the Pacific Northwest.

The Northwest . . .

Current home of Jed Turney.

Gina's mind considered those names again: Jed, Teo, Cal. Somewhere deep inside, she still paced those halls of romantic possibility, brushing the various doorknobs with her fingertips. When it came to these three, was there a right choice? A wrong one? Or solely good and bad consequences to accompany whichever decision she made?

She reached the top steps leading into the castle, where a guide warned her that the facilities would be closing in a few minutes. She started to turn back.

"Gina."

"Teodor?"

He appeared from the dank recesses of the entryway. "Good to see you. I wasn't sure you would make it." He was tall, angular, with a jutting chin.

"And I shouldn't have doubted my friend."

His flinty eyes turned tender. "I've been waiting nearly two hours."

"And you made me climb all these steps? Thanks a lot."

"I just came up a few minutes ago to see if you were here. You're small, but I know how strong you are. You did hike all the way from Busteni, da?"

"Strong? Worn-out is more like it."

Teo moved to wrap an arm around her.

"No." Gina raised both hands and stepped back.

"What's wrong?"

"Nothing. A few cuts. Are we going to do the tour or not?"

"It's too late. I already walked around, but they're closing things for the night. If you'd like, we can still make a wish and drop a coin down the well."

"Are you trying to flirt with me?"

"Why, after driving here from Arad on short notice, I think my feelings are not so secret."

"Teo, I'm glad you came."

"The courtyard's still open, if we hurry. You can make your own wish, Gina. You do not have to reveal it."

She wished for a cool drink and a warm bed. She wished to have back her smooth, tanned left arm. She wished to be a mother again, cradling her newborn son in her arms and never letting him go.

"Lead the way," she said.

The archway into the courtyard was a step back through time. High walls and balconies blocked the setting sun from this space, yet a few rays managed to bounce down off the upper level's lead-paned windows. There were no ghostly wisps or gothic symbols, only this rustic fortress of black timbers and stone.

"Over here," Teo said. "We must hurry."

"Okay, okay."

"I know what my wish is." He stood at the well, screwed his eyes shut as though mustering some arcane magic, then let a Romanian leu fall through a crack in the wooden cover. He looked her direction. "Your turn."

She checked Roxana's purse. Nothing left.

"Do you need a coin?" he said.

"No, I . . ."

Gina reached in her pocket for the coin gathered this morning from the cave floor. What'd she care about some old piece of silver or tin? It'd belonged to a Collector, and that alone was reason to toss the thing. Plus, here in Teo's presence, she felt safe and relaxed. She'd tasted first love on his lips, tasted blackberries and goat's milk and the musk of his young desire.

Oh, to go back and start over again . . . With him? Maybe that's what she would wish for.

"Look." She lifted the coin. "I came prepared."

Teo's eyes widened, and he plucked the object from her fingertips. "You can't use that." From his mouth, that same creamy scent wafted.

"Give it back. It's my wish we're talking about."

"But this is very old, perhaps even valuable."

"So is my wish."

"I can't let you throw this away, Gina." He studied the engravings, then pressed it back into her palm and curled her fingers around it. "Use one of mine," he said.

She dropped in the provided coin, but it sailed downward without wings. She had been so close, so vulnerable, almost opened her heart to him. For now, though, the choice would have to wait.

"It was a happy wish, I hope?" said Teo.

She slid a soft kiss across his cheek, then turned toward the archway before he could see the melancholy in her eyes. "We need to go."

"Where? What is this mischief you've involved me in?"

"You're taking me to Bucharest."

THE SECOND TASTE: EX ARDESCO

They spill each other's blood with great vigor? Do you believe it? . . .
In this land, it seems the more you have the more aggressive you become.

—STEPHEN KING, *'SALEM'S LOT*

What sorrow awaits them . . . For they follow in the footsteps of Cain.

—JUDE 1:11

Journal Entry

July 7

With the ferry plowing through the waters of Puget Sound, the diesel smell's making me queasy. I'm not used to the motion, even though I've lived here in the San Juan Islands all these years. Funny how you can think you know so much about something, but it's a whole different deal when you actually jump into the middle of it.

I have an overwhelming urge to rush back to the island, to the refuge I've trusted for as long as I can remember. What impact can I have by leaving anyway? I mean, who am I? Nobody, that's who.

Even with the dock drawing near, my mind is stuck on the things encapsulated in Gina's droplet. I not only got peeks into her experiences but into Cal's and the Collectors' as well, and that's left me confused. How'd all of this come to be in Gina's blood? Where is Erota? What about Natira? Something's gone on between him and Cal, and I hate to think what'll happen should they ever confront each other again.

We're getting closer to the other side now. Here I am about to take my first steps off Lummi Island, and the captain's giving me this funny expression like he's worried about me. Does he know something I don't? Or is it the way I look?

Let him stare. I figure I have a few minutes still, so I'm going to explore more of this story's layers through another taste from Gina's droplet.

Who sent me this map? Will I find answers or only more questions?

Time to taste and see.

CHAPTER
EIGHTEEN

En route to Bucharest

The hum of the Opel's motor and the glow of the dashboard dredged images from Gina's past. She grasped at them like a shipwreck survivor reaching for flotsam, only to have them drift away.

"You're quiet," Teo said.

She looked off through the window, where the wide swath of the headlights pushed back an orange-black dusk.

"Can you tell me what we're doing once we arrive in the capital?"

"I don't know," she said.

"Is this your way of forcing my hand?" His tone was playful. "We run off together and leave the folks in Cuvin buzzing about our elopement?"

"Teodor." She shook her head. "You think you're so bad."

"I could be."

"Bad?"

"Only if you . . ." Teo adjusted the rearview mirror. "Gina, I've wanted you for a long time. I've tried to be respectful, never imposed myself on you, but it's not been an easy task."

"I'm that irresistible, huh?"

"If you wish to know the truth."

"You've been good to me." She rewarded him with a half grin. "Taking care of my dog after I left, standing up for the orphans at Tomorrow's Hope, giving me the space to pull my thoughts together."

He downshifted into a curved descent, his face merging with the deepening shadows of the night.

"Honestly," she said. "This isn't even about you, Teo."

"I wish that it were."

She almost blurted out "*I wish that too*," but the words would've been a reactionary sentiment rather than heartfelt certainty.

Instead she rested her elbow on the window jamb, knocked at the glass with her knuckles, then shifted both hands to her lap. She had a vague recollection of Teo's waving hand long ago as she was carted away, and she had vowed she would never again let her mother dictate her decisions. Now, beside her, this childhood sweetheart was a full-grown man.

"I've wanted you for a long time."

His words echoed her own feelings from another lifetime, yet so much had changed. She still wasn't sure who she was. Or, more pressing, who she was meant to become.

There seemed to be something larger at work in her life, woven into the very fabric. Even the blackest threads had a purpose, contrasting with the brightest to create elaborate patterns, but she had little clue as to their intended design. She feared that the slightest tug might make it all unravel.

Teo was speaking again.

"What?" she said. "I'm sorry. I was . . ."

"That's all right, Gina. I was saying that it's my privilege to help in whatever way I can. I'm glad you called. And, as your friend, I'd like to understand what it is that's upsetting you."

"Once I figure that out, I'll make sure to let you know. How 'bout that?"

"Fair enough." He pointed at a road sign. "Ninety-two kilometers to go."

They stopped once for fuel. Teo bought milk chocolate and cold drinks to share. Gina took two more aspirin from the supplies Roxana had provided. She then pressed back against the headrest with her left arm cradled in her lap, and reflected on her last moments with Cal Nichols at Sinaia's train depot. She tried picking out clues from their conversation, anything that might direct her to a specific rendezvous point within the capital's sprawling boundaries.

Her words to him: *"We meet back up . . . Say, tomorrow in Bucharest."*

Why hadn't they set a time, a place?

So much had gone wrong. And yet here she sat, warm and alive with an old friend at her side. She had much to be grateful for, so much to . . .

She closed her eyes, and for the first time in two days she slept.

Bucegi Mountains

The impact at the base of the precipice had snapped Erota's legs, ripped a hole through her torso, cracked her skull wide open. But by some malignant luck, she'd rolled beneath a cornice and remained hidden from Cal's and Dov's prying eyes.

Doubly dead?

Well, let the world take notice once more.

She was a revenant on the rise. A vampire revamped. A Collector collecting her thoughts—as well as the remnants of a shattered knee, chipped teeth, and a chunk of scalp that went back into place like an ill-fitted toupee.

Her reconstruction had taken her into the evening, a procedure made possible by the Master Collector's same animus that had led to her cluster's rising.

The moon was peeking over the ridge by the time she stood and cracked her neck both ways, letting vertebrae shift back into place.

Undead. Unrequited. Understandably thirsty and cold.

She gazed up the rock face. She had to believe Cal and Dov were gone, or by now they would've found her and banished her to the Restless Desert. So what if she'd let a few things slip out while Cal played out his little Q&A session with the lebben? At least she'd made her escape.

Monastery bells sounded from down in the valley as Erota lurched her way through these mountains. What a sham. What did Easter week-end really mean to those who bent their knees for one, and only one, morning of the year? Oh, if these two-leggers had any idea.

A killing at Golgotha . . . *And we believed we had won.*

A corpse in a rich man's tomb . . . *Dead and gone, or so we thought.*

And then the Nazarene had risen from the grave, defying the Separation and the efforts of Collectors everywhere.

Yeshua . . . Didn't the very name mean "to save"?

Well, let Him splash His Blood about in morbid displays of forgive-ness. Let the humans lap it up like witless lambs, so long as they viewed it as chore and ceremony, a form of godliness and nothing more.

What did He see in them anyway? The majority of Those Who Resist kept silent and hidden, often nursing their secret infections. Erota herself had compromised and tapped a few of them, watching men and women writhe as they questioned the Almighty's purposes.

Such thoughts spurred her over the uneven terrain as she traced an unmistakable odor that stewed somewhere close. Minutes later, she con-firmed her suspicions that Shalom's Collector had been dispatched. Though the two women had never been close, Erota shook her head at the loss of yet another at the hands of Ms. Lazarescu.

We're not done yet, Gina. I have others on the lookout for you, you and your baa-baa *bad little lambs.*

Bucharest

Gina awoke to farmlands and oil fields on the outskirts of Bucharest. Here in the evening hours, small derricks were pistoning up and down along the highway, sucking up the earth's black blood. She moaned. Wiped at dry lips.

"I'm glad you could rest," Teo said.

"Me too."

"Where are we going once we reach the city?"

"Uh . . ." She straightened in her seat. "Still working on that. Do you have a map I can look at?"

"Da." He pointed to the glove box. "In there."

She selected one from his stack of cartography, spread it across the dashboard. A grid overlaid the capital, providing coordinates for each library, museum, street, and park. She poured over the locations: People's Palace, the Village Museum, Hotels Capsa and Persepolis, the Arch of Triumph, and so on.

Though any one of these could be a meeting place, none triggered a response. Where would Cal think to go? What would link them in this large city?

C'mon, Gina. Put yourself in his shoes.

She ran her eyes over the ranks and files of coordinates. In chess, a similar grid was used to record the moves of a game. For example, Bf4 meant the bishop had moved to the f4 square.

Wait. Could it be that obvious?

Her finger found the fifth column over from the left, then slipped down to the row marked *e*. The map showed a residential sector east of the city center. Not much in the way of government buildings. Very few places of distinction.

"*e5* . . ." Cal had mentioned to her. "*A great spot for a knight.*"

Gina studied the corresponding square and noted one particular location. "I've got it," she told Teo. "We're going to Avram Iancu Street."

"What're we after?"

"I'm meeting someone."

"A man?"

"Does it matter?"

He repositioned his hands on the wheel, checked his rearview and sideview mirrors. "I suppose not. I'm here to keep an eye on you either way."

"What's that supposed to mean?" she said, half kidding.

"To help you, of course."

"Multumesc."

"You will give me the directions to get there?"

"Don't worry, pal. I'm actually good with a map."

"Considering your chess mind, this is no surprise to me." The rutted highway shook the steering wheel in his hands. "What place are we seeking?"

"Elvis's Villa Hostel."

"We came all this way for a youth hostel?"

"Chess . . . don't you see?" She flashed a cryptic smile, heart racing at the thought of a reunion. She could only hope Cal would make the connection. "It's not just any hostel, Teo. It's Elvis's."

"And?"

"Long live the king."

CHAPTER
NINETEEN

The night clerk at the hostel was efficient and kind. A metallic-blue ring pierced his lower lip, and his hair was spiked in a manner meant to look haphazard. He wore peg-leg jeans and a cowboy shirt with pearl buttons.

The beds were filling up, he explained, and he would have to separate Teo and Gina. Would that be okay?

Gina nodded. Yes, no problem.

Teo was less pleased with the arrangement, but as a travel agent he seemed to find some consolation in the hostel's affordable rates.

Gina accepted sheets and blankets for her bunk, then followed the clerk up the stairs between yellow- and pink-painted walls. He pointed out a shared toilet and small dormitory rooms, told her the showers and kitchen were downstairs.

She loved the place already. It made her think of the free and easy existence that might've been hers if not for her work among the orphans. Not that she would change a thing. She'd seen in Cal's eyes, heard in his voice, the loneliness that tempered a vagabond lifestyle.

Was he okay? Would he find her here?

Once Teodor was out of earshot, she asked had there been any recent check-ins, and the clerk replied that it'd been a typical busy Saturday.

"How 'bout a teenage boy and a man around your age?"

"Nu." He pursed his lips. "Not since I came in this afternoon."

"Okay. Do you have a first-aid kit?"

"You don't feel well?"

She set her jaw. "Couple scrapes and bruises, that's all."

"There's one at the front desk. I'll bring it to you."

She thanked him and spread out her bedding. Travelers snored in nearby bunks, while a corner bed showed signs of use but sat empty for the time being.

With the first-aid kit at her disposal, she waited her turn for the shower on the lower level. The moment the spray hit her thorn-furrowed arm, she felt the world tilt away, and she buttressed herself against the tiles. Her feet burned with blisters. The root stiffened on the left side of her neck. She crouched in the tub enclosure, awash in steam, and began digging the grit from her lacerations, watching dirt, blood, and tears spiral down the drain. Regardless, she'd never been more appreciative of hot water on aching muscles.

She was still here, still alive. Couldn't keep a good woman down.

Gina toweled off, applied medicated cream to her wounds, and wrapped them in fresh gauze. Her hair was still damp. Without any other clothing, she eased back into the same attire and padded barefoot to the community area, where she joined Teo on a lumpy couch.

He said, "You feel better, I hope?"

"Like a million bucks." She leaned back in mock evaluation of the hostel's pastel walls and mismatched furniture. "What do you think of this place?"

"For tonight it's okay. But tomorrow I will call my boss in Arad and arrange better lodging through our tourist bureau."

"What? And miss out on this great vibe?"

"Elvis?" Teo shook his head. "He is not the king."

"Watch it."

"You are in Romania now, Gina. Not Tennessee. We hear rumors in our office that Michael Jackson might be coming here on his next tour."

"You think Michael wears the crown? He can't even find his other glove."

"And that is worse than Elvis, who wore sequins and pantsuits?"

"Hey," she shot back. "Those years don't count."

"Neither should Neverland."

At the desk, the clerk was stamping and stacking registration forms in a valiant effort to hide his eavesdropping.

"What about this, Teo? More number ones than any other male artist."

"But whose is the bestselling album of all time?"

"*Thriller*-diller," she scoffed. "If nothing else, Elvis should win because he was Michael's father-in-law."

"But it was Lisa Marie who wore Michael's ring."

"Not to mention the pants in the family."

The clerk choked back a giggle.

"Checkmate," Gina said.

"No. A stalemate, I think."

"Two kings left standing, one white and one black." She shrugged. "Stalemate sounds about right to me."

Teo decided he was spent after the long day of traveling. He headed upstairs, probably still wondering what she'd coerced him into. She closed her eyes and listened to the city's night life that hummed outside the lobby's louvered windows. Tipsy guests bumbled in and out, past the registration desk.

Would Cal come? Were Dov and the other orphans okay?

She flipped through dog-eared paperbacks that were free for the taking, her attention diverted each time the front door opened. She crossed her legs on the couch and selected a book by a British writer. As a young girl, his land of Narnia had captivated her, but this book had a gargoyle's image on the cover.

The Screwtape Letters, by C. S. Lewis.

The literary exposé turned her mind inside out, detailing fictional demons' schemes to undermine the life of an average citizen. In many ways, it read like her struggles against the Collectors.

Eleven p.m. Still no sign of her men. And she drifted to sleep.

She was awakened at midnight by church bells pealing in Easter celebration. *"Hristos a inviat!"* she said to the desk clerk. *Christ is risen.*

The traditional greeting brought a look of skepticism to his face, but Gina wasn't offended. She, too, had begrudged those days when Nikki foisted such sayings and rituals upon her. To her surprise, however, she now tasted very little acidity in the words that flowed from her tongue. They felt right, even necessary.

"My shift was over ten minutes ago," the clerk grumbled, toying with his lip ring. "The night watchman better get here soon."

"I know what you mean," Gina said, and settled herself for a long wait.

When Cal did appear the next morning, he came bearing secrets and surprises that would change her life forever.

CHAPTER
TWENTY

En route to Kerioth-Hezron, Israel

Erota was here on business, here to sample the latest vintages. At least that's what she told the white-shirted official at Ben Gurion Airport.

"You have tried Israeli wines before?" he said, using that tone of suspicion perfected by customs agents around the world.

"Of course," she said. "Hevron Heights is making quite a name for itself."

"What about Alon Winery?"

"Don't you mean Alona?"

He stared at her, grunted, then added another stamp to her passport. She'd used company funds, as Totorcea Vineyards' operations manager, to grab the earliest flight out of Bucharest.

Now, instead of taking a morning train toward the fledgling wine regions of Galilee, she headed for Beer Sheva, capital of the Negev Desert. From there, a bus carried her over dun-colored landscape toward Arad.

Erota stared out the window at acacia trees and camels, and reflected on the misadventures of the last twenty-four hours.

Atop the Bucegi Mastiff, she'd found Shalom's human shell not far from the cabana, as well as a dead sow a few kilometers along the trail to Bran Castle. Erota had counted on help from her fellow Collectors—Lord Ariston, Nehemiah, Auge, and Shalom—yet they'd all been vanquished. She had hoped for word from one of her informers, those who'd allowed thorns to dilute their Power of Choice, but there, too, she had come up empty-handed.

In particular, Gina's friend, Teodor, had never called.

Teo had long resisted Erota's sexual tactics, as well as ploys with money or alcohol. Only recently had she identified his pitfall, a chronic depression rooted in boyhood beatings from his Uncle Vasile—former host to a local Collector.

Aside from his damaged psyche, Teo bore an empathy for others that became poisonous when focused inward; and it was in moments of self-pity that Erota tapped, numbed, and infested him. In fact, by tasting from his veins a few months back, she'd attained some of the necessary details for the Sinaia ambush.

Even so, Dov and Cal had vanished. And Gina, as well.

So much for Teo's help. By some coincidence, the poor fool had found a repellent, a taste for goat's milk that gave him momentary reprieves.

And to think he's not even one of Those Who Resist!

Once again, it was the Almighty's all-nauseating grace at work. Did He think He might draw more into His arms by such folly? Did He still hope to feast one day with His two-legged neophytes, sharing with them Yeshua's New Wine?

Well, Erota and Totorcea Vineyards would take things in the opposite direction, growing drunk on the blood of the wicked.

They could not accomplish this alone, though. She hated, oh how she hated, to grovel—especially to Megiste—but she'd already seen other clusters bogged down by petty rivalries. After this latest fiasco, she believed the Akeldama Cluster's best chance for success would come by mending the schism between the Houses of Ariston and Eros.

Even if that meant kissing the hand of her former priestess.

And what if she was turned down? What then? She knew of Megiste's cunning ways and wondered if such a request might only precipitate a war.

An Israeli soldier-girl boarded at the next bus stop, an M-I machine gun slung over her shoulder. She was Erota's age. Nineteen, maybe twenty. As a military conscript, she was excused from paying for public transport.

The girl slipped into a nearby seat. If Erota had not been focused on her destination, she might've investigated the capabilities of such a victim.

Instead, at a signpost for Tel Arad, the Collector stepped from the bus into the heat. Archaeologists had turned up temple ruins at this ancient mound, a reminder that so much of Israel's history centered around places of worship. Even the Ninth of Av, feared as a day of ill fortune, was based on two temple incidents—first, the destruction of Solomon's Temple by the Babylonians, and, later, the Romans' tearing down of the Second Temple.

And now, because of the Nazarene, each and every human was a potential residence for the Almighty. Had He no standards at all?

Ah, well. So many temples. So much more to destroy.

Erota watched the bus chug off toward the palm trees of modern Arad, while she headed north for the Betrayer's birthplace.

Bucharest

Cal's clothing was dingy like hers, his hair disheveled. He leaned against the hostel desk in his casual manner, shoulders tapered to trim hips, his face young and flawless. A familiar JanSport daypack hung from his back. The mustache that'd been part of his bus-driver disguise now seemed almost comical.

"Excuse me." He addressed the morning desk clerk. "I'm looking for a friend of mine who might've checked in yesterday."

"Name?"

"Regina."

Gina eased into the lobby, convinced by that smooth voice of Cal

Nichols' identity. She said, "Honestly, Cal. Why don't you just take a look around?"

"Gina?" He turned, his eyes sparkling. "You're . . ."

"Alive."

"And beautiful."

"You think I'm falling for that one, buddy boy?" She shook out her brunette locks with curled fingers. "This hair's out of control after sleeping on it wet. I looked in the mirror and thought I'd turned into Medusa."

"Not even funny. That woman was evil."

"Careful. I haven't had my coffee yet."

"Well then," Cal said, "treat's on me."

Gina's defenses came down as he slipped a hand through her hair and drew her close. He held her the way a returning soldier might after years of fighting upon foreign shores. In normal circumstances, she would've refused to accept a handout, but all that came out of her mouth was: "I think I'd like that."

"We have lots to talk about. There's a nice little bakery on Calea Mosilor."

She looked up at him, wondering why it felt so right to be in his arms, when Teo was just up the stairs and her husband was so far away.

"I wasn't sure I'd find you," Cal said. "Spent all night checking around, but it didn't click till this morning, while I was on a trolley car staring at a city map."

"'A great spot for a knight.'"

"That's me."

From above, the stairs creaked beneath the weight of Teo's lanky frame. His eyes were hooded, his chin rigid, as he reached the ground level. "So this is your reason for coming to Bucharest," he said.

"Meet Cal," Gina said.

Cal stretched forth his hand, and Teo gave it one firm pump.

"Teodor's the one who met me yesterday after I'd hiked to Bran Castle."

"And a friend of yours since way back," Cal said. "Yeah, I remember."

"I too." Teo took a step toward him. "Your face, it is still young. I was at the curb the day you sped off with Gina in your dented red Dacia."

"He saved my life, Teo."

"He took you away. What business has he in your affairs?"

Gina set a hand on the arm of her childhood companion. "Don't get yourself worked up. Cal knew my mother, and she enlisted his help long ago. If it weren't for him, she and I would've never made it to Chattanooga."

"Does he keep you from trouble? Or draw you to it?"

"Hey." Cal set down his daypack and leaned forward, chest to chest with the thinner man. "She's mine to watch after, you got that?"

Teo snatched his arm from Gina's touch. "Is this true?"

She stood beside them, thinking how silly it was that men postured like this. Was it really so necessary to establish the alpha male? Why couldn't they just play nice while strolling with her through the corridors of her heart?

"You phoned me, Gina. You said you needed me. And I drove nearly the length of the country, playing carriage driver to your highness, the queen."

Cal bumped Teo's chest. "Better show her some respect."

"Teo's right," Gina said, causing both men to turn her direction. "I shouldn't have called. I'm torn, okay? I care about both of you, and I definitely wasn't meaning to abuse your trust in any way, Teo."

"Do you love this man?" he insisted.

"Yes."

"And your feelings for me?"

"Please don't ask me that now. Of course you'll always be special."

"But it was only between children, is that it?"

"How do you want me to answer? We're adults now."

She felt his gaze slide off over her shoulder, while a brooding unrest took up residence in his eyes. She'd seen this same look in their childhood, though he'd never spoken of its source, and she wanted now to ease his despair. Ol' muddy waters. That was her. The more she attempted to settle these issues, the more sullied they seemed to become.

Beside her, Cal was a statue, his gaze locked on the other man.

Teo squirmed and swiveled away. "I'll wait until checkout, Gina. If you're still in need of my help, I will offer it. Otherwise, I must be returning home."

"*Calatorie placuta*," Cal mouthed. *Pleasant journey.*

Gina jabbed him in the ribs.

Teo paused, seemed to think better of it, then carried himself up the stairs.

"Guess that leaves coffee for two," Cal told Gina.

"Why not three?"

He shot her a look.

"Not Teo," she said. "I'm wondering where Dov is."

"Living up to his name," Cal said. "He's Concealed. It may be a while—a long, long while—but I have a sneaky feeling you'll see him again before it's all said and done." He hefted his pack and angled outside. "Let's go grab a bite."

"You take that thing with you everywhere, don't you?"

"If possible. I think of it as my Super-Duper Crush-a-Collector Bag."

"Ohh-kay." Gina wore a wry grin. "I think I'll just stick with 'pack.'"

Her feet were already throbbing, each blister chafing in her hiking boots. Her other shoes were on the charter bus, but considering the dogs that roamed Bucharest's alleyways, going barefoot could end in a messy misstep.

"Lead the way," she said. "We have a lot to catch up on."

"Man, you have no idea."

Ruins of Kerioth-Hezron

Barabbas met Erota at the crumbling walls of the old winepress and clamped a huge hand on her shoulder. She saw spots of red glimmering in his beard like sparks from a Beduoin campfire, and a tan shirt clung to his chest's contours.

"You're afraid of me?" he said.

"I forgot how big you were," Erota said. "You're . . . imposing."

His fingers dug into her skin. Though the sun was only now making an appearance, she could accept the dampening of her clothes in this desert climate, but refused to let the bodyguard see her pain.

"I'm here for Megiste," she said.

"She knew you were coming."

"A little birdy told her so?"

"Something like that," Barabbas said.

"You don't belong here," Erota said, slipping free of his grip. "You were once loyal to the House of Ariston."

"We've switched places, then. You once belonged to the House of Eros."

"Naturally, Barabbas. Eros was my father."

"And Megiste is still your priestess."

Erota cleared her throat, almost choked. "Yes," she managed to spit out.

The henchman's expression was flat. "Come with me."

Eleven years earlier, the entire cluster had reenervated the bones beneath the Akeldama, then answered the culling call of these desolate ruins. Here in this region, where Judas had played as a child, they had hunted and gathered before migrating to Eastern Europe in their efforts to track Gina and the Nistarim.

Despite the setbacks, that same hunt was still on.

And when all else fails, Erota told herself, *start back at the beginning.*

CHAPTER
TWENTY-ONE

Bucharest

Cal led Gina through the hostel's wrought-iron gate onto the street, his mind buzzing with things to be revealed. "You're limping," he noticed. "You okay?"

"Still breaking in these boots. I wore them from Busteni to Bran."

Cal empathized. Nearly eight centuries earlier, he'd been part of a trek that left many wounded and dead. He still remembered the wan faces of young children as they crossed the Italian Apennines on a tragic quest for peace.

"Listen," he told her. "We're just going around the corner."

"Sure, no problem."

"I can carry you if you want." And he meant it.

"What do you think I am?" she said. "Some wimpy girl?"

Although he wanted to answer, *"Don't you think every dad should be willing to carry his daughter,"* he knew it would sound abrupt, even manipulative. Instead he pointed to her bandaged limb. "How'd you get hurt? I've heard of people giving their right arm for something, but it looks like you gave up your left."

"Still works. And at least I knocked Ariston off the board."

"You went toe-to-toe and won?"

"Someone should've warned him to decline the queen sacrifice."

Cal chuckled.

"As for Shalom," Gina said, tapping her earlobe, "I had to give up something even more precious than my arm to put her down for good."

"Your earrings?"

"I still have this one left. See? Coming from you, it has sentimental value."

"Well, it was meant to be used."

"It sure did a number on the Collectors." She gave a brief rundown of her encounters in the cave and along the cliff. "Oh, here . . ." She produced the medieval coin from her pocket. "Ariston left something behind. Might be nothing, but when I kicked at him, I heard it clatter to the ground."

Cal accepted it from her. "Mind if I hold onto it for a while?"

"All yours. Just share the profits if you sell it on eBay."

"Uh, what's eBay?"

"This place on the Internet where you can . . . Never mind."

"Dov tells me I need to catch up with the times."

Cal turned his attention from her smirk to the distinctive coinage in his palm. During the Crusades, the Knights Templar had minted money to finance their wars. What started as quests in the name of God and country soon raged into atrocities spanning decades and ensnaring numerous races and creeds.

"I haven't seen these in ages," he said. "Not since my days in Italy."

"You really do get around, don't you?"

"Occupational hazard."

He tucked the item into his pack. Had Ariston used antique coins such as this to finance Totorcea Vineyards, as he'd done years ago with a jeweled armband from his burial cave? Or had this particular coin been mixed in with the rest of the Akeldama's relics, a clue to Natira's whereabouts? Why else would Ariston have toted around such a thing?

Nearly two thousand years earlier, Jerusalem's Field of Blood had been established as a cemetery for foreigners. Centuries later, the Knights Templar had built upon that same soil, with the ruins of their boneyard still standing to this day, visible to all who dared climb the dusty slope.

Had the knights inadvertently compromised the burial caves underneath, perhaps letting this coin slip during their digging?

How, though, would that fit with Erota's enigmatic clues?

At his side, Gina was trying to disguise her limp, and he told her they were almost there. He led her around the corner onto Calea Mosilor, and Gina stepped aside to make room for a lady in a head scarf, exchanging Easter greetings with her as nearby church bells chimed.

Cal's thoughts were still on the coin.

Years ago, he'd pored over Israel Antiquities Authority reports and read that the burial box next to Ariston's had been empty, smashed into orange-tinted shards. When fitted together, those shards bore an engraving that identified Ariston's warrior son.

"Do you know, Gina, that an Akeldama Collector is still missing?"

"And do we know where all the others are?"

"The House of Ariston, or what remains, is still over in Lipova at the vineyard. As for the House of Eros, they're back in Israel at Kerioth-Hezron."

"Never heard of it."

"Some old ruins out in the desert. A haunt of jackals."

Gina raised an eyebrow. "Why does that sound familiar?"

"In the Hebrew Bible, or *Tanakh*, it's the term for a number of different cities. Specifically, places that God left lifeless and desolate because of iniquity."

"Sounds, uh . . . fire and brimstone-ish. So who's this missing Collector?"

"Natira," Cal said. "Next in line as the cluster leader."

"Great. Just when I think we're getting ahead in this game."

"What I'm wondering is if the Knights Templar had something to do with Natira's disappearance. You know, in the thirteenth century they shipped tons of soil from Jerusalem to towns across Italy, believing it had supernatural properties. Hmm." Cal's fingers tapped his cheek. "Maybe they were onto something. Didn't the Renaissance, the 'rebirth,' start soon after that?"

"So you think Natira's down there somewhere, enjoying an espresso?"

"Or 'fava beans and nice Chianti.'"

"Uggh. That's not even funny, Hannibal."

"Sorry." He smiled. "Couldn't resist one of the few movie references I know. But yes, the big question is where's Natira? If I can determine his starting point, it'll help me track him down before he decides to come after me again."

Greeted by the aroma of fresh bread and pastries, Cal guided Gina through a glass-paned door marked *Brutarie*. He ordered coffee and pastries for two and chose a table at the window, where he could watch for potential foes.

"Least I don't have to worry about the calories," Gina said, biting into a cream-filled delight. "I might bloat up like a balloon, but hey—me being immortal and all—that shouldn't be any problem, right?"

"Hey, don't abuse it. Technically, you're only half-immortal."

"Ah, because of that whole three-day limitation dealie-whopper. Stretch me out on the rack, or put me under the guillotine—no problem, so long as I'm revived within seventy-two hours?"

"Pretty much."

"Handy bit of info." Gina relished another bite.

"You know what your birth date is?"

"July twenty-fourth."

"What year?" he asked.

"I'll be twenty-three in a few months. You tell me."

"1965."

"Those are some shaky math skills there, buddy boy."

"You're aging at half the normal rate, Gina. You're almost thirty-six, but you look eighteen. In 1989, when your physical body hit womanhood—age twelve by Jewish standards, which is why the letter Tav showed up—you were actually twenty-four. Your mom falsified your documents to show you being born in '77, a bogus date to match up with your appearance at the time."

"Go, Nikki. So you're saying when I'm sixty, I'll look thirty?"

"Not a bad gig," Cal remarked.

"Shoot, I'll have to change my name to Sophia Loren."

"Not a bad example. She looked thirty at age eighteen, and eighteen at age thirty. As close to the Unfallen as they come."

"Down, boy."

"Okay. I deserved that." He tilted his cup, dropped a sugar cube into the swill. He waited until a woman and her daughter had ordered and gone, leaving the bakery empty again. "As for you, I'm guessing you'll top out in your late seventies, maybe early eighties. But looking a very healthy forty, by my guess."

"And that's where I'll plateau?"

"Until Final Vengeance. Barring some accident, of course."

"How 'bout an attack? What if I had died in that cave on Friday night, and you weren't able to find me?"

"Lights out."

"So then why didn't you come after me, Cal?"

"If you hadn't shown up here, I would've still had a day or two to go looking for you. And in case you've forgotten, Dov and I had our hands full with a bear. Couldn't just up and leave the kid, could I? In fact, he and I faced off with Erota in a couple of different forms, but she managed to get away."

"You're sure Dov's safe now?"

"He's on his way to . . ." Cal winked. "Shelter, I guess you could say."

"He's not alone, is he?"

"Never again. By the way, he told me to let you know how much he appreciates you watching after him at the orphanage. You're probably the closest thing he now has to a mother."

"Will I . . . ?" Gina set down her coffee. "Will I get to see him again?"

"Like I said, could be a long time."

She tilted her head, coming to terms with that. "What about the orphans? Tell me they're tucked away and out of sight. Tell me no one else got hurt."

"They're under police protection."

"How'd that happen?"

"The muncitors, they panicked in Sinaia. Can hardly blame them, can you? After everything that'd happened, they drove straight to the main station here and the cops jumped all over it, putting the children in secure cells and holding the muncitors for questioning about the body on board."

"Petre?"

Cal nodded. "Petre Podran."

A sob caught in Gina's throat. Her nostrils flared. Cal reached across the table and covered her hand with his, more than aware of the guilt she must be feeling. Hadn't he borne that same weight on previous occasions?

"Gina?"

She gripped his fingers, a climber holding on for dear life.

"You fought hard," he said. "You helped save Dov."

"I lost Petre."

"You can't do it all on your own."

"How's Pavel taking it?"

"Hasn't said a word. Won't talk to anyone, especially the cops."

She met Cal's eyes. "He likes me. Maybe, if I go, he'll—"

"You can't." He waved off her objection. "You have to trust me."

"Where have I heard that before?"

"Listen, Gina." His voice turned stern. "You've gone through a lot— no argument from me—but that's no excuse for the attitude. I need you to work with me here. There's no way you can go back to Arad, not with the Collectors keeping an eye on Tomorrow's Hope, looking for you, me, anyone who might lead them to their coveted prize."

"The Nistarim. And Dov."

"That's right. It's now time for you to lay low, to disappear."

She withdrew her hand and began ripping bits of dough from her pastry. "What about me having a destiny, a purpose? You can't just ask me to do nothing."

"I haven't asked you anything yet."

"You told me to lay low."

"That was an order, not a request. I do have one crazy idea, though, something specifically suited to you."

Gina popped in a bite and chewed, her eyes never leaving his.

"See, under President Isarescu, there's been talk of putting a moratorium on all foreign adoptions. That's bad news for lots of people, but you've got dual citizenship as a Romanian, which means you could still pull this off."

"Do I want to hear the rest?"

"You tell me. How do you feel about adopting Pavel Podran, and—hold on a sec, hold on—moving back to the U.S. of A.?"

CHAPTER
TWENTY-TWO

Ruins of Kerioth-Hezron

Erota followed Barabbas along a hillside path. In the open area below, outlines of primitive houses and pathways squatted beside the remnants of a Byzantine-era monastery. Sand played about their legs, driven by wilderness winds, and the presence of simmering malediction heated the soles of her feet.

It's true, Erota realized. *This place is cursed even where I walk.*

"How'd you get to Israel?" Barabbas said over his shoulder. "By plane?"

"Much better than overland. You remember our first trek to Romania, in the backs of those trucks and that boat from Zonguldak?"

"And the stings of those jellyfish. Lord Ariston did try to warn us."

"Traveling has its toils, certainly. Considering my earthen vessel's limitations"—Erota patted the fashion jeans that shaped her backside—"even the plane's padded seats didn't give me much comfort."

"I, uh . . ." The henchman licked his lips. "I see what you mean."

His reaction was the very sort Erota hoped to evoke. Yes, she intended to forge a pact between the divided houses, but in the event that failed she might be able to lure away this testosterone-driven oaf.

Barabbas came to a halt at a wide bush. Erota wondered what could possibly be of any interest in this arid basin, then smiled as he pushed aside prickly branches to expose a cavity in the rock.

"Enter," he said.

"Where's Megiste?"

"She'll speak to us soon. Please, if you'd remove your shoes inside."

Erota cocked an eyebrow, humored by the incongruous image of being welcomed into a British manor by a butler in a black suit. Then she slipped through the crack and found herself gaping at a domed cavern's opulence. Six stone steps lowered her onto a carpet of plush animal pelts, where she toed off her shoes and sank weary feet into cushioned fur. Candlelight lent the space a sensuous glow that played between dips and depressions in the ceiling and trickled down over statuary, textiles, glittering baubles and gemstones. Some of the jewelry bore lockets and etched initials, and one gold timepiece looked to be of European origin.

Were these the House of Eros' spoils? Or merely stolen goods? Either way, Erota was impressed.

"Do you like it?" Barabbas said.

"It's beautiful. And more than enough room for your household, I see."

"What? No, this is only one chamber, shared by me and Megiste."

"How many are there?"

He pointed toward a thick drapery. "Through there, you'll find a warren of dens and tunnels. We've chosen the best-hidden ones with the easiest access."

Erota caught a sickly sweet odor from the direction of the passageway, and imagined what further wonders might lie beyond this room. "So," she said. "Is Megiste on her way?"

"She's already here," Barabbas replied.

His gruff voice brought to life an alabaster statue across the chamber. The kneeling figure was adorned in a cream-colored robe with a hood, her thin waist belted by a string of tan and black jackal tails. The priestess rose with the grace of a budding rose, the long curls framing her high cheekbones a velvety red no less resplendent.

"Shalom," Erota said in Hebrew. "I've come here in peace."

"Is that so, my young seductress."

Erota stiffened at the reminder of her days in the pagan temple, there to do the bidding of this priestess and her paying devotees. However, as a Collector, she'd been well served by such skills, and she told herself to remain focused on this trip's goal.

"So what brings you to our humble abode?" said Megiste.

"I've come to . . ."

"Yes, dear? Please don't hesitate. 'Ask and you shall receive.' Or is it, 'Ask and you shall deceive'? That *does* have a nicer ring, don't you think?"

"Megiste, I've come to discuss our cluster's future."

"*Our* future? Dear, dear, you speak as though we have something to share. Why *ever* would I want to give up what I've taken so easily on my own?"

"We need each other," Erota said. "I see that now."

She stepped forward, her golden anklets trailing over soft carpet. When Barabbas moved to stop her, he was gestured away by his leader, and Erota bent a knee before the willowy woman. She took the outstretched hand, lowered her eyes, and forced herself to kiss the ring upon Megiste's finger.

All for the greater purpose of destruction. For an end to the Concealed Ones and Gina Lazarescu; for Final Vengeance and the bleeding out of mankind.

"And to what do I owe this change of heart?" Megiste said.

"We are two houses divided. I believe it's time to join forces again and become stronger as one cluster."

"Oh? When you and I were last together—a few years back in Atlanta, if you've not forgotten—you chose to run off and pursue your own methods. I could've told you, dear, that you'd have little success among the American clusters. As a whole, their Consortium is egocentric and imperialistic. Though that may've wooed you to their way of thinking for a time, your cultural DNA is more suited to the tribal mind-set, don't you think?"

"That's why I'm here, my priestess. Is an apology what you want?"

"Not necessarily." Megiste shook her hand from Erota's grasp. "Stand, my dear. I'd *sooo* like to know your *true* motives for this long overdue visit."

"We are leaderless. Lord Ariston has gone to the Restless Desert."

"Gone?" Barabbas, Ariston's long-time acolyte, looked stunned.

"It happened two nights ago. In Zalmoxis Cave."

"At our own memorial site?"

"Now, now, Barabbas." Megiste flicked away his sentimentality while her eyes twinkled with new prospects. "It's merely one more added to the list."

"More than one," Erota corrected. And she spent the next minutes detailing the weekend's events, including the banishments of Shalom, Auge, and Nehemiah, as well as the disappearances of Cal, Dov, and Gina.

"We're a household in disarray," she said in conclusion. "Natira would be next in line to lead us, but long ago we came to a dead end—if you'll pardon the expression—in our search for him. Ariston and I were able to trace his steps to the end of Hitler's regime, and then . . . nothing."

Megiste's stare floated past Erota's head. Emotions pulled at her shaped eyebrows in a mixture of trepidation and hope.

"What're you thinking?" Barabbas said.

"Well, if he was up and about, I have to believe he would've found us by *now*. Or perhaps you've been mistaken all along, Erota, and his cherished bones were turned into hairpins by some crafty graverobbers of yesteryear."

Erota suppressed a flare of anger. "Not likely. In our long wait at the Akeldama, we never saw the graves compromised."

"Please, dear. In nineteen hundred years we never stumbled in our duty? We never looked away, or went flitting about Jerusalem? Come now, we all had our moments of impatience. We wandered—never far, but we did."

"I didn't," Barabbas stated.

"You mean to tell me," Megiste said in her honey voice, "you never trailed after a desirous woman or became transfixed by the trappings of a sultan?"

"Never."

"To be quite blunt, my dear—hogwash. Even in our Separated state, there were always *hints* of passing diversions."

The henchman clenched his teeth and fell silent.

Why was it, Erota wondered, that the very enmity Collectors tried to spill onto mortals seemed to slosh back and infect them as well? Divisions. Strife. Jealousies. All of it, diverting them from their primary task.

"And you?" Megiste was addressing her. "Did you ever stray?"

The priestess wanted substantiation for her theory that Natira was out of the picture, in which case there would be no rightful heirs to dethrone her. Nevertheless, Erota had seen with her own eyes the Knights Templar coin found at Natira's grave by Lord Ariston. She'd tested its residue, eliminated possibilities, then followed the most likely path from Italy into the heart of Nazi Germany.

"Megiste," she said, "I really didn't come all this way to nitpick."

"I know, I know. You came to seek unity, to bury the hatchet—an expression from the American Indians, perhaps?"

"Where is my sister?"

Barabbas stepped forward. "Domna is out hunting."

"Are you hoping to mend family bonds?" Megiste cooed.

"Not just family," Erota said. "The entire cluster. Or haven't I made that clear?"

"No need to be testy. Peace, peace, we all want peace." The candles' luster lent Megiste and her hooded robe an ethereal air. "Domna has her own furnished space down the way, while Hermione and Dorotheus share another chamber that's only slightly less palatial than the one in which we stand."

"But this land, this household, our cluster—we have a purpose that goes beyond such creature comforts."

"'Creature comforts.'" Megiste twirled a tail of her belt. "I like that."

"Did I waste my time in coming here, priestess?"

"That's for you to decide, I should think."

Erota swallowed her growing frustration. "Our vineyard is producing some deliciously human wines. Perhaps we can come to some agreement, whereby you are beneficiaries of our vintages while partnering in our work."

"Oh, most definitely not. It's a beautiful property there in Lipova, so idyllic, but it's tainted by some awful memories. Your own father, for example—a spike through the head out in that warehouse. Simply *awful.*"

Erota felt the bile rise in her throat.

"No," Megiste went on, "we're quite happy here on our own."

"Doing what, exactly? Accomplishing what?"

The priestess pulled her shoulders back, as she'd once done at pagan altars, arms spread wide and ringlets playing past her collarbone. "My dear, don't think you can come in and *presume* to know our activities. Have you yourself become *sooo* caught up in your humanity that you have no sense of horrific beauty even as it travels beneath those thin nostrils of yours?"

At that, the same cloying scent Erota had noticed earlier seemed to intensify, emanating from the tunnels beyond this room, undulating over the rugs. The smell was pregnant with dread and muffled pain.

"If you think you're up for it," Megiste said, "let me show you what we've been up to. Though it's vastly entertaining, you will need to look with your undead eyes, to view that which is darkened even to Collectors in mortal shells."

She nodded, struck dumb by anticipation.

"Come along then, Erota. Let's visit our palace of thorns."

Erota glided through the sandstone labyrinth in the wake of Barabbas and his robed leader. From sconces cut into the walls, candles sent wings of golden light fluttering along the corridor. A stranger thrust into this scenario might've mistaken it as a hall in a Saracen fort or a walkway in a

Tibetan monastery, but in reality it was a subterranean palace for Jerusalem's Undead.

Megiste came to a stop. "You see this tendril here?" She ran fingers over a strand that writhed along the wall at waist level. "We are the plants, if you will, Erota, living off this root system's nutrients. Each chamber is fed by such a tendril, for those moments when a sip of blood is needed."

"And where's its source?"

"That, my dear, is something to be witnessed firsthand. There's really no sense trying to put it into words, is there, Barabbas?"

"No sense at all."

Megiste turned and gave Erota a sly wink. "You'd think the big oaf was describing himself."

Erota said nothing. A lizard scurried past, hugging the wall.

"Don't mind those. Here between the Judean and Negev Deserts, and with the Dead Sea but a day's walk away, we find all *sorts* of creatures roaming about. Jackals being what they are, is it really any wonder they should scavenge the area? Even to this day, the biblical name for this place remains accurate, and the location has been verified for me by men of great learning."

"Students from Ben Gurion University?"

"That too. Actually, I was referring to certain ultra-Orthodox men."

"You've found a foothold among them?"

"Not all are susceptible, mind you."

"But the ones in Arad," Erota said, recalling their cluster's encounter years ago with a black-hatted man from the nearby town.

"Yes. It's not so difficult to twist their pious knowledge into hate."

"Then you have been busy?"

Megiste responded with a thin smile.

"Sodom's salt," Barabbas exclaimed. "You do underestimate her, Erota."

An almost putrid sweetness wafted down the hall, and Erota said, "Are we getting close? I already had quite a walk from the bus."

Megiste slowed her steps. "My masterpiece is in the next chamber.

Well, not mine com*pletely,* no. The household does deserve some credit, as well." She shot Barabbas a fey look. "Now as for your suggestion that we join forces, let me first say that I'm honored, Erota. But you must understand a saying we have here in Israel: '*Kachol lavan.*' Quite simply, it means we will do things for ourselves rather than relying on others. A laudable stance, considering the Jews' precarious position in this armpit of the Middle East."

"You're not Jewish, though. You have nothing to do with the God of Abraham, Isaac, and Jacob."

"And you do? Have you lost your *mind*, my precious one?"

Erota knew she'd overstepped her bounds. "That's not what I meant."

"What you need, it's quite clear, is replenishment. Come along."

In times past, the priestess had possessed an uncanny ability to undermine and infest. Now she seemed flighty, almost whimsical. Had she gone soft out here in the desert heat?

Ahead, Barabbas skirted a protrusion in the sandstone tunnel and moved out of view. When he reappeared, he gave Megiste an all-clear signal and stepped aside for the women to enter an earthen chamber.

CHAPTER
TWENTY-THREE

Bucharest

"You . . . you would trust me with that?" Gina scooted back from the bakery table, feeling unworthy of raising one of the orphans as her own.

Cal showed no hesitation. "You're the top of my list."

She stood to her feet and paced the tiled floor. Two days ago, she'd been on an excursion with her beloved kids—some with HIV, others with the scars of abuse, all with detachment issues. She was their sister, full of love without pity, and after the heartache of nearly three years ago, she'd found renewed meaning among them.

Two nights ago, however, that hope had been snatched away, stabbed and brutalized while she stood by.

Stop, Gina. Don't even go there.

"You'd make a good mom," Cal was saying. "So what do you think?"

She gazed out the front window. "I . . . I can't."

"You can."

"Isn't there someone else? Someone less . . . ?"

"What?"

"Likely to make a mess of things?"

"You'll never find purpose without risk, Gina. It comes with the territory."

"Where would I take him? Where would we live?"

"I'm working on that."

"Not Chattanooga. I can't go back there."

"Nowhere even close," he said. "Scout's honor."

She sat back down, brushed the crumbs from the table.

"I need to pull a few strings," Cal said, "with the Romanian Adoption Committee. Meantime, I'll set you up with a place to stay till things're done. You'll have papers to fill out, some questionnaires and legal stuff. Once I get the ball rolling, though, you and I will have to stop all direct contact."

"Where'll Pavel be during this?"

"A foster farm, you might say. Comforting a couple who lost their son."

"Near Bucharest?"

"There are some things it's best you don't know, Gina. You and Pavel will undergo identity changes for your protection, and of course his new name will be kept secret as part of the adoption."

"Won't the Collectors start suspecting something?"

"For the moment, I think we're off their radar. My plan is that Pavel Podran and Gina Lazarescu will have ceased to exist by the time they catch up. I've made lots of friends over the years, in lots of countries. Time to call in a few favors."

The bakery's front door opened, and Gina watched a pudgy man enter, his bushy eyebrows toggling in anticipation at the items behind the glass. She returned to her ruminations. What would it be like to raise a nine-year-old son? Would such an arrangement end any chance of her and Jed getting back together?

"And just in case you're wondering . . ." Cal whispered. "He's next."

She looked up. "Who?"

"Pavel. From what I can tell, he's lining up to be a Concealed One. Which could explain why the Collectors targeted his twin in the parking lot. Maybe they mistook Petre for Pavel and tried taking him out with a preemptive strike."

"How could they know?"

"Based on years of observation, they're able to come up with some pretty good guesses. If anything, my presence was a major clue."

"Are you saying you can detect the next Concealed Ones?"

Cal patted the air, indicating to keep the volume down. Bushy Brows was squeezed into a seat behind them with his treats. "It's a role I've taken on," Cal said, "narrowing my focus to find those who might fill a role among the Thirty-Six, the Lamed Vov. I've even spotted the Letters on their expectant mothers."

"Like me." Gina cringed at that memory. "Not that it did any good."

"This is . . ." He paused. "Based on the past, I don't blame you for doubting some of things I say. This is my way of trying to make amends."

"For losing Jacob? I meant what I said the other night: I forgive you."

Across the table, the sun shown on Cal's face and caused the gold flecks in his irises to draw closer, like metal shavings to a magnet. Was that moisture in his eyes? In the past forty-eight hours, Gina had felt her world coming apart, yet here sat a man willing to put everything on the line to give her a second chance.

A new name. New life.

Another shot at being a mother.

"Doesn't it ever get old?" she said, her heart swelling in appreciation. "All the secrecy and hiding, the solitude. It must drive you crazy."

"I've been accused of worse."

What was it about Cal Nichols? She loved her husband, despite the miles now separating them, and she would always have a soft spot for Teo. But with Cal she felt something . . . beyond words.

"You're a good man," she told him. "I don't care what anyone else thinks."

"Gina." He hesitated, then touched her hand again. "I need to clear the air. I need you to know that I've made some big mistakes along the way."

"Wouldn't be human if you hadn't."

"Then again, I'm not exactly mortal anymore, am I?"

"Not exactly 'died and gone to heaven,' either."

"Okay, I need to say this." He shifted. "I should've said it long ago."

" 'Hit me with your best shot.' "

He grinned. " 'You're a tough cookie.' "

"You're kidding me. You know Pat Benatar? See, you're not as out of touch as Dov thinks. Now stop procrastinating and spit it out already."

Ruins of Kerioth-Hezron

The scent grew heady. A lusty luminescence drew Erota in. She found herself in a cavern that dwarfed the previous one, a space rising into darkness that even hundreds of tapered candles failed to penetrate. Barabbas took up his post at the far end of the chamber—an exit to the outer world by the look of it—while Megiste pushed back her hood and took hold of a candelabrum.

"Behold . . . ," she said, lifting the object in melodramatic fashion. "This here is where we share our household meals—the breaking of bread, the drinking of wine. If you will, it's where we come when it's time to . . . prey."

Erota squinted into the shadows, aroused by moans and trickles and the taste of anguish in the air. She followed the circle of light, as Megiste paraded along the room's perimeter, casting panels of artwork into bas relief, then painting them again in shades of crimson and gold.

It was a living collage, Erota realized.

But just barely.

As though conjured by the willowy priestess, vines curled out from the individual panels, climbing toward the ceiling and sliding onto the floor. Brambles knotted in the air, twining through and around each other, forming arches and bowers of intricate design, each of their thorns engorged and pulsing red. The entire cavern had transmogrified into a palace of gothic beauty.

"Isn't it lovely?" Megiste said, gazing upward. "And it smells so *rich.*"

"What is the purpose of such a place?"

"Look closely with undead eyes, and I think you'll understand."

Erota adjusted her gaze and picked out the first inklings of human limbs, breathing bodies, a macabre Collection woven into the walls and layered with various skin tones and seductive shapes. The artwork glistened, dripping with fresh wounds and recent tortures. Students and clergy, tourists and worldy-wise backpackers, soldiers in uniform and women in traditional garb—all were represented. Some were whole, hanging onto life, while others had been vivisected by their thorns, sacrificed for the sake of composition.

The Collector took a step back, overwhelmed.

"Tell me now," said Megiste. "Is it clear what I've been up to?"

"You're out to break the Concealed Ones' backs," Erota whispered.

"To put it delicately."

"If even one should stumble beneath the weight . . ."

"That's correct. Out of our rage, we've produced agonies that now claw at the Nistarim's ears. Why gallivant the globe in search of thirty-six wretched men when we can escalate sorrows from this forlorn patch of soil? Don't you see? We'll not only cause them to stumble, we'll drive them to their knees and *crush* them into dust."

"But other clusters have—"

"Have what, my dear? Done it all before, with a tad less *style?*" Megiste tilted the candelabrum to spotlight a section where severed legs hung knitted together with morbid flair. "While you and your household bemoaned your situation, we've taken full advantage of ours. What can multiply humanity's anguish more effectively than striking at the things most grievous to the Ever-so-Fickle One? We have here 'six, no seven things the Lord detests.' "

The premise, Erota knew, was yanked from the book of Proverbs, and she reveled at its audacity. She stepped closer.

For a full hour, maybe more, she moved about the chamber, admiring the handiwork—to Megiste's great pleasure—and comparing the wall's overlapped panels with the list as she knew it.

It was all here on display. Six, No, Seven Things:

Haughty eyes . . . These trophies of manhood and womanhood were arranged in lurid positions, memorializing those whose bold eyes and smooth lips lured others into depravity. Interspersed throughout the panel, dozens of skulls—many capped in religious accoutrements—showed the cracks of hubris and self-righteous duty.

Lying tongues . . . What seemed a casual thing revealed itself in images of black humor, with a sea of wagging tongues, their tips slathered with the venom of verbal abuse and malicious rumors.

Hands that killed the innocent . . . Here, fists and fingers gripped rifles and knives, revealing their lust for violence. The atrocities were no less heinous than any serial killer's work, and yet Erota was most moved by the subtleties of a doctor who stretched forth a suction tube for the most innocent ones of all.

Hearts that plotted evil . . . Behind sandstone polished to a glassy sheen, blackness oozed from beating hearts, staining rib cages that rose and fell with the breath of guilty schemers. From suicide bombers to back-alley muggers to executives who skimmed from retirement funds, depravity was on display.

Feet that raced to do wrong . . . Boots, sandals, high heels, and tennis shoes formed a stampede of men and women, young and old, who pursued wickedness in its fleeting glory. Mobs and robberies, rapes and promiscuities were sculpted from real-life subjects.

False witnesses who poured out lies . . . Placed in boxes like stacked TVs, the mouths of these talking heads were raw and ragged from their constant sibilation of untruths. Reputations were undone; family men, children, and wives brought low. One prosecutor, still dressed in suit and tie, prattled on in his courtroom manner unaware that the jury had long ago adjourned.

And those who sowed discord among brothers . . . By speech and innuendo, these insidious souls had filed swords more deadly than bronze or steel, slicing homes, shops, even townships in two. A pair of half-dead churchgoers were still frozen in a clench, hissing careless, cutting words, while blinded by wooden staves through their eyes.

"What do you think, Erota?"

It was glorious, a pantheon of horrific grandeur.

"Have you had any trouble with the police?" she asked.

"You're wondering about the missing victims, I suppose? Well, we do take precautions, with Barabbas doing the more tawdry work, and Hermione and Dorotheus keeping active watch. Like our dear jackals, we most often forage at night—in hospitals, side roads, bomb zones, and so on. A body a day, maybe two—and as you've seen, the numbers *do* grow rapidly."

Erota was having a hard time concentrating. She felt light-headed. Tendrils extended from human veins and arteries in the wall's transparent panels, swarming overhead, summoning her thirst like a beast from the deep.

"Yes, oh yes," Megiste said. "I can see you'd like a drink."

Hypnotized by these blasphemous vintages—please, just one tannic spurt into her mouth—Erota found her thoughts turning to sludge. She lifted a hand toward an archway of throbbing thistles.

"Yes, dear," said Megiste. "I see that forbidden desire . . ."

Forbidden?

The guidelines of the Collector Procedure Manual were the furthest thing from Erota's mind. She pincered a thorn between pinkie and thumb.

Broke it loose.

Recoiling en masse, the vines braided themselves into one mighty strand and encircled the cavern like purse strings drawn to protect one's valuables.

She blinked, fighting off slumber, and told herself she could not partake. Why? Because these vines were not hers, not of her vineyard. Staring at the thorn-cup between her fingers, enraptured by its scent, she recalled the penalty of stealing from another household's Collection. With even one unauthorized sip, she would find herself bound to Megiste, a slave to her schemes.

"I . . . can't."

"You can." The alabaster face floated into view.

Erota tilted the cup, imagined her tongue lapping up its liquid, her throat working it down in great, greedy—

"Not again," she stammered. "Not . . . not to you, Megiste."

"Oh? But I should've known that you would not submit. Nevertheless, I remain this household's leader."

"A role you usurped."

"It was left empty, actually."

"Only because Dov Amit drove a skewer through my father's head. And now you're trying to benefit from my family's misfortune."

The woman patted Erota's cheek. "And that's as it should be. You see, dear, the Almighty tries to work all things together for good, whereas we do just the opposite. Is that *sooo* hard to understand? By directing our efforts to these Six, No, Seven Things, we've already seen signs of erosion."

"What're you saying?"

"The Concealed Ones, they are quavering even now beneath this burden. Earthquakes. Tsunamis. Wars and rumors of wars."

"You don't think that you're actually responsible for—"

"Think what you will, Erota, but don't expect us to share our glories. No, and again, no. You'll only go on failing, as you did in Chattanooga, Sinaia, and so forth. Your House of Ariston is a crippled, fatherless bunch."

Erota shook off her fuzzy thoughts. She had to get out of this place. She and her household would find their own methods for accelerating Final Vengeance.

"Show me the way out," she said.

Megiste brushed aside coiled hair that had fallen into her eyes. "My sweet dear, in light of your teenage petulance, I cannot allow you to roam wild."

"Petulance? I came here for reconciliation."

"And *that*, my dear, is something I've never been much in favor of."

Barabbas was upon Erota in a flash, sprung by an imperceptible signal—the flick of his leader's hair? His thick thighs and arms covered the distance before she could react, and one huge hand slammed upward into her throat. She could not breath, could not bite. Her fangs dropped down to retaliate, but she was staring into the darkness above, her toes lifted from the cave floor.

"Do with her as you will," Megiste said.

The household henchman had always wanted Erota. A raspy growl signaled his anticipation as he started toward the corridor.

"No, no," the priestess said. "Do it in here, you brawny oaf."

A low grunt.

Erota, seizing their moment of discord, hooked her legs around her captor's rock solid hips, then locked her ankles. As his pupils widened in desire, the hand loosened at her neck. She clawed her fingernails up through his wiry beard and threw herself backward, drawing him down with her.

Barabbas' expectation flared further as her teeth ripped into his lower lip. His blood was salty and hot. He groaned.

Still caught in their downward tumble, Erota used his own weight against him, releasing the leg-lock and tossing him back over her head. He struck the earth with a shuddering jolt, while she hopped back to her feet and darted for the outside exit. Ghostly fingers caught at her. She tore free. Megiste called out, and in response, the monstrous braid of scarlet-tinged vines coiled through the air and tried to catch Erota midstride. She jump-roped twice through the thorny loops, tripped, righted herself, and dove outside through the fissure in the rock.

A bed of warm desert sand eased her fall, but gravity was not done with her. She rolled, tried to catch herself, rolled again, flipped, then landed atop a jagged knob.

What was this? How strange.

Like the Man from Kerioth two millennia earlier, her belly had ruptured and her juices now sizzled down the face of the rock. She peeled herself away, finding in this connection to Judas some respite from her human pain.

She pressed a fist into the wound, trusting her undead frame to stitch itself back together, and took off in a lurching gallop. Her path led past the ruins toward a gap between the slopes.

"Erota, come back!"

She threw a glance at Barabbas' form in the opening up the slope. Did he really think that she'd be so foolish? That he could still have a shot with her?

Beside him, Megiste appeared with her mouth curled in bland amusement. It was an expression Erota had seen during her days of temple service, one that disguised the woman's most dangerous moods.

Still running, Erota gave the pair one more look.

Barabbas had his eyes glued to Erota, but his lids were already drooping as the priestess ministered to his injured lip with gnawing, anesthetizing bites.

CHAPTER
TWENTY-FOUR

Bucharest

"Gina, there's a lot you don't know about me." Cal's demeanor was guarded, his voice touched by anxiety, and in the bakery's sunlit glow, he saw concern blossom in his daughter's deep-brown eyes. Despite his miscues and untold secrets, it was clear she still cared for him, and this only intensified his fear of earning her permanent rejection.

"Well," she said, turning playful. "I know that you're immortal."

"Never say die."

"And good-looking."

"Runs in the genes," he said, though she failed to get his gist.

"And, uh, you're good at different languages and disguises. Speaking of which, that mustache has got to go. No offense."

"Thing's scratchy anyway."

"One question." Gina drained the last of her coffee. "I know my mom didn't like you coming around me when I was younger. I heard her say she couldn't trust you. Why? What'd you do that made her so upset?"

"What's she told you about me?"

"Nothing. Nada. Zippo."

"Well, she swore me to silence long ago. You need to know that, because it's the reason I've kept quiet all this time. For your protection, Gina. And for the sake of Nikki's pride, I guess. Your mom lives every day with her own shame, and she tends to take things seriously."

"Tell me about it."

"Not that I'm excusing her." Cal knew Nikki's peddling of self-help to the masses was an effort to find some solace of her own. "But now that you've seen the Collectors up close, maybe her paranoia makes a little more sense."

"I'm trying to understand. I am."

"They infected her, and that's the part she can't forgive herself for."

"So she took it out on a little girl?"

"It was her way of trying to keep you safe, keep you pure."

Gina's eyes trailed off through the store window, while her hand moved to the mottled skin of her neck. At the table against the wall, Bushy Brows was applying a napkin to his mouth.

"She didn't want to lose you," Cal said.

"Well, she almost did."

"You can still start fresh, you know? Doubly alive."

Gina wiggled her remaining earring. "With this?"

"Just one drop."

From down the boulevard, Easter bells chimed once more. Though Cal feared Gina's resentment for his years of silence, for Nikki's extreme measures, he now marveled at life's poetic beauty. It had all led to this moment—at a table in a Bucharest bakery, with sunbeams reaching over the rooftops and peals of renewal ringing in the air.

"You can drink it now," he offered.

"You know how twisted that sounds? How do I know I'm not jumping onboard with all the religious wackos out there? I know I can't keep holding on to what Nikki's done. I get that. But it doesn't mean I want to be like her."

"The point is to be like Him."

"The Nazarene?"

"His Blood purifies. Not yours or your mother's."

Gina's fingers trembled as she touched the earring. "I've seen what it does to the Collectors. It's going to hurt, isn't it?"

"Yes."

"Gee, thanks. You could've at least softened the blow."

"It's a complete transfusion, Gina. When the Blood washes through, it pinpoints each place the thorns've tried taking hold. That's the worst part, but also the part that makes everything else worthwhile. Think of it like plucking a bunch of splinters or trying to remove a tumor. As they say: no pain, no gain."

"Ahh," she said. "Well, in that case . . ."

Cal watched her rise again from the table, her forehead furrowed, eyes unfathomable. Wincing, she took long strides to the trash can, where she crumpled her plastic cup and shoved it through the opening. She stared off through the glass, hand slipping from her ear to the wound on her neck.

She came back and faced him. "There's something you said . . . If I'm half-immortal, what about my mom? Is she immortal, like you?"

"Nikki? No."

"How does that make any sense? We already know your math's lame, but it seems your biology's not exactly top-notch either. If I'm half-immortal, that would make her fully immortal."

"Either that," he said, "or fully human."

She studied his face. "If that were the case, it would mean that . . . that my father . . ."

He nodded.

She took a moment to let that sink in, narrowed her gaze, and fixed her lips into a frown, then struck his cheek with a stinging slap.

"Gina, I—"

"You lied to me. You never told me."

"I couldn't. I was sworn to secrecy by your mother."

"You let me grow up without a dad? You let Nikki carry out her little cutting rituals, figuring I was strong enough to handle it? Heck, you even *helped* her that one night outside of Borsa. My own *parents*, bleeding me of my sins."

Head down, Bushy Eyebrows scurried from the premises.

"It was the only time I ever did that," Cal said.

"How restrained of you."

"I was trying to mislead the Collectors. There was one of them almost upon us that night—right on our tails, if you remember—and that was the only way I could send them hoofing it in the wrong direction, using your blood to feed them misinformation. Gina, you've got to understand that."

"Get away from me."

"Please. Let me explain."

"Now? After twenty-two . . . uh, thirty-six years? Whatever. All of this, it's ridiculous, Cal. Or am I supposed to start calling you Dad now?"

Cal's eyes brimmed. For so long, he had hoped to hear that word from her lips, and here she hurled it like a spear into his chest. Freed from the Separation, he knew sorrow would one day be no more, and it was this certainty that most often kept his own tears at bay. Right now, however, there was no stopping the hot trickles that worked their way down his face.

"Why the waterworks?" she said. "Shouldn't I be the one crying?"

"I love you."

"Love?" She swiped a hand at her own eyes.

"It was lonely," he said, "being one of only thirty-six. Not that it's any excuse. I ended up losing my Letter, all for one night with Nikki."

"Okay. TMI. You think I really want to hear this?"

"But then *you* came along, Gina—the most perfect little baby I had ever seen. I've adored you since that very first day in Seattle."

"Seattle?"

"Where you were born. When Nikki took you to Romania a few years later, she changed your papers to show that you'd been born in Cuvin."

Gina's gaze shifted out the window again.

"Back then," Cal said, ignoring another tear as it rolled off his chin, "fathers couldn't go in during delivery. The moment they brought you out, though? I took you in my arms and never wanted to let go. Believe *that*, if nothing else. From the moment I first laid eyes on you, I was in love. Later, your mother insisted we all stay apart, for your safety and mine. Despite that dragon-lady persona of hers, she was just trying to keep any sort of evil from getting its hooks into you."

"How ironic." Gina reached up and gripped the bulge on her neck. "The real hooks came from her misguided little surgeries."

"Funny how parents end up doing that. I'm sorry."

Her countenance softened. "Cal, I want to believe you. I do. Just tell me, is there anything else to divulge while we're getting things off your chest?"

"Nothing that can be said right now."

"So there is more."

"There's always more, isn't there?"

"Apparently so."

Contrary to his fatherly instincts, Cal decided there were matters she was still better off not knowing. How would she react, for example, to hearing about a twin brother who'd been lost years ago? She was upset enough as it was.

"We need to get moving," he said. "Every second we stay here is another second gained by the Collectors."

"In that case, why not just give me another cut?" Gina nudged her dagger from its sheath. "Go ahead. Create a little diversion again."

"Gina." He stood and removed the weapon from her hand. "I will never—you hear me?—*never* do that again."

Her curved brown eyes searched his.

"Now, please," he said, "put this away, and let's get you out of here."

"What if I say no?"

"I won't make you. I'm only asking as your father."

She weighed that. Blinking, she took a half-step toward him.

At the sight of her deflated posture, he did that which came naturally. He reached out and gently enfolded her petite frame in his arms, grasping at grace, and hoping in some small way he might impart it as well.

Gina walked a bit taller, a bit quicker, as she followed Cal Nichols back to Elvis's Villa Hostel. Her indignation had melted into relief, even joy, knowing the intense feelings she harbored for him had a basis in a biological connection.

She, Regina Lazarescu, was not fatherless.

Never had been.

Fragments of her childhood now fitted together into mosaics with a specific pattern, points at which her father had shown himself. Her twelfth birthday—and a young provocateur bearing earrings as a gift for his daughter. Her chess mastery—and a handsome instructor challenging her at the board with lessons of honor, duty, and combat.

There were still gaps, but she could live with that for now. Here she was, strolling the streets of Bucharest with her dad.

Which meant Teodor, back at the hostel, deserved an explanation.

Oh, Teo, I'm sorry. Don't you see, it had nothing to do with you? I'm his daughter. No wonder I felt all this love for him. No wonder.

By the time they returned, however, Teo was gone. The clerk explained that the tall, thin man had covered Gina's expenses and left something for her here in a paper bag. She took it. The scent of blackberries, and their juicy tang in her mouth, stirred those childhood flirtations in the village of Cuvin.

"I don't trust him," Cal said. "Why would he pay for you to stay here?"

"Relax. I'm a grown woman, not a little girl."

"Yeah, and he seems to be fully aware of that."

"Teo's a travel agent, that's all. It's his job to make arrangements."

"I still don't trust him."

"You know, Cal, now you're even sounding like a dad."

"Really?"

"Really."

Even with the silly mustache that he'd grown for his role as orphanage bus driver, even with his Romanesque nose and mesmerizing eyes and the thick waves of hair that had been dyed so many times Gina had no idea of its true color, there was no hiding his ear-to-ear grin.

CHAPTER TWENTY-FIVE

Jerusalem, Israel

Cal Nichols met two weeks later with one of the Concealed Ones, in a spice shop on David Street. It was a nondescript place, lost in the shuffle, a perfect spot for him to broker his latest intel.

Cal loved this city, always had. Although born on the island of Cyprus, he'd lived and married here, been buried here.

It was good to visit. Good to be doubly alive.

Here within the walls of Jerusalem's Old City, crowds pressed through covered alleyways on this Friday afternoon. They came from all directions and through different city gates—the Jaffa Gate, the Dung Gate, Herod's Gate, and so on—their very passage a reminder of those who had gone before, invaders and defenders, redeemers and kings, the rich and poor and the poorest of the poor, all carrying on their business in this revered location.

Shabat, the Sabbath, would soon usher in a day of rest—even as the Lord had rested on the seventh day—and dancing and singing would take place down by the Western Wall, while the Dome of the Rock gleamed just beyond.

Until then, tourists from around the world took photos before the prohibitions of such at sundown. Orthodox rabbis and Russian Jews race-walked to and fro, side locks swinging beneath traditional kipas and tall fur hats. Israeli flags fluttered above the broad square, and a police vehicle stood guard, a reminder that even with cries of *shalom, shalom,* peace was threatened by those who knew only strife.

Stalwart and silent amidst the bustle, the old temple's remaining stones turned gold then pastel pink with the setting of the sun.

One more day, in a line of thousands upon thousands.

One day closer, the rabbis believed, to their place of worship being rebuilt. It was written that the Almighty's presence would never leave His temple, and even now He hovered to hear the wailing of His people.

"You bring me news, Nickel? Good. When you visit, I am made happy."

"Are you ever *not* happy?"

"I am what I am, and you know this more than most."

Isaac, the spice shop owner, was a slight fellow, with dark curly hair and a smile so irrepressible that tourists often assumed something was not quite right with him, harmless as he seemed to be.

In one way, Cal thought, they were correct. Isaac numbered among the original Nistarim, changed from mortal to immortal after being marked in the days of Ezekiel. His smile was a brave cover for the torments he'd carried two thousand years, and if this Holy City in any way magnified mankind's griefs, then Isaac had the toughest assignment of them all.

"Sometimes I wonder how you keep smiling," Cal said.

"It is no big task." Isaac topped off his rows of vibrantly colored spices, then stabbed display markers into each of the heaps at precise diagonal angles. "I have seen the glory that awaits."

"But we . . . we were never given a glimpse of heaven, were we?"

"Oy, but I have seen the Nazarene."

Chastised by the man's faithfulness, Cal remembered again how he had once strayed from the simple joy of serving Yeshua. Now, each day, he learned more, growing in his own knowledge of the Nazarene Blood.

"You are not finished," Isaac said.

"Yeah? Well, between you and me, there are times I'm not so sure."

"No, Nickel, you misunderstand. I mean you are not finished with what you were telling me."

"Oh, yeah. Of course."

"Come to the back, where we speak beyond the ears of these people."

Isaac eyed the throng in the shadowed alleyway, the press of stocky Europeans and Arabian women in flowing *burkas*. He gestured to his assistant to take over the shop, then hooked an arm through Cal's and dragged him through curtains that billowed with aromas of cardamon, zăatar, and tumeric. He pointed to a bulging sack. The coarse material wore a coat of reddish powder as it tried to contain its contents.

"Sit," Isaac said.

Cal sat.

The Concealed One smiled his irrepressible smile.

"How's Dov?" Cal said.

"Safe and hidden away. We'll make sure he doesn't forget the things you taught him."

"He's a good kid."

"But this is not why you are here, no?"

"I came to tell you what I've learned about the Akeldama Collectors," Cal said. "I was able to question one of them—"

"With the lebben? This is tricky."

"It seems some of them are entrenched again here in Israel. I went this morning to the Kerioth-Hezron ruins, but I couldn't get too close. Still, I was able to verify things through some bloodstains on a rock. Megiste's there, and her crew."

"Yes, yes. I have seen this myself." Isaac waved off Cal's look of concern. "It was weeks ago, a trip to gauge their threat, and I saw Barabbas there. Tell me, have you found the missing warrior yet?"

"Getting closer."

"Not too close, no? We know what happened last time, and the other thirty-five still wonder that you did not call for help. We were so very nearby."

"I know, Isaac. I know. Believe me, I'm done fighting alone."

"Good. Now tell me of your daughter. How is she?"

"She's my daughter, and she's . . . she's fantastic." Cal swelled with pride at being able to claim her as his own. "She's still healing, still on the run, but about to be hidden away—until the time comes."

"It's as it should be. She was a young girl when I saw her last, a brown-eyed beauty at that! You must keep watch after her."

"The Unfallen are on duty as we speak."

"As they always are. Very good. This search of yours, now where does it lead you?"

"The next step is still unclear. I'll be going back to Bucharest soon, but three days ago I was in Pisa, and I flew in from Frankfurt last night."

"Oy, to be young and adventurous again."

"Ah-ah." Cal wagged a finger. "You can't fool me."

"We are what we are, Nickel. So there was something in Pisa?"

"As you already know, soil here from Jerusalem was shipped to Italy hundreds of years ago and turned into numerous graveyards. Did you know, though, that World War II planes bombed one of those cemeteries?"

"The Campo Santo."

"Exactly."

"And you think this warrior's bones—"

"Natira."

"He was released at that date?"

"July 1944. Only a theory, but it matches with this coin." Cal relinquished the Knights Templar item, watched Isaac's eyes sparkle with intrigue. From outside came the city's late afternoon murmur. "That dates from the thirteenth century, so what would it be doing in the Akeldama, right? I believe Natira was dug up and carted off, only to be buried again in Pisa."

"Yes, yes. I see this." In a habit from the past, Isaac bit the edge of the coin to test its mettle. "But he did not stay there, no?"

"He joined the Nazis."

The smile faltered, though so briefly a casual observer would've missed it. "What makes you sure of this?"

Cal explained how the time frame of the Campo Santo's bombing had forced him to reconsider Erota's clues, ridiculous as they had first sounded. *"He's in knotsies . . . he has a gift . . ."* In context, the first part was simple to see; with Cal's language proficiency, the second was only slightly harder to decipher.

Gift . . . In German, it was the word for "poison."

There in Pisa, Cal pored over history books, studied the details of the Allied bombing, and discovered that German tanks had been retreating from battles in North Africa and southern Italy.

A half-day later, Cal came upon a possible link. It seemed a Doktor Ubelhaar had been among the fleeing battalions, passing through the vicinity on his return to Germany. Later, at his Nazi laboratory, he would milk the venom of his captured African boomslangs in the development of Gift 12, a poison gas.

Snakes? Cal curled his lip at the thought. Well, at least it wasn't spiders.

"And so, Nickel, you have been to Frankfurt to find this doctor?"

"He's long dead, actually, due to a mishandling of his own snakes." Cal shifted his weight on the spice sack. Once this meeting was done, he would smell like a falafel. "I did go to check the records of his work, though. Thanks to German efficiency, the paper trail was easy to follow. Took me only a day to find it."

"Go on. I have work to do, Nickel."

Cal handed the Concealed One a yellowed photo, dated January 1945 in the corner. It showed a group of scientists and assistants stood in three rows, blank-faced before a low concrete building. Cal had circled the person of interest, a Goliathan fellow who towered over the others from the back row.

"That's Natira?"

"I'll never forget his face."

"He came hunting after you many years later, and what then?"

Cal, however, was lost in a memory. The sounds of Jerusalem faded, as well as the colorful dust that wafted in the shop's storeroom.

He was back at a riverbank, stunned by the death of his loved one. He was grappling with his undead foe, slapped by the stench of that fetid breath. It seemed the Collector's physique had been chiseled from a monster piece of granite, broad blows used to define his musculature. Though Natira's face had been given more attention to detail, the eyes were crude hollows, scooped from stone and finished in a hurry with chunks of obsidian thrust into the sockets.

"Hello?" Isaac said. "This Natira, where did he go?"

"That's still anyone's guess. The more I know, and the less he knows that I know, the better chance of us knowing how to find him."

Isaac looked off toward the curtains, putting that together in his head. Satisfied, he patted Cal's shoulder, returned the coin and the photo. He seemed in a sudden rush to be done with their chat, and knowing the man's trained instincts, Cal assumed it was for a good reason.

As Cal rose to go, Isaac wedged a small jar into his pocket.

"A mix of best spices. You take it," the curly-haired man said with a conspiratorial nod. "Maybe you will find something to your taste, something to . . . Oy, to give energy for your search. Yes, yes. I think you will appreciate, no?"

"No," Cal said. "I mean, yes."

And still that irrepressible smile.

Bucharest

For three weeks now, the reality of Gina's lineage had seeped into her marrow. For three weeks, she'd been holed up here under a false identity. Soon she'd be on her way to the U.S. with a doctored passport and nine-year-old son in tow.

Cal's instructions had been clear: "Talk to no one. You stay out of sight and off the radar. You have to trust me till this is done, you got that?"

She'd nodded like a good girl, sensing that dad-daughter connection. Despite ramifications that were too deep to fathom, she knew she wouldn't shrink from the purposes set before her. Yes, she would do all that her father stipulated.

Except for this one little thing.

Two evenings ago, she'd placed a surreptitious call to Teo. With Cal's identity now revealed, her heart's romantic choices had narrowed to her estranged husband in Oregon and the Romanian love of her youth.

Teo said he would pick her up if she'd only tell him where she was staying, and she had almost let it slip—a quaint *pensione* outside the capital city—then checked herself. Perhaps a neutral place would be better. She'd suggested the Village Museum in Bucharest, and he agreed to make the long drive for one last get-together.

Today was the day.

Gina took a morning bus into the city, where she transferred to another. As she rode past road workers, prancing young women, and grocery-laden shoppers, she felt her pulse quickening.

Was this really the best move? In chess terms, it was "dubious."

A quote popped into her mind, something from George Eliot that she'd learned as a child: *"Fancy what a game of chess would be if all the chessmen had passions and intellects . . . if you were not only uncertain about your adversary's men, but a little uncertain also about your own . . ."*

Gina was still uncertain of many things, especially her own heart. Although she scolded herself for defying her father, she felt the need to pursue this, this one selfish desire. She needed to explain things to Teo.

And if not now, when?

Soon she would be nestled away on a far corner of the chessboard—to be forgotten or, perhaps, to reenter the skirmish at a later date. Until recent years, she'd been a playing piece unaware of Those Who Hunt; now she was moving as part of a larger strategy, coordinating, resisting along with her other *piese de sah.*

What would happen in America? How would she adjust to living in the Pacific Northwest, renting a modest home in an Oregonian town?

"Close to Jed again," Cal had pointed out during their last discussion. "I'll have to give the okay before you try making any contact with him."

That was more than Gina could think about. "How's Pavel doing?" she'd asked her father. "Is he talking yet?"

"A little, but he's still in shock. Nothing will bring back Petre."

"Isn't there some way we can wash away those images?"

"You tell me. Sounds like something your mother would've tried."

That was the last they had spoken of the matter. For the first time, Gina understood Nikki Lazarescu's efforts to protect her all those years, with genuine care behind her distorted methods. The bleedings, the slice of the blade . . . They were attempts not only to cleanse but to blur her daughter's memories.

The crazy part was that Gina now found herself considering similar methods for her soon-to-be son. None of that hocus-pocus stuff. It'd be for his good, of course. To purge his sorrow. Wouldn't Pavel be happier if his mind no longer replayed the impaling of his twin brother?

Enough of that.

Gina stepped off the bus a few blocks from the Village Museum. Even as she walked the tree-lined boulevard toward the tourist site, she mulled the new name on her passport, the one she would be answering to in the U.S. of Everyone-for-Themselves A.

Kate Preston . . .

"Hi," she practiced aloud, feeling her lips form around the name. "I'm Kate Preston. Yes, good to meet you. We just moved into town."

At her side would stand Pavel Podran, recently adopted from Romania. He would have his hair combed back, shiny and black like his eyes. He would straighten his shoulders and push out his little chest, ever-courageous and ready for this new adventure.

"And this is my son," she'd tell people, with that motherly care in her voice. "Full name's Kenneth, but he goes by Kenny. Kenny Preston."

Yep, she liked these names. Solid and secure.

Raindrops were dimpling the thatched rooftops as she paid to enter the Village Museum grounds. It was a sprawling exhibition that showcased Romania's various traditions and lifestyles.

Seemed a fitting place for parting ways.

She strolled the paths between full-size cottages, gardens of wild-flowers, and ornate black-timbered steeples. An old stone well reminded her of life in Cuvin.

She checked the time with another sightseer. Ten twenty-five.

Where was Teo?

Lounging near the front entry, she shifted from foot to foot. A stab of pain shot from her fingertips to her left elbow, then subsided. The healing process had gone better than hoped, accelerated by Cal's washing with droplets from his vial.

Eleven. Eleven twenty.

Still no Teo.

At noon, she trundled back toward the bus stop. It had been wrong to come here in the first place, an act that defied Cal's stipulations and served only her own interest. Now that she thought about it, Teo's voice had sounded guarded on the phone, even fearful. Maybe he'd never intended to come.

What did it matter now?

She pushed pricks of moisture from her eyes. She would not call again, wouldn't risk it. She was Kate. She had a new life to lead.

So I guess that's it. Good-bye.

CHAPTER
TWENTY-SIX

The phone woke Gina from her bed in yet another grim communist-era hotel. She'd lost the comfort of the pensione weeks ago, due to her father's heightened demands for safety and secrecy.

Two rings, a long pause . . .

She waited.

Then, according to their preset signal, another ring.

She rolled over and snatched up the phone. Cal's voice eased through the receiver, but his words were a call to action. "You ready to go, Kate?"

Kate?

Could this be it, so soon? He'd warned that the bureaucracy and red tape could drag on, but now after only a month of waiting, after a string of restless nights, it seemed the day of departure was upon them.

"Uh . . . Okay, sure. Right this instant?"

"Sooner the better," he said.

"The paperwork's done? Everything's good to go?"

"You know, just because Collectors have worked their way into the government offices doesn't mean the Unfallen have gone to sleep. How do you think I've pulled this off? Since day one, I've been working with a lady here at the Adoption Committee . . . A real angel."

Gina groaned. "It's too early for bad puns."

"No pun intended. So you ready to get out of here or not?"

For Gina it was more complicated than that. Would it ever be safe to return to Romania? In all likelihood, no. That was a strong dose of reality, as she now prepared to leave behind places from childhood and the orphans she loved.

On the other hand, she would have a son to raise and protect.

"I'm ready," she said. "Let's do this."

"Ah-ha, that's my girl. So here's the deal . . . A driver'll be there for you in an hour. You need to be packed and standing at the door, because your flight leaves Otopeni International at 9:40 a.m. Your new son, Kenny, will be waiting at the airport with a police escort. I've got the guys here at the station convinced that someone's after him, especially after what happened to . . . to his—"

"To Petre. Yes, Dad. I got it." He had told her to avoid the familial term, even on the phone, but it slipped out before she could stop it. Or maybe that was her intention.

"Dad." He paused. "I like it."

"Me too."

"From now on, though—just Nickel. In case of eavesdroppers."

"Yes, sir."

"And you'll be Kate to me. Kate and Kenny Preston. In my mind, though, you'll always be my baby girl. Now, one other thing."

Gina swung her feet off the mattress and sat up. "Yeah?"

"The driver'll have a manila envelope for you—a wad of U.S. dollars, your plane tickets, a set of house keys, new passports, et cetera, et cetera. But I don't want you trying out the last part until you're on that plane."

"What last part?" She tried to pat down her bed-hair.

"A little something from me. We're the same flesh and blood, right?

Well, I wiped a drop on a postcard, and once you're in flight all you have to do is touch it to your tongue."

"Your blood? Yuck."

"A taste, that's all. Enough to pull up some of the things I've experienced. No lingering, though. It'll be like flipping back through a Rolodex until—"

"People still use those things?"

"Until," Cal huffed, "you get to our weekend in the Bucegis, and to some scenes in Italy and Germany from a week or two ago. For now, you and I have shaken loose from the Collectors, but I think I'm closing in on the missing one. You with me, Kate?"

"You're scaring me. How's the postcard supposed to help?"

"Recent research seems to show that some of our junk DNA is actually used to encode our memories. Which means that it's all in that drop."

"And you want me to taste it?"

"You have to trust me on this. Don't go snooping around, trying to dig up more than I've suggested. There are some things that're none of your business."

"So it sounds like you'll have to trust me too."

"Exactly. We're in this together," he said. "Just do it."

Five and a half hours later, seated on the airplane with Kenny Preston's head of black hair resting against her shoulder, she did.

Westbound Flight over Central Europe

The postcard featured the Campo Santo, the Holy Field, a walled cemetery situated near Pisa's famed Leaning Tower. A real snooze-fest, as far as Gina was concerned. Here she sat in economy class, thirty thousand feet up, bound for Portland, Oregon, while Adam Sandler yukked it up on the featured film, and all she wanted to do was hold the boy in the window seat beside her.

Pavel. Young Kenny.

Of the twins, he was the one who'd played board games with Gina at the orphanage, saying little and leaving it to his gregarious sibling to state his feelings toward her: *"You know, my brother thinks you're pretty."*

This morning in the airport terminal, after weeks of near silence, Kenny had lifted his head at the sound of her voice. She'd put out her hand. Without a word, he stepped away from the stern-faced police officer and took it.

Mother and son?

Her heart burst with relief and pride.

Now, with his head growing heavy on her arm, she decided it was time to venture a taste, a flip back into Cal's—Nickel's—memories. Sounded bizarre. Except recent experiences confirmed all the things her dad had ever told her.

"Just do it . . ."

The stain was burgundy, a smear on the postcard's glossy top corner. She slid it to her lips, let her tongue flick across it. At first this produced nothing, but as she allowed the moisture to work into the paper, hazy images materialized, smudged yet undeniably real.

With her thoughts fixed on the Bucegi Mountains, the Rolodex started riffling through its memory markers—Nickel and Dov in the Prahova River, a blackbird and a pile of wood, bits of Shalom's and Erota's thoughts, a stint in Israel—then thumbed forward to more recent events.

A cool evening . . .

A Mediterranean breeze through a grove of olive trees . . .

Nickel appearing quite suddenly from a cobblestone street. How, Gina wondered, had he ended up here?

That question was forgotten as she found herself looking through his eyes, moving between Italian homes, coming to stop at a museum that catalogued Pisa's part in World War II. Inside, Nickel skimmed book after book. He ended his search with a long examination of a magazine photo.

The subject was a Red Cross tent, where U.S. Army MPs guarded a corpse. It was a nurse in a white uniform. Her arms and legs had been straightened upon the folding cot, but the angles of her bones seemed unnatural, and her entire body was parched and peeling. Facial muscles remained locked in the rictus of death, a result of puckered wounds like a necklace around her throat.

Her eyes were closed. *"Thank God,"* Gina heard Nickel mumble.

Aside from a few incidents of lycanthropy or vampirism, initiated by the most opportunistic of Those Who Hunt, this woman's torn flesh was something rarely seen before the Akeldama Cluster's rising.

Yes, Nickel had witnessed Collectors' gruesome acts before, with human, canine, even feline vessels possessed to wreak mayhem. Such unhallowed deeds had led to tales of werewolves and hobgoblins, zombies and ghouls. Yet even here in 1944, in the midst of war, the ruthlessness visited upon this nurse stood out. She'd been drained, the report said, of every last ounce of blood.

Later, after his time in the museum, Nickel strolled the pilloried walkways of the Campo Santo and stepped into the inner courtyard, where bombs had broken open graves decades earlier.

He knew this: Natira, the nineteenth revenant, was still on the loose.

And now, heading out over the Atlantic, Gina Lazarescu Turney—Kate Preston—knew it too.

THE THIRD TASTE:
EX SILENCIO

Alone . . . the most awful word in the English tongue. Murder doesn't hold a candle to it and hell is only a poor synonym.

—STEPHEN KING, *'SALEM'S LOT*

Show mercy to those whose faith is wavering.

—JUDE 1:22

Journal Entry

July 7—continued

I stumbled off the ferry not long ago. Seagulls floated overhead, hoping for crumbs from the passengers, and the beach's briny odor made me think of the smell sometimes attributed to the Collectors. Even as I write, I wonder if they're closing in? Am I heading into a trap?

The last taste from Gina's memories flipped my thoughts around. It's clear now that Cal's postcard and personal experiences gave her access to all sorts of information she didn't expect. It was through him that she got glimpses into Barabbas' mind-set, as well as Shalom's and Erota's. She only siphoned the parts her dad authorized, but it might've helped me if she'd gone deeper.

From the dock, I passed up a ride to the closest town here in Washington State. The man behind the wheel seemed nice and all, just one of the Lummi islanders showing some common courtesy. I told him no, thanks anyway, and raised a hand to shield my face, but he gave me a pitying look and asked again.

That was it. Already on edge, I simply turned and walked away. I walked like I've always done, taking the chance to wrap my head around things. Somehow, I must play a part in all this, though my guesses are only shots in the dark.

The Open sign shone from the window of a small diner and I went in. Now, sitting here sipping a Dr Pepper, I'm caught between going on a search for answers or waiting to see if someone comes for me.

Erota's blood calls from the map in my pocket. Maybe she was able to find out more about Natira. At this point, I'll take any info I can get.

CHAPTER
TWENTY-SEVEN

July 2000—Beijing, China

Natira rode a taxi to the edge of Tianamen Square. Even with his head ducked, his cropped hair scraped the roof and his shoulders spanned a space equal to two, maybe three, Mandarin-speaking passengers. He'd been here ten months already, and still he pondered the diminutive size of these people. Didn't they eat? Were chopsticks their obstacles to putting down man-sized meals?

The more urgent question, of course: how was he supposed to find a Concealed One amidst this country's billion teeming souls?

Today he believed that he had done just that.

The Collector shoved a handful of bills into the driver's hand, then squeezed out onto the square's endless expanse.

The summer air was stifling and hazy. He tugged a blue Chairman Mao cap over his skull, unzipped his seam-stretched sport jacket, and pocketed his pincered right hand the way an assassin might hide his weapon of choice. He headed north. He would approach his prey by shuffling amid a pack of lanky Dutch tourists. If he stayed bowed and hid his swarthy skin, he might get close without being noticed.

From the square beneath his feet, the blood of China's massacred students still murmured, still cried for freedom and justice.

Natira knew all about such things. Nineteen hundred years ago he'd fought Israel's Roman oppressors. In a final skirmish at Jotapata, he'd made corpses of thirteen of them before being rent asunder by a foreign sword. He was a warrior and he'd died as one. Not quite the merchant his father had wanted, but what honor was there in bartering and slapping shoulders while cutting another's purse strings? For Natira, it was better to slice a man's throat while staring him in the eyes than to torture him with the pinpricks of interest and usury.

As for his family, had the Houses of Ariston and Eros finally found release from the Akeldama? If so, it seemed they'd made little effort to come looking for him.

Did Natira even care? Sure, he and Erota had once exchanged desirous glances, but he had gone on to fight the Romans. What good would it do to surrender again to such human vagrancies?

These days, Natira trusted in his own strength, his own intelligence. While dealing with local Collector clusters, he kept his chest wounds hidden, his right hand in a glove. Why make his identity known to the weak and unfaithful? No, he'd marked out his own path and had little interest in kowtowing to the wishes of his shrewd father. Wherever the family might be, let Ariston and his cluster fend for themselves. Let older brother Sol have his fill of buying and selling. Let Sol kiss Ariston's wide—and ever-widening—Syrian posterior.

Natira moved on, bringing up the rear of the Dutch tour group. Despite a pale-yellow smog over Beijing, there was no muting the red fortress walls of the Forbidden City, former palace to China's great emperors. The broad courtyards and intricate designs bespoke riches and grandeur.

None of this interested the Collector. Through this host, hadn't he seen his share of Hebrew and Italian wonders? Not to mention Hitler's proud technological feats?

The Dutch guide rambled on about the history of the palace while Natira's eyes roved from beneath his cap. He searched the grounds, the passersby, the pair of local policemen. He planned to exit at the far end of the Forbidden City and step onto a regular city street with its shops and taxis and bicycles and shade trees and alleyway pool tables where Chinamen in white tank tops and flip-flops smoked cheap cancer sticks.

Nothing had changed, had it? The human spirit, in its attempts to rise above, kept stepping in piles of its own steaming waste.

At last, the tour neared the final gate.

Natira pressed his thumb and pinkie together in his pocket. They were giant tongs, ready to latch onto and pop brains from fractured skulls. He slid into the street's flow of traffic, using it to mask his approach. He moved in shadows here, still humid and sweating yet hidden from the sun's diffused light.

Would he get close enough? Would he confirm the letter Tav on the forehead of the man at the bicycle rental shop?

For over three decades, Natira had stalked these meek and mostly mild Nistarim. He marked their locations and identities, with plans to annihilate all of them in one simultaneous offensive. They'd survived in the past by refilling their ranks as they fell, but what if he were to strike down all thirty-six at once?

May it be so, Master. I'm over halfway to my goal.

He'd found nineteen so far, a decent result on a planet numbering in the billions. Of course, in his undead state he had an advantage over typical Collectors in that he could spot the Letter's ethereal glow.

The pattern of his findings indicated that Concealed Ones hid evenly distributed, five per landmass—Europe, Africa, Australia, Asia, South America, North America, and the Middle East. That would constitute thirty-five total, and he could only assume a thirty-sixth functioned as the preeminent personality for the bunch. If so, such a man comprised his last and most difficult target.

Now, with those first three regions checked off his list, Natira focused his efforts on Asia. He'd found one man in Sri Lanka, a farmer. One in South Korea, a house church leader. Another taught in a missionary school in Papau New Guinea, and the fourth served on a Japanese fishing vessel.

Today, here in Beijing, he hoped to close the door on his seven-year Asian search. If he could only get close enough to verify the man's Letter for himself and then—

Look there. Could this be Number Twenty?

The owner of the bicycle shop emerged from his shanty wearing an American baseball cap and a thin white shirt, but it was his repairman who riveted Natira's attention. The man embodied subservience, his shaggy head of hair bowed and his hands stained from fixing a flat for a New Zealand tourist—a pretty young thing whose strong calves showed beneath knee-length shorts.

During his vigil south of the equator, Natira had supped from her sort, and those recollections caused taste buds along his tongue to contract in expectation. The woman's voice pricked at his ears, at his memories . . . an accent just like hers, and moans of pleasure that then spiraled into torment.

Ahhh, fresh blood. How long had it been?

His last tapping of a substantial artery had been days ago, and he now longed to veer from his task, if only for an hour or two. Who could blame him? It was in a warrior's nature to vent aggression, particularly if his mission required years of quiet reconnaissance.

He bit into his lower lip, dragging upper incisors along chapped flesh. Hot droplets slipped over his tongue, cannibalized nourishment.

They would have to do for the time being. His goal—his only respectable goal—was to nail down the identity of this twentieth subject without alerting him, then inform local Collectors so they could maintain round-the-clock surveillance using various mortal hosts.

Which meant no attacks on the attractive Kiwi tourist.

No swinging of the sword or baring of fangs.

None of the secondhand torture Natira had inflicted during his work in the Nazi biochemist's lab, in the airtight testing rooms, where he'd watched human vermin bleed out through every orifice in response to his special "gift."

But my thirst . . . Master, how do I slake it?

Across the street, the repairman nodded in humble acceptance of the tourist's thanks. He brushed at his brow with his hand and, for a fraction of a second, blue flashed beneath the pass of his grubby hand.

Natira stiffened. The letter Tav? Was that it?

Dark hair fell back over the repairman's broad forehead before he slipped back into the shanty and closed a door behind him.

Natira grinned. So his instincts had been correct. Recent years had shown a resurgence of Those Who Resist in northern China, a reliable indicator that Concealed Ones lived close by. Beijing's local Collectors had spoken of a humble, righteous man at this shop, and their intel was on the mark.

The thirst now prickled along Natira's skin and convulsed against the steel bands of his stomach. He had to act. He took a step onto the pavement, slipped between bikes and taxis and a work truck. He came at the bicycle shop from the left, hugging the wall of a building from which the shanty jutted. The owner stood concluding his business with the Kiwi girl, and that allowed Natira to dash behind a row of rentals, through the door into which the repairman had disappeared.

For a moment, the contrast of darkness and light left the Collector disoriented. He widened his eyes and realized the shaggy-haired target was only feet away, gaping at him from a workbench on which sat a dented tub of water and a bottle of liquid soap.

"I help you?" the man said.

Natira hadn't meant to overplay his hand here. If this was his desired Concealed One, then it was best to act like a tourist and get out quickly.

The repairman wiped his brow again, and this time Natira recognized the flash of blue for what it was. The man's hands were soiled by not only chain oil but also streaks of colored pencil that he used for circling tire-tube punctures.

The grease pencil . . . It was there on the bench. Electric blue.

A false positive, if Natira had ever encountered one.

In a flurry of rage, he hopped onto the bench, sending the water tub crashing to the floor. He crouched there, a gargoyle of monstrous proportions, and feasted on the repairman's fear. He fixed his hand upon the man's cranium and brought pinkie and thumb together until they had sunk deep into opposite ear canals. His victim's eyes bulged from the growing pressure, lips parting in a cry that never made it beyond Natira's clamped left hand.

Another squeeze of thumb and pinkie. Mighty tongs.

Locals often referred to lichee fruit as "dragon eyes," and Natira thought it a fitting description of the objects that popped from their sockets onto the wet floor.

From outside, a stifled scream seemed to come as a direct response to the dying man's pain. Natira dropped the repairman and bounded out the door.

The Kiwi had cycled away on her rental while the shop owner stumbled off the other direction. The owner dropped to a knee, lost his baseball cap in the gutter, then hopped back up and dove into the backseat of a hailed cab.

He turned to stare through the rear window, his Letter burning like blue flame along his exposed forehead.

How interesting. A Concealed One had been here at the shop, after all, but he'd chosen—wisely, considering the implications—to protect his own skin over the repairman's. That being so, Natira would have to summon one of the more trustworthy local clusters to keep an eye on the owner.

First, the Collector had a meal to finish. He turned back inside.

CHAPTER
TWENTY-EIGHT

September—Junction City, Oregon

Coffee. Mmm. Kate had liked caffeine since her years in Chattanooga, at Rembrandt's Coffee House, and after only a few days in this new hometown she'd chosen locally owned Espresso Yourself as her latest supplier of all things roasted and brewed to perfection.

"How ya doin' today?" said the owner from his narrow booth.

He was tall, thin, his head bobbing to the sounds of King's X through small speakers. Yesterday, the band's name had segued into talk about the game of kings. It seemed the owner was a chess aficionado himself.

She leaned on the counter. "Good."

"It's Kate, right?"

"Kate Preston. Good memory."

"Well, with you coming by a coupla times a week, I shouldn't even have to ask. So what're you in the mood for?"

"A white mocha."

"One of my personal favorites."

"No big shocker. You and your wife make them the best."

"We just make 'em the way we like 'em."

She smiled and watched him tamp the espresso grind before fitting the portafilter into the sturdy Faema machine. She found comfort in the routine, the consistent results. Why couldn't life operate with that same reliability?

No complaints, though. She and Kenny had been in town nearly four months now. Her son, still shy, was making some friends at the local elementary school and improving his English. His teachers remarked that he was withdrawn in classroom settings but more sociable one-on-one.

Kate, too, was adjusting to life in Junction City—or J.C. as the townspeople called it. Home to five thousand, the place lay nestled between the soaring Cascade Mountains and the less formidable range along the Pacific Ocean. Many who lived here claimed Nordic descent, a fact they celebrated during the annual Scandinavian Festival that drew crowds from around the world each August.

Small Town, U.S.A. . . . A great place to disappear.

And wasn't that the goal? Eat, work, study, sleep, and do the things average citizens do. Keep a low profile and avoid drawing attention.

For now, that also meant no contact with her loved ones.

As an alternative, Kate watched her mother's new late-night television show, *Beyond the Stars*. N. K. Lazarescu wore her trademark purple head scarf and delivered self-help mantras on a platter of religious ideas and quasi-scientific theory. She called her studio audience "life students," and they gobbled up her offerings with wide-eyed appreciation.

Kate was also unable to speak with her husband, Jed Turney, who lived in nearby Corvallis with his uncle, Sergeant Turney. She'd hoped to see Jed within days of arriving in Oregon, even imagined what it might be like to raise a son together—the way they'd once dreamed.

Back in Bucharest, however, Nickel had cautioned her that a sharp-eyed Collector might watch for such a rendezvous, and made her agree to wait until he gave her the okay.

"I want you to settle in with your new son, Kate. Take time to heal—both of you, you hear me?—and care for this kid like he's your own. From what I've seen, a mother's love can work wonders in the Nistarim."

"Here ya go." The man in the espresso booth handed over her white mocha. "Hope it's up to your standards."

She took a sip. "Perfect."

"It's on us today."

"What? No." She reached for the money in her cargo skirt, the one with the flared hem and black belt that matched her boots. Her fingers brushed the hilt of her dagger. Despite J.C.'s relative security, she never walked unarmed.

"Seriously," the owner said. "You're a good customer."

"But I—"

"I know. You have this overblown sense of duty, like it's some sin to accept a freebie. Take it. I mean it."

"Thanks," she said. "If you insist."

The moment he turned to knock the coffee grounds from the porta-filter, she stuffed a five-dollar bill into the tip jar and strolled away.

A few blocks south, Kate settled on a bench in Founder's Park. She brushed back her hair, now trimmed to shoulder length and colored with caramel streaks, and her fingernails ticked against her remaining ruby ear-ring. She took a sip from her drink, then crossed her legs and lifted her chin toward the sun.

How long, she wondered, could this peace last? How long could she play the role of a single mother, covering bills as a cashier at the Ace Hardware store on Sixth Avenue, forking over rent for their two-bedroom home on Oak Street?

How long?

Till the day I die. Or . . . Kate sat taller on the park bench. *Well, at least until I look older than Sophia Loren.*

The simple life. She loved it. As far back as Cuvin, she'd found plea-sure in the back-straining work at the village well, in the endless sweeping of kitchen and walkway. Weary muscles made sleep that much sweeter.

Here in J.C., she'd already found the bond between her and Kenny strengthening by the day. They played chess and other games as they'd done at Tomorrow's Hope. He'd learned some basic English at the orphanage, and they now took turns reading aloud from the first book of *The Chronicles of Narnia*. This not only helped Kenny's vocabulary, it allowed Kate to share something nostalgic from her own childhood—one fragment that still shone clearly.

At her bedside rested a copy of *The Screwtape Letters*. She found it unsettling, yet invaluable. A handbook for unmasking the Collectors.

"Why, you look deep in thought, dear."

Kate squinted into the sunlight, saw a white-haired woman wearing silver wire bifocals and leading a Chihuahua on a leash. "Hi, there. Yeah, I . . . What a beautiful day, huh?"

"It is, at that. Is there room beside you on the bench?"

"Sure. I don't bite."

"Thank you, dear. I didn't suspect that you would." The elderly woman took a seat and lifted her pet into her lap, where it perched like a small purse. "I must say, you do look happy. Is he a good man to you?"

"What?"

"I couldn't help but notice your ring."

"We're separated, to tell the truth." Kate wrapped her right hand over her left. For the first time in over a year, she wore her wedding band. It not only deflected unwanted attention, it reminded her of the love she and Jed shared. Had shared.

Maybe again, someday.

"But you're right," she told the lady. "He's a good guy."

"Chiara here is my companion. She's a bit skittish—as you would be, if you weighed less than a rubber boot—but she's a marvelous judge of character, and she seems to have no qualms about you, dear. That's more than I can say for the attendant at the gas station."

"You still drive?"

"At my age, is that what you're implying?"

"No, I . . . I don't know," Kate said. "Sometimes I think about getting older and I just wonder how I'll handle it. You're my new hero. More power to you."

"I don't drive."

"I thought you said—"

"I have other responsibilities."

"Oh?"

"Such as this train here." The woman's creased hand fluttered, bird-like, in the direction of the nearby fenced display. "Engine 418. One of only two such engines remaining, it saw action in four separate wars."

Kate had read the placard explaining this Finnish locomotive's transfer from across the ocean in token of J.C.'s Scandinavian roots. Locals speculated Vladimir Lenin had once ridden this vehicle over the Russian-Finnish border before starting his revolution. The world was a small place, and the more Kate traveled, the more she willingly considered such improbabilities. History, relics, and people linked in ways most could never know.

Who, for example, would guess her dagger's past role in Gethsemane? Or the circuitous journey of a Knights Templar coin?

"This engine was built in 1904," the white-haired woman was saying. "It came to our town a few decades ago, and I've been guarding it ever since."

Kate played along. "From what?"

"You think I jest, dear?" The lady scratched her pooch's chin, which had fewer white hairs than her own. "I'm quite sure that one day they'll be coming after it, hoping to collect their little trinket."

Collect?

A quiver spread over Kate's shoulders, despite the sun's warmth.

"I'm telling you this, dear, so that you won't fret. Like any curious child, your own son has tried climbing through the fence to play on the train, but—"

"You saw this with your own eyes?"

"I'm always on guard," the woman said, "always attentive. Put it out of your mind, and trust me to keep watch. He'll be safe, of this I assure you."

"How'd you even know I have a son?"

"Dear, there's no hiding the love in those light-blue eyes of yours."

Kate stood. This attention was making her uncomfortable.

"Or," the woman amended, "should I say deep brown?"

"Excuse me?"

"Your irises. Naturally deep brown. I assume those're colored contacts you're wearing."

"Who are you?" Kate's hand slipped toward her thigh.

"Are you familiar with the Life Alert ads?"

"On TV?" Kate wondered what this had to do with anything. It seemed the old lady was six biscuits short of a baker's half dozen.

"Surely you've heard the phrase, 'I've fallen and I can't get up'?"

"Yeah," Kate said, losing patience. "Who hasn't?"

"Well, to be truthful"—the woman gave a wink—"it doesn't describe me at all. Quite the opposite, in fact."

"You *can* get up? Great. Good for you."

"The other part is what I meant."

"You haven't fallen."

"Precisely, dear."

"Are you saying that . . . Hold on. You're . . . Are you Unfallen?"

"And ever at your service. Now I must be on my way."

Before Kate could wrap her head around this, the woman had vanished from the park with Chiara still clutched to her side. They hadn't taken off at a breakneck gallop, and neither had they loafed it. It was more like—and yes, Kate knew this sounded a little out-there—more like they'd defied time and space for their own brief purposes. Whereas Collectors required hosts to manipulate the natural world, the Unfallen moved unrestrained between spiritual and physical.

Nickel had told her about these counterparts to the Collectors, beings who walked free of the Separation's tethers, but she'd never encountered one firsthand. Or if she had, it'd been unawares.

What had the woman said?

"One day they'll be coming . . . hoping to collect . . ."

Were the Collectors already close, sniffing out Kenny's location? Were they waiting for him to reach the age of thirteen? They definitely hadn't waited in Chattanooga, three years ago. They'd killed Jacob only hours after she pushed him into this world, this cruel unforgiving place.

"Put it out of your mind . . . trust me to keep watch . . ."

Kate's motherly instincts made that almost impossible.

She guzzled her drink and hurried home, buzzing with caffeine and concern for her adopted son.

CHAPTER
TWENTY-NINE

Kate faced the bathroom mirror, her dagger held to the wound at her throat. The colored contacts meant to disguise could not hide the rising unease in her light-blue eyes. Despite the peace and anonymity since their move here at the end of May, she still seemed seconds away from the memories—and lack thereof—that defined her life.

She'd seen the Unfallen woman twice more, caught glimpses of that white head of hair from across the lawn at Founder's Park, but the words meant to comfort Kate had only increased her worries.

Was it only a matter of time before Those Who Hunt closed in?

"He'll be safe."

Coming from the Unfallen, Kate knew she should take this as a promise worth holding on to, but it didn't help her son overcome his own unsettling memories.

Kenny had seen his brother killed before his eyes. Also had seen Kate try, but fail, to stop the attack.

Some nights she still found him curled into a ball and groaning on his bed, or with his eyes closed as he thudded the back of his head against the wall, over and over, over and over, till it seemed she would go crazy with grief for him. How could he ever find solace? How could she? Would it be so wrong to apply the knife to his skin, just once, to see if it would bleed away his pain?

Was this the quandary Nikki Lazarescu had faced, hating herself every moment as she did what she thought best for young Gina?

The front door opened, signaling that Kenny was home from school. Tennis shoes squeaked in the entryway and textbooks dropped to the floor.

Should she try it? Kate wondered. At least once?

"Mom?"

No, Gina. Never!

"Be right out," she called. "There's cran-apple juice in the fridge."

She pried the strand of thorns from her neck and severed it, knowing it would return in the same way the mythical Hydra had sprouted new heads. She'd seen this thing shrivel over time as she rejected her bitterness against her mother, yet its roots still clung.

She cleaned the exit point, shoved her dagger back into its sheath, then fingered the crimson sphere of her earring.

It felt warm, almost soft to the touch.

On some level, she believed. She did. But to take it in, to make it part of her, would mean shoving aside all other options and choosing to receive the healing in "just one drop." For now, she could survive on her own, thank you. By leaving it untested, she could hold onto its abstract hope the way others held onto the idea of falling in love.

Kate met Kenny in the kitchen. He already had a glass of juice in hand.

"Whadda we got to eat?" he said. At this impressionable age, his accent was giving way to American speech patterns by the week. "I'm starving."

"Sun-dried raisins?" she offered.

He wrinkled his nose.

"Rice cakes? Carrot sticks?"

More wrinkles.

"How 'bout we run down to DQ?"

Kenny's black eyes gleamed. If he had it his way, he'd live each day on Peanut Buster Parfaits alone, but Kate could afford once-a-week treats at best. And the dentist bills would be the real killer, if she didn't keep on Kenny about his brushing.

Future Nistarim or not, he was all boy. Just like Dov.

Kate's mind swirled as she led the way to their Nissan in the driveway. Like the other Nistarim, Dov even now lived concealed somewhere on this earth, back bowed by the world's woes. According to Nickel, Kenny still lacked a few years until such an assignment, though he already showed signs of deep empathy.

Were there others standing by, ready to join the Concealed Ones? If not, did this mean this planet was, at every moment, a breath away from collapse?

She fired up the engine and watched Kenny plunk down beside her.

He lifted his hand. "I brought quarters to help pay."

"Save it for another day, sweetie. I've got it."

"Mom, I'm hungry. I'm gonna need a Full Meal Deal to fill me up."

"My treat," she insisted. She made a mental note to skip her espresso stops this week. "Now buckle up, okay? Dairy Queen, here we come."

Early October—Totorcea Vineyards, Romania

Erota navigated her motorcycle through the curves that hugged the Mures River. With months gone by since her fiasco at the haunt of jackals, her split belly had come back together, as had her roiling thoughts, and she warmed herself with images of the item in her pocket.

She had a plan, a blueprint for ascendance and dominion.

But she could not carry it out alone.

As she rode, her head ached from the splayed rays of the winter sun, and she wished once again that she could have her old sunglasses back.

There was nothing like a pair of fashion shades to heighten a slim brunette's mystique, and this new pair was simply not as effective as her beloved Ray-Bans.

Blame it on Cal Nichols, the ever-elusive immortal. He'd stolen them from her up there in the mountain cave. Then, in a maneuver archaic and rare, he'd attempted to subdue her with goat's milk. She'd fallen under that accursed sedation, only faintly aware of their Q&A session.

Not that she had much to hide. She herself still wondered about Natira's present whereabouts. As for the location of the House of Eros, let Cal chase the wayward Collectors into Israeli wastelands while she helped bolster the fragmented House of Ariston.

The very thought of that cave-floor interrogation brought the milky aftertaste to her tongue, reminding her of the goat's figurative purpose. In Mosaic Law, the animal was an object of wrath, loaded down symbolically with the sins of the community then herded off into the desert.

Quite literally: the scapegoat. Taking away the guilt.

Never for long, though, Erota told herself. Never for long. Thanks to the Power of Choice, these humans had a way of wallowing right back into the muck.

Speaking of goats, a pair grazed the roadside just ahead. She aimed her motorcycle their way and watched them scatter. One hung himself up in the barbed wire of a farmer's fence, bleating in pain.

Who was the scapegoat now?

From a nearby hill, the ruins of Soimos Castle peered over the trellised rows of Totorcea Vineyards. The village of Lipova was a welcome sight after Erota's months of far-flung travels. Utilizing various modes of transport, beastly or human, she'd sought a strategy, a vision—to borrow that cherished biblical word—by which to reinvigorate this household.

Who was still here, anyway? A handful, at best.

Lord Ariston's wives, Shelamzion and Helene, had survived by infecting and bleeding local souls for their autumn harvest. Three orphans also remained—Ariston's nephew and niece, Shabtai and Matrona; and his granddaughter, Kyria.

Seeing as Gina Lazarescu had mustered resilience from the kids of Tomorrow's Hope, Erota knew she could do the same from this ragtag group.

She halted to open the vineyard's main gate. A dirt road then carried her to the farmhouse, where she heeled down the kickstand and propped the bike next to a mossy wall. Across the yard, a dilapidated warehouse held machinery, stainless-steel vats, and aged oak barrels on wooden racks.

In there, three years ago, Dov Amit had tried to protect his mother by thrusting a metal tent peg through the temple of Erota's father. True, Eros had been vanquished. As for Dov's parents, though? They'd been sucked dry.

Orphans here, there, everywhere.

And so the cycle of grief made its heady spirals.

Revenge appealed to Erota's human host, and she despised young Dov almost as much as she did Cal and Gina. All of them, trying to gird the eroding bastions of mankind. Did they truly see something there worth saving? Or were they only trying to save themselves?

She shook long shiny hair from her helmet and stood to meet doe-eyed Helene and sturdy Shelamzion.

"We're glad to see you, at last," Shelamzion said.

"I didn't come back empty-handed."

"No, that would not be your style, would it? So tell me, what do you think?" Helene gestured at the grapevines. "Is this a fitting tribute to my late husband?"

"And mine," Shelamzion noted.

"Well, let's take a look."

Erota led the way, strolling and evaluating the slopes, where afternoon light spilled through dusty leaves and glowed amidst clusters of deep purple grapes. This harvest would be bountiful, watered with rain and fertilized with the spillage from swollen human veins.

Soon, in the old warehouse, the vats would fill with crushed Pinot Noirs and Cabernets, to be swilled and settled and fermented.

Soon the life flow of wretched two-leggers would enter the mix, to be bottled and shipped to restaurants and dining rooms across the continent.

Oh, yes, let the infestations spread . . .

Dancing upon tongues.

Slipping down throats.

Finding root in the drunkards' bellies, the abusers' fists, and the fornicators' slurred invitations.

"Yes," Erota said at last. "I think Lord Ariston would be happy."

Both wives stood taller with satisfaction.

"I'd like to think so," Helene said, touching the sleeve of Erota's leather jacket. "Local workers have maintained the fields, while Shelamzion and I have done our best to tap the most . . . juicy, shall I say, of the region's inhabitants."

"Impressive."

"We now have a self-sustaining vineyard, and thanks to the contacts made by Lord Ariston, we've been assisted by vintners from the Rhine region, the French Alsace, and Oregon's Willamette Valley. He had a passion for turning this soil into something productive, and envisioned celebrating with a lavish feast."

"A Collection of Souls," Erota said. "I remember him talking about it."

"A harvest," Shelamzion added, "of the very best—thorns curling from human veins, blood swirling into our goblets."

"Pure sacrilege."

"Oh." Helene squeezed her arm. "I wish he could hear you say so."

Erota's mind cringed at that. In that desert of restless sands and isolation existed no chance of banished Ariston listening in on Earth's dealings. Two-leggers, on the other hand, might be able to do just that from the afterlife, lending an ear from the heavens above. When Those Who Resist gave up the ghost, so to speak, they were no longer Separated by the confines of time and space.

And the Almighty saw fit to grant them such reprieve? *Ha!*

Were a few splashes of Nazarene Blood supposed to rinse humanity's blemishes from this planet? *Double ha!*

"Let's go inside," Erota snapped. "I'm chilled to the bone."

"Understandably so, after your long ride."

"Come along," Shelamzion said.

Following the pair of widows, Erota let long legs carry her into the farmhouse where flames crackled on the stone hearth. Helene had prepared a traditional Romanian meal, and the aromas were rapturous. Though the food would disintegrate soon after sliding down their undead throats, they'd have a fleeting cornucopia of flavors to enjoy.

And to think that humans complained. Given two minutes in even the fanciest of eateries, Erota was sure to hear the snivelers start sniveling.

"Almost time." Helene gestured for her to sit at the large birch table. "Shelamzion's heating things up."

"Are the kids coming?" Erota said.

"They'll be here momentarily, but please don't let them hear you call them that. They are Collectors, after all, and Shabtai, being a teenager, is especially sensitive to such things. He's a proud young man."

"Aren't they all?"

"Teenagers?"

"Men. Seems to be part of their genetic makeup."

"Oh, I don't know," Helene said. "The way I see it, they're merely covering for their deficiencies in other areas."

"Try telling that to—" Erota put the brakes on that thought.

"To whom?" Shelamzion said, sticking her head in from the kitchen.

Erota wanted to reply: *To the Master Collector. To that most prideful of all male beings, the one who urged us to join him in rebellion.*

His same arrogance had also wrought trouble amongst the two-leggers. Had they been so wrong in wanting to embody the Almighty? To themselves become all knowing? A mere bite was all they'd taken, a taste.

The knowledge of good and evil.

And now they knew. Ah, yes, did they ever know.

It was this very disobedience that had polluted their bloodlines and passed through man's seed ever since. Only One had been conceived apart from that seed, born through a woman's womb with blood unspoiled and pure.

Yeshua . . . He who saves.

Not if I can help it!

Erota unzipped her black leather jacket and reassured herself that the packet was still tucked in the pocket. Over dinner, she would divulge her new scheme.

CHAPTER
THIRTY

"Here you are, Erota."

"Thank you." She accepted from Shelamzion a bowl of steaming *supa* and dipped in with her spoon. The broth was flavorful, and potato chunks gave the illusion of hearty sustenance. "It's delicious."

A tinny squeal interrupted her next bite, and she turned to see Kyria bound in through the farmhouse door, followed by Shabtai and his sister Matrona.

Their young countenances disguised full-grown vehemence. These particular Collectors had a knack for picking out adult victims and bringing them down with ease, preying on deviant tendencies. The fruit of their work was evident in the ripe clusters draping the trellises outside.

"You're back," Kyria said. "We worried about you."

"I'm safe and sound. How are you, darling?"

"Did you hear the news?" the girl blurted.

"News?"

"Back in May, we read that Regina Lazarescu was struck down by a bus, killed while crossing the street."

"Where?"

"At the Piata Universitatii, in downtown Buchar—"

"No. Where did you read this?"

"A small article from the *Cronica Romana*," Shelamzion said, distributing bowls around the table. She and Helene exchanged a glance. "It was tucked away under a feature about a jazz festival."

Satisfied slurps put the conversation on hold. Matrona wiggled in her seat, while Kyria scooted away, clearly hoping to be counted among the adults. Helene, elegant as always, ate with her back straight and her eyes down. Shabtai, the teenager, sat with long hair flopped in front of his face, tufted hands clawing his spoon to dark lips.

"Seems convenient, don't you think?" said Erota.

The entire table turned toward her.

She downed another spoonful of supa. Although its warmth worked down her esophagus, she'd need something richer to take the chill from her bones.

"What do you mean?" Kyria asked.

"Well." Erota tapped a finger against the girl's button nose. "We all know how Ms. Lazarescu destroyed Shalom on her way to Bran Castle. Records also show that she made it to Bucharest and spent time at Elvis's Youth Hostel. Who really believes she would've come to such a mundane end?"

"Accidents do happen," Shabtai snorted. "These knuckle-draggers are dumb as they come. You lived in Georgia, didn't you? So you should know."

"What're you referring to?"

"Who's that lady, the one who wrote *Gone With the Wind*?"

"Margaret Mitchell."

"Yeah. Her. There she was, famous and all, and she steps off a curb right in front of a city bus." He donned a jaunty look. "Wham, bam, thank you, ma'am."

"Where do you come up with this stuff?"

"It's true," he said. "Look it up on the Internet."

Erota pushed back from the table and wiped her lips. She could think of better online diversions, some of which she'd employed to great effect in an Atlanta suburb against her now-deceased husband. Modern technologies could be so effective in exploiting lustful minds and eyes.

"Very well," she conceded. "We'll debate Gina's demise at a later date, once I've called a witness to the stand."

"Who?" Shabtai said.

"Teodor. He grew up not far from here, in the village of Cuvin."

"With Gina," Kyria said.

"That's right, darling. He now works at a travel bureau in Arad, and it was his name that was signed to the receipts at the youth hostel in Bucharest. He might be pressured into coughing up some helpful information."

"He'll also know where she was buried, won't he?"

"*If* she was buried."

"Perhaps he helped hide her away."

"Perhaps." Erota brushed aside these speculations and reached into the pocket of her black jacket. True, she would've loved to bury her teeth into Gina's tender throat, but personal vendettas would have to be postponed for the more urgent goal of bringing the Nistarim to their knees. "Right now," she said, "since we're all gathered here as a household, there's something more important I'd like to show you."

The others leaned forward.

This, Erota told herself, had always been a strength of hers, the ability to compartmentalize tasks and human emotion. It was the reason Lord Ariston had called upon her in times past to lend a hand in bookkeeping and accounting duties.

Even now the townspeople of Lipova thought of Erota as the vineyard's operations manager. She dealt with distribution contracts, overseas tariff issues, and purchase of varietals. She rubbed shoulders at occasional wine festivals. Moonlighting as a vampire was a fringe benefit, with opportunities for draining life from all who would offer a drink.

"You gonna show us now, or what?" Shabtai said.

"Yes," Erota replied with a grin. "Glad to have an attentive audience."

The teenager yawned and scratched his scruffy chin.

"What I have here is something that's been hidden away for decades, and if we can tap its potential, it'll put pesky Dov and his Concealed companions at risk. Gina's survival will become a moot point—which seems fortuitous, since she's the one who led me to this."

Helene cleared bowls from the table. "How did she do so?"

"It was her trek to Bran Castle that made me curious. She has—or perhaps, had—an uncanny knack for stumbling upon places of importance. I wondered what I might find if I took on a stealthier form and searched the fortress myself, particularly its secret chambers and passageways. It doesn't hurt that the place has sentimental significance for us, due to its ties with Vlad Tepes."

"Count Dracula," Shabtai said, waving the fingers of both hands and speaking the name in a ghoulish voice. "Whadda we care? He was just a man."

"Dracula means 'son of the devil,'" Kyria said.

"That's right." Erota winked at her. "But a man, nonetheless."

"So why the reputation?"

"Actually, many Romanians think him a hero for holding waves of invaders at bay. He also ruled with an iron fist, dispensing justice in grisly fashion. Decapitations. Impalings. Whatever would make his point."

Shabtai's brows shoved together, forming a thick, furry line.

"Last century," Erota said, "Bran Castle was home to Queen Marie, a relative of the tsars. Before revolutionaries gunned down the royal family, many imperial treasures were smuggled out of Russia by the Brotherhood of Tobolsk, and some of those made their way into the queen's hands. No one knows all the details, but the missing items included jeweled eggs, reliquaries, and some of Rasputin's unpublished prophecies."

"Sounds boring," Shabtai said.

"Then you don't know much about the man. He was a backwoods priest who weaseled his way into the tsars' favor, using sexual prowess and mystical ramblings to great effect. Eventually the people assassinated him, but many historians believe he was responsible—at least, in part—for the monarchy's downfall. Sure, most of his words were pseudo-spiritual bunk, but some came to him by covert knowledge dredged up from his cluster leader."

"This is true?" Helene said. "He hosted Collectors?"

"An entire cluster."

"Who cares?" Shabtai snarled. "That was a long time ago."

"You're just rude," Kyria told him. "Why, you're . . . you're a cad."

"Gimme a dog any day. Or a wolf. That's even better."

Kyria sighed. "The man-child proves my point by his ignorance."

"Don't worry about it." Erota rubbed her temples, reminded again how tricky it could be for these habitations to stay on task, with their distinct foibles and idiosyncrasies. She added, "He can't help it, darling. He's a he."

The teenager blew out air in disdain. Beside him, his little sister bounced in her seat, whispering requests for dessert.

"Patience, Matrona. Patience," Shelamzion said.

"So," Erota said. "Here's what I found."

With all eyes upon her, she removed a green plastic folder from her jacket and set it on the table. She had stalked Bran Castle during the off hours and zeroed in on Queen Marie's sleeping quarters, where she'd discovered a hidden panel in a wooden pillar. The space held a jewelry box, and this packet of writings had been tucked beneath the ring tray, aged and curled at the edges.

"Tell us what this is," Shelamzion said.

"These papers contain Rasputin's most potent prophecy."

" 'An immoral, no-good person,' " Kyria said.

"Ah-ah," Shelamzion chided. "Now who are you to judge?"

"I'm not judging. That's what *rasputa* means in Russian."

"That's correct," said Erota. "And oh, I do love an earthy man of the cloth. Don't you wish we could've been available for that particular hosting?"

Even circumspect Helene seemed to find pleasure in the thought.

"Now, let me show you what he wrote."

As though prompted by Erota's words, the packet began to glow from beneath the translucent plastic with the intensity of a neon moon. The pages lay like layers of flayed skin, each a tribute to unspoken horrors, while the inky Cyrillic scrawls turned into writhing larvae, squirming over each other as they awaited maturation.

She smoothed her hand over the packet, taming the vile essence of these writings. "*The Black King,*" she said. "That was Rasputin's title for this. He'd worked wonders with the tsar's hemophiliac son, causing the tsarina—unrest her soul—to place great faith in his words. And why not? He'd trained as a priest. Traveled in Israel. He'd also heard tales of the *lamedvovnik,* the thirty-six humble ones, and in his younger years may've even fancied himself to be one of them."

"Rasputin?" Helene frowned over steepled fingers. "What would possess the man to think such a thing?"

"Pride. What else?"

"Quite the opposite of the required humility."

"True enough. While we may devalue such meekness, the Ever-so-Bewildering One looks for those who put others before themselves."

"Survival of the weakest?" Shabtai said. "What a joke."

"The priest also had other disqualifying traits, including an unquench-able thirst for young virgins. Some believe he kept a Collection of their hair buried in glass jars in his garden."

"Now there's a real man."

Kyria rolled her eyes. "Like you're one to speak, Shabtai."

He kicked at her chair and the table lurched.

Erota drew them back to the subject at hand. "This is going to take a group effort. The point is that Rasputin penned these words with the Concealed Ones in mind. If he couldn't join them, he was more than will-ing to speak ill of them, and his writings here provide an antidote for the scourge of the Nistarim. I believe this prophecy is the key to our success."

"Well." Shabtai folded his arms. "Why didn't you say that?"

"I just did."

"It's always blab, blab, blab with you women. Me, being the only man around this place . . . I'm going bonkers."

"There's one word for that," Kyria said. "Hormones."

Choosing to ignore the bickering, Erota drew the writings into view. She'd learned passable Russian while living in Kiev years ago, and she thought now was the time to put it to use.

"Are you ready," she said, "to hear Rasputin's words for yourselves?"

CHAPTER
THIRTY-ONE

April 2001—Junction City

Seated on her black-and-gold bedspread, Kate let her mind wander as Kenny read a chapter from their latest in *The Chronicles of Narnia*. She rubbed her thumb over the Italian postcard in her hand. It served not only as their bookmark but as a reminder of her dad.

Cal Nichols. Nickel.

Nearly a year had gone by without a word from him.

Back in Bucharest, he'd told her he would come when it was safe, when the Collectors looked elsewhere, but she'd still seen no sign of him. Meanwhile, she'd gone back to her old pattern of searching crowds and passersby for a glimpse of his wheat-colored hair and distinctive eyes.

Kate stared now at the cemetery pictured on the card. With white marble walls and open arcades, the Campo Santo's beauty masked the macabre realities of buried bones and sarcophagi. In the same way, the smudge of dried blood in the corner—from her own father's veins, no less—concealed secrets both numerous and grim.

Would it be wrong to delve deeper by taking another taste?

"Don't go snooping around."

Despite Nickel's words, she'd come close to trying a few times over the last year, but never crossed that line. To do so would be even more invasive than thumbing through someone's personal diary. She vowed, however, that the next time she saw him she would get his permission. Surely she had the right to know more details of her own past.

"You want me to keep reading?" Kenny said.

"Uh, was that the end of the chapter?"

He gave a reluctant nod.

"Okay, then." Kate slipped the postcard between the pages. "That's it."

"We're done? No fair."

"You have school in the morning. Time for bed."

The truth, though, was that she cherished these moments with her growing boy, and even to herself she sounded unconvincing. How long before he was too embarrassed or too busy to hang out with Mom? For now, ten-year-old Kenny seemed to enjoy their nightly reading sessions, and he often used these occasions to feather his fingers over the scars on her arm.

"How'd you get hurt?" he once asked her.

"I got caught in some thorns," she said. "Had to rip loose."

"Does it still hurt?"

"You ever heard of phantom pains?" He shook his head. "It's when your nerves lock down on a past injury and keep sending distress signals to your brain. You think you're getting cut again, even though there's nothing really there."

"So it's not real?"

She shrugged. "Sometimes it sure feels like it."

"I don't want you to hurt, Mom. Not even phantom pains."

That's when Kenny began the habit of soothing her with his fingertips. His own burdened shoulders always lifted while he did so, as though he found the comfort he himself needed by first giving it away.

Now, propped on the edge of her bed, he pleaded with big round eyes. "One more chapter, *te rog?*"

"Please," Kate corrected. "Remember, use your English."

"One more, *please.* It'll be good practice for me."

"Hmm, you think you're real slick, don't you?"

"Well, it will be. You said so yourself."

"Okay," she capitulated. "But after this you brush your teeth and go straight to bed—no complaining, no messing around. You promise?"

"Promise."

She removed the postcard and handed over the book again. "Make sure to enunciate. Read slower if that helps."

Kenny nodded and continued. Propped against her ebony headboard, his naturally tanned legs stretched out before him.

She watched him with adoring eyes. She refused to let her own failures or personal loss barricade her heart. He was a good kid. He deserved her best. Soon she'd have to instruct him to wear something other than tightie-whities about the house; for now, though, she didn't want to put restrictions on what little innocence of his remained.

Kenny's voice filled with excitement as he plunged into the adventures of a dutiful boy named Shasta. He seemed to relate to this fictional kid.

As her son read, Kate clutched Nickel's Italian postcard to her chest and closed her eyes, reflecting on the way her dad had always been there, seen and unseen, threading in and out of her life's fabric.

What other secrets were contained in his drop of blood?

By telling her not to snoop, had he shielded his own past? Or hers?

For now, it was enough to know she was Nickel's daughter—half-immortal and fully loved.

Arad, Romania

Teodor put down the phone and pushed back in his chair. On the desk, stacks of brochures highlighted tours of Prague, St. Petersburg, and cruises through the Rhine's wine district, while posters on the walls showed happy families and scantily clad newlyweds exploring the shores of the Black Sea.

And here he sat.

For years he had booked tickets and tours from this travel bureau in downtown Arad, alternating between the two suits he owned. He'd left the country only once, and that was to visit his ailing grandmother in Moldova.

None of this bothered him. Teo liked making other people happy. *"Faithful Teo."* Isn't that what Gina had called him?

He had not been so faithful, though. He'd fed bits of information to Erota while letting thorns infest his limbs and leech his strength. And yet a year ago, out of fear for Gina's life, he'd abandoned their plans to meet at the Village Museum, knowing his journey there would be tracked by the Collectors.

What could he have expected from such a meeting anyway?

Gina's feelings did not match his own. He'd fooled himself into hoping the old flames between them still burned, and he would never forget coming down the hostel staircase in Bucharest to find her in another man's arms. A familiar chill had come over him in that instant, accentuating the arthritic tightness in his joints.

The chill was one that had haunted him since his younger years. His parents had been imprisoned for revolutionary ideas, leaving him stuck with his uncle Vasile in a thatched-roof house. Vasile was the village prefect. Not only had he turned in Teo's parents to the communists, he'd eyed all that went on in Cuvin and spied with great glee upon the local women.

Vasile's appetites had other outlets as well. Some nights, he'd been possessed by a dark presence that struck out at Teo with balled fists and a belt.

Teo still despised that presence. Despised his uncle, who had died two years ago from cirrhosis of the liver.

To this day that vile presence still hovered at Teo's back.

Cradling him. Corrupting him.

Medicine is what I need, he told himself. *A cold drink.*

He rolled back in his swivel chair until he reached the small refrigerator that served also as a counter for the coffeemaker. He opened the door, seeking the natural elixir he kept stored in a bottle. For years, nothing had subdued his anxiety so consistently as a few gulps of local goat's milk, slightly soured.

From the bureau's front entry, the bell rang. A customer.

He sighed. "*Buna dimineata*," he called out in greeting as he leaned back for a view of the office.

"A good morning, indeed," said the young woman who entered.

"Erota?"

"You act surprised to see me."

Surprised, yes. Also titillated. She was slim, shapely, with long brown hair brushing the twin swells beneath her white sweater. Almond-shaped eyes studied him with a predatory gleam.

He looked away. "It's your custom to call when you need travel arrangements. Really, there was no need to come all this way."

"Lipova is not so far."

"You are here for tickets? Where is it you wish to go this time?"

"I'm hoping," Erota said, "you can help me figure that out."

The lack of milk left Teo feeling weak. In times past, it had girded him against this woman's soporific voice and seductive glances, and he was tempted to turn back to the refrigerator. Maybe he could swig some down, coat his lips and throat with its cool balm before she realized what he was up to.

"Come on out here, won't you, Teo?"

He eased his chair back toward the desk. They were alone. His boss spent most days in Timisoara to the south, leaving him to oversee this regional office, and clients would be minimal on a midweek morning such as this. For now, Erota could harass him as she so desired.

He ventured, "You want to take a holiday, perhaps?"

"More like a visit to an old friend."

Teo straightened the items on his desk and paper-clipped a customer's tickets into a travel folder. He tried not to look at the Collector, even as he felt something coil within, tightening along his back and his buttocks—at the points where his uncle's belt buckle had once drawn welts from his skin.

"I'm hoping," Erota said, "to visit Gina."

"A common name here."

"Regina Lazarescu, if that helps. From Cuvin."

Teo blurted out, "Da, this name I know." Self-loathing filled his confession.

"Where is she?"

"I . . . am not sure."

"Of course you'd tell me if you knew, wouldn't you?" The she-vampire came around his desk, trailing her fingers from his shoulder down his back. Though his skin crawled, the wounds of his past bulged beneath his shirt, responsive to her touch.

"Sit," he said. "And I will help you."

"No, no, Teo. You stay seated. You may not always be the most compliant of my sources, but it seems today you were a bit late in fortifying yourself. I can smell the sickness on you. Here, let me help ease the pressure."

Fingernails worked up under his shirttails, circling sores where the pressure she spoke of festered with pus and infection. He flinched as the nails broke through his skin. Seepage, hot and sticky, ran down his spine.

Then: a sharp tug.

"Ahhh," he groaned. His head started spinning. The blend of anguish and desire squeezed salty drops from his tear ducts, and he collapsed over the desk, begging her for more, begging her to stop.

Thuwappp, wappp, wappp . . .

One by one, the crusty thorns popped loose from his lower back. Begging, begging—

Snip, snip!

Erota held a pair of thorn-cups before his eyes, swirling their contents in a wash of red and purple. "Let's see what we shall see," she purred in his ear.

Teo cried noiselessly into his batch of travel brochures. Tears of regret for the bitternesses spawned by his uncle's abuse; tears of relief because there was no new information that could endanger his childhood love. He knew he had thrown away his chances of winning Gina's heart when he skipped their last meeting in Bucharest, but by doing so he'd saved her from the monsters to which he'd already succumbed.

"Hmm." Erota licked his blood from her lips. "No recent signs of Ms. Lazarescu."

"You see?" he gasped. "I told you the truth."

"She's alive, though, isn't she, Teo? If you happen to hear from her, I do expect that you'll give me a jingle. Is that clear?"

A nod was all he could offer, but even that seemed like a betrayal.

CHAPTER
THIRTY-TWO

Mid-May—Junction City

"You're not falling asleep, are you?" Kenny said.

Kate opened one eye. Sometimes they skipped bedtime reading, if Kenny had homework or a school function, but this evening they'd agreed to get in an extra chapter or two. Now, stretched out on the foot of his mattress, she found herself fighting drowsiness after a long work day.

"Keep reading. I'm fine." She closed her eye again.

He slapped the book shut.

"What's wrong?" When she got no response, she added, "How am I supposed to listen if you won't read?"

"You have to pay attention."

She shot him a look and saw his brows butt together above a simmering glare. She'd witnessed his mood swings before, and they were no shocker, considering the detachment he'd suffered while shifting from center to center in Romania's orphanage system.

"Be nice, Kenny. No need to act that way to your mother."

"You're not my mom. Not really."

"Yeah? Well, I'm as real as it's going to get."

"Where's my dad? I want my dad."

Though Kate knew such a thing could never happen, she still had hopes of reuniting with Jed and raising this adopted son together. Maybe.

"For right now," she said, "it's just you and me."

Kenny shoved up to the headboard and thudded the back of his skull against hard wood. "I want my brother back."

She thought of nudging closer in an effort to placate him, but such a move would only reward his behavior. Again she contemplated using her dagger to bleed away his memories, a quick purging just to —

Absolutely not. Out of the question.

"I love you, Kenny," she said. "I do want to read with you."

He folded his arms.

"But we can't do that while you're making a scene." She stood. "I'm going to make some tea, and you let me know when you're ready to finish the chapter."

"You closed your eyes."

"I did. That's true. Listen, though, we're not back in Romania. You won't get special treatment because of things that happened to you there, and for the most part we can't even bring those things up here. You and I, we're both scarred, both hurt inside. That's why we have to look out for each other."

He stomped a foot on his bed. "I wanna go back."

"That's not possible."

"I want a puppy."

"And I want my old friends. I want to see the kids in Arad, and my friend Teo, and I want . . . I want my husband." She threaded fingers through her hair, trying to hold on. "Kenny, I'm still learning how to be a good mom, okay? I'm not perfect. Whether you ever get your puppy or I ever get what I want, we're a family now. We have to give each other a little leeway."

Kenny sulked, refusing to lift his eyes.

"Be back in a few minutes," she said.

Standing at the kitchen stove, she listened to water boiling in the kettle. A framed carving on the wall reminded her of her Romanian roots. She was convinced it came from her homeland, a villager's craftwork placed here by Nickel as a memento for her.

The thudding from the bedroom stopped.

Kate filled a mug, watched flavor ooze from the Stash tea bag, and imagined the turmoil going through her son's head. Sure, she could give him affection and empathy, but he needed a man in his life. A father figure. Kenny's own parentage was unknown, since Tomorrow's Hope had sealed the children's pasts—often too terrible to dwell upon. Here in J.C., Kate had spun a cover story about his father being a womanizer who took off to Alaska and wrote only once every few years, and Kenny embraced the fabrication. It not only silenced his schoolmates' questions, it kept his own at bay.

"You coming, Mom?" he called from down in his bedroom. "We're not done with our chapter."

With that softening on her son's part, she let the tension melt away. She eased back down the stairs and sat herself on the corner of the mattress with the mug cradled in her hands. "Where were we?"

"We're . . ." Kenny opened his copy of *The Horse and His Boy.* "At the part in the desert, just outside the tombs."

"Ooooh." Kate quivered in imaginary terror.

"Shasta thinks he's being chased, and then he hears this eerie noise."

"What kind of noise?"

Kenny was caught up again in the tale. "A jackal."

Hot tea sloshed onto Kate's leg and she coughed out a Romanian curse.

"Mom," Kenny chastised. "Only in English, remember?"

"Forgive me. That wasn't nice to say in any language."

"I forgive you."

"Thank you." She dabbed at her leg with the bedspread. "Now go on with your reading. We were at the tombs, I think."

Her mind traveled elsewhere, though. Reeling. Flooding with images.

A haunt of jackals . . .

She hated the way a word or phrase could knock her off balance, but Nickel had spoken last year of Akeldama Collectors who'd gathered at sandy ruins in Israel. Despite the site's notoriety, it had lain desolate for eons. What sort of vile creatures would gather there? What schemes were the Collectors working on even as the Prestons settled in halfway around the globe?

Kate did find some comfort in knowing the Unfallen were on patrol—even those with white hair and bifocals—but she felt unworthy, ill equipped. How was she supposed to mother a Concealed One? What if they hunted him down?

"Mom?"

This home's unique construction did give her some security. Nickel actually oversaw the property—"*But paying rent keeps you honest*," he'd told her with a fatherly smile—and he had built a reinforced basement bedroom. With its own ventilation and back-up generator, the self-contained living area served as Kenny's bedroom. If necessary, the stairway leading to ground level could be closed off with a trapdoor and locked from below.

"Mom?"

She'd even drilled him on dashing down while she slid the trapdoor shut and covered it with a hallway throw rug.

"You're not *listening* again."

"I'm sorry." Kate shook off her musings. "What's wrong?"

"I'm not done reading."

"I did it again, didn't I? Kenny, you know how your mind gets stuck on something and you can't stop thinking about it? Well, sometimes I . . . I get scared. Do you think we . . . ?" She hesitated. This was so out of the norm for her. "Can we can stop for just a second to pray?"

"Pray?"

"Talk to God. Assuming He's up there listening."

"Sure. What for?"

"For our protection, I guess. I don't know. I'm winging it here, okay?"

"Is that why you have the angel tattoo on your back?"

"Did you just make a joke?"

He gave her a shy grin.

"And in your second language, even." She rewarded him with a high five. "Actually, my mom used to call me her angel, so at first I got the tattoo to annoy her. It's also a reminder that I'm not alone, that there's someone out there watching out for us. Just don't ask me to explain any of it, because I don't know how it works. In fact . . ." She paused. "I'm not even sure *if* it works."

Kate's and Kenny's eyes met, locking in on the shared memory of young Petre's death and letting it pass unspoken between them.

"Mom?"

"Yeah?"

"You're *my* angel."

"Thanks." Kate felt a lump rise in her throat. "Not sure I deserve that."

"If you wanna pray, that's okay. But I don't know how to do it."

"Join the club."

"Maybe we could say the Ten Commandments. I think I can remember most of them from when we had them posted in our classroom in Arad."

"In Romania? Things were still communist when I was in school there, so that wasn't allowed."

"They're not in my classroom here either."

"Strange how the world changes, huh? C'mon," Kate said, grabbing hold of his small hand. She figured a good mother was supposed to feed her young one some line about trust and leaps of faith, but this was a subject in which she had zero tolerance for clichés. "We'll just say whatever comes to mind. I mean, either we get credit for trying or it's all a big joke anyway, right?"

He clamped his eyelids shut and squeezed her fingers.

"Kenny?"

"Yeah?" He was cutting off her circulation.

"You okay, sweetie?"

Eyes still closed, he nodded, and she realized his hunched posture had nothing to do with supplication and everything to do with discomfort.

He was taking deep breaths, his shoulders bowed beneath an unseen weight. She drew him close. She felt helpless. A few years from thirteen, and already Kenny experienced these first tremors of the burden he would carry night and day.

As she pleaded for her son to receive some divine mercy and strength, he began trembling in her arms. She sensed no personal assurance, no relief. Her voice faltered, her tongue tripping over hollow words.

Was anyone listening?

She whispered now, barely able to complete full sentences, yet drawing words from the depths the way she'd once retrieved water from the village well.

CHAPTER
THIRTY-THREE

Early June—Junction City

Some nights, Kate's sleep was graced with images of Jacob's snuggly wrapped body in his incubator, while others included broken glass and walls mangled by that pipe bomb, or crimson blossoming against the side of a charter bus. Though the nightmares often seemed to intensify during her monthly cycles, last evening had broken the pattern by conjuring one of her worst yet.

"Mom? Mom, are you okay?"

She bolted up from pillow. "Jacob." Her forehead was cold with sweat.

"Uh, no. It's me, Kenny."

"I . . . I'm sorry. I thought he was . . . What time is it?"

"A little after nine. You want me to make you pancakes?"

"I need coffee."

Kenny scrunched his nose. "I don't know how to make it."

She pulled him into an embrace and, since no one was watching, he let her hold him longer than usual. She wondered how his friends at Tomorrow's Hope were doing, halfway around the world, tucking into their beds for the night. And what about Dov? At least Nickel had promised he was no longer alone.

Her mind flipped back to visions of coffee and double-tall lattes. How long had it been since she dropped by her local espresso hangout? A week? Ten days? She'd been wringing every dollar from her paychecks, but today she was going to splurge.

"Hey," she said. "Let's go to Espresso Yourself. I'll buy you a hot chocolate, if you want."

"With marshmallows?" One of Kenny's favorite American treats.

"Lots of them."

"Can we ride our bikes?"

"You have your helmet?"

"Ahh, Mom. I look stupid with it on."

"What're you talking about? You look like a racecar driver."

He brightened. "Like Jeff Gordon?"

"Sure, I guess. Is that Flash Gordon's real name?" She swung her legs from beneath the covers and shuffled into the adjoining bathroom. "Anyway," she said, "it's for your own protection. It's my job to look out for you."

"You can't watch me every second."

"I know." She stared into the mirror over the sink. "But I can try."

Fifteen minutes later they lifted the garage door and headed out onto Oak Street. Kate loved the way Kenny stood up on the pedals and gave it his all. He had so much energy, and she felt so inadequate at this task of raising a boy. When his muscles didn't move, his imagination often did, pretending to be a superhero, superspy, or—and this part she never quite understood—superfly. It all made her feel old, at least twice her age.

Which, according to Nickel, would be just about right.

Was this a blessing or a curse for her, to look like a late teen and have the maturity and experience of a woman in her thirties? What had taken place in those years of which she had no recollection?

Just ahead, Kenny led the way across Ivy Street, the main thoroughfare that split Junction City down the middle. Although traffic was light, Kate's heart lurched, and she bit back the flurry of warnings on her tongue.

She had to let him go, let him grow.

The Unfallen woman's words echoed again through her head: *"I'm always on guard . . . he'll be safe, of this I assure you."*

She wanted to believe it, the same way she wanted to believe cleansing and hope were contained in her remaining earring. Still, best to be cautious.

She scanned the sidewalks. No sign of the old lady.

"You coming, Mom?" Kenny was across. He was okay.

"Hold your horses, pal. I'll be right there."

Belo Horizonte, Brazil

Another year. Another country. Another taxi.

From the radio, Neil Diamond's gravelly tones assailed Natira's ears. Did the driver think this would impress a foreigner? The Collector cared nothing about "Sweet Caroline," and all it did was exacerbate his foul mood.

Here in Belo Horizonte, a metropolis of millions, Natira's search for the twenty-first Concealed One seemed interminable. The Almighty had been setting up camp in local late-night meetings, and it was this gathering strength of Those Who Resist that had drawn Natira here the way raw meat drew flies.

Still no sign of his prey, though.

Master, my Lord of the Flies, please guide me this day.

Up front, the taxi driver tapped his fingers to the music, singing along with all the machismo of a drunken karaoke singer. A Catholic saint dangled from a chain against his hairy chest, flashing gold in the rearview mirror, and Natira contemplated the possibilities of strangling the man with it.

These knuckle-draggers and their beloved icons. Sometimes the symbols carried heartfelt and therefore dangerous meaning; usually, though, they were nothing more than emblems of superstition.

Number Twenty-One. Where was he?

Natira directed the taxi driver to a street where tourists and locals milled around vendors selling pocket sandwiches. He felt the need to satisfy the cravings of his human belly. Leaving the driver without a tip, he stepped from the car and slammed the door on the final strains of Mr. Diamond.

The pop tune was replaced by the sounds of teens clumped near a brightly lit vendor's cart. It looked to be an informal get-together, and they broke into song in Portuguese, bronzed bodies swaying, hands clapping, eyes sparkling with joy as their mouths honored the . . .

The Almighty?

Natira took a step back. Even here? Was there no escape?

Such folly made him want to tear limbs from their shoulders, to rip flesh from their throats with bare teeth. Subtlety, though, was his current mode of operation. Best to keep a rein on his aggression.

He parted the kids with a sweep of his arm and spat his order at the vendor. His eyes watched the man fry an egg, adding spices and meat, but his ears could not block the strains of adoration that rose all around. Sounds of war undergirded these happy melodies, and even as the singing grew louder, it grew more jumbled in the Collector's ears. He had to get away from here.

With sandwich locked at last between his pincers, Natira hurried down the sidewalk. "Sweet Caroline . . ." he mumbled through a bite. Hating himself for turning to Neil Diamond for relief, he nevertheless broke into the chorus at full volume and continued his rapid retreat.

Anything to drown out the youthful praises. Anything at all.

"Ohhh, sweet Caroline . . ."

Nobody minded his singing. Brazilians were easygoing, fun-loving people, with a much less constrictive view of personal space than the average Westerner, so it came as no surprise when a woman pushed away from a store window with her foot and stepped into his path.

"I like this song," she said in halting English.

"You do?"

"*Sim.* Very much." A coy grin. "My name, it is Carolina."

"Are you sweet as well?"

She smoothed the fringes of her miniskirt, then tossed her hair and laughed. "You want me be?"

Natira took a bite of his sandwich, felt the juices run down his chin as he mulled her question. A warrior needed his momentary diversions, and in fact this might give an outlet for the violent tendencies he'd kept in check. If things got out of hand—as he suspected they might—who would miss a woman of the streets in a city of over five million?

"You are shy?" the hooker said.

He took another bite, wiped his mouth, and tossed the sandwich. "I'm thirsty."

"I see this. You and me, we might need find private place."

"You have a place in mind, my sweet Carolina?"

Junction City

In Kate's experience, it was the little things that pushed a person over the edge. She'd faced paralyzing grief and managed to move on, dragging her limbs until they regained the ability to respond. She'd been struck with jolting truths and deceits from her past, and assimilated them into her daily life.

But the little things . . .

"They're gone?" she said. "What do you mean?"

"There's a sign on the window." Kenny pointed. "Says they moved."

Kate braked her bike beside his, next to the closed espresso booth. The menus were still in place, the Torani flavoring bottles still on display behind the overhead glass. This was her local hook-up. Espresso Yourself. How could she express herself without a trusty place to get her jolts of caffeine?

"Read the whole thing, Kenny. Maybe they're still within riding distance."

"I read it."

"And?"

"They moved, it says. To Tennessee."

Kate wrinkled her mouth. This one couple had helped her feel welcome in town, and now they'd taken off for the state she had left behind
years ago. It was only a little thing, yet it seemed that everyone she cared
about was taken away.

For over a year now, Kate and Kenny had embraced J.C.'s serenity. She'd
convinced herself this was the life she wanted, nothing fancy, just enough
to meet her obligations and enjoy quiet evenings with her son. Her son was
growing, though—ten years old. Soon a candidate for the Nistarim.

What if he was called away? Was she ready to be alone?

She thought about Teo and the way things had ended in Romania at
the youth hostel, and his no-show at the Village Museum. Was she destined to remain isolated from everyone she cared about? Had her desire for
some sort of connection pushed him away? She owed him an explanation,
or at least an apology.

And what about Jed? It killed her inside that she couldn't drive to his
uncle's house a half-hour away and talk things over. Her dad had prohibited
all contact with Nikki or Jed, and she'd been obedient. Here, over a year
later, though, she was sure that any Collectors shadowing her husband had
moved on to better—or worse—things.

What would happen if she and Jed saw each other again? They'd parted
ways two years ago, time enough to let things settle. Maybe now they could
join again as man and wife to rebuild the life they'd once imagined. Although
nothing could bring back Jacob, they would still have each other.

"So what're we gonna do?" Kenny said.

"I was just wondering that very thing," she replied.

"What about DQ? They have MooLattes."

"Sure, sweetheart. I guess that'll work."

Kenny adjusted his helmet, ready to pedal away, then doubled over the
handlebars and emitted a throaty groan. He tried to stand. Cried out again.

"What's wrong?" Kate let her bike clatter to the pavement and moved
to his side. She recognized his sudden onrush of pain, similar to the ones

she'd experienced while sharing Jacob's empathy in her womb. "Are you okay?"

He nodded.

"No, you're not."

Kenny straightened and donned a thin smile. "I'm fine, Mom. It just felt like . . . like I'd swallowed a buncha thorns."

She winced at the imagery.

"For a second," he said, "I thought I was gonna hurl."

Hurl?

Okay, if he could work in his slang words, he must not be too bad off. These were only the first symptoms he was experiencing, the warm-ups for a lifetime of suffering. Nonetheless, she offered up another silent prayer.

Belo Horizonte

"Good times never seem so good . . ."

Natira embraced the inane lyrics, having basked in all five senses for the last hour or so. A tasty sandwich. A spicy side dish. Sure, it'd been a bit self-indulgent for a warrior on a mission, but even the best of soldiers needed reminders of the sweet life—or sweet, sweet death—for which they were fighting.

In case the Master Collector disagreed, Natira had found justification for his actions by chancing upon the very man he sought.

Number Twenty-One.

He was a squat Brazilian with lively eyes beneath a shock of salt-and-pepper hair. The Letter glowed upon his forehead even as he mingled with ten-dollar hookers near the tree-shaded benches of a city park.

One of the Nistarim? Here?

"You know that fellow there?" Natira asked Carolina as she led him back through the park toward the downtown streets. "Has he come here before?"

"The older one, with white in hair? Luiz, he come every week."

Natira let a sneer curl across his lips.

"To talk to ladies," Carolina said.

"To talk?"

"Only talk. Tell about love from God. Luiz is making us mad at first, but he keep coming. Some listen. Not me, but some say he nice. Look them in eye only, not like other men who visit."

"You got that right. He's not anything like other men."

Natira's eyes traced his prey's translucent blue mark, and Luiz stiffened the way a deer might come alert to the scent of a hunter. The Collector pulled the woman closer, knowing his own height was impossible to hide but hoping he would appear as simply one more john in the park.

"Oh," said Carolina, with a grin. "You still have energy?"

"I'm a warrior, after all."

"Sim, *senhor.* And warrior has more *dinheiro?*"

Natira sighed at the tedium of such transactions. Avoiding loneliness always came at a price, and he flashed a wad of bills before following her away from the Concealed One's wary eyes. He wanted nothing more than to vivisect that man's body here and now, making him scream, but to do so would undermine Natira's greater purpose. For now, a cheap hooker would have to do.

CHAPTER
THIRTY-FOUR

Late November—Portland, Oregon

"See, we made it. Everything's fine," Kate said.

"We're not there yet."

"It's just over the bridge. Look." She pointed through the fogged bus window, directing her son's attention across the Willamette River to the submarine harbored permanently outside the Oregon Museum of Science and Industry. "You're going to love this place. Lots of hands-on exhibits and stuff."

"Do I get to do the sub tour?"

"I'm just one of the chaperones. That'll be up to your teachers."

This field trip to the OMSI was not only their first journey out of Lane County since the terrorist attacks on 9/11, it was also the first time since Romania either of them had boarded a bus of any kind. On mornings when it wasn't raining, Kenny rode his bike to school; otherwise Kate drove him in their old Nissan.

"Just so you know, Mom, you don't have to follow me around in there."

"Who, me?"

"Yeah. Sometimes, you know, you . . ."

"What?"

"You hover."

"Hey, pal, you're the one who begged me to sit by you."

"Shh." Kenny looked back over the seat, then pushed his hands into the front fold of his sweatshirt, which he wore rain or shine. "Thanks, Mom. But I'm just saying, you know, once we're inside I'll be okay by myself."

"You're a big kid, I know that. Practically a man now."

He fielded that with a timid grin.

"No problem, anyway," she said. "While you're running around looking at exhibits, I'm going to grab a drink and maybe chat with some of the other parents. Of course, if you need anything I'll be right there."

"Okay."

"You know what else? I think you're one handsome young man, Shasta."

"Not Shasta anymore," he said.

"Since when?"

"I'm David Beckham."

"Did you skip books? I don't remember any characters with that name."

"Mom."

"He's a big soccer star," the bus driver called from behind the wheel.

Twenty minutes later, school kids were spreading out through the OMSI, using the buddy system, and Kate found a seat near the front where she could read the *Oregonian* while sipping fresh-brewed coffee from the cafe.

She felt so domesticated, so soccer mom-ish. In fact, Kenny had joined the team this year and even scored goals in their last two games.

She felt soothed by the everyday routines and responsibilities: taking her son to school, going to work at the hardware store, then running to pick him up from practice before getting him home for dinner, homework, a little TV and Xbox, maybe another chapter ventured into Narnia.

Most days, she felt safe, secluded, and . . . alone.

Sometimes she contemplated breaking Nickel's rules and calling Jed or even showing up at his uncle's house. With Thanksgiving coming up, the temptation was that much stronger.

Christmas, she decided. She'd break the silence, if nothing changed.

She flipped open the newspaper, thumbed past the celebrity gossip, and rolled her eyes at a political cartoon.

On the front page of the third section, she read about the thirtieth anniversary of the D. B. Cooper hijacking, an event that'd started here in Portland and still ranked as one of the FBI's greatest unsolved mysteries. She'd seen bits and pieces about it before, even heard it mentioned in movies, but it intrigued her more now that she knew of her own birth in this area of the country.

She sipped her coffee and panned the museum's entrance area, including a colorful display for the current *Grossology* exhibit. Kenny would be into that.

On cue, her son darted into view. "Mom," he said. "Guess what?"

"Oh, no. This is going to be disgusting, isn't it?"

"It's cool. Did you know that the acid in your stomach—"

"Hydrochloric acid."

"It can dissolve razor blades."

"Don't get any ideas, Kenny."

"Did you know that you swallow a quart of snot every day?"

She shook her head. "Not true. Only boys do that."

"How much is a quart, anyway? About the same as a liter?"

"It's more than anyone should be swallowing, okay?"

"Okay. See ya."

Kate watched him dash off, joining back up with his buddy. She turned her eyes again to the Cooper newspaper article in her lap.

On November 24, 1971, a nondescript man had purchased a one-way plane ticket for Flight 305 from Portland to Seattle. He wore a black raincoat, loafers, and wraparound sunglasses. He said his name was Dan Cooper.

While waiting for takeoff, he handed the stewardess a note indicating a bomb was in his attaché case. He opened it to show her a mess of wires and red-colored sticks that appeared to be dynamite. He said he would release the thirty-six passengers onboard in Seattle if he could receive four parachutes in exchange. Oh, and as an afterthought: two hundred thousand dollars.

All went as planned at SeaTac Airport. The thirty-six deboarded, the parachutes and money were handed over, and Mr. Cooper ordered the Boeing 727 to depart for Mexico City. Not long after leaving Seattle, however, he commanded the pilot to level out at ten thousand feet and to lower the landing gear. It was 8:11 p.m. when he jumped from the rear stairway, out over the forests of Washington State, just north of Portland.

No trace of the man or his parachute was ever found.

In 1980, a boy camping with his family near the Columbia River found six thousand dollars in a rotted package, the bills matching the serial numbers of those given in ransom to the legendary figure now known as D. B. Cooper.

"He didn't jump alone," a reedy voice said from Kate's right. She recognized the man as one of the fathers from their group. He was wearing blue and red Nike exercise gear.

"Excuse me?"

"Cooper. He wasn't alone."

"It happened a long time ago." Kate pushed caramel-highlighted hair back over her ear. "How do you know?"

"Why would a guy need four parachutes?"

"I don't know. In case the cops tried tricking him with a faulty one?"

"But they could've all been faulty." He pointed at the empty spot beside her on the plastic bench. "Mind if I join you?"

"You're not hitting on me, are you? Not during a school outing."

"Do I look that desperate?"

"Hey, buddy." Kate sat up and closed the paper. "Thanks a lot."

"Not that I'd have to be desperate. I'm not saying that you're . . . Listen, who first jumped to conclusions here, huh?" The man's hair was feathered back, almost as red as the stripes on his Nike jacket, and his eyes were dark green between pointed sideburns. He slid in beside Kate. "Let's start over."

She shrugged.

"You're Kenny's mom, aren't you?"

She nodded.

"Funny how that happens, isn't it?" he said. "Maybe someday we'll have our own names again. For now, we're just 'Kenny's mom' and 'Jessica's dad.'"

She wanted to remain annoyed with him, but he had a nice smile and a pleasant smell—one of those sporty Mennen deodorants. Good hygiene was always a bonus, and for a woman who lived each day with unspoken worry balled up in her tummy, she found his easy manner disarming.

"Hi, I'm Kate."

"Hi, I'm Jessica's dad."

She shot him a smirk.

"Also known as Dan Cooper," he said.

"Nope. Wrong hair color."

"How do you know? By all accounts, he was one of those guys who blended in. They looked at over eight hundred suspects in the first five years, and there's still a big fat goose egg on the FBI scoreboard."

"Where'd you learn all that? It's not in the article."

"Firsthand knowledge, baby."

"I'll let that slide, buddy boy."

"Just call me Dan."

"How 'bout D. B.?"

"Nah," he said. "That's something the press made up. If it helps you any, though, you can think of it as Daddy's Back."

"Daddy? As in . . . No. Is it you?"

"Kate, please." He bounced his palm in the air. "Keep it down. We don't want to go making a scene."

"Nickel?"

"I like 'Daddy' better. But you can imagine the rumors that'll start flying around if anyone hears you calling me that, suave fellow that I am."

Kate pushed away, her eyes brimming with tears.

"Sorry," he said, "if I startled you. I'm supposed to be in disguise here."

"I should've known. Guess it's the red hair that threw me. And by the way, I like your normal voice better—if I even know what your normal voice is."

He leaned her direction and whispered in baritone. "I've missed you, Gina. I've been busy like you wouldn't believe."

"There's a lot I'm having a hard time believing. Where've you been?"

"Guarding, guiding—mostly far, far away from here. It's better if I don't go into details."

"Figures. So who's Jessica?"

"Jessica?"

"You know, your *other* daughter?"

Nickel let out a belly laugh, even leaned back and wiped at his eyes.

"And that's funny, why?"

"Because you sound downright jealous." He was back to the reedy tones, one school parent shooting the breeze with another. Although there was no one else within earshot, he played the role for any suspicious onlookers. "You don't have to worry, Kate. You're my only daughter."

"Then how'd you get onto the bus?"

"Same as you. I walked on and took a seat."

"But only parents were allowed."

"I'm your father. I belonged on there as much as anyone."

"Yeah. Well, anyway."

"I talked with a few kids before we left the school, and stayed by them as we got onboard. I told the driver I was with my daughter—a true statement. Plus, you bought it, didn't you? You thought I was just one of the other dads."

"That's . . . that's flat-out scary. It shouldn't be that easy."

"Hey, I've been doing this—the whole disguise, other persona thing—for a long time. Too long. I'm supposed to make it look easy."

"You made me feel like a fool."

"I wanted to see you, to pass along the latest news. We have a good block of time here, while the kids explore the museum. Plus, I didn't think I should make contact in Junction City since there are Collectors there, and—"

"In J.C.? Great. Fantastic."

Kate snapped to attention, surveying the exhibit area for a glimpse of Kenny. She didn't know if she had the emotional capacity to change names and locations again. Not now. Not after they'd settled into regular family life.

"Stay calm," Nickel told her. "Don't make a scene."

"Fine. Okay. So, tell me the plan then. What is it you want us to do about it this time?"

CHAPTER
THIRTY-FIVE

"Nothing."

"Nothing?" Kate said.

"The Akeldama Collectors haven't shown up. Least not yet."

"What's the difference, Nickel?"

"Are you serious?" He unzipped his jacket, revealing a T-shirt with a large Nike swoosh beneath the words *Just Do It*. "The Akeldama vampires are undead, immortal. They can spot the letter Tav. Your average Collectors, they use mortal hosts and they're restricted by that mortality. If their host has to take a leak, they have to tag along. Their host misses a flight? They've got to wait like everyone else—unless, of course, they're inhabiting a raven or mosquito or whatever."

"Mosquitoes. No wonder I hate those things."

"Filthy little bloodsuckers."

"Nikki used to make me wear this smelly garlic ointment to keep them away. One got me anyway, and out came the trusty dagger."

"It does have its healing properties."

"The dagger? Ha. Not for the Collectors, it doesn't."

"For them, it's a curse. I told you how it once belonged to the Apostle Peter, before Judas nabbed it in Gethsemane. Well, it goes back even further than that. The bronze handle, that part came from the *Nehustan*."

"The whadda-what?"

"Nehustan. The Bronze Serpent."

Kate had that sense of sliding down into another labyrinth of mysteries, of fumbling in the musty caverns of her past, hoping for a torch to light her way. This time, however, she was better prepared. She straightened on the plastic bench, glugged from her coffee cup, and said, "Spill it, buddy boy."

"Atta girl," Nickel said. "The Nehustan's actually mentioned in the Hebrew Bible, the Old Testament. When this plague of poisonous snakes attacked the people of Israel, God told Moses to fashion a bronze serpent on a pole. Each person who was bitten could look upon the pole and be saved."

"This happened?"

"You ever wonder why pharmacies use that snake-around-a-pole symbol? It's taken from this story. And later, Yeshua compared Himself to that 'serpent lifted up in the wilderness.' When He was lifted onto the cross, He offered salvation to all those who would look upon Him and believe."

"And this has *what* to do with the dagger?"

"When some of the Israelites started worshiping the Nehustan, treating it like some kind of idol, King Hezekiah got mad. He broke the thing down and put an end to their little cult. But, just being efficient and all, the bronze was refashioned into tools and weaponry."

"Are you saying my dagger's from that Nehusta-thingie?"

"Not to be idolized, of course. Yes, though, it has symbolic power over Collectors the same way it destroyed the work of those desert snakes."

Kate found herself accepting her father's words. Hadn't she, with her own eyes, witnessed Ariston's rapid demise in that cave, skewered upon her blade?

Down the way, a group of kids spilled from the planetarium, while from the OMSI front doors a wave of cold air swept over her. She felt grounded here, planted in the real world.

"You still have the thing with you, I hope," said Nickel.

She ran a hand down to her shin. "Always close by."

"Ah-ha. So that explains the baggy cargo pants."

"They're comfortable."

"No complaints here, Kate. As your dad, I don't want you running around in tight jeans anyway. Do girls really think it's attractive to have their thongs showing?"

"Makes the guys look."

"It's like driving past an accident. You don't want to look, but sometimes you can't help it. And believe me, it's not always pretty."

She took a sip of her coffee. "Men are such dogs."

"Can't argue there." He changed the subject. "I see you still have your earring."

"Is this your version of a subtle hint? 'Time to drink up'?"

"Nazarene Blood's a gift. Nobody's going to force it on you."

She raised an eyebrow. "I beg to differ. You ever been to some of the churches around here? Kenny and I have visited a couple, since he seems interested in all that biblical hero stuff. Figured we could meet some nice people, find some friends his age. Most of the places we went, they either sounded like my mom's TV show—self-help and lots of *rah-rah-rah*—or they were itching to sell us the latest brand of fire insurance."

"Fire insurance, huh?"

"You know . . . 'turn or burn,' 'fly or fry,' 'pay into our building fund and your life will be swell.' I mean, shouldn't we be helping the poor or something?"

"Not a real popular idea these days."

"You're telling me."

"And not real popular with the Betrayer either. Judas was the one in charge of the disciples' money, and it was his job to distribute it to those in need. The moment a woman went dumping expensive perfume on the

Nazarene's feet, Judas got torqued. Big-time. From there, he hurried off to sell out his leader."

"And now it's all come back to haunt us," Kate said.

"That's right. Those thirty silver shekels were the ones used to buy the Field of Blood. If it weren't for a little envy, a little greed, we might not be facing off Jerusalem's Undead, and we might still have Petre with us."

"And Jacob," she breathed.

Nickel peered off toward the *Grossology* display. Even with dark-green contacts, he was unable to hide the swirl of emotion in his eyes. "There's more I should tell you, Kate."

"Do I dare ask?"

"I . . ." He hesitated. "I lost a child too."

"I thought you said I was your only daughter."

"Daughter, that's right. I said nothing about a son."

"What're you talking about?"

"When Nikki and I came together that one night, back in 1965, she got pregnant with not just one child. She gave birth in Seattle to twins."

"You're saying I have a brother?"

"Had, Kate."

"What do you mean?"

"He died thirty years ago."

Kate blinked. Her lips felt numb. She wanted to scream or get up and run; instead she sat frozen on the bench. "Is this why you didn't want me exploring your drop of blood on the postcard? You think I don't deserve to know these things?"

"I'm trying to protect you."

"The way you did my brother?" Her eyes trailed down the hallway, and the frustration in her voice faded into a whisper. "When did he die?"

"November 1971," Nickel said. "That same night Cooper parachuted from the plane, not more than an hour north of where we're sitting right now."

Soimos Castle, Romania

Frost glistened in the starlight that fell upon these slopes, where only weeks earlier grapes had been harvested for the latest vintage. Viewed from the heights of these medieval ruins, the Totorcea Vineyards farmhouse was a rectangular stone box with a thread of chimney smoke slithering away on the river breeze.

Erota thought that the stone-box image was a fitting one. Hadn't their entire cluster risen from their ossuaries after two millennia trapped in limestone burial caves? Hadn't they been released for a purpose?

And that purpose remained undermined by the divisions so endemic to their cluster. Rather than working toward a common goal, Megiste was still bent on her Six, No, Seven strategy, commandeering the House of Eros for her own.

"Don't blame yourself," Helene said, her eyes sympathetic.

"For what?"

"For what's transpired between our two households."

"I don't," Erota said, leaning against one of the old bastion walls. "I'm upset because I haven't been able to decipher Rasputin's meanings. We need someone more familiar with Russian culture and the era in which he penned his words. If there's a Black King—and I'm convinced there is—we need to figure out where he is and how to unchain him for our purposes."

"To bring down the Nistarim."

"What else, Helene?"

Erota thought of Rasputin's papers, sealed and pressed closed to her breast, despite the fact she had their contents committed to memory. His scrawls of squirming ink had come to life in her mind. Taken form. Spread their wings . . .

Before my bones have lain a century in the grave, humanity will be pressed to the brink of lunacy. Wise men will stand in chains while fools masquerade as

*lords. Only the powerful One's arrival will coax new order from the chaos. He
will emerge, this Black King, from the holy ground, and wage war against Those
Who Resist. From the haunt of jackals, he will take dominion with authority.
Yes, the Black King is key. His likeness shall unlock riches to strengthen his campaign, and many shall bow, finding peace in the arms of the strongman. He will
take back by force his kingdom, despite the thirty-six who oppose him.*

What did it all mean, though? Potent as she knew them to be, these
words were now nothing more than dragonflies pinned alive to a board—
tiny feet scrabbling, antennae waving, as they fought to give wing to devilish
prophecies.

"I don't mean to be impatient," Erota added, "but I can't do this on my
own. You and Shelamzion spend most of your time at the vineyard, and
Shabtai's off hunting and gathering, keeping you two sustained."

"A worthy task for any boy of his age and size."

"Meanwhile, I'm hopping from wine festival to festival and, in between,
trying to dredge up some information that'll connect the prophecy's dots."

"We are with you in our thoughts, Erota. I hope you know that."

"I'm missing something, some stone still unturned."

"It'll come to you." Helene rubbed Erota's back, played long fingers
through her silky brown hair. "Each season we have to rake the vineyard's
soil and clear the rocks, and in the same manner you have to churn up
these bits of history and find what it is that's been hidden, hmm?"

"I've been doing that."

"Of course you have, of course."

Erota fumed. Was she the only one committed to their goals—to
feed, breed, persuade, and possess? Here in Romania, the household was
myopic in their vision of a bloody harvest, while off in the Negev, Megiste
and crew were fixed upon their own schemes.

The prophecy did speak of the haunt of jackals, though surely the
priestess could not be the one to "take dominion with authority."

No, the Black King was still out there, waiting to be released.

Encumbered by human ennui, Erota's mind rolled back through the past to her encounters with Ariston's idealistic son. Natira: strapping, strong, and serious. He was the type of man she needed now. Where was he? Would they ever reunite? Imagine the threat of Akeldama Collectors united for one purpose.

"Do you know how close we came?" Erota muttered.

"My apologies," Helene said. "I couldn't hear you over this wind."

Erota turned, facing Lord Ariston's widow. "A few decades back, we nearly demolished the Nistarim, all thirty-six of them in one blow. Not our cluster, per se. Collectors, in general. This was before the Akeldama was broken open."

"I don't know that I'm familiar with this story."

"It happened in the Pacific Northwest, in 1971. It seems the Concealed Ones were convening from around the globe for the first time in centuries. No one knows what their intention was, but the Consortium in the U.S. tells me the tale is true. Drawn from around the world, these humble, hard-to-find souls were to be gathered simultaneously under one roof."

"An irresistible target, I should think."

"Except Cal Nichols showed up." Erota glared down over the vineyard and town of Lipova. "Before contingency plans could be arranged, he took the Nistarim and vanished into thin air. Only in retrospect were we able to piece together his escape route—on an evening flight to Seattle, Washington. To this day, the local clusters and Consortium are still kicking themselves. If they couldn't solve the mystery, it's no wonder the FBI's been unable to do so."

Portland

Kenny Preston appeared from the OMSI gift shop and bounded over to Kate and Nickel in the waiting area. He looked so young, full of life. Kate hated to think of anyone trying to squelch that vibrancy in his smile.

"You okay, Mom?"

"Hey, sweetie. You having fun?"

"Mm-hmm. You didn't answer my question."

"I'm fine," she said.

Kenny narrowed his gaze at Nickel. "Is he bugging you?"

"I told you, I'm fine." Kate was thankful for her son's protective instincts. As man of the home, he took it upon his almost-eleven-year-old shoulders to watch after her. "This here's a . . . a close friend of mine."

"Then why have I never seen him before?"

"Actually," Nickel said, "you have."

"Where?"

"I've been to a few of your soccer games."

That caused Kate to whip her head around. "Really?"

"We first met," Nickel said, "while you were at the orphanage, Kenny."

"*Mom.* That was supposed to be between you and me."

"And me." Nickel thumped his own chest. "I was with you in Sinaia."

Kenny tilted his head. "In Romania?"

"Unless you know another Sinaia. I was the one driving the bus, the one who fought that bear at the train station."

"But you're a carrottop."

"Kenny, where'd you pick that up?" Kate chastised. "That's rude."

"School."

"Well, you're home-schooling next year, pal."

"I think she's pulling your leg," Nickel said in response to Kenny's long face. "Listen, why don't you call me, uh . . . Uncle Terry."

Kenny turned to his mom for guidance.

She was unsure where this was leading, but if her dad wanted to create another persona on the spot, she'd let him have his fun. It would keep Kenny from divulging Nickel's true identity to others while providing an explanation for the new man on the scene.

"Don't worry," she told her son. "Yeah, uh, Uncle Terry here is one of the good guys. Almost like a father figure."

"Cool."

"Tubular," Nickel said.

Kenny stared at him, unfamiliar with the eighties phraseology.

"As in very cool. One day I'll come around and teach you some things, such as inner-tubing and river rafting. How to pitch a tent. How to hammer in those metal tent pegs." Nickel shot Kate a look as she cleared her throat, then carried on. "I bet you're an outdoorsy kind of guy. You've got that good Romanian blood. I might even teach you some of my personal moves."

"What? Like karate?"

"If it's okay with your mother."

"Really, Mom? Could I?"

Inside, she swelled with hope. For a while, she'd thought that her father had left her and her son to fend for themselves, yet here he was offering to mentor Kenny in the ways of the Nistarim. Questions still crowded her head, though: *If it's been thirty years, why did Cal and Nikki never tell me I had a brother? That means he was six years old when he died.*

"We can work out the details later," she answered. "Kenny, go on back to your buddy over there and see if you can get in the rest of the exhibits before it's time to leave. Have you done the submarine tour yet?"

"Nuh-uh."

"You have to see it," Nickel said. "You'll love it."

Kenny turned and gave a small wave, then headed off.

"Nickel?" Kate said, turning toward him in her seat. "This twin of mine—how come he died if he was half-immortal like me?"

CHAPTER
THIRTY-SIX

Regret carved furrows into Nickel's brow and pulled at the corners of his mouth. His perpetual youth seemed to disappear, if only for a moment, as the sorrow of his son's death darkened his eyes.

"It was my fault," he said. "Maybe if I'd . . ."

Giggling over crumbs of gossip, a group of mothers passed the plastic benches on their way from the museum's café at the end of the hall.

"Kate, let's go outside. Seems kind of warm in here, don't you think?"

She followed him out front, dragging legs as heavy as sandbags. The November chill was a slap across the face, but at this point she felt she needed something to break through her numbness. They leaned against the wall, in view of the glass entry doors.

"That night, I honestly thought I had it all figured out," Nickel said. "We were going to escape—you, me, Nikki, and Reginald."

"That was my brother's name?"

Nickel's chin moved up and down.

"Regina and Reginald." She blinked, struck by the loss of that relationship. She tried to laugh it off. "Not too creative, but hey—a set of twins, right?"

"It was gonna be 'Reggie' and 'Gina.'"

"Go on with the story."

"Like I told you, my name—one of many I've used—was Dan Cooper. Your mother was a flight attendant for Northwest Orient. That's how I first met her, on some of my travels."

"Nikki? A stewardess?"

"And a total knockout. She was based out of Seattle, which is where you all lived in secrecy for those first few years."

Kate's feeling of paralysis had returned, spreading down her arms and legs. Children's voices echoed from around the building, from the area of the submarine, yet here on the concrete she stood cocooned in the pounding sounds of her own heartbeat.

"Your mom snuck you kids onto the plane that night," Nickel said, "in violation of the airline's rules. Of course, it was all part of our plan. I boarded along with the thirty-six other passengers and—"

"Thirty-six. Is there some significance to that?"

"Does everything in that chess mind of yours have to have a purpose?" Nickel gave her a wink. "Now like I was saying, we took off from PDX."

"Portland. Got it. And you were carrying a bomb in your case?"

"With a few loose wires."

"Sounds like you had a few loose screws. What were you thinking, Nickel? A bomb? You had your wife and kids onboard."

"Not my wife. Nikki and I never married."

"Because that was off limits to you, right? Your only stipulation."

"I lost my Letter. I failed everyone, the Nazarene first and foremost."

"So, just to make things better, you hijacked a plane?"

"Flight 305."

Kate closed her eyes, exhausted. What must it feel like to be an average citizen, with mortal blood? None of these immortal responsibilities.

"Even mortals don't get off easy," Nickel said, as though reading her thoughts. "Thing is, you and your brother were already specific targets. I thought this was our best chance of sliding off the Collectors' maps once and for all. We landed in Seattle, said farewell to the other passengers, and got our parachutes."

"All four of them."

"Yep. I thought we were home free."

She glanced over. "What about the two hundred thousand bucks?"

"Meant as a diversion, nothing more. Stealing was never my intent."

"Hijacking, on the other hand . . . No problem."

"I was desperate." He ran a hand back through his dyed red hair. "After nearly two thousand years of feeling the guilt of others, I had no idea how to carry my own."

She tapped the vial that hung from his neck. "What about this? Isn't it like the miracle cure, the magic elixir?"

"The Blood cleanses, absolutely. But I'd stopped drinking it."

"I thought it was a daily thing—dying to yourself, coming alive again. All that stuff you told me."

"The answer dies within. That's right."

"So why'd you stop?"

He kicked at a weed poking through the concrete. "I got tired."

"That's your big excuse?"

"When you're young," he said, "you imagine giving your life for a cause, or maybe throwing yourself in the path of a bullet to save the one you love. Well, that's all good. We need those kinds of people. The real heroes in my book, though, are the ones willing to die over the long haul— twenty years, fifty, a hundred. When it comes down to it, Kate, it's a lot harder to give your life not just one time but every single day."

"Okay, I think I see what you're saying."

"And that's what it means to have the Nazarene Blood flowing through your veins. It means letting go of your own selfish desires and giving in to the desire of your Maker. It's self-sacrifice. Day by day by day."

"So you caved," she said. "You gave in to your desire to be with a woman, then you stopped partaking of the Blood because of your guilt."

"For many years, yes. I didn't feel worthy."

She thought of her own thorns and looked away.

"There we were, all four of us," Nickel said, returning to his narrative. "The plane headed south and started climbing into the darkness. I could see I-5 down below, car lights moving in both directions. I went to the rear stairwell, where your mom was waiting with the two of you."

"Me and my brother."

"That's right. I cinched the packs on yours and Reggie's backs and told you how to pull the ripcords, letting you feel them with your own fingers. Things were going to get rough, I warned. You'd have to land with your knees bent and relaxed, and then—no matter how long it took—you were to sit tight while I came looking for you."

"And?"

"One by one, we jumped into the dark."

Kate was incredulous. "Reggie and I were just kids."

"With immortal blood in the mix. I believed—truly, down in my deepest heart of hearts—believed that you'd survive the landing. At that point, Nikki and I had been living in fear since the day you two were born. Stalked by Natira, the one you saw in my blood. This seemed worth a shot at finally breaking free."

"Yet, years later, here we are . . . Still running. Still hiding."

Nickel zipped his jacket back over the *Just Do It* slogan.

"And my twin," Kate said, "my brother that I don't even remember, is dead. Explain that part to me, because right now my head's spinning."

"I found him too late."

"What do you mean, too late?"

"You and I, we drifted past a stand of trees and landed in a cow pasture. With the rain that'd fallen, the ground was muddy and soft. We both came down okay. Little banged up but not bad. Your mom got tangled in some evergreens about a half mile away. I cut her down and we gathered up the chutes."

"How 'bout Reggie?"

"We searched everywhere for him. All through the woods, the pastures
. . . Nothing. With the wind currents, he could've been blown miles away.
The cops were already out in force, but their search radius was farther north
and they were also having a hard time gauging which direction we'd drifted
in the night. By this time, Nikki was hysterical. I knew if we stayed in the
open much longer, we'd be done before we started, so I got you two tucked
away in an ol' feed shed that looked like it hadn't been used in ages. You
snuggled together to keep warm while I went out looking again. Daybreak
came. Still nothing."

Kate began pacing the OMSI's entry area. She wanted to drive away
these unwanted images, wanted to beat her head against the wall the way
Kenny used to, yet she needed to know how the story ended.

This was her history.

At last.

"I walked," her father continued, "with you and Nikki to a rural road.
Your mom was in shock, I think. We went until I saw a convenience store,
a rundown place. I told her to take you, get you to a bus station, and head
for the Motel 6 in Yakima, on the other side of the state. I'd find Reggie
and meet you there."

"That was the big plan?"

"I'd already told her we couldn't be together, not as man and wife, but
I would do everything in my power to be a good father. We had agreed
we'd lay low for a while, then make a fresh start somewhere else. No strings
attached."

"And she picked Romania? Why?"

"She was born there. That wasn't her first pick, though. Up until
then, she'd been committed to staying close by me, wherever that would
be."

"What changed?"

"Well, for the next two and a half days, I hid out in the woods and
avoided the authorities by using my skills picked up over time—immortal
and otherwise."

Kate raised an eyebrow.

"I'll explain that part later." His voice was weary as he butted up to the conclusion of his narrative. "When at last I found Reggie . . ."

She waited.

"He was gone."

"Dead, you mean?"

"Facedown in a stream." Nickel swallowed hard. "Caught up under a bunch of branches, like he'd been shoved there on purpose. His throat was all chewed up, and I was sure an animal had gotten to him. I pulled the vial from around my neck and went to revive him, and that's when Natira appeared."

"The Collector from the Campo Santo."

"Yes. From the Akeldama, originally."

"He's the one who shoved my brother under there? He did that?"

"I didn't have time to ask questions. He came pounding down from the tree line along the river, caught me in midair, and took me under the water in a monstrous splash. We clawed at each other even under the surface, then came up sputtering. On his right hand he had only a pinkie and a thumb, but he clamped them over my head and into my ears—like a stinkin' bowling ball—and pulled me under again. Strong as steel. Digging in. I thought I'd drown, but Reggie needed my help and I kept fighting. We thrashed into the shallows. I caught his head in my own hands and drove a knee into his face. Felt like a block of granite, but he let go for a second and I slipped loose. He tackled me. We wrestled in the water, taking turns dunking, coughing, spitting, swinging fists, kicking legs. His shirt tore off in my hands, and I caught a glimpse of his muscular chest and stomach split by a ghostly white scar from his right shoulder to his left hip. He stared at me with deep-set eyes, black as hell, and chuckled."

"Chuckled?"

"He was mocking me. Here I was at the end of my strength, and he was toying with me. That's when I got scared."

Kate was spellbound.

"All I could think about was getting back to Reginald. I tried over and over again, tried dodging, twisting, fighting, spinning. I threw rocks, big ol' rocks. I yelled at Natira and screamed at God to do something. My own choices had gotten me in this mess, but couldn't He intervene? The whole time, Natira batted me away, ducked my blows and rocks, and laughed with open glee at my yells."

Tears pooled in Kate's eyes.

"As night fell, as we hit the end of that third day since the parachute jump, Natira simply turned and walked away—like he knew something I didn't. He called back over those massive shoulders, 'So much for raising your own line of Concealed Ones.'"

"He knew Reggie was your son?"

"He'd been hunting me from the day I fell. By my own actions, I'd been left vulnerable, and he must've found out Nikki was pregnant. All along, it was his goal to stop me from siring more of the Nistarim, as though my sins could reap such a thing. I didn't even believe that was possible, but he seemed to know more about the Almighty's grace than me."

"You think Reggie would've been a Concealed One?"

"I don't know. But I do know you bore one from your own womb."

Kate's eyelids fluttered and she let them close.

"Natira must have never known, though, that Nikki had twins. He never found out about you, and for that I have Nikki to thank."

"What happened to my brother?"

"By that time, it was too late. Even though I tried giving him Nazarene Blood, three days were up. That's when I first realized the limitations to your half immortality."

"How did Natira know it, though?" Tossing back her hair, Kate squared her shoulders and wiped away the last of her tears. She needed answers as much as comfort. "Why," she persisted, "was he so convinced Reggie would be gone for good?"

Nickel nodded. "That's the real question, isn't it?"

"Any ideas?"

"We're dealing with the mix of mortal and immortal blood. As far as I know, you and Reggie were the only ones to qualify for that category, but for Natira to be so smugly confident, he must've had knowledge of . . . of someone else."

"Another half immortal, you mean."

"Yes."

"Do you think one of the other Concealed Ones could've—"

"No!" Nickel rested a hand on her arm and quieted his voice. "No, I'm the only one who's ever broken that trust. Why do you think we're in this predicament? And it's my mistakes that turned Nikki against me. Even though this big plan of ours had worked, it came at the cost of my only son. Her son."

"So that's why she's always been so overbearing with me."

"Trying to guard you from harm. Trying to pay for her own guilt. Sure, Nikki pointed the finger at me, but she could never forgive herself. She made me promise to never tell you what'd happened."

"Why?"

"She didn't want you carrying those memories, that grief. Didn't want you blaming her in any way. Didn't want anyone connecting you and me and the Nistarim. She was done trusting other people—especially me—and decided she'd save you by herself, by her own methods. That's why she ran off with you to Romania."

The tears spilled over now, running down Kate's face. The trails burned down past her lips, turned frosty in the November air.

Just water, she told herself. So what? And a little salt.

But they kept running, kept digging.

Although she felt physically nauseated from Nickel's account, the truth was out in the open. Nikki. Reggie. Natira. Her own father. So much pain and shame, hidden behind years of secrecy. In her mind, Kate could see the chess moves playing across the board's black-and-white squares—combinations and gambits, attacks and sacrifice. Although the pieces—her beloved piese de sah—were able to coordinate efforts, there was no avoiding the fact that victory always came at a price.

Kate wiped at her face and faced the museum doors. She refused to topple her king and resign. She would fight this out to the very end.

Day by day by day.

CHAPTER
THIRTY-SEVEN

August 2002—Ensenada, Mexico

Natira strolled the boardwalk, moving past a dry-docked fishing boat and breathing in the odor of kelp and barnacles. That briny scent was a comforting one, familiar and foul. In the harbor, a cruise ship stood proud and white against a sunset of bruised plum and peach, while strings of light festooned the Pacific seawall, sparkling beneath a huge Mexican flag that rolled in the balmy breeze.

If ever there was an evening for a Collector to relax, this was it.

But no, that is not the choice of this warrior.

Natira had picked up the pace during the past year, identifying four of South America's five Nistarim. That first fellow, in Belo Horizonte, had been the most slippery only because he chose to mingle on the streets, concealed by the very filth of those he served. Did Luiz think that earned him points? Ha!

Now, with one more to go for this region, Natira had zeroed in on the seaside town of Ensenada—the "city of science," as it was called by some, due to the numerous scientific disciplines practiced here.

Only a hundred miles to the north lay the United States. Was Cal Nichols still loitering there, still blubbering over the loss of his murdered son?

Natira smirked, remembering the anguish on Cal's face, the humiliation and helplessness of that piddly shell of a former Nistarim. The humble one had been humbled. The ageless man had been left to rot in ageless shame.

And, as Natira had known would happen, the half-immortal child had been vanquished.

The Collector paused now beside a palm tree, his attention drawn by lovers walking hand in hand, gaggles of bar-hopping American girls, and obese tourists who waddled back toward their cruise ship. One day these mammals would become taproots of pulsing nourishment.

Oh, what a day that would be. Final Vengeance . . .

According to the Master Collector, mankind would be once and for all annihilated, their rivers of blood seeding the earth for a time of Collective prosperity and peace. The time was drawing closer, nearly in sight.

Toward the end of World War II, Natira had believed that very day was upon them. After his bloodstained bones had been churned up from the Campo Santo in 1944, he'd found a ride to safety in the sidecar of a Nazi motorcycle, then met up once more with his friend, Doktor Ubelhaar. This biochemist who'd played temporary host in the past had recognized Natira immediately as a familiar spirit and extended an invitation:

"*You want to join me in my work, ja?* Kein problem. *You will be Igor*"—he gave a mirthless smile—"*to my* Doktor *Frankenstein.*"

But Ubelhaar's experiments had nothing to do with creating life. Death was his goal, and Natira had joined in, serving willingly, gathering strength, assimilating languages and customs of the new era in which he found himself.

He'd even befriended Doktor Ubelhaar's teenage daughter. Seduced her, to be more accurate, and—

Well, that was another story, wasn't it?

Natira pushed off from the tree, scattering the nearest tourists like cockroaches. In times past their unease would've delighted him, whereas now he worried only that he did not blend in.

He fixed his eyes on a boat chugging into the harbor. An official crest marked it as an oceanography vessel, and he hoped to spot a particular marine biologist on board.

A quiet man. An ugly man. A man of faith, he was told.

Number Twenty-Five?

The Collector watched the vessel ease between the docks and berth beside a gleaming yacht.

A portly fellow in white shorts and a tie-dyed tank top hopped onto the wharf and moored the boat to wooden bollards. He stood straight again, beads of sweat dripping from his neck into curls of black chest hair, and called out to the captain, who shut down the electric motor. Together the two went about cleaning the deck, rolling the sails, and battening down the hatches. All this while nodding their heads to music from the cabin radio.

Carrying over the water, the song's lyrics were fitting if a bit trite: "Gone looking for things we used to find . . . in Ensenada."

Natira raised an eyebrow in bemusement. He recognized those raspy tones of Neil Diamond. A sign, perhaps?

"In Ensenada . . ."

With his pincers, the undead creature fished small binoculars from his pocket and held them to his eyes. He adjusted the focus and watched the portly man lift his shirt to wipe his brow. A corpulent, hairy belly sagged into view for a few moments, then the shirt dropped back down. Along the sloped forehead, squiggles of blue shone even brighter than the tie-dyed material.

So then, this was his vaunted foe?

It would seem the Almighty had no standards at all. Only the Deluded Deity Himself would choose a roly-poly scientist without any sense of style to be part of His plans. How embarrassing.

All the easier for Those Who Hunt, though. All the easier.

With this target acquired, Natira's thoughts turned to the next leg of his journey. The Nistarim throughout Europe, Africa, Australia, Asia, and

South America were now accounted for, leaving only two landmasses to explore: the ever-tricky Middle East and North America's materialistic hellhole.

Which should he sift through first?

From the cabin radio, Mr. Diamond offered a suggestion: "They're coming to America, they're coming to America . . . today!"

The revenant shrugged and nodded, as though choosing between something as innocuous as paper or plastic for bagging one's groceries. Well, why not? When all else failed, let pop culture guide the way.

That evening, after entrusting the marine biologist's identity and location to a local cluster, Natira wandered along the La Primera shopping street and bought himself a hat and woven poncho to keep warm during the coming night. His fake passport was in order, but border guard questions prompted by his size and grisly scars could be avoided simply by joining a late-hour exodus with some of the illegals who gathered along the U.S. frontier.

He flagged down a taxi and waved a handful of bills before the driver's gleaming eyes. "America," he said.

"You want go through Tijuana?"

"*Sí*. But not through Customs."

"*Bueno, señor.* I take you. Extra for road toll."

Natira heaved a weary sigh and climbed into the back. With the poncho wrapped around his broad chest, he was soon rocked to sleep by the car's motion just as he'd once been rocked by his mother, Helene. Encoded in his DNA, those first-century AD memories provided him with her likeness, a graceful woman who'd played second wife to his father, Ariston.

Where was she? As far as he knew, she had never come looking for him.

In a dream, he imagined her roving the earth in tents, bartering for souls, offering immoral pursuits at a price. She was too busy to search for him. No harm done. It was a silly human connection, nothing more. And yet the warrior's own idealism felt slighted by her disinterest.

The bright lights and susurrus of Tijuana's nightlife shook him from his slumber. A few minutes later he saw the stark facade and endless lines of the San Ysidro border before darkness swallowed the taxi again as it angled off toward an illegal crossing point.

Natira fought off his fears of the Restless Desert as he stepped out onto the sand and watched the taxi zip away. He was not alone, though. Crouched in the shadows of cacti and sagebrush, dozens of men, women, and children awaited their signal to make the moonlit dash.

Their tension invigorated him. So what if this was against the law? All had sinned, had they not? All had fallen short.

In fact, humanity's wrongdoings were what qualified him as *hostis humani generis*: "the enemy of mankind." He'd overheard this phrase from a Roman shield bearer long ago, and he clung to it these days as his calling card. There was a price to be collected for mankind's sins—and he was, after all, a Collector.

CHAPTER
THIRTY-EIGHT

Late August—Junction City

There was Nikki. Even on the thirteen-inch screen, N. K. Lazarescu was as beautiful as ever. Raven-haired, with delicate features, she made eye contact with her late-night studio audience and seemed to impart personal revelations. It was an intimate experience, undeniable in its appeal, and from the lumpy living room sofa Kate wished her own childhood had been warmed by such closeness.

She pointed the remote, determined to shut her mother out of her life once again—not that Nikki had made much effort to open that door—and then remembered Cal's words from last November.

"She could never forgive herself . . . She didn't want you carrying those memories, that grief . . ."

Kate hugged her knees to her chest, snuggling toes beneath a blanket.

"We are all destined to be God's children," Nikki said now. "But we must cut away our failures the same way a leech sucks infection from a wound. It's through this very suffering we find purification and release."

Kate knew there were elements of truth in the statement. Wasn't her own scarred arm testimony to a suffering that led to release?

And yet, Cal said there was another way. *Just one drop . . .*

From Kate's right earlobe, the sphere of Nazarene Blood seemed to hum a low, soothing tone. It resonated through her being, a reminder—or so Cal claimed—of the torments the Nazarene had endured to bring about mankind's purification, as opposed to individuals purchasing it by their own good behavior.

This general concept squared well with Kate's heritage. After all, wasn't the sacrificial lamb a wholly Jewish custom, dating back to the original Passover? On that inauspicious night, the Angel of Death had passed over Israelite homes, sparing those who'd daubed their doorframes with a sheep's unblemished blood.

Nikki prattled on from the television. "Once you've been purified, you discover you are not alone. You're part of a family, a collective consciousness."

"A family." Oh, really? And how long has it been since we talked?

"Collective consciousness." You even realize what you're saying?

A tendril wormed along Kate's neck. Though her dagger had carved at and weakened the root, it persisted.

She jabbed a finger at the remote and watched the screen go black. Rolling onto her side, she pulled the blanket over her head, cocooned in the glow of the table lamp.

Her thoughts went back to a bitter encounter five years ago, on the porch of her mother's antebellum home in Chattanooga's St. Elmo's District. Then had come their meeting in the hospital room, moments before the concussive blast that stole away little Jacob's life and blew a chunk from the side of Erlanger East Medical. And their last face-to-face, over lunch three years ago, before she'd headed off to Tomorrow's Hope in Romania.

And all this time, Nikki had been trying to shield her from harm?

Although this failed to dissolve the tendril twitching beneath Kate's skin, she held onto the realization like a woman clinging to a lifeline.

Could she be a good mother to Kenny? To a possible Concealed One? She'd done just fine as a big sister for the orphans in Arad, but she wondered if she had the maternal instincts to be all that her son now needed.

"Mom?"

Kate's eyes popped open.

"You okay?" Kenny said.

"Hmm?" She propped herself up and lowered the blanket into her lap. "Yeah. Just, uh . . . What're you doing out of bed, young man? It's time we start getting back on a school schedule, you know."

"I had a bad dream."

"Again?"

"There was a werewolf right outside my window."

"You don't have a window in your room."

"I did in my dream, and he was glaring at me with slobber dripping from his fangs."

"Werewolves aren't real."

Kenny plopped onto the sofa and slipped beneath her arm. "His eyes were the same color as that bear's in Sinaia, glowing green."

"Let's not talk about that. It's late."

"Can I sleep in your room?"

"*May* I," she corrected.

"May I?"

"No, you may not."

"Why? It's so unfair."

Kate planted a kiss on her son's thick head of hair. In another eighteen months, her half-immortal eyes would be able to detect whether or not he stood among the Nistarim. She told herself he would be safe from such a burden; at worst, he might serve as a substitute, never even called into the deadly game.

"Maybe," he said, "there's something on TV. You had it on, didn't you?"

"A few minutes ago. Yes, I did."

"What were you watching?"

"Some late-night show. It doesn't matter, Kenny."

"Derrick says that Conan's better than Leno or Letterman."

"Listen, I see what you're up to here and it's not going to work. Back to bed, okay?"

"I love you, Mom." He cuddled closer, the smell of his changing body rising from his armpits.

"Love you too." She cupped his chin and looked into his eyes. "How 'bout this? Why don't you go take a shower to help you relax, and from there head straight to bed. No ifs, ands, or buts."

"In your room?"

"Ah-ah-ah. Not even going to answer that one."

His feet scuffled down the hallway. She heard the bathroom door close and the shower-curtain rings rattle. With both hands, she hugged the blanket to her throat and chewed on her lower lip, telling herself that she'd done good by sticking to her guns while finding a practical compromise.

Mental note: *buy the little man some deodorant.*

That thought pasted a grin on her face as she remembered her own mother teaching her to wash herself and change her undergarments daily. Maybe Kate had picked up a few parental tidbits after all.

The phone call came moments after Kenny had gone to bed.

≁

"Hello, Regina."

"*Mamica?*" Kate whispered.

Her mother's voice was a crowbar, prying open a locked door and flooding Kate's cell with dingy light. She was a prisoner, trapped in darkness and befriended by its anonymity. This sudden exposure sent her reeling into the corner, sliding down the wall, clutching her arms over her eyes, and hoping the memories would scurry back into the shadows where their teeth did not show.

"My angel," Nikki said. "Your father gave me this number. He says it's better if we don't meet in person, for fear of arousing the Collectors, but he thought it might benefit us to talk, particularly now that he's spilled things he was supposed to keep secret. I can't say I'm pleased. What's done is done though."

"You lied to me."

"For your protection, dear. Surely you can understand."

Kate understood better than she wanted to admit. Along the corridor and down the basement stairs, her son slept, unscathed by the same dagger that had once been misemployed by her mother's tactics.

"What do you want, Nikki?" She felt the twist of the gnarled vine at her throat, and she edged into the kitchen where this conversation would not wake Kenny. "After two or three years without communication, you want me to act like everything's A-OK?"

"I want purification."

"Oh, of course. 'Let Bygones be Bye, Gone,' and all that slop you shovel out to the masses. It's all about you, about pacifying your own guilt, right?"

"We all have our crosses to bear."

"Sure, but Dad says the Nazarene came to carry those burdens for us."

"Explain, then, the need for the Nistarim. Why were they commissioned to walk among us, bearing the world's weight on their backs?"

"Who knows?" Kate braced herself against the Formica countertop, standing tall once more in her cell and facing the light. "Call it what you like, Nikki. You lied to me and kept me away from my own father."

"Not entirely. He was there when you were younger, playing games with you, taking you on walks. And don't forget his assistance in our flight from Cuvin. He was instrumental throughout your childhood."

"You told me I was born in Romania."

"Again, it was for your—"

"Protection. Yeah, I got that part."

"I couldn't risk losing you, not after . . ." Nikki's voice cracked.

For the first time in her life, Kate heard weakness in that maternal tone, realized in that moment that her mother was in the darkness with her, a prisoner of her own sorrows and regret. The earlier crowbar at the cell door had been applied from within, not without. Nikki, too, was trying to break free.

"For years," Nikki said, "I lived in daily fear that the Collectors would track you down. Everything I did—and I'm not claiming my methods were always the best—I did with your welfare in mind."

"Mom, it wasn't your fault that Reggie died."

"He was but a child." A small gasp. "Only six years old."

"Same as me."

"Yes. Yes, the same as you."

Grasping for her mother's hand in the stale confines of their cell, Kate said, "They took my son's life as well. Jacob would've been five this year."

"I'll never forget that day. I'm so sorry, dear."

Kate closed her eyes. "It's okay."

"For everything," Nikki added. "Please, I do hope you'll believe that."

"I want to, Mom." Kate clamped a hand to her neck. "I really do."

CHAPTER
THIRTY-NINE

May 2003—Ekaterinburg, Russia

Erota gazed up at the gold-domed structure under construction. In another year or so, it would be christened in honor of the tsars who had died at this spot.

Cathedral-on-the-Blood. How apropos.

Over eighty years ago, Bolsheviks had revolted and promised equality to the masses—with disastrous results, as time would tell. They'd exiled the pampered royalty in Tobolsk in 1918, then moved them here where they were gathered in a basement and mowed down by gunfire.

"This was a great loss to Mother Russia," said the man named Dmitri.

"Terrible," Erota said.

"But we will bring back to life our great-grandfathers' dreams, *nyet?*"

"That is the goal, and I can help you do that. It's why I tracked you down and e-mailed you in the first place."

Dmitri Derevenko turned toward Erota. Above his solid jaw, idealism burned in intense blue eyes. Not a bad-looking specimen, as humans went.

Beside him, Oleg Volovnik had the voice and groomed look of a choirboy, but Erota recognized and respected the greed that coiled behind his eyes.

These two were descendants of the Brotherhood of Tobolsk. Those original "good Russian men" had plotted to sneak the tsars out of the country, but their dream had died in the soil beneath this cathedral. Except . . . over the years, rumors had persisted that one fortunate soul had escaped the bloodbath: young Alexei Romanov, next in line for the throne.

Now this new breed of the Brotherhood had risen up, hoping to restore national pride to their great land, to resurrect the monarchy.

If Erota could only convince them that Alexei was the fulfillment of Rasputin's Black King prophecy, they would ransack the globe for their destined ruler, doing the work she could not accomplish alone.

No thanks to Megiste and Barabbas, holed up in their desert enclave.

"Dmitri and Oleg, I want to help you," Erota said.

She explained that she was seeking the Black King, he who would, in Rasputin's words, *"take back by force his kingdom, despite the Thirty-Six who oppose him."*

If the words had been scribbles from a mere madman, she would have laughed at their melodramatic tone, but they came from a defiled priest who had yielded himself to Collectors. That which had gone unexplored for nearly eight decades was now at her fingertips.

"The thing is," she added, "I will need your help in return."

The Brothers acknowledged her with sharp nods.

"I will show you the prophecy, and then it's up to you to play your cards right and to bring the stars—or should I say tsars—into alignment."

"Da," Dmitri said, too serious for even a smile. "We are ready."

"You know this prophecy is genuine?" Oleg asked.

"I found it among the possessions of Queen Marie of Romania. These writings of Rasputin were closely guarded by the tsarina—she probably believed they pointed to her son Alexei's future dynasty—and then smuggled out by your own great-grandfathers. Few others have seen what I'm about to show you."

Oleg looked unconvinced. A breeze mussed the hair beneath his hat as he turned and studied the scaffolding around the cathedral.

"Do you believe Alexei is alive?" Dmitri said.

"Hmm." Erota pursed her lips and noted the flicker of attraction that passed through his gaze. She could use that to her advantage. "I suppose it's possible," she said, "but he would be in his nineties now."

"He is the rightful heir, though. This is what matters."

She gave Dmitri a wink. "It's always about the bloodline, isn't it?"

"Very important, da. We Russians put great merit in such things."

"And well you should."

In all truth, Erota had no concern for such trifling loyalties. She believed that the prophecy spoke of something more insidious, but she would let these men read into Rasputin's words what they wanted—a Russian tsar; a powerful ruler; destruction to all foes. *"He will emerge, this Black King, from the holy ground, and wage war against Those Who Resist. Yes, the Black King is key. His likeness shall unlock riches to strengthen his campaign, and many shall bow, finding peace in the arms of the strongman."*

"If Alexei's alive," Oleg said, "if he's fathered a son, who is going to finance this rise back to glory? Political leaders now stand in our way. Yeltsin himself was born in this city and would've opposed the rise of a tsar."

Erota smiled. "I like you, Oleg. You're a practical man."

"Ideas are worthless without the means to make them happen, nyet?"

"But," Dmitri said, not to be outdone, "who supplies the ideas, if not me?"

"A Brotherhood at work," Erota said. "It's good to see. Now, if you'll allow the interruption of a sister, I'd like to take you back to my hotel, where the prophecy is stored in a safe. You can look"—she cocked her head toward both men—"and decide if you like what you see."

Oleg stayed fixed on the details. "What do you want in exchange?"

"I need for you and the rest of your Brothers to spread far and wide, using your cultural insights to ferret out the clues in Rasputin's writings. All I ask is that you let me know when you've found the missing piece from his chess set."

"A paltry chess piece?"

"A black king, with its obvious symbolic parallels. I've studied the prophecy myself, and it seems this king may be one that Rasputin fashioned to access his hidden collection of relics and treasures—the Tmu Tarakhan, it was called—all of which he dedicated to the rise of a new ruler."

"Far-fetched, I should say."

"You may be right, Oleg. But I think you'll feel differently after reading the words yourself. '*Yes, the Black King is key.*'"

"I am ready," Dmitri said again, his jaw set and his eyes afire.

"That's what I want to hear." She touched his arm and spoke in bedroom tones. "I believe you have the *man*power and the *desire* to do as you please."

"I will prove this to you."

"The sooner the better."

"Dmitri." Oleg threw his hands up. "I see she's finally getting through to you."

Erota said, "What does it take to get through to *you*, Oleg?"

"Women are of no interest to me."

"Is that so? Because I know a few—"

"I put trust in more dependable treasure. Gold, for example. Diamonds."

"All of which are yours, if you can locate Rasputin's key. In the meantime," she cooed, "would you be interested in some Romanian wine, harvested from my family's own vineyard?"

"Wine can be treacherous, just like a woman."

"Oh, I don't think you really mean that."

"Don't listen to him," Dmitri said. "I know how to appreciate both."

Oleg shot him a scowl.

"If nothing else," Erota said, "I insist that you two join me for a drink while we look over the writings. Surely, you can do that at least, can't you?"

"A single drink," Oleg conceded. "And that's it."

Isn't that what they all say?

She pasted on a coy smile. "Come along, then."

Linking arms with the pair of Brothers, she jaunted forward. Already she knew their weaknesses, the points at which she could pass along infection and make them pliable for other Collectors down the road. In a few minutes she would show them the writings, as promised. Then she would uncork the vintage brought in her suitcase as a gift from Totorcea Vineyards.

Why not take this opportunity for blasphemous communion? Together they would drink the wine—insipid as their blood might be. Together she'd break the bread—of their chalky male skin.

White bread, at that. How patently un-Russian.

CHAPTER
FORTY

Early September—Corvallis, Oregon

The begging had paid off. Today she was going to see Jed.

With Nickel's grudging permission and his promise that someone would be keeping an eye on her, Kate Preston made the drive toward Sergeant Turney's home. She had found some measure of peace in her dialogue with Nikki, and she hoped to also talk things through with her husband, using these few hours while Kenny was away at school.

"So this is it," she said to herself as she passed the sign that welcomed her into Corvallis. "Heart of the Willamette Valley."

Yesterday, Kenny had printed MapQuest directions for her in Oaklea Middle's computer lab. Another year had gone by without incident, and her son was growing up, all of twelve now.

She wondered what her own brother would've been like at this age. Little Reggie, running around and—

Don't, she told herself. *Don't even go there.*

Kate returned her thoughts to Kenny. She was proud of the way he helped around the house, kept up—with some motherly urging—on his homework, and even mowed neighbors' lawns to pay for his soccer cleats.

Though she qualified for food stamps on her income, she felt like a negligent mother for making him cover his own costs.

"I like helping," Kenny had told her. "Don't worry about it, Mom."

"I'd pay for it all in a heartbeat if I could."

"I know you would." Then, "Hey, you think we can get a puppy? *Please.* I'll pay for his food."

"It adds up, you know?"

"I can build a doghouse for him all by myself."

"Is that something else Uncle Terry's taught you how to do?"

Uncle Terry. Dan Cooper. Cal Nichols . . .

The revelations there at the OMSI in Portland had been mind boggling, and she was still letting them settle.

Kenny had nodded. "He says he's never seen a kid hammer as fast as me. Don't worry, I know how to be careful."

Kate did worry, though, each time she dropped Kenny off at her father's, an hour up the McKenzie River. Thick forests surrounded the property, and alarm wires ran its entire ten-acre perimeter. Once a small summer camp, the place was an adventureland for a boy with Kenny's energy and imagination. In strict confidence, Nickel admitted to Kate that he had trained others here as well. This was the base from which he made journeys around the globe, gathering intel and data for the protection and instruction of prospective Nistarim.

He'd also opened a storefront business on Sixth Avenue in Junction City, a local hangout for the town's youth. The walls were lined with video games, new and old, and a Mario Brothers clock hung above the front register. Recent high-school grads ran the place for him, keeping the doors open six days a week.

Nickel's Arcade, he called it.

"Isn't that asking for trouble?" Kate had inquired.

"It's not my real name. Anyway, customers pay for a monthly membership card, then play anything they want for only a nickel per game."

"As if kids don't spend enough time in front of the computer and TV."

"It's my way of giving them vision."

"Vision? I've got to hear this."

"It's something Dov told me, how playing games helped him visualize doing heroic things. In the meantime, it lets me keep an eye on Kenny and other potential Concealed Ones without looking like some kinda weirdo."

"You are some kinda weirdo."

"Ahh, Kate—you're just saying that because I'm your dad and already starting to look younger than you."

"Not even."

"Give it a few years."

"Not going to happen, buddy boy. Young Sophia Loren, remember?"

"Did I say that? I'm busted, huh?"

Heading deeper into Corvallis, Kate glanced now in the Nissan's rearview mirror. According to her dad, she was thirty-eight years old, yet with the appearance of someone nineteen. Based on her doctored passport, she told acquaintances she was twenty-nine, a pronouncement most often met with surprise and compliments.

She brushed back her hair, gave herself another once-over in the mirror. Her heart thudded against her ribs.

How would Jed react to her?

Would he like her colored contacts?

Did he look any different? Or did he still cover those big baby blues of his with thick-rimmed glasses, like he was the singer in some emo band?

Four years, Kate realized. That's how long it'd been since she and her husband parted ways. Six years since Jacob's death in Chattanooga.

In 2000, she had returned to Romania and found purpose again in Tomorrow's Hope. He'd come here to wrap his head around things while hanging out with Sarge. The few letters she'd received while at the orphanage described Jed's steelhead fishing on the Umpqua River, walking the waterfall trails around Silver Falls State Park, and skiing Mt. Hood. He drove delivery for Lochmead Dairy, while his uncle patrolled the streets of Corvallis.

She eased through traffic into the center of town, then followed the printed directions and made a left turn off Highway 99.

Okay. Here goes nothing.

With heart galloping, she edged to the curb in front of Sarge's address. It was an older townhouse with some personality, nothing too fancy. She tossed her hair and mounted the steps, hope and love and desire twining through her thoughts. One glance would tell her all she needed to know.

Her hand was poised to knock on the door, when she noticed a folded note taped to the wood. That was her name on the front, in Jed's slanted handwriting. She tugged it loose and read it over.

Felt her knees almost give way.

Was this a mistake? Surely, he wouldn't do this to her. She forced herself to read through it once more.

I know you're going to be mad. I know I said you could come today, and I meant it. Sweetheart, I do want to see you. Please forgive me, but I guess I'm just not ready yet. It's not you, okay? It's me.

She looked up and down the street. Checked the townhouse windows, in case Jed was watching from inside. Feeling angry, she knocked on the door but got no response. She couldn't believe this. He didn't even have the backbone to face his wife? To sign his name to the stinkin' note?

Crumpling the paper, she started to shove it deep into the keyhole.

"Whatcha doin' there?"

"Oh." Kate turned. "Sorry. Are you Sergeant Turney?"

"You got it. Sarge'll work just fine, though."

He was a large man, with eyes as creamy brown as Hershey's Kisses. His hair was buzz-cut, his stomach pushing against the buttons of his police uniform. He looked to be about thirty, younger than she had expected. Considering his sizable frame, he had come up behind her with surprising stealth.

"I was supposed to meet Jed here," she told him.

"Mondays are his day off. He's gone fishing."

"Figures."

"You Gina?"

"That's what Jed calls me."

"He's told me lots about you. All of it good, mind you."

"But he couldn't stick around to chat, huh?"

"You know, that boy blames himself for what happened at the hospital."

"In Chattanooga, you mean? That makes no sense."

"I've been in his position," Sarge said. "It ain't easy talkin' yourself outta something like that, no matter how hard you try. He says that he went off to make a phone call, and if he hadn't have done that, your kid would still be alive."

"That's not true. It wasn't his fault, not even close."

"He seems to think so."

Kate wanted to lash out at this police officer for even bringing it up. What right did he have, giving her details about her husband and the events surrounding their son's loss? Who did he think he was?

Despite this indignation, she found herself silenced by the expression in the man's eyes. She saw there nothing but genuine care.

"Well, listen." Sarge shifted his weight from one foot to the other. "I ain't gonna poke my nose in where it don't belong, but I will tell you that man of yours is torn up and twisted sideways. Done about all I can do. Jed's gotta take that next step, you hear what I'm sayin'?"

She nodded, wondering how long such a step would take.

"Don't you give up on him, though."

"I won't," she said.

"I know you won't. Otherwise, you wouldn't have come here today."

"Thanks, Sarge. I should get going."

"Sure thing." He pointed a stubby finger. "Uh, you mind fishin' that paper outta the keyhole first?"

Kate was on the outskirts of Corvallis when the Nissan cut out on her. She coasted to a stop along a railroad embankment. She knew squat about mechanics, but it felt ridiculous to sit in the driver's seat and pout. Tall grass brushed the boots beneath her cargo skirt as she climbed out and opened the hood. She turned and gazed both directions. Far down the road, a tractor crept along. Moments later, an elderly couple passed in a Dodge Duster.

Was that a head of white hair? Was the Unfallen lady sitting in the passenger seat, perhaps with a Chihuahua lazing in her lap?

Ridiculous. Here Kate was, grasping at straws again—just like she'd done by driving to this stinkin' town in the first place.

A crushing loneliness settled over her. What had made her think Jed would follow through, when he was the one who'd bailed on her years ago, unable to share his grief with her?

She climbed back into the car, fell over the steering wheel, and sobbed.

Junction City

It felt like a countdown to upheaval. Kate paid someone to replace the fuel pump on her vehicle and life pressed on as it had for the past few years. She and her son had dwelled in relative peace, drawing strength out of the silence, yet she had a sense their small-town normalcy was coming to a close the same way she sensed a rising resolve in her son. For him, it was more than the prelude to manhood; it was a steeling of his will and submission of his skills to the Almighty.

Kate could relate to those families whose sons and daughters served in Iraq and Afghanistan, putting it all on the line for what they believed in. How many had already fallen? The cost of freedom was never cheap.

She found herself toying with her earring, contemplating the price that had been paid to offer healing.

"Mom, I'm never gonna get this homework done."

"Sure you will." Standing in their kitchen, she wrapped an arm around Kenny's shoulders. "The work's getting harder because you're getting older, that's all. Can you believe it? A seventh grader."

"It's no big deal."

"No big deal? By next March you'll be a teenager."

He beamed. "Does that mean I can get a paper route?"

"We'll see."

What it did mean—and this was the part that worried her—was that he would be a man by Jewish standards. If he were to be one of the Nistarim, the old Hebraic letter would appear on his skin, visible not only to Kate and Nickel but to the Collectors of the Akeldama.

Kate took a sip of her tea. In the steam that rose from the mug, she saw glimpses of the carnage inflicted by Erota in Chattanooga and Sinaia. From what her father told her, Erota's Collector inhabited a host similar in build and coloring to Kate Preston herself. To Gina Lazarescu.

One day, Kate suspected, they would face off again. Do or die.

"Mom, are we gonna read before bed?"

"I, uh . . . Aren't we done with that series now?"

"I'm talking about that other book of yours, *The Screwtape Letters*. When you read it out loud, it makes more sense to me."

"Sometimes I'm not even certain what it means."

"Uncle Terry, he's good at explaining."

For most of the summer, Nickel had been away on covert assignments. Nevertheless, on a handful of occasions, he'd invited Kenny upriver to the wooded property. Kate valued those trips, knowing her son was getting the mentoring he would soon need, should he take up that momentous burden.

"Sorry. Time to brush your teeth, and—nope! No arguing, pal." She'd been pressing upon Kenny the importance of diligence and focus, of doing one's best. And that all started with a good night's sleep, right? "Here's some motivation for you . . . Keep up your grades, and we'll talk seriously about that puppy you want."

"Really, Mom? If I get that paper route, I could even pay for—"

"Teeth. Bed. Go."

She watched him hop down the stairs into his reinforced basement bedroom. She had to trust the measures Nickel put into place, as well as the watchful eyes of the Unfallen. If her son became a Concealed One, he would serve Yeshua Himself.

Kate propped herself before the dining room computer. Into the search window, she typed: *the nazarene.*

She knew the things Nickel had told her about this man, knew the power in His Blood, but history's abuses—as well as more personal ones—carried out in His name made her hesitate in surrendering her allegiance.

For half an hour she perused articles, encyclopedic entries, and blogs. It was overwhelming, the disparity in people's reactions. Some called Him a man of peace. Others a man of war. Some blamed the world's ills on His radical ideas, while others claimed that lasting peace could come through Him alone.

What did respected Jews say about Him?

On a whim, she added *albert einstein* to her search and hit Enter.

The results were instant, and she clicked on one of the first links. She clicked on another, then another, each one confirming the veracity of a quote from the Nobel Prize winner himself: *"I am a Jew, but I am enthralled by the luminous figure of the Nazarene . . . No one can read the Gospels without feeling his actual presence . . . His personality pulsates in every word."*

Stunned, Kate pushed back from the computer.

What kept her from experiencing that same enthrallment as Einstein, that sense of presence and personality? Was it her own fear? Her desire to remain in control?

Five minutes later, in front of her bathroom mirror, she combed out her dark-chestnut hair. Her job at the hardware store sometimes entailed pulling sheets of plywood, stocking bins of sixteen-penny nails, or stacking bags of fertilizer. In her tan tank top, she could see not only the scars on her left arm but the muscle tone in her biceps and shoulders.

She brushed her teeth and swished water in her mouth. Throughout the routine, she avoided the crimson glow of the orb hanging from her ear.

In the darkness of her room, beneath her black-and-gold bedspread, she did her best to block out the looming countdown that ticked louder and louder in her head. She found herself tiptoeing along the old corridors of her heart, rattling doorknobs and pondering possibilities.

Cal Nichols . . . A few years ago, she'd opened the door upon the truth of his role as her father.

Jed Turney . . . Earlier in the month, she'd found emptiness waiting in the room that'd been occupied by her estranged husband. He'd called once since her visit, apologized, and they'd even discussed a weekend date. So far, no go.

One door remained.

She fell asleep, her dreams blending blackberries and goat's milk and the flint-eyed stare of a lanky Romanian man.

CHAPTER
FORTY-ONE

Arad, Romania

Teo paced between his desk and the travel bureau's front window. His suit was wrinkled, his tie loose around his neck, symptoms of a restlessness that had come over him these last few months. Here it was, the end of September, and already he could see another year fading away with nothing to show for it.

Why was he still alone? Was there some defect that made him abhorrent to the fairer sex—not counting his belt-buckle scars, of course?

He paused to consider his reflection in the glass. Midtwenties, diligent on the job, with modest savings in his Banca Transilvania account, he also owned the home his Uncle Vasile had left behind.

And still he had no one to share these things with.

For Gina's own safety, he'd squandered his last shot at love by failing to appear for their date, and she'd disappeared from his life since then. Where was she now? Had she reunited with her husband?

In his right hand, Teo cupped the milk bottle from the fridge. It was

a balm for hurtful memories, a salve for the thorns that pricked at his
lower back. Though it held off the Collectors for short periods, his restlessness continued to grow.

He tilted the bottle to his lips, but lowered it before partaking. No,
he was tired of fighting them, tired of embracing loneliness. The Power
of Choice was his, and as manipulative as Erota could be, he preferred
being her puppet to being nothing at all, to nobody at all.

I'll call her, he decided. *If she wants control, let her have it.*

Before he could dial, the phone jangled beneath his outstretched hand.
He lifted it to his ear and gave the standard office greeting, the one he'd
regurgitated thousands of times the past few years.

"Teo?" a female said. "You sound tired."

One of his regulars? But who called him by his shortened name?

"Hello?" she said. "Did I lose you?"

Fluent Romanian. So this wasn't one of his German or Hungarian
customers. He said, "I am here. May I help you?"

"I'm a childhood friend of yours, but I'd rather not share my name
over the phone. In fact, I shouldn't even be calling."

"Can I help you with travel arrangements?" he offered.

"Don't you recognize my voice, Teo? Maybe you remember a certain
three-legged dog of mine. That's the only clue you're going to get."

"Treia."

"Yes, that dog."

"Where are you?"

"A long ways away."

Teo covered the transmitter with his palm for fear Gina would hear
the trembling in his voice. How he had longed for this moment, a chance
to set things right. "How far?" he said. "Are you here in Romania? I can
come to you."

"You mean, the way you did at the Village Museum?"

"There was a reason for that."

"I'm sorry for throwing that at you. Listen, I'm living in America now,
and I was just calling to touch base with you, for old times' sake."

He jutted his angular jaw at the window, cracked his neck. So that's all this was? A nostalgic chat? A frivolous call? It would be lunacy to believe there was anything more significant to it, and treacherous thoughts began rumbling between his ears as a result.

"Teo?"

"Where in America?" he said.

"Does it matter? I'm halfway around the world."

His spine tingled as he recalled Erota's earlier injunction: *"If you happen to hear from her, I do expect that you'll give me a jingle."*

"Please, Gina, you can tell me." Then, "Forgive me. I understand your wish to remain anonymous. In my line of work, though, this distance is not so far. Perhaps I could visit you."

"C'mon. You know how expensive that'd be?"

"I can travel very cheap, nu? Is it nice weather in the place you live?"

"Rains a lot, but that's Oregon for you. It's a small town, lots of farmland, not much different than Cuvin."

"Is he there, this other man? Cal?"

A hesitation. "Are he and I together, you mean? No, it's not like that, Teo. He . . . he's related to me."

"But he's there?"

"He stops by now and then. He has no idea I'm even calling you."

"I would like very much to see you." The words gushed from Teo's lips. "Da, I believe I need to do this. We are friends, and sometimes it is good for friends to—how do you put it?—touch base."

"You would make the trip? Seriously?"

"It would be good for me to get away. Is Portland the best to fly into? Okay, then, this is not so difficult." Sincere as his words were, he felt that treachery still coiling through his head. "Or . . . Nu, perhaps this is not a good plan."

"Of course it is. Long as you don't skip out on me again."

The prickling intensified along his back, a thousand pinpricks roiling into one wave of pain that left him irritable. Whereas his good intentions had led to solitude and regret in the past, this time he would serve his own desires. After all, wasn't Gina reaching out, despite the potential danger? Time to reciprocate.

"Is there a hotel near you?" he asked. "A cheap place to stay?"

"Like I said, it's Small Town, U.S.A., but I'm sure we can find something that'll work. I know of apartments that rent for a week at a time."

"I have holidays at the end of October, if this will work for you."

"This October? Perfect."

"Thank you for phoning. I will let you know once my dates are confirmed."

"Sounds good, Teo. Ciao."

He bid farewell, then leaned over the desk and worked his knuckles along his spine. Muscles writhed at his touch. Snatching up the phone again, he placed a call to Totorcea Vineyards and told Erota of his plans.

For the first time in weeks, his restlessness gave him reprieve.

Junction City

"Coming to J.C.?" Nickel's volume rose in the receiver. "You invited him?"

"Teo wants to see me. Is that some big shocker?"

"No, Kate. The shocker is that you seem to forget you're in hiding. This isn't just about you. It's about the Concealed Ones, your son specifically."

She gazed out the kitchen window, where dusk drew a blanket over the backyard. "It's not as if Kenny has the Letter yet, assuming he ever will."

"I still don't like it. Something about that guy gets under my skin. Sure, Teo's your childhood friend and all, but it bugs me to think of him coming after you."

"He's not coming *after* me. He's coming to see me. Anyway, it's not till the end of next month and I still have my earring for protection, right?"

"It's not some lucky talisman. You're leaving yourself vulnerable."

"You'll be back around by then, won't you?"

"To cover for your disobedience?"

"Well, it's not like you've been here to discuss things," Kate fumed. She grabbed a pot of boiling water from the stove, and the spillover sizzled on the burner. "Seems you've been gone a lot these past few months."

"Putting out fires. Keeping watch."

"You could at least call every once in a while."

"I've been busy," Nickel said. "Based on my descriptions of him, a number of the Nistarim believe they've seen Natira skulking around. My guess is he's marking their locations, preparing for an assault, and the last thing we need is some impetuous move of yours drawing his attention to you and Kenny."

"Relax, okay? I've spent most of my life in hiding, so I know how to blend in." She dumped pasta into a colander in the sink, draining the hot water. "Plus, I'm a grown woman now, not Daddy's little girl."

"Like that's supposed to put my mind at ease."

"Bye for now, Nickel. I have to feed my son."

Mid-October—Seattle, Washington

The Greyhound bus delivered Natira into downtown Seattle on a dismal rainy day. With these sorts of seasonal conditions, it was no wonder the suicide rates were high. His own humanity felt saddled with the despair of this place, and he turned to memories of Erota, of her warm skin and sensual lips.

Where was she now? What might they accomplish together?

His lone crusade against the Nistarim felt that much lonelier, and he questioned the decisions that had left him wandering this mortal coil on his own.

Shrouded in self-doubt, the Collector walked through the streets looking like some hulking homeless man. The few bicyclists and pedestrians who braved the downpour gave him wide berth in his tattered wool

overcoat and huge leather work boots. He didn't stop until he reached the
Space Needle. He paid the fare and took the elevator to the observation
deck.

What a wretched view. Mist and gray clouds and drizzle. Barely a
glimpse of towering Mt. Hood to the southeast, or the San Juan Islands
to the north.

An island. That's where I'd hide if I was one of the Nistarim.

This was Natira's first visit back to the Pacific Northwest since that
fateful November evening in 1971, when he'd tracked Cal Nichols to this
region and put to death the fellow's hopes of siring an immortal bloodline. Now, to wipe out the Concealed Ones—and this putrid planet along
with them—the Collector needed only to locate the final eight.

Two more in North America. Five in the Middle East.

And, of course, Number Thirty-Six, wherever he might be.

Despite the gloomy weather, this area had exerted itself as a strong-
hold for Those Who Resist. They thrived against all odds in this liberal,
highly educated environment, feeding off the Almighty's natural handiwork and building relationships without artifice.

This was an ominous sign for Collectors. It was harder to operate
when Those Who Resist started branching beyond the traditional church
structures.

The rain came down even harder now, pelting the Space Needle's
roof and streaking the windows in angry rivulets. Barometric pressure rose
in Natira's skull till he thought it might split apart at the temples, and he
determined that this portion of his search would have to end quickly.

The search was twofold. Not only did he hope to unearth his twenty-
ninth target, he was seeking his former lover.

Rumor had it that Trudi Ubelhaar, teen daughter of Doktor Ubelhaar,
had been brought to the Northwest as part of the American's post-WWII
struggle for technological superiority over the Russians. Trudi was a skilled
deceiver—this Natira knew firsthand—and she must've convinced U.S.
counterintelligence that she held invaluable Nazi secrets in her pretty
young head.

Perhaps she did. If nothing else, she would've been capable of stealing biochemical nuggets from her deceased father's files.

Trudi, Natira calculated, would be seventy-five years old now, no longer the Aryan beauty he'd once seduced. For a time, she had been part of Hitler's SS breeding program, but then claimed she was barren.

Another of her deceptions.

The Collector circled the Space Needle's perimeter one more time, then decided to return to ground level. Time to visit the Seattle Public Library and see if he could dig up any information on Nazi war criminals still living in Oregon or Washington State.

Later, once this infernal rain had abated, he would go back to hunting Number Twenty-Nine.

CHAPTER
FORTY-TWO

Late October—Totorcea Vineyards

Howls came from the crenellated ruins of hilltop Soimos Castle. Through the farmhouse window, Erota could see a pale yellow moon above the fortress towers and movement among the rocks below. Wolves were not uncommon along these fringes of the Carpathian and Transylvanian mountain chains. This region, once home to the Dacians, had long nurtured tales of werewolves.

In Romanian: *vircolac.* The name *Dacia* itself meant "wolf."

Erota continued packing her soft-sided suitcase. Tailored skirts and jackets went in with silk blouses, fashion jeans, scoop-back dresses, heels, and an assortment of jeweled accessories. She would use her looks to full advantage, for business connections as well as personal pleasure.

Destination: Wiesbaden, Germany.

Event: 15th Annual Glorious Rheingau Days.

She had a side event planned, as well, a private rendezvous at a castle north of Frankfurt. All her travel arrangements had been made through Teodor's office in Arad. He, too, was on his way out of the country—with a report to bring her upon his return, regarding Gina Lazarescu's precise whereabouts.

A louder howl than before rolled down the slopes into Lipova, and Erota suspected it came from surly but strapping Shabtai. Would he ever learn to control himself?

Of late, the man-child had been toying with the use of wolfish habitations, adding a new dimension to the term Those Who Hunt. As was the risk, however, in long-term usage of temporary hosts, he'd begun taking on doglike behaviors and appearance. By moonlight, he embodied the traditional traits of a werewolf, even scratching at himself and complaining of fleas.

"Keep quiet, would you?" Erota said aloud. "You're drawing attention we don't need here at the vineyards."

Despite his adolescent indiscretions, Shabtai would make a capable partner for her upcoming trip. They'd take a train to Frankfurt, then rent a car by which to explore the Rhine's wine district. After scoping out the land for a week or two, they'd join the official Rheingau event for eight days of feasting and drinking.

And for dessert?

The blood of the rich and inebriated.

During the festivities, Erota would meet with her cohort from the Brotherhood of Tobolsk. Dmitri Derevenko had unearthed new clues he wished to discuss. It seemed Adolf Hitler had made attempts in the mid-1940s to track down Alexei Romanov, the missing son of the tsars, and documents related to that search were in storage at local Kransberg Castle.

Perhaps she would find her Black King.

Then, together, they would take dominion at the haunt of jackals.

This was part of Erota's gift, squeezing all she could from her trips, locations, and those she encountered.

In many ways, however, she felt like a shipwreck survivor, treading water in hopes of reaching land. The narrow vision of other Collectors and clusters annoyed her to no end. How much quicker things would go if the Houses of Ariston and Eros reunited, or if missing Natira were to join forces with them.

Instead, Megiste and crew pursued their strategy of Six, No, Seven—cave walls squirming with gutted flesh and carnality.

Erota, with the Brotherhood's help, hoped to trigger Rasputin's dire prophecies by identifying and releasing the Black King.

And who knew what ends Natira served, if any.

Erota yanked the zipper tight on her suitcase and was dragging it off the bed when Shabtai appeared in her doorway. His hands clawed into the wooden frame, and he lowered his head as though sizing her up.

"Are you ready for our trip?" she said.

His stubbled visage and shaggy sideburns shook from side to side. Lupine drool lay wet upon his chin, and silver tufts gave his ears a pointy look.

"You'll need to get ready." Erota smoothed a sheer dress over her hips. "We'll travel as we are now, in our permanent hosts. Once in Germany, though, you'll be able to hunt at will."

His words came out in a growl. "Like you could stop me."

"You should be careful, Shabtai. The more time you stray off in these temporary vessels, the more of their traits you assimilate. Look at you. You're sounding more canine by the day, and your eyes are almost yellow."

"The better to see you with, my dear."

"I'm familiar with *Grimm's Fairy Tales.* Enough of your mocking."

"You're not my boss, you know?"

"For now, I am the *de facto* household leader, and the Collector Procedure Manual gives me the right to banish any mutinous members. I'll put up with you only so long as your goals remain in line with the House of Ariston."

"Ariston? Ha. That pudgy ol' man was taken down by a girl."

Erota vaulted the bed in a single bound and caught the teenager by the throat. Her curved nails turned luminescent green, notched for disembowelment, and incisors dropped down through her gums, poised for a long draught from this troublemaker. "Who do you think you are?" she said.

Shabtai gurgled. "I'm . . . the man here."

"Is that so?"

"I should . . . be the one leading us."

"You're a man-*child*, that's all you are—with much to learn." Erota's face hovered an inch from his, the blaze from her irises casting a waxen pall over his angular cheekbones. "I asked for you as a partner on this trip. Take that as a sign that I trust your abilities, but not that I trust your decisions."

Shabtai stopped resisting. As he lowered his guard, his body reacted to the nearness of her nineteen-year-old host, and he seemed to realize the possibilities there. He checked the hallway for others, his cheeks reddening.

"I can learn," he said.

"That's what I'm counting on. Your virility needs to be harnessed."

"What is virility?"

"It means"—she gave a cold grin—"that you have what it takes."

"Thanks."

"Together, we can make this a good trip, Shabtai. I have this sense that something unexpected will happen, something fated for our benefit. For now, you should go pack—and that doesn't mean roaming the hills as a wolf. Gather your belongings. We leave first thing in the morning."

As she watched him lope down the farmhouse hall, she could've sworn she saw tufts of silvery-blue fur rippling through his hair.

Junction City

"There's something I need to give you, Kate. Could be a matter of life or death."

"Can't it wait?"

"Which part of life or death didn't you understand?"

"No, I got that." Kate straightened a keychain display next to Ace Hardware's front register. "It's that I can't drop the phone and just leave work."

"Let's meet for lunch," Nickel suggested. "Over in Founder's Park."

"You're in town today?"

"Right across the street. See me waving?"

She leaned back from the register and peered past a bin of garden rakes. There, on the corner of Sixth and Front Street, sat Nickel's Arcade. Or, as her dad referred to it: "*A training ground for the kiddos.*" As opposed to his secluded property along the McKenzie: "*A boot camp for the kiddos.*"

Cordless phone to his ear, he lifted a hand from the main doorway.

She waved back. "Founder's Park. See you at noon."

Two hours later, still clothed in her hardware uniform—yeah, didn't she look snazzy?—Kate walked to the park with sack lunch in hand. From across the lawn, the storied Finnish locomotive bore a majesty that belied its need for a paint job.

"A beautiful machine, huh?"

She stifled a gasp. "Nickel?" She turned. "Where'd you come from, Mr. Ninja-man?"

"The back of the arcade."

"I didn't know there was a rear exit."

"There's not." He winked. "It's called *bridging*."

"Bridging, huh? Is this one of the tricks you've been saying you'll teach me, or something you're hogging for yourself?"

"Remember *Star Trek*, how they'd get beamed from one place to another? It's something along those lines."

"But that is not logical, Captain."

Nickel rewarded Kate's Spock impersonation with a smile. "Takes a little practice, but with my genes you should be able to get the hang of it in no time. Right now, though, we need to make sure you're armed for Teo's arrival."

"Armed? I have my dagger."

"He's arriving tonight, right?"

"I'm picking him up from PDX after work. Plane comes in around seven."

"I still think you should've checked with me first. Here." Nickel patted the bench. They both sat, and he hefted a JanSport daypack, his intrepid traveling companion, into his lap. "While you're eating, we can play a game."

"Bring it, buddy boy."

Nickel pulled out a portable chess set and started placing the black pieces. True to form, he left her to arrange her own piese de sah. As queen of her own destiny, she was responsible for coordinating her forces. Between bites of a tomato-cucumber sandwich, she made her opening moves and offered the Evans Gambit.

"Ah-ha." Nickel snatched the free pawn. "Preparing an attack, huh?"

"Just like the Evergreen Game."

"Anderssen's better known for the Immortal Game, but his Evergreen was even prettier if you ask me. What's the man do? He peers deep into the position and finds a daring attack while poised on the edge of defeat."

She took another bite, then moved her queen's pawn to drive away his bishop. "Speaking of edges, you don't think my dagger's enough to handle things? It took down Ariston." She castled, sliding her king to a safe spot.

"It'll work, sure. It's just that Kenny's getting pretty handy with his MTPs, and I want to be sure you've got two or three around." He shook his daypack, producing a metallic cacophony. "Just in case."

"In case what?"

"Well . . ." He moved his queen's knight. "You know how guys can be."

"Oh, so that's what this is about? Overprotective dad, making sure I tell the boys to keep their hands to themselves? Don't worry, Nickel. Me big girl."

"I still want you to have them."

"Because you don't trust Teo."

"Only as far as I can throw him." Nickel responded to her bishop's development with an aggressive pawn move. "Which, come to think of it, might be far enough. Only problem is that I've got to be somewhere else by tomorrow morning. There are hints that Natira's sniffing around the Northwest."

"Seriously? That's not good."

"No, it's not." Nickel's eyes glazed over, the sparkles of gold in his irises turned dull by worry. "I'm leaving as soon as we're done here."

"More like once I've checkmated you."

"We'll see." He pointed. "Are you planning to sac that knight of yours?"

"Shhh, I'm trying to play a game."

"You know, that was Anderssen's first step toward victory—the sacrifice at f6. Giving up the queen a few moves later was just an added touch."

In silence, father and daughter completed ten more moves in rapid succession. The brisk autumn air marched dried leaves past their feet, while Engine 418 stood guard in its fenced enclosure. Though Nickel had answered her attack with sharp counterplay, his king now stood exposed, and Kate waited for his response as she downed the last of her sandwich.

"The black king is key," he mumbled.

"Better believe it. I'm coming after him."

"Atta girl." Nickel snapped from his thoughts. "That's what I like to hear."

"Move, scaredy-cat."

"Only if you promise to take the MTPs."

"I promise." She saw a mate in three moves, with only one way he could stop it. "What's the deal with these, anyway? I know Sisera took a stake through the head and all, but is there something else I'm missing?"

Nickel reached into his pack. "As Jews, we believe the Scriptures speak of a coming Messiah. He's given lots of names—Cornerstone, Lion of Judah, Prince of Peace. The prophet Zechariah also called him the Tent Peg."

"As in . . . ?"

"Metal tent peg, that's right." Nickel pulled tapered spikes into view and handed them over. "I believe Yeshua is that Messiah. Think of Him each time you hammer these into the skulls of the undead. Whether it's your dagger, MTPs, or Nazarene Blood, the Collectors'll be in for a rude awakening."

Kate weighed one of the metal objects in her hand. Though crudely fashioned, it was well balanced. She tucked the whole set into the deep pants pocket of her work uniform, feeling a little awkward yet comforted by their nearness.

"There you go," Nickel said. "So's it my move, right?"

" 'Hit me with your best shot,' mister."

Grinning at their old Pat Benatar reference, he thwarted her threat of checkmate with his bishop, and she groaned.

"Sorry," he said. "But as you know . . . 'love is a battlefield.' "

She groaned again, even louder.

Minutes later, he ground out a victory in the endgame.

CHAPTER
FORTY-THREE

Portland, Oregon

Teo wondered how his travel clients ever managed. The space was cramped on these planes, the overhead bins so low his black hair scraped against them and gave him the sense that something crawled over his scalp. He fidgeted, battling claustrophobia, as though forced to share his seat with an unseen interloper.

When a fellow passenger offered the window seat, Teo found some temporary distraction in the views of patchwork farmlands and snowcapped Rockies tinged teal and maroon. But his tension never completely dissolved until the moment he made it through the Arrivals area to Baggage Claim.

There, not ten strides away, stood Gina. She wore casual cargo pants with black boots and a fitted black jacket over a red Joan Jett T-shirt. Her straight hair fell to shoulder length, with caramel highlights streaking the section that dipped down over her left eyebrow.

They met halfway, and he set down his briefcase. When they embraced, he brushed a traditional kiss of greeting past her cheek. She stiffened for a second, then relaxed and returned the favor.

"How was the flight, Teo?"

"Worth every moment." He cocked his head. "Your eyes look blue."

"Contacts," she said. "It's fun to try different things. I even go by a . . . a nickname here. Most people call me Kate."

"Kate? But it's no shorter than Gina."

She shrugged. "I like it. Don't you?"

The lilt of her voice assuaged his concerns. He held her at arm's length and gazed at her. She was the first girl he'd ever kissed, and the memory of those lips still warmed his dreams.

"You look nice . . . Kate. And still so young. Look at me." He touched his receding hairline. "Not yet thirty, and already I lose some of my hair."

"You should try parenting. That'll really do it to you."

"You are making a suggestion?"

"I . . . Teo, no. What's that supposed to mean?"

"A joke. Nothing more."

"I have a son," she said, elbowing him. "That's what I was getting at."

"A son? I did not know this."

"I adopted."

"A Romanian?"

"You'd never know it, with his American accent. Kenny's a great kid." She turned from him. "Well, let's get your luggage and get on the road. I'm sure you're worn-out, but you can meet him tomorrow. Tonight, I'll drop you at the apartment. They gave us a good discount for the two weeks you'll be here."

"Thank you," Teo said in English.

"Hey. Very good."

"I've been listening to language CDs."

"You'll learn tons just by being here. C'mon."

They located the correct baggage carousel, but as they waited, all Teo wanted to do was snatch up his suitcase and scurry to the nearest departure gate. Did he think he could control the darkness that lingered always at his back? He should not be here. Kate did not need the trouble of his presence.

"How old is he?" he heard himself ask. "Your son."

"Twelve," Kate said. "He thinks he's big enough to be on his own, but I had one of the, uh . . . one of my elderly friends come over till I get home."

"It is wise to be careful, nu? I bet you make a good mother."

Kate nodded, her lips pressed into a determined line. "I try."

Teo saw his suitcase on the conveyor. He'd come this far, and he would do his best to enjoy the time allotted. He'd deal with the consequences as they surfaced, and when Erota demanded information upon his return, he would lie. He would do nothing to compromise Kate's safety.

That's what he told himself as he retrieved his luggage and followed her out to her car.

Eastbound Flight, Somewhere over Europe

When possible, Natira avoided sudden schedule changes, but there was no skirting this. Usually not one to subscribe to the whims of fate, he sensed that the cogs of a greater plan were now turning.

Tonight, Master, I shall take wing and fly.

Seattle boasted a number of local airfields, and without much difficulty he found a flight logged for Frankfurt, Germany. Utilizing his undead abilities, he crept over the tarmac in darkness and found a hiding spot in the belly of the Army transport plane. Now, wedged between machinery and munitions, he pondered what lay ahead.

It had all started with the crumbling of a Concealed One. What the American clusters lacked in overt supernatural abilities, they made up for in organizational prowess, and Natira had been impressed by the speed in which their Consortium delivered to him the news.

The miserably humble soul, it seemed, had been posted in the northeastern tip of France—a location Natira had cataloged years ago.

Very well, then. Check Number Four from his list.

As satisfying as this was—a sign that Collectors were piling up the world's iniquities—it meant setbacks for Natira while he tried to pinpoint the fallen man's latest replacement. His best bet was to act quickly. The new fellows were like wobbly-legged foals, fresh in their roles and easier to sniff out. The longer he delayed, the more protracted the search became.

Number Twenty-Nine could wait. Trudi Ubelhaar could wait.

With metallic reverberations shaking his resting place, Natira marveled at the excitement that stirred in his human chest. As fickle as these habitations could be, he had a sense of being drawn toward the embrace of friends or family.

Of Erota?

But, no. He was self-sufficient, quite capable of functioning without the compromising influence of relationships and emotion. He was a warrior.

Regardless, his excitement continued to mount as the airplane droned through the night. To think that a manmade contraption could transport him back here in one night, as opposed to the flittering upon the wind he would be subject to as Collector without a physical host. Only in this century had he enjoyed such a luxury, whereas Collectors in ages past had been more limited.

The Separation had robbed them of so much. Even the Master Collector, called the "prince of the power of the air" by the Christian Bible, was no longer able to enjoy this fleshly realm without manipulating hapless humans.

Master, my eternal allegiance to one who understands.

The plane began a slow descent through the clouds toward a region in which Natira had dwelled soon after his rise from the Campo Santo.

"Heil Hitler!" "Deutschland uber Alles!" . . . And all that nonsense.

Still, the mousy man named Hitler had wanted all true-blood Germans to have *lebensraum,* or space to live, and this was also the desire of Collectors everywhere. They wanted room to roam . . . without humans spoiling the fun.

Natira's recollections of World War II took him to a castle not far north of Frankfurt. There, he and his Nazi sidekicks had gathered as the Third Reich began to implode.

Kransberg Castle . . .

A simple medieval edifice that watched over a small village below, it was not so spectacular as to draw crowds. He knew the rolling hills that surrounded the site, knew the fortress itself, and it might serve as a good base for his coming search. If nothing else, it would be a functional place to rest his human frame after this cramped and icy ride.

Junction City

As a protective parent, Kate avoided neighborhood trick-or-treating. Typically, she picked up Kenny after school and took him to various businesses and banks around town that offered free goodies for the kids. She knew razor-in-the-apple stories were urban legends, but hated to think what it would be like facing a bona fide Akeldama Collector in Halloween garb.

Those fangs . . . *Oh, you mean they're not fake?*

The tapered fingernails . . . *Don't even let those things near me.*

That ax through the skull . . . *Hmm, does that have the same effect as an MTP? Or does it just leave a killer headache?*

She stood at the hardware store register and debated what to do this evening, particularly with her Romanian friend in town. At the moment, he slept off jet lag, but she knew Teo would enjoy this aspect of American culture—carved pumpkins, plastic spiders, and the sidewalk parade of Freddy Kruegers, Sleeping Beauties, and Count Draculas.

Yesterday, during the drive from Portland to J.C., they'd caught up on old news before she dropped him at the Holly Street Apartments. Per her father's instructions, she had shared only the surface details of her new life.

What reason was there to fear? Hadn't Teo always come to her aid? Hadn't he been with her when they discovered Dov Amit living on the streets?

Nickel's words: *"Something about that guy gets under my skin."*

Dads would be dads. It was only natural.

Nevertheless, last night's TV news had given Kate reason to think. The wife of a Corvallis winemaker had vanished from their home at Addison Ridge Vineyards, and her BMW Z3 had been discovered in a ravine. The police had a suspect in custody, yet warned that an anarchic terrorist ring might be involved. With the 9/11 attacks still fresh in people's minds, the authorities weren't taking any chances. You never knew what sort of crazies were out there.

Kate shook off her foreboding. She didn't need a straightjacket of fear here; she needed a sound mind to survive All Hallows' Eve.

She picked up the phone. She had a plan.

"*Buna zuia,*" she greeted Teo in Romanian.

"Good day," he said in English, his voice still groggy.

"Sorry if I woke you up, but we want to make the most of your time here, right? Here's the deal. I'll pick up Kenny after school, then swing by so we can go out for pizza together. After that, we'll make the candy rounds. Sound good?"

"You speak too fast for me, I think. But yes, pizza is good."

"I'll be there around five-thirty. You get back to sleep."

"*Multume*—" He stopped himself. "Thanks."

Teo followed Kate down the stairs from his corner apartment. A video store sat next door, and a park across the street featured a large locomotive that looked like something from pre-WWII Russia. He was surprised to see such an engine halfway across the world.

"Jump on in," Kate said, gesturing to her car.

He climbed into the passenger seat. He wore gray slacks, a belt, and a white dress shirt. Back in the apartment, he'd tossed off his navy-blue tie, deciding it too obvious an attempt to make a good impression.

"Hi, Teodor," said the boy in the backseat. "I'm Kenny."

"I am good to meet you," Teo said, stumbling over the words.

"*Glad* to meet . . ."

"Da. I mean, yes."

"Don't worry 'bout it. I still mess up sometimes," Kenny said. "Hey, my mom says she knew you back in Romania. That's cool."

"Cool," Teo said. He knew that word, at least.

They headed for Abby's Pizza and ordered a large pepperoni-and-olives. Teo looked around, amused. He'd seen witches and goblins depicted in his native folklore, as well as werewolves and vampires, but the addition of iconic Hollywood figures turned this evening into a monsters' parade. Parents ran through the place, chasing children dressed as princes and princesses, angels and demons; one boy hopped from table to table, waving an orange goody bag and chanting, "Trick or treat, trick or treat, trick or treat."

"Here." Kenny held out a handful of candy from his own stash.

The boy grabbed the offered bounty and darted away.

"This was nice of you, Kenny," Teo said.

"I have plenty."

"Like that kid didn't have enough sugar already." Kate leaned toward Teo in the booth. "We train our drug addicts young here in the States."

Despite his English courses as a travel agent, Teo was having difficulty fielding words in this raucous environment. He nodded toward the exit, and Kate nodded back. Kenny grabbed the to-go box.

On the way to Kate's house, Kenny pointed out seasonal decorations ranging from the ghoulish to cute. A sign in one yard called it the Cemetery of Sin. Draped in fake spiderwebs, plastic tombstones depicted an array of biblical transgressions.

"D'ya see that one, Mom?" He read aloud the saying at the bottom of the sign. " 'The wages of sin is death'—Romans 6:23."

"I see it," Kate said from the driver's seat.

Teo's upbringing gave him limited familiarity with the Bible. He watched the "cemetery" pass by and thought of Uncle Vasile in his grave.

"Kenny?" Kate glanced back. "You okay?"

Teo looked into the back and saw the boy's lips locked shut, his shoulders shaking. Was it a seizure? A sudden attack of the flu? Kenny's bag of treats had slipped from his hand onto the floor, spilling Reese's Peanut Butter bats and triangular, orange-white candies that looked to Teo like decayed teeth.

Kate pulled the car to the side of the road. "Sweetheart?"

"It's . . . it's over," Kenny said. "I'm fine."

Teo saw concern in Kate's eyes. He knew she'd lost a child in Chattanooga, and she'd taken a bold step by opening her heart again as a mother. It made him want to stay in this small town, by her side.

From Cuvin, he had watched her ride off years ago in a dented red Dacia, and he'd never let go of the hope that one day they would be together again—and not only as friends. He'd never loved anyone else. He had tried dating a few times, then given up and focused his energies on the travel bureau.

At his spine, the thorns coiled even now.

He was infected. He did not deserve a woman's love. Yet with just one of Kate's smiles, she could almost convince him otherwise.

CHAPTER
FORTY-FOUR

Kate Preston shooed Kenny off to bed. Together they whispered a good-night prayer, and she gave him a kiss on the forehead. She pictured for a moment what it would be like to see the letter Tav shimmering beneath his dark bangs. His thirteenth birthday was only five months away.

On the selfish side, she hoped the symbol would never appear, that they could live in continued tranquility—if such a thing were possible with a teenager.

What was it Nickel had told her? *"You're doing a good thing, Kate. Remember that 'pure and lasting religion . . . means that we must care for orphans and widows in their troubles, and refuse to let the world corrupt us.'"*

Caring for orphans? That'd been her desire since childhood. As for dealing with the world's corruption, that was a battle to which she was still adjusting.

She leaned over and switched off the bedside light. "Love ya."

"Love ya more," Kenny said.

"Okay, pal. Spit out the gum." With the unmistakable scent of watermelon Koolerz in the air, she ignored his expression of innocence. "Out."

Once he'd obeyed, she climbed the stairs, closed the panel, and covered it with the hall rug. He would be safe and sound in his ventilated hideaway.

"What you are doing?"

Teo's broken English startled Kate, and she rose from her work. He faced her from the doorway at the end of the hall, his eyes scanning the floor. Although lamps glowed from the living room, they failed to illuminate this end of the corridor.

"Just straightening things up," she said. She took a step forward, planting both feet on the basement panel. "You ready for some coffee?"

"It's late."

"Yeah. Well, I think I need something. Plus, I don't have to work in the morning, so I can sleep in."

Teo studied her face, as though trying to read her meaning.

"Alone," she made clear. "Don't go getting any ideas, buddy boy."

"I . . . No," he said. "I am here as your friend."

Kate admitted to herself that she still had mixed feelings for this man, but none of this negated her dad's concerns or her marital status. After Jed's failure to make an appearance she had removed her wedding ring, but legally they were still joined. She knew if anything were to happen between her and Teo over these next fourteen days, it would have to move at its own pace.

Ten minutes later, they were seated apart on the couch with mugs of coffee in hand. Aside from a few late trick-or-treaters, they were able to chat uninterrupted about his itinerary while in Oregon—trips to the beach, the mountains, waterfalls, and to Crater Lake, the deepest in North America.

The conversation turned to how things had changed since Ceausecu's execution in Romania, the country's possibility of joining the European Union, and the continued plight of her state-run orphanages.

Teo said, "We still do not know why there was this HIV outbreak in '89. Thousands of children have already died."

"I know why."

"You? Even scientists do not know."

"The kids were infected on purpose," Kate stated.

"What makes you say this, I must ask?"

She swirled her coffee. She cared for him, and if this relationship was going to progress, it could only do so on full disclosure. Nickel had cautioned her about this, but she chalked it up to fatherly overprotectiveness. Teo had come all this way, and he deserved to know where things stood. So did she.

Time to lay it all on the table.

"Teo, I know you're not much of one for religion," she said. "Neither am I. In fact, all that mumbo-jumbo turns me off."

He sipped his coffee.

"Thing is there is a whole other world out there. The superstitions we grew up around—frying the hearts of corpses, cutting off the heads, all these things to keep a vampire from coming out of the grave—they're distractions from the real deal. Or maybe lame variations of it."

"This is how you explain the outbreak? I don't understand."

"It's . . ." She switched to Romanian in hopes of clearer communication. "I believe the children were attacked by creatures who already carried the virus."

"Who would do such a thing?"

"The *strigoi mort*. The undead. These are vampires out to suck not just your blood, but your time, your energy, whatever."

"Fairy tales. Stories to frighten the children."

"I've seen them, Teo—up close and very personal. And they'll do whatever it takes to collect your strength for their own. They're the ones who bit the orphans and started the spread of that particular HIV strain."

He stared at her, his expression flat, his eyes hooded.

"Be honest," she said. "We're all diseased, right? I mean, we all have evil in our hearts. If we say we don't, we're fooling ourselves. Any given day I could do stuff that'd put me in prison for life, and I'd deserve to be there."

"Nu, Kate. You should not believe these things your mamica told you. You are a good person."

"Maybe. But isn't it a form of escapism to think we don't have to deal with the infection in our hearts, in our minds? It's like it's there in our blood. We've all done things, and had things done to us, that make us susceptible."

Teo lowered his eyes, his knuckles turning white around his mug.

"Yes, my mom tried shoving it down my throat, which has made it hard to accept even the real morsels of truth. I know you got the opposite, with almost zero talk from your uncle about—"

Teo's coffee sloshed onto his shirt as he jolted from the couch.

Kate stopped. What had she said wrong?

"Vasile is dead," he said.

"I'm sorry. I didn't—"

"Do not be sorry. He should've died long ago, before he ever got his hands on me. He . . ." Teo risked a glance her direction, his pupils oily black.

"What, Teo?"

"It doesn't matter," he barked at her. "The man is gone."

Near Wiesbaden, Germany

"A werewolf did this?" Erota said.

"That is what some are saying."

"And what about you, Dmitri?" She hooked her arm through the Brother's and guided him away from the estate courtyard. Outside the doors, terraced slopes descended toward the Rhine and basked in the midday glow of late autumn. "Do you believe such a thing in our modern times?"

"I'm not sure what to believe."

"A publicity stunt, I suspect."

"Not according to those who saw the bodies."

Erota laughed to cover her own dismay. She'd seen cadavers before, even instigated their mutilation, but the brazen display outside Schloss Johannisberg's stately walls was too much.

Once a monastery, this hilltop estate dated back to Charlemagne and had been owned by Napoleon in the 1800s. Now it enjoyed a worldwide reputation for quality wines—Johannisberg Rieslings, Eiswein, and Spätlese. The world's oldest Riesling vineyard had been planted here, a fact around which the Glorious Rheingau Days revolved.

Which only made three gutted human pelts that much more distasteful.

How could Shabtai be so uncouth?

"Believe me," Erota told Dmitri Derevenko. "I'm a regular at such wine festivals, and they'll do anything to cause a stir. It makes for higher attendance and greater profits, that's all."

"Then why were the police in such a hurry to clean things up?"

"They don't have time for these games."

"I think they wish to quell panic and find those responsible."

Erota grimaced. Once Shabtai showed his face again, she would berate him for this indiscretion. Could he not fathom the results of such behavior?

This was Germany, a bastion of reason. In her experience, there was little to gain by stirring the primal fears—and spiritual curiosity—of these preoccupied masses. It was easier to gather souls and tap blood while their worries were centered on the value of the Euro or the Bundestag's latest scandals.

"Such a beautiful day," she said, hoping to divert Dmitri's attention. "And wait till you see the meal they have planned: duet of pigeon, red-pepper couscous, and a saffron mousseline."

"I prefer good Russian *borsch*."

"Oh, don't be a bore." She twirled away, letting her burgundy gown shimmer about her slender frame. A moonstone pendant clung to her neck.

He said, "I am here for one reason only."

"Hmm." She gave him a sultry smile. "Is that so, comrade?"

Dmitri took a step back. He wore a threadbare jacket over brown trousers, and a cell phone clung to his belt. He was a solid specimen, with a sturdy jaw, and though he'd given himself to her briefly in Ekaterinburg,

she knew him to be a man on a mission. He viewed the Brotherhood of
Tobolsk as God's agency, seeking out the rightful heir who would lead
their motherland back to glory.

She, too, had a mission. And his zeal could be put to good use.

"Very well," she said. "I'm anxious to hear your latest news. A clue to
the Black King, I hope? Some insight into Rasputin's writings?"

Before he could answer, a taxi turned from the highway and rumbled
up the estate drive. It dropped off a man in gray slacks and Arin Mundazi
loafers.

"*Entschuldigung,*" the man said to them in rough German. "Excuse me,
do you speak English?"

They both nodded.

"My name's Marsh. Marsh Addison."

Erota tried to place that. His accent went along with his American
mind-set that expected them to know and/or care who he was.

"I'm from the U.S."

"Da." Dmitri's expression remained flat. "We can see this."

"*Es tut mir leid,*" Marsh said, in a passable German apology. "I'm still
disoriented after my long flight. So is this where it's all happening? And
where am I supposed to register?"

"In through those gates," Erota told him. "Correct me if I'm wrong,
but I believe I know you. Don't you own a vineyard in the Willamette
Valley?"

"In Oregon, that's right. And you are . . . ?"

"Erota. I represent Totorcea Vineyards, from Romania."

"That's right. We e-mailed back and forth about Pinot Noirs and
other varietals." He reached to shake her hand. "Good to finally meet
you."

The moment their palms met, his grip stiffened and his gaze narrowed, fixing on her as though trying to identify a person behind a mask.
She had the unsettling suspicion he'd discerned her undead nature.

Is he one of Those Who Resist? He must be.

"Well, I better get inside," Marsh said.

Catching her breath, she smoothed her dress as he strode off. She was both repulsed and attracted to him. His blood smelled rich.

Shabtai, at least, seemed to be getting his fill. She anticipated there would be more carnage as he prowled the hills tonight.

It wasn't the killing that bothered her so much as his flaunting of it. Whereas a vampiric attack could spread infection through the blood, reaping a harvest capable of sustaining Collectors for years to come, a lupine ravaging left only one creature gratified: the werewolf.

Food. Erota felt prone to her human craving for fuel. She turned to Dmitri, who carried himself with that staunch old Russian demeanor. "The duet of pigeon is calling to me. Are you ready to eat?"

"If you are ready, Erota, I can show you my latest news now."

"Can't it wait till after lunch and the festivities?"

"If you wish. Afterward, we'll drive to Kransberg Castle, over by Usingen." He set his hand on his cell phone, the way a bodyguard might touch his gun for reassurance. "Near the end of World War II," he said, "the Allies used the castle as an internment camp. Countless Nazi scientists passed through its gates, and many secrets were divulged. Not all have been made public."

"Well, Dmitri, I do hope this secret is worth both our whiles."

CHAPTER FORTY-FIVE

Junction City

Teodor paced the living room of his good friend, moving back and forth between pools of golden lamplight and shadow. He felt that familiar presence clawing into his back, with thorns that matched the length of his bitter memories. How could he ever forget the lashes of the belt, the breaking of his skin?

And why would he want to?

To do so would be to release Vasile from the deeds for which he was accountable.

"Teo," Kate said, "I'm not here to judge your uncle."

"Let him rot in hell, I say."

"I can only imagine the things he did to you, but this is the way Collectors hook into you. Through one small wound, they can trigger the disease in your veins and produce an entire tangle of thorns. If you don't flush away that hatred or lust or whatever, the infestation keeps spreading."

"Bah."

"Seriously," she said. "You're probably already at risk."

He paced—lamplight to shadow, lamplight to shadow. With fingers threaded through his hair, he tried to hold together his thoughts. They spiraled, whipping faster, gaining centrifugal force so that it seemed they would explode outward through his cranium.

Cuvin, Romania. The thatched-roof house.

The man who was his uncle, who was the village prefect, who was a godless man and proud of it.

The nights without anyone to protect him, no answers from the skies above or the earth below. Only darkness.

Teo came to a stop in the shadows. He turned next to an armchair and faced Kate, latching onto the memory of her lips against his. He wished he had goat's milk on hand, something to subdue these briars. Surely he could find something to drink in this rural community. Surely so.

At the base of his spine, the infection dug deeper,

"You believe these creatures exist?" he scoffed. "You have seen these Collectors with your own eyes?"

"You're being harassed by one now, by its evil."

"You . . ." His anger dissolved into relief. She understood this struggle he endured, meaning he was not alone in his insanity. Despite the reality of his shame, she saw behind that black curtain.

"How long has it been there, Teo?"

"Since Cuvin."

"Since we were kids?"

His chin moved up and down. The pressure increased. He watched her hand touch the hem of her skirt, as though reaching for something hidden. He felt knots of tissue move up the vertebrae to his neck, angling his head forward so that his eyes slipped to her cleavage.

"Teo. Up here."

Humiliated, he met her gaze.

"There's a cure for the disease," she said. "None of us are strong enough to fight it on our own, and even if you hold it off for a while, it's still there."

"My uncle called this our evolutionary struggle to survive."

"At the expense of others?"

"Survival of the fittest."

"Yeah? Well, pushed to its extreme, only one person is left standing."

"Or," Teo said, "we accept that systems and the rule of law will safe-guard our collective survival."

"Collective, huh? And who makes these rules? Who decides between right and wrong? Do we cut away the weak ones so that the strong can thrive?"

Uncle Vasile's words: *"You are weak, that's what you are. You're nothing."*

"Tell me this," Teo said. "If there is a God, why was He deaf to my cries?"

"You won't get easy answers from me." Kate leaned forward, elbows on knees. "Maybe He tried sending help, but the help refused to cooper-ate. Who knows? I do know you're here with me now, all the way from Romania."

"What can you do?"

"Nothing. I'm not sure. Each of us has a chance to choose, to receive or reject the evil." She tapped her earring. "In here, there's Nazarene Blood. From what I'm told, drinking it can cleanse you and help you start new."

"A ritual to perform? Nu, Kate, I am not interested."

"It's more than that."

"You have drunk this Blood? Nu? Why not?"

"I will." She fidgeted on the couch. "When I'm ready."

Teo slipped next to her, felt her warmth at his arm. Kate tried to offer a cure, but all he wanted was *her*—not her ideals, her imaginary comforts. A woman to love and love him back. Was that too much to ask?

"Are you ready now?" he whispered.

She closed her eyes, her long dark lashes curling in the golden light, her defined jaw and the movement of her full lips teasing him. Tawdry sugges-tions slipped into his thoughts, and he listened with rising interest.

Kate's lips were still moving, her eyes still closed.

He ran his eyes over his friend's bronze skin and a raised scar on her neck. He'd never been this close to her, for this long, without the subduing tonic of the goat's milk. It would be wrong to violate her trust, and a part of him wanted nothing more than to share a proper relationship. Another part wanted her this instant, on his own terms.

The Power of Choice?

After years of longing, waiting, it seemed his choice was already made.

Kate felt uneasy as Teo nudged up beside her. At her shin, the dagger was in its sheath; shoved into the inner pocket of her fitted jacket, an MTP waited. Despite these precautions, she wished she could give Nickel a phone call, but he was off looking into the threat of Natira's return.

She pressed her eyelids shut and began to pray. She could come up with no flowery words, only a desire to see this friend of hers freed from his past. Teo had been infected long ago, and she felt his eyes upon her now.

As for his Uncle Vasile? Kate remembered the man's advances at the village well, and her refusal to play along.

Her thoughts turned to Kenny's safety in the room below her. Though the trapdoor was closed and the rug covering its location, it was doubtful Kenny would've thrown the bolt that locked it down. Why would he? Teo was his mother's friend, right?

God, please. I should've listened to Nickel.

In other circumstances, her friend's nearness might've kindled her desire, but instead she felt only trepidation. What was she supposed to do? This was no undead foe she was facing. Teo was a living, intelligent human, fashioned in the image of the Almighty.

"Gina," he said softly, using her real name. "You are the only woman I've ever desired."

Her hand moved beneath the fold of her jacket.

He said, "You were raised a Romanian Jew, da? You have heard the story of Esau and Jacob, of course, how Jacob stole the birthright from his older brother. Have you heard, though, what some scholars and rabbis believe?"

She shook her head.

"There is conjecture that Esau was one of the first vampires." Teo chuckled at the hilarity of the idea, but Kate remained silent. "Redheaded Esau had a temper to go with his hair, and later, when he went to meet his kid brother, he leaned down to greet his brother with a kiss. You know what happened?"

Another shake of the head.

"It was no kiss, according to these scholars. It was a bite to the neck."

"A bite?"

"That's what they say." Teo's breath ran hot and heavy over her earlobe. "He meant to clamp his teeth into Jacob's neck, only to find that his brother's skin had been turned to marble by God's hand."

Kate shivered, uncertain whether the story was delivered as a warning to her, or as some bizarre stimulant for her friend. Her fingers wrapped around the MTP in her jacket pocket.

"Do you think," Teo said, "that same thing would happen now?"

"If what?"

In response, his lips locked onto her throat, teeth probing at her flesh and drawing forth a trickle of blood.

"Teodor!" She tore away and leapt to her feet. With the metal spike in full view, she stood out of reach and bore her eyes into his. "You come near me again and I'll slam this through your temple, you hear me?"

His lips were still open, glistening with unanswered desire.

"You hear me?"

In his eyes, the vile hunger slowly dissolved into self-loathing, and at last he looked away, embarrassed.

"Why?" Gina insisted. "Why did you do that?"

"I don't know. I . . . I have no one."

Although her nurturing instincts nudged her toward him, the rough metal in hand reminded her of the conflict's true nature, of its potential brutality. Confusion gnawed away her empathy. "You need to go."

"Please, I—"

"Not now, Teo."

"I . . . I'm sorry. This was not why I came. I beg you to believe me."

"If you care about me at all, you'll understand that I can't have you here tonight. Tell me you can understand that much at least."

Crestfallen, he mouthed an affirmative.

She waggled the MTP toward the door. "Go."

CHAPTER
FORTY-SIX

Kransberg Castle, Germany

Natira despised the fragility of this human tent—skin, bones, tissue, and sinew, and this infernal demand for sleep.

Driven by his need, he'd slipped away into the morning fog soon after his arrival in Frankfurt and made his way to the town of Usingen. From there, it was a good stretch of the legs to Kransberg Castle.

He was surprised at how little had changed since his stint here in the 1940s. The abandoned fortress was a haphazard affair, with an ancient tower rising above gabled roofs, timbered eaves, and stone partitions. A chapel huddled beneath a tree's branches. The nearby village consisted of pristine, quiet streets.

He waited in the surrounding woods till dusk, then crept onto the premises. Now, curled up in the medieval turret, he was awakened by sounds from below: snuffling, growls, as well as shifting pebbles and dirt.

When this persisted, he rose and stared down over the stone ramparts. Was that a dog down there, digging up the chapel graveyard?

It looked to be a very large dog. A human, perhaps.

Time to go investigate.

Dmitri Derevenko parked the rental car in an alleyway a half-kilometer away from the castle. Tonight, he assured Erota, they would be left alone, and despite soft purple moonlight that filtered through the clouds, their trespassing did indeed seem to go unnoticed.

Erota fought the constraints of her burgundy dress, but made it over a battlement and slinked behind Dmitri into an enclosed courtyard. They paused at a heavy door that he said fed into subterranean storerooms and passageways.

"Did you hear that?"

She feigned innocence. "Hear what?"

Dmitri cocked his head, his hand moving to the phone on his belt. From the tree-studded hills, another woeful howl went up.

"The werewolf," he said.

"Please," Erota said. "We passed signs to a forested nature reserve not far from here. It's not so surprising, is it, to hear a wolf baying at the moon?"

"I saw one of the bodies outside Schloss Johannisberg. I will not forget."

"A victim of a rogue, perhaps."

"Does a bullet kill a werewolf?" Dmitri unclipped his phone. "This is a Maksalov IV, a functioning cell phone that also fires four .22 caliber cartridges."

"An impressive device. But don't you need silver bullets?"

"Silver?"

"That's what the legends say. Please, comrade, if you'll open the door we won't need to find out."

His fingers seemed to take longer than necessary jimmying the old skeleton lock. The door creaked open, followed by another spine-tingling howl.

With Dmitri leading the way, Erota followed the bouncing beams of his red flashlight down the steps into the castle's bowels. Stone pillars braced the ceiling. Were these old dungeons? Cobwebs and undisturbed dust lay everywhere, while oxygen seemed in short supply.

She was impressed at this Brother's thoroughness in exploring a place where nearly six decades ago U.S. counterintelligence personnel had plied their captives for information. Had they used psychological ploys or resorted to actual torture? At the end of the war, documents had been gathered by the ton from similar facilities across Germany.

"Take this." Dmitri handed over the flashlight, then applied his back to a huge iron tender box still loaded with coal.

On rusty rollers, the box screeched away from the wall and revealed a small opening where a handful of metal file boxes awaited inspection.

"I removed nothing, Erota. I wanted you to see for yourself. These are U.S. and British files, forgotten, I think, in the aftermath of the war. Transcripts of conversations between interrogators and prisoners."

The boxes represented a fraction of the information gathered, and Erota guessed that these contained the least credible tidbits, the leftovers. Given enough crumbs, though, one could form an entire loaf of bread.

"Let's see what you've managed to dig up," she said.

Crouched in the musty space, Erota used long fingernails to riffle through the files, through page upon page of Q&A between interrogators and detainees. At her shoulder, Dmitri held the flashlight and kept an eye on the corridor through which they had come.

"Don't delay," he whispered.

"There are no werewolves, Dmitri. Relax."

From her study of the time period, Erota knew that the Pentagon had authorized the secret recruitment of German missile and chemical engineers after the war. The transfer of supplies and personnel had started from this castle and two other facilities, then funneled through docks at Bremen on their way to American shores. Interesting stuff, but not the reason she or her Russian cohort were here.

The Black King . . . Who was this fabled ruler? Where was he?

For some time now, Erota had hedged her bets on Rasputin's words. The hypnotic advisor to the tsars had operated under the guidance of a

Collector cluster, and she believed it was from so great a pool of hind- and foresight that he had penned his final prophecy.

In 1916, shortly before Rasputin's death at the hand of conspirators—poisoned, shot, and finally drowned in the Neva River—he had said of himself: *"I perish, I have perished already, and I am no longer among the living."*

Those words proved spookily accurate.

Erota believed a similar accuracy marked the papers she had found at Bran Castle, if only she could nail down the details. She had their most pertinent sections memorized:

"Before my bones have lain a century in the grave." Rasputin had died eighty-seven years ago.

"From the haunt of jackals, he will take dominion." She knew the spot well and could be the one to lead him there.

"He will . . . wage war against Those Who Resist. He will take back by force his kingdom, despite the thirty-six." The Lamed Vov. The Nistarim. Their opposition would give way.

On the other side of this prophetic coin, the Brotherhood of Tobolsk had been doing their best to assist Erota. They'd read the words—written in Russian, by a Russian—and made their assumptions about who the Black King would be.

Alexei Romanov?

Sure, let them hold on to that hope. Erota was viewing matters on a larger scale. Throughout history, Collectors had utilized hosts both lowly and powerful. Paupers, priests, and princes had followed the designs of the Master Collector, employing thievery, usury, and taxation to demoralize humans everywhere. With last century's fall of longstanding monarchies, Those Who Hunt had been forced to learn less overt, more pestiferous, methods. Even now, at the haunt of jackals, Megiste and her loyalists corrupted the sacred injunctions of the Six, No, Seven Things, breeding thorns of depravity.

But Erota's own efforts had not been in vain. She had to believe that.

She had to trust that Rasputin's words were true, and judging by his murder in 1916, the clock was winding down on this final prophecy.

"I recognize this name," Dmitri said, cutting into her thoughts.

She followed his pointing finger to the page in her own hands and saw: *First Lieutenant Addison*. "Yes, it's the same family name as the man we met outside the winery."

"It is a sign, I think."

"Perhaps."

She perused the recorded dialogue between the American first lieutenant and a German woman, daughter of a Doktor Ubelhaar.

Trudi Ubelhaar's claims were preposterous, surely met with skepticism by those conducting the interview. Who would believe that Hitler had not only located but brought the missing tsar out of exile? Or that he'd encouraged Trudi to bed with Alexei Romanov, in hopes of birthing an heir who could forge a blood pact between beleaguered Russia and Germany?

Erota could believe it. Only Collectors would implement so wild a scheme.

Portland

Teodor was a travel agent. He had little trouble finding his way from Junction City to the international terminal at PDX. He paid the fee to change his ticket and spent a half day awaiting his flight. The time now flashed on the departure board, and he angled toward his gate.

He could not stay here. Not after what he'd done.

For all these years he'd clutched onto the hope of a relationship with Kate. With Gina. He'd calmed his inner turmoil with sips of goat's milk, never sure why the curdled liquid worked, except that it conjured in his mind that light tingle of touching lips and his fantasy of a life spent together.

He ran his tongue along his lips.

What'd happened there on the couch? While attempting to draw her into a forceful embrace, he'd tasted for a split second the richness of her blood.

He hated his actions, the way he'd listened to that lingering presence and chosen to assert himself. He fled Kate's house, knowing he could never again face her after what he'd done. He had let Vasile's old poison pump through him, that need to inflict pain, to dominate, to be in control.

He shuffled through security to the boarding gate, then onto the plane.

Was any torment worse than having to live with one's shame?

Rather than resisting the claustrophobia this time, he slid into his seat and let despair crush him—down, down, down, where he knew he belonged.

Kransberg Castle

Years later, in retrospect, Erota realized how fate had plotted against her. Even as she made the connections between an abandoned transcript and Rasputin's prophecy, she found herself now distracted by a more urgent matter, one that would tease her along a different path.

As she followed Dmitri Derevenko up the stairs into Kransberg's courtyard, that fateful crossroad was only moments away.

The moon had slipped from behind the clouds, a cadaverous eye tracking their movements over the battlement wall. They descended a grassy slope and headed toward the car. Though Erota had the Addison/Ubelhaar file in hand, the gist of its contents was already imprinted upon her undead brain.

"Do you think this Trudi Ubelhaar actually gave birth?" Dmitri asked.

"That's what we need to find out."

"If so, she has prolonged the bloodline of the tsars. This could be our Black King, nyet? The one who will restore the motherland."

" *'He will take back by force his kingdom.'* "

"Da. It is what Rasputin spoke of. He saw this day approaching."

Erota allowed this Brotherhood representative his little fantasy, sus-pecting that the 'kingdom' was one much broader.

A spine-tingling howl stopped her in her tracks. It was close.

Coming closer.

From the copse of trees on their right, the wolf appeared. Silver-gray and slope-backed, it stood upright on hind legs. Its claws were stained with blood, its fangs dripping with saliva, and its pointed ears turned toward the fear in Dmitri's gasp.

"A *werewolf*? See here, I told you it was so," the Russian hissed.

"It's all right," she said. "Go to the car and I'll meet you there."

To his credit, Dmitri swallowed his panic and refused to abandon an attractive woman to the will of a threatening beast. He angled his stance for stability and reached for the Maksalov IV concealed in his cell phone.

She shook her head and touched his wrist to calm him. To the were-wolf, she said: "Shabtai, enough with your games."

The man-creature snarled. ·

"If you insist on feeding so brutally, could you at least do it farther back in the forest? You're being selfish, you know. A typical teen."

Another snarl. His eyes burned yellowish-green.

"Why are you here, anyway?" she said. "Did you follow us?"

"You followed *me*," Shabtai rasped, seeming annoyed by this perceived lack of trust. In the light of day, he would've looked like many pubescent males—downcast eyes, fits of rage and irritability, as well as uneven facial hair.

"We did no such thing," Erota said. "In fact, we——"

"But I'm glad you're here," he growled. "I dug up a few bones for you."

Dmitri's gaze flitted from woman to werewolf, his ice-blue eyes show-ing disbelief, his hand clenching the loaded cell phone. "Give the word and I will kill this . . . this thing."

"It's quite all right. He wants to share a bone with you."

"A . . . a bone. You understand what the beast is saying, Erota? Nyet." He shook his head. "I have had enough of this for one day."

In her clinging gown, Erota shrugged. "Let's see what he means, at least."

Hairy Shabtai thrust a hand to his left, the spaces between his padded fingers dripping chunks of loam and dirt from his earlier hunt. "There you go. Take a look."

CHAPTER
FORTY-SEVEN

From over the rise came a giant human male, his strides shaking the ground beneath their feet. He seemed to be missing a few ribs on one side, evidenced by a sunken area that flexed and collapsed with each breath, but his chest was expansive, his pectoral regions squared and solid like battleshields. Ladders of rib and muscle worked their way down his abdomen to powerful hips.

"Who is this?" Erota said.

"I was eating earlier," Shabtai said. "Chewing on fresh flesh that I had dragged into the castle courtyard from the graves. Bam! Outta nowhere, who shows up but this guy. Says he was napping in the Kransberg turret."

The monster came alongside the werewolf.

"You don't have to worry," Shabtai added. "He's one of us."

Erota was more awestruck than anything. She'd thought she would never again lay eyes on this man, the son of Helene and Lord Ariston.

"Natira?"

His eyes flashed in recognition.

"It's really you?" she said, switching to the ancient Hebrew they'd once spoken between their households.

"And you are Erota."

"That's correct. I survived in Jerusalem for a few more years after you were cut down"—she pointed at his chest—"by the Romans at Jotapata."

He tensed. In the moonlight, his mat of curly bronze hair couldn't hide the diagonal mark running from his collarbone to lower left stomach. On his right hand, he bore nothing but a gnarled pinkie and massive thumb.

Dmitri eased into a shooter's stance and raised his Maksalov phone.

"No," Erota told him. "He's one of us."

"I don't like the look of him. Are you not aware that he's half-naked?"

"Oh, very aware."

"I stripped off my shirt and coat," Natira said, "to show Shabtai my wounds and convince him of my rank among the Akeldama Collectors. He's careless and impetuous, but a bright young fellow. He's fortunate I didn't tear him apart before asking questions."

Erota shook her head in joyful disbelief. "This is . . . it's truly fortuitous. Lord Ariston and I tracked you to Pisa, then here to Germany, but I was unable to find your steps after that. Where have you been?"

"I've worked alone. In silence. Tracking the Nistarim, one by one."

"We've made similar attempts."

"To date, I have identified twenty-eight of them, minus one who's crumbled not far from here. Give me one day and I'm sure I can track his replacement."

She was impressed beyond words.

Natira took a step forward. "Where's my family? My father, my brother?"

Failing to take into account his reanimated humanity, she answered with a Collector's bluntness. "Both banished, I'm afraid."

Natira threw back his arms and roared. In this departure from his years of silence, Erota detected a longing for companionship, for those who would validate his self-imposed exile and the ideals he shared with Collectors at large. His chest expanded, tendons rippled, and then he launched himself in a burst of hellish energy at this bearer of bad news.

She held her ground. Surely he would snap out of this rage.

Eyes blazing, he came in long strides.

Beside Erota, Dmitri was done with restraint. He jutted his phone forward and it coughed twice through chambers in its shell. The rounds sliced the air and buried themselves in the giant's left pectoral. Bits of flesh and bone erupted from the wounds in a bloody spray, and Natira blinked once against the sensation of pain before continuing his charge with his pincers swooping toward Erota's head of streaming brown hair.

Dmitri yelled, and fired off two more small-caliber shots.

Not even a blink this time.

At Natira's back, Shabtai seemed to realize the danger he'd unleashed. On lean, furry legs, he vaulted forward and overtook the monster as it was almost upon Erota. His claws raked the broad back and caused the warrior to stumble. Snarling, Shabtai's long jaws snapped at the scruff of exposed neck.

Before the fangs could latch on, Natira dropped to a knee and rolled with the wolf's weight. He brought his arm around, hooked into the silvery pelt, and catapulted Shabtai into Dmitri Derevenko. The pair hit the grass in a pile of blue eyes, frothy teeth, claws, and disheveled blond hair.

"Wait! Your mother," Erota shouted at the revenant. "She's alive."

Natira let out another roar as he rose to his feet. His chest was dimpled by two bullets, his thigh by another. The fourth round must've gone astray. He faced Erota, his hand cocked and ready to strike.

"Helene is alive," she said.

"Helene?"

"She'll be happy to see you. We all are."

Erota recalled the way Natira had run off to combat Roman oppression, in defiance of Ariston's wishes. He was an idealist, ever loyal to his cause. And here he was, the cluster's rightful leader—just the person to give her an advantage over their rival household in Kerioth-Hezron.

"Natira, please," she cooed. "Let me take you to her."

The fire wavered in his eyes.

"Helene's only a day's journey from here, okay?"

At last he nodded his head.

Erota helped Dmitri to his feet. He bore mere scratches, but his lungs heaved with fear and indignation. "I want you to forget what you've seen here," she said to him. "You're Russian. You know the sort of things that determined men can do—criminal things, violent things. Take this." She handed him the stolen file, while his wary gaze remained fixed upon Natira. "Stay focused on your task. That should lead you and the Brotherhood to your precious tsar."

Gripping the file, Dmitri Derevenko retreated a few steps, then turned and scrambled away with the occasional backward glances of a man trying to verify that this scenario was a nightmare and nothing more.

Erota turned to Shabtai. "As for you? Meet us at Frankfurt's Nord Banhof two mornings from now. We'll be taking the train back to Lipova."

"You think it's safe?"

"Safe for whom? I say it's time for a reunion."

He loped off, dropping to all fours as he reached the wooded slope.

"Natira, Natira." Erota sighed and reached a soothing hand to his cheek. "You're a fine specimen, but this half-nakedness is unbecoming for a king. Come along. I think it could only be destiny that we crossed paths tonight."

En Route to Lipova

Destiny, indeed.

Through the window, Erota watched snow-dusted fields stretch toward the breaking dawn. Within the hour, the train would arrive at the station in Arad.

Moody Shabtai slouched beside her, modish jeans and a long overcoat concealing the bulk of his hairy skin. On the bench across from her, Natira filled the space of two average males, his tattered overcoat stretched tight over colossal shoulders and thighs.

Here was the nineteenth Collector. Their lost member. Last night he'd confirmed that, yes, he had sailed aboard a Knights Templar ship from Jaffa in hopes of accessing Natira's stalwart frame. And now, after nearly eight centuries outside a Pisan cemetery, he was back with his cluster.

"We've suffered some losses," she told him.

His face was grim. "Ariston?"

"Yes."

"And Sol?"

"He and Auge, both. A few others, as well."

"Who has wrought such violence amongst us? I don't understand."

"We'll discuss it more, once you've settled in at the vineyard and seen your mother. We also need to strategize."

"To strike back at our enemies?"

"Ever the warrior, aren't you?" She gripped his solid arm. "Yes, Natira, we have foes all around, but we first need to clean house—starting with the muddle that's been made of the House of Eros."

Most days, Erota wrestled with a profound sense of futility. It seemed her fellow Collectors had hamstrung themselves with ceaseless infighting and Machiavellian deceits—though, of course, that very description came from an Italian prince inspired by Collectors more deceitful than he.

Truth be told, Erota's fealty to their aloof Master had wavered.

No longer.

She recognized now that the Master Collector had been guiding her all along, leading her to the serendipitous convergence at Kransberg Castle. How else could she explain finding long-lost Natira?

Erota saw her own reflection in the window as she imagined the Brotherhood of Tobolsk's excitement.

Dmitri Derevenko had taken the castle file to confirm his findings to his other Brothers. Soon they'd traipse the globe in search of their new ruler. And if such a man existed? If Alexei Romanov and his kin still lived? Dmitri and Oleg would wet themselves in ecstasy and go marching with their beloved tsar across Red Square.

She smirked at herself. She knew the truth.

Sitting here in this train cabin, breathing the same air she breathed, the actual "powerful one," "the strongman," the one who had risen from "the holy ground" of the Campo Santo was at her disposal.

Natira . . . the Black King.

Here, she believed, was the true fulfillment of Rasputin's prophecy.

CHAPTER
FORTY-EIGHT

Totorcea Vineyards

Jubilant tears and shouts met Natira's arrival at the farmhouse. Shabtai and Matrona adored having a man around; Erota was enamored with him; and, although Shelamzion was less responsive, Helene seemed overjoyed to have her son back in her arms.

Natira, too, was thankful. Nevertheless, he found it unsettling that his human vessel could wring out such emotion, from himself as well as others. This was the result of their trying to dodge the Separation's curse and yet knowing that only by persuading or possessing a host could they directly impact the physical realm.

It was Friday. Already Lipova's workforce was on the move, sleek autos and belching trucks passing along the road at the foot of the vineyards. A river wended through the valley, between trees stripped of their leaves and turned ghostly white by frost.

"What do you think, dear?" said Helene. "Isn't the property beautiful?"

"You're more beautiful by far, Mother."

She gazed up at Natira and smiled.

"But," he said, "I don't like that you are alone."

"A widow, you mean? I have Shelamzion to commiserate, and in all honesty, Lord Ariston was not an easy man with whom to live."

"Even when he wasn't living?"

"Oh, he was even more irascible while undead."

Natira drew his mother to his chest. She showed no repulsion to his two-fingered grip, leaning in and sighing, patting his hard belly with a soft hand.

"I am glad you found us," she said. "Your strength will be a great help during our next harvest."

"I may be elsewhere."

"He has warrior blood in his veins," Erota interjected from nearby. She spread straw on the front steps to lessen the morning ice's treachery.

"To be precise, dear," said Helene, "he has only the residual seepage of blood that he's tapped from others."

"It was an expression," Erota clarified. "Modern science tells us that our genetics are locked within the DNA of our hosts."

"The Nazis," Natira mused. "They also spoke of genetics."

Helene said, "I always knew my son to be a bright young man."

"Father thought otherwise."

"No." His mother patted his chest. "No, that's not accurate. He admired many things about you, and it was only your warmongering that riled him."

"Warmongering? I fought for justice."

"Whose justice? Is any one side more right than the other?"

Erota finished her task and stepped closer. "Do you actually believe all two-leggers are equal, Helene? Don't let the Master Collector catch you saying so. Plus, being equal has little to do with being right or wrong."

"I *was* in the right," Natira said. "My job was to oppose the Roman invaders, those who came to steal our rights. And they killed me for it. Those filthy Italians not only took my life, they locked me in one of their graves as well."

"Why is it that men resort to weapons rather than words?"

Natira pushed away from Helene. "You're worse than Father. What is this lukewarm drivel you're spewing?"

"Dear, you are not listening."

"For good reason. Even stone can be whittled away by driving sands, and that's all that your words are: sand and more sand. Not all are as level-headed as you seem to believe."

"You refer to Megiste, I assume."

"The priestess." Natira remembered her well—her thin curved lips against lily-white skin and those auburn ringlets framing fine features. He knew from experience that she was not as delicate as she appeared. "She's the one who delivered my brother's fatal wound. Isn't that what you told me, Erota?"

"She did, but she was punishing Sol's insolence, within the guidelines."

"I will send her to the grave on my brother's heels."

Erota showed him a half smile.

"You, my dear son, are our rightful leader," Helene said. "If Megiste and her desert crew refuse to acknowledge that, then we have no choice but to unite the Akeldama Cluster by force."

"And Lord Ariston? Who banished him?"

Erota and Helene exchanged a glance.

"Is there more you wish to tell me?" Natira said. "Speak."

"It was another woman," Erota responded. "A half immortal."

"Half?"

"Gina Lazarescu. Her father was one of the original Nistarim, so she carries his immortal genes—or DNA, as we mentioned earlier. She wore the letter Tav for a time, as a prequel to giving birth, but I wasted my own energies thinking I'd identified her son as a Lamed Vov."

"What happened?" Natira questioned.

"I struck down the child as planned. And yet, we are still here."

"But the Letter on the mother's head? You saw it through undead eyes?"

"Perhaps it was a birthmark that faded over time, or a genetic anomaly.

In fact, she may have been deluded into thinking she was of greater importance than she is."

"And yet she killed Ariston."

"And Shalom," Helene noted.

"What sort of human could pull off such a thing?" Natira said.

Erota and Helene both paused at their tasks, and he tried to decipher their shared furtive glance. These females guarded information like hens did fresh eggs.

A suspicion formed in his thoughts. "I might well know the name of this woman's father. And if he sired a child, he violated his oath to the Nazarene."

"He's of no consequence." Erota pulled her coat tighter around her thin frame. "For now we have more pressing priorities. Until the House of Eros comes alongside, our efforts will remain halfhearted."

"Agreed," Helene said. "'A house divided against itself shall surely fall.'"

"His name," Natira demanded. "Was it Cal Nichols?"

"You know the man?"

Natira grimaced, his pinkie and thumb *clack-clack-clacking* together like crab pincers, tendons stiffening along his neck. "I killed his son. I thought I had destroyed his bloodline for good."

"Sad to say, but his daughter is alive and well." Erota turned, her coat swishing about her hips, and spoke back over her shoulder. "Come along, and you'll have a chance to peer by proxy into her piffling life."

"Here?" Helene said. "I'm not sure I understand."

"We have a new vintage to try, a man who calls himself her friend. He's just returned from America, and he claims that he saw her."

"As we suspected, then. The news reports in Bucharest were lies."

"She's alive, yes, but not as dangerous as she once was," Erota said. "Teo even swiped some blood from her before darting back here to share the details."

Clack-clack, clack-clack . . .

"Take me to him," said Natira.

Teodor heard their steps on the hardpacked ground. He tried again to break free from his restraints. He sat in a warehouse, pressed against a wagon wheel, his arms pulled back between the spokes and bound so tightly he'd lost circulation in his wrists. A wine-stained rag cut across his mouth.

The warehouse door slid open. Gray light washed over him.

"There he is," Erota said. "He came by his own choice."

That fact burrowed through Teo's mind like a worm. Why *had* he come? What had propelled him to drive here? He still had nearly two weeks of scheduled holidays, so there was no reason to have climbed out of his bed in Arad where he'd sulked for the past few days.

Erota's words: *"If you happen to hear from her . . ."*

Not only did he have a duty to inform the Collector, he cradled newborn hostility toward his childhood sweetheart. She had spurned his affections.

"He looks cold," Helene said.

"He's been here since early this morning," Erota said.

Teo was familiar with Erota and Helene, his uncle's companions from years ago. However, the monster that ducked through the door behind them was something new. The man's chest swelled to eye-popping proportions as he studied this captive on the ground. Emerald light glowed through his pupils.

Had Teo lost his mind?

Yes, he realized, that's exactly what he had done. Robed in his uncle's bitter scent, he'd let these Collectors linger. He'd quelled his anxieties with a temporary cure, never chasing off these familiar spirits once and for all.

Now he'd come full circle, at the mercy of those stronger than he.

Maybe he could crack one of these wooden spokes and pull his arms through. He flexed and tried to wrench free. For his efforts, he received a sliver in the meat of his forearm, and his yelp of pain swelled into a cloth-muffled scream.

"Please," Erota said to him. "There's no need to panic. You already told me all I needed to know. You're familiar with Helene, and this here is Natira. We want only a few sips, enough to see what Gina's been up to. Or, should I say, dear Kate?"

Teo knew what was coming.

The trio kneeled around him, with the huge male taking up position on his right. They were supplicants preparing to partake in blasphemous sacrament, and Teo was their goblet of wine.

A small seed of resistance sprouted up from his soul. He waited till the monster's breath was cold as ice against his cheek, then, imagining Vasile there, he slammed his forehead into that prominent nose.

Natira grunted. Blood spurted. Helene and Erota lapped at the air, refusing to let any go to waste, letting it dot their cheeks and paint their lips deep scarlet.

Then they turned upon Teo, three at once. He tried the head butt trick again, but it was averted with ease, and they came in as one to tap his arteries—at his neck, his thigh, and forearm. The pain was short-lived. A prickling sensation radiated from the smaller two sets of punctures. The third was a ravenous bite accompanied by a sharp jerk as large mandibles latched on.

Slurping sounds were interrupted by an amused laugh.

"So Cal Nichols went searching for me," Natira said, "even as I caught a plane heading this direction. The poor fellow, he is ever bumbling about."

"As bumbling as he and his daughter may be, they are trouble."

"On this we agree, Mother. I will destroy them."

"All in good time," Erota said, pulling back from her tapping point. "As I suspected, Kate—or Gina—is still living in her guilt-driven delusions. Once again she thinks she's the appointed custodian of a Concealed One."

"It's a possibility," Helene said.

"Bah. It's another distraction, at best. Why chase personal grudges when we have our Black King here among us, the haunt of jackals before us? I've shown you the prophecy. Nothing should divert us from that."

Natira grunted in reluctant agreement.

"To put our minds at ease," Erota added, "we could at least send Shabtai to Junction City to investigate."

"The werewolf?" Natira scowled. "How does his sort cross a border?"

"Oh, he's much tamer during daylight hours," Helene explained. "Years ago, we as a cluster procured falsified travel documents just as you have, so it's a simple matter of scheduling the appropriate flight. What do you say, Erota?"

"Hmm. Yes, I like it. Let the man-child run off and have his fun."

Teo was an eavesdropper in their morbid confessional booth. He stayed still, convincing himself that he might be forgotten while they headed off to implement new strategies. Maybe he could escape and warn Kate. No matter how much she had hurt him, she didn't deserve this.

"Look here." Erota gave Teo a playful slap. "He's been spoiled."

Natira and Helene turned their attention back to him.

"Already," Erota said, "I see resistance welling in his eyes. Perhaps we should offer Teo to Shabtai as a hearty meal before he goes off on his trip. We all know how teenagers are, don't we? They'll eat nearly anything."

And she was right.

By early afternoon, Shabtai was holding a full belly and licking streaks of red from his claws and furry jowls.

THE FOURTH TASTE:
EX NIHILO

*A deeper watchman than her five senses had been wakened
after a long season of sleep. And there was no ignoring it.*

—STEPHEN KING, 'SALEM'S LOT

I find that I must write . . . urging you to defend the faith.

—JUDE 1:3

Journal Entry

July 7—continued

Earlier today, through the diner window, I noticed a rickety fishing boat flipped upside down on the rocks across the street. That boat was me. I feel older than I should, beat up and stranded. Was coming here to the mainland even the right thing to do? What am I thinking? My guess is that being one of Those Who Resist takes an extra dose of strength. Already, I feel so tired. Why would they want me? Or maybe negativity is just what Those Who Hunt want.

As I sipped my Dr Pepper, I wrote out some of my questions. I wanted to get down all that I'd just seen in Erota's blood. All sorts of thoughts tumbled around in my head, and I wondered if I should just go back to the island—you know, forget this little excursion of mine.

By the time I'd closed my journal and hurried outside, the ferry was already chugging across the channel. I guess the next one'll come along soon enough, but the captain's going to think it's strange that I ever crossed in the first place.

I came back here to my booth in the diner, knowing I don't belong here. Already people are giving me pitying looks, suspicious stares. What do I care? I think I'll spread out my blood-dotted map here on the table and let them all really wonder what's going on. As though I have any clue.

Why'd it get sent to me? Where'd it come from, anyway, a place in Israel or Romania?

What I'm hoping is that I can squeeze the last bits of info from Gina's—or, should I say, Kate's—droplet. It's her story. Has been from the very start. With all of my questions buzzing, I guess I'll give it one last try.

CHAPTER
FORTY-NINE

Early November—Willamette Valley, Oregon

Kate spent the entire weekend indoors, keeping Kenny occupied and within her line of vision. They played Scrabble, watched cartoons in their pajamas, and she even ventured with him into the world of Xbox. While she never won a game, she did win her son's approval. That was good enough for her.

Where was Teo, though? Would he come back?

Early Saturday morning, she had stopped by his apartment. The place was paid up through the middle of the month, but she got no response to her determined knocks and saw no activity behind the half-drawn curtains.

Teo's attack on the couch had unnerved her. Though he'd drawn blood, he'd done little damage, locking onto the spot where a root already lay beneath her skin. Maybe his feelings toward his uncle had been attracted to her old bitterness toward her mom.

Despite everything, she was concerned for her friend. She wanted him to know that she forgave him. Couldn't they just forget it'd ever happened? Of course, that didn't mean throwing all caution out the window.

On Monday, still uncertain of Teo's whereabouts, Kate decided to keep Kenny out of school.

"You sure, Mom? I feel fine."

"Let's take the day off."

"What about the hardware store? Don'tcha have to work?"

"Called my manager already and requested a sick day. It's the first one I've ever taken, so it's all good."

They stopped by the Dairy Queen on their way out of town. The highway heading north carried them between fields and rolling hills. Kenny lapped at a butterscotch Dilly Bar while she worked on a Pumpkin Pie Blizzard.

Without intending to, she steered her Nissan to the outskirts of Corvallis. Or maybe it *was* intentional. Didn't Jed have Mondays off?

Probably out fishing, so it's not like it'll even matter.

She followed the same route as last time to Sergeant Turney's townhouse. The shades were open. On the porch, a scarecrow sat in coveralls on a hay bale, cradling a bowl of empty candy wrappers from a few nights ago.

"What's this place?" Kenny asked.

"It's . . . There's a cop who lives here."

"You in trouble, Mom? Does this hafta do with that Teo guy?"

"Everything's fine."

"Because I liked him and all, but he kinda scared me."

"Yeah?" She ran her hand across her son's shoulders. "Me too."

"You want me to go in with you?"

"Just sit tight, sweetie, while I run up to the door."

He gave her one of his searching gazes, filled with empathy beyond his twelve and a half years. She tousled his hair and hopped out. There were no other cars within twenty feet, but she figured there must be a garage around back. Hadn't Sarge appeared out of nowhere last time around?

She knocked. She was raising her hand for another try when Sarge opened the door, a box of Peanut Butter Crunch cereal dangling from his fleshy hand. "Heyya. Kate, right?"

"That's me."

"Sorry 'bout the bathrobe and slippers, but it's an improvement over what I looked like five minutes ago. Pulled a late shift last night. This job—whoo boy, it's takin' it outta me."

"Listen, is Jed around?"

"He moved out a few months back. Ain't seen him in a coupla days, but he's got himself a place over in Silverton, near Silver Falls State Park."

"I've walked the trails there. It's gorgeous."

"God's country, I'm tellin' ya. Doesn't get much better."

"You mind giving me an address or number? We're still married, at least on paper, and I promise there won't be any of that 'bad ex' stuff. I want to see what he's up to, that's all."

"Did ya know he still wears his ring? That's right," Sarge said as she shook her head. "You can take heart in that."

She absorbed this information the way her scarred arm soaked up lotion. It wasn't so much that she was on the rebound after her encounter with Teo as she was more committed to giving her marriage another chance.

Jed, lovable Jed.

She knew the same sensitive side she'd fallen in love with was what kept him knotted in guilt and grief. Was she looking to him to be her savior, drawing her out of her cynicism? He was only human. He had his own issues. What was it going to take for her to flip the script?

"Kate?" Sarge's rich brown eyes met hers. "I know he cares deeply for you. The fact that he's moved out is a sign he's getting back on his own two feet."

"I'm glad to hear it."

"It's a good thing for me too. Jed paid his rent and pulled his weight around here with chores and all, but that nephew o' mine . . . He likes singing in the shower, and when I'm tryin' to sleep, that is a no-no."

"Singing?" Kate grinned. "Well, that's a new one to me."

"Oh, yeah. He's changin', all right. The new and improved Jed Turney."

"Why're we stopping?" Kenny sat up in his seat. "Something wrong?"

"I don't know. I think so."

On the edge of Corvallis, Kate braked to a halt by the same railroad tracks where she had broken down nearly two months ago. A large rook fluttered from the thicket on the embankment's other side, taking wing in the slate-gray sky.

"We run outta gas?"

That was one way of putting it.

As a young woman, Kate had traced the translucent blue squiggles on her own forehead, evidence of a conflict unseen. She'd faced off with Collectors and witnessed the effects of her dagger and Nazarene Blood. In a Bucharest bakery, she'd felt the love from Cal Nichols' gold-flecked eyes as he revealed his identity as her biological father.

So why had she held onto her attitude? Was she so arrogant as to think that she alone understood the ways spirit and flesh coincided? Was she so broken, so weak, that she would hide forever behind walls of pessimism while the battle raged outside the castle ramparts?

A hissing sound lifted from the thicket beyond the railroad tracks.

Leaves rustling in the wind? A snake in the grass?

Kate ignored it and lifted her hand to her neck, where the last tendrils of bitterness still moved beneath her scar. She ran her fingers to the other side, to her earring.

"Just one drop . . ."

What was stopping her? What more convincing did she need?

"Kenny, let's get out for a minute," she said.

"Okay."

She smiled at his unquestioning obedience. Not that he was always so compliant, but to be that trusting, that childlike . . . How long had it been since she showed such qualities? She'd been doing all the work on her own faulty wisdom and strength.

No wonder her tanks were running low.

She propped herself next to her son against the passenger side of the car, away from passing traffic, facing foliage that marched in green rows toward a nearby hillside. She eased the ruby orb from her ear, felt it pulse between her fingertips. "You know what this is, Kenny?"

"An earring."

"I mean, you know what's in it?"

"Nazarene Blood. Uncle Terry told me all about it, and he says it has a way of dealing with infection like nothing else. Kills it on the spot."

"That's right." Her voice turned husky. "The answer dies within."

"What's it taste like, you think? Just normal ol' blood?"

She wrapped her arm over his shoulder. "You want to find out?"

Kenny's mouth dropped in astonishment at such a suggestion from her. "For real?" He glanced both ways, then settled into her embrace.

"We could do it together. You and me."

"Once you drink it, Mom, you'll never be the same. It's like a transfusion, a whole new start."

"That's what I want."

"I wanna serve the Nazarene, same as Uncle Terry."

She swallowed the lump in her throat, thinking of that luminous figure, that resonating presence. "Me too."

"What if it hurts, though?"

"It will," she said. "At first."

"No pain, no gain. Right?"

"Yeah, I can guess who told you that." In her palm, the earring thawed and warmed, reminding her of its counterpart's effects on a foul-scented wild boar. "Did he also tell you that we all have infection in our systems, that it hooks in and tries to drain us dry?"

"He said the Blood heals all of that by bonding us to the Nazarene." Kenny grew somber, thoughts churning behind wide black eyes. "Okay, I'm ready."

"Just like that?"

"Mm-hmm. But do you think you can go first?"

Kate stared down at the glowing sphere. What would happen if its

contents pinpointed all of her doubts and fears, her resentments and iniquities? Was she pure enough to survive?

I know I'm not. She closed her eyes. *And that's the whole point. I need You,
Yeshua. If it means dying to myself, then so be it.*

"Day by day by day," she said in a hush.

Then set the droplet on her tongue.

Drippp, drippp . . .

The sphere softened, a gel tablet releasing drops of its sweet coppery
liquid. It was hot in her mouth. Alive. She ingested the life of the Nazarene,
gazing through His eyes, and for a moment she was overwhelmed by the
sense that she would shrivel and die. She was not ready. Not worthy.

Her throat and stomach constricted against the oozing warmth, then
a blaze of light seared images into her brain that were hideous and lovely,
beyond anything she'd ever seen. There was that serpent lifted in the wilderness, a symbol of healing. And there was Yeshua—He who saves—nailed
to rough wood while soldiers mocked from below and religious leaders
railed against him.

The torment was excruciating.

Sin and disease. Sorrow beyond words. Wicked things done under the
guise of religion. Vile acts performed in rituals pagan and godless.

Drippp, drippp . . .

The thorns dug in under her skin, desperate to survive this sacred
flow.

She felt Kenny's fingers take the earring from her lips, like a baby bird
receiving sustenance from its mother. That mental picture blurred as her
thoughts zoomed in on incidents from her past, including ones she'd
thought permanently purged from her mind. It was all there—the good,
bad, and ugly. She had tried molding herself into a strong person, capable
of dealing with anything and everything, yet now she saw only a girl with
a pink ribbon in her hair, a child fashioned for a purpose from the womb,
by the hands of the Almighty Artisan.

What had Nickel told her at the Sinaia train station? *"You'll always have
a mother's heart, and there'll always be more kids for you to watch after."*

But she'd already failed twice.

Dripp . . .

Kate let the moisture slide down into her innermost being, where it was absorbed into her bloodstream and distributed to her extremities.

Heat swelled from her very core and burned outward, a consuming flame that roared into her neck and caused the subcutaneous vines to recoil and disintegrate. In an expulsion of dry air and hot ash, the growth burst from the long-infected wound.

She collapsed beside the car, spent. Kenny kneeled next to her.

It was finished.

Then from out of nowhere, from out of nothing . . .

Ex nihilo.

Life was breathed into her, through her. Arteries began driving blood back into her heart. As though her five senses were being stirred from a near-comatose state, she felt vitality surge along her skin and muscles, followed by a purging dose that washed through her mind and brought clarity.

She felt along her neck. The swollen area was gone. Nevertheless, she still bore small dagger marks from Nikki's impassioned attempts to protect her, marks Kate would always wear as reminders of what not to do.

Paying no attention to the hiss of the breeze in the tall grass or to the rumble of a passing tractor, she pulled her son close. No longer adopted and adoptee, they were now related by Blood. They looked into each other's eyes, both scarcely able to see beyond their tears. She wiped at his face and her own, then he took a turn, his young hands moving over her cheeks. The moment they removed one teardrop, another took its place.

With consensual shrugs, Kate and Kenny surrendered themselves to this situation and collapsed into a hug of messy, unabashed laughter.

CHAPTER FIFTY

The next afternoon, Kate picked up a puppy from the Greenhill Humane Society. She'd hinted at this for months, and Kenny was proving responsible at school and around the house. She told him this was his early Christmas present, and that he'd better expect nothing more than candy canes on December 25.

Her secondary motive was early detection.

Of all the dogs, this little girl had exhibited the meanest growl, one that erupted into a bark much larger than her size. Perfect. If Teo—if anyone—came to the Prestons' door, they'd have to wonder what stood on the other side.

"Who cares about presents?" Kenny was bouncing. "I won't need anything else, Mom. Not ever."

"She won't get much bigger than that."

"I love her, I love her," Kenny said. "Her name's Gussy."

"Gussy?"

"That's what she is. She's a Gussy." He ignored his mom's earlier warnings and lifted the ball of fur to his face. Gussy nipped at his nose and he scolded her. "No, girl. No! You save that for the bad guys."

"Or for the twelve-year-old boys who won't listen."

"Mom."

"Kenny. Now let's lay down some newspaper in the bathroom, and we'll start housetraining her."

He hefted the day's *Register Guard.* "The newspaper . . ." he said.

"What about it?"

"Don'tcha think I should get that paper route now? I'll have to pay for her food, and I wanna build her a doghouse too. Uncle Terry already gave me my own hammer and a coffee can full of nails."

"I know, I know. He says you're the fastest around."

"You could do it, too, Mom. If you just practiced."

She thought about that fateful night in Sinaia, over three years ago. She'd watched Nickel and Dov confront a bear with MTPs, seen Collectors felled by blows through the head. If she had it her way, she would never again see a spike or a nail—a stinkin' thumbtack, for that matter—raised in defense.

But sometimes that's what it took.

After all, she and Kenny were now part of Those Who Resist.

This Blood now washing through her was energizing and sobering, unlike anything she'd experienced before. It was liberation. It was life. It had nothing to do with cuttings or a list of do's and don'ts, and everything to do with knowing the One who'd taken upon Himself that awful Crown of Thorns.

How had she missed it all these years? There, in a single drop.

Kate realized that the path ahead would still be fraught with danger, with brief rests between the raging storms. Aside from Teo's assault, the past few years had been more restful than any she'd ever known. Sure, there had been serial killers and school shooters in the news, not to mention terrorist attacks—including a recent plot by a local anarchic group—but she and Kenny had enjoyed a sunny patch here in J.C.

She knew, deep in her gut, it was coming to an end.

Soon her little man would turn thirteen.

Where was his Uncle Terry anyway? Good ol' Nickel. Daddy-o. He'd left her with a handful of MTPs and cryptic references to "bridging." He'd parried her blows over the chessboard. He'd spoken of a "black king" as though he knew things he wasn't sharing.

"Where are you, Dad?" she whispered to her bathroom mirror after tucking Kenny and Gussy into bed. "The least you could do is call."

Nickel did call two days later. They agreed to meet in Founder's Park again, despite the dropping temperature. With Thanksgiving only a few weeks away, she hoped he'd be in a family frame of mind, but she had a feeling that would not be the case.

From the fence that guarded Engine 418, she stared at the silent beast of burden and thought about the stories it could tell. She admired this workhorse. Though she wished she could be as dependable, she sometimes questioned if she had the endurance.

"Hold still," Nickel said, coming up from behind. He looped a braided cord around her neck, from which hung a silver vial. "It's yours, as one of Those Who Resist. And I have one here for Kenny too."

She gripped the vial in her hand. "Thank you."

"Like father, like daughter."

Kate liked the sound of that.

"Things are about to get rough," he added. "I have some stuff to tell you, and I don't want you freaking out."

"Me? C'mon, Nickel, do I ever freak out?"

"Maybe not on the outside."

"Well, it would help if you called every now and then, while you're off doing whatever it is you do."

"Identifying and mentoring the Nistarim."

"Yeah, that."

"Raising red flags."

"Okay."

"Seeking out more of Those Who Resist."

"All good things, of course. But what about staying in contact with your daughter? Maybe, instead of carting around metal spikes and ancient daggers, we could try carrying cell phones. Hello? We're in the modern world now."

"Hey, I do try. See this Nike shirt? You hear the way I try tossing slang into conversation? Those're my ways of blending in. It hasn't been easy over all these centuries, you know. You think it's fun always being the fifth wheel?"

"Third."

"What?"

"A fifth wheel is a type of RV."

"Okay, smarty-pants."

"I should know," she said. "J.C. is one of the RV capitals of the world."

"Cell phones, huh? What about high-frequency signals and all that?"

"You mean the potential brain damage from using one? Don't worry, buddy boy. I think the damage is already done."

"Whoa, now, this is your old man you're speaking to."

"'Old' being the understatement of the year. What are you? Two thousand, plus whatever you'd lived before that? Since the days of Ezekiel, right?"

"You really want to hear this?" Nickel saw her beckon with both hands, and he shrugged. "By traditional dating, I figure I was born in 617 BC."

"Just. Incredibly. Weird."

"Meaning, you were born when I was over twenty-five-hundred years old. So, you see, I think I deserve a little respect."

"I'm sorry," she said, and she meant it. "Still, it doesn't change the fact that you're a little out of touch."

"'Reach out and touch someone,'" he said.

She raised a quizzical eyebrow.

"An ad for the Yellow Pages. It was an eighties thing."

"See, there you go again. Time to catch up with the times."

"You're not going to let this go till I agree to cell phones, are you?" She shook her head.

"Okay," he said. "Let's get them."

"Really? We can sign up for a friends-and-family plan to keep down the cost. The bill can come to my address, as long as you pay your part."

He plucked a handful of change from his pocket. "It's all yours."

"Even that one?"

Nickel looked down, where she had pinpointed the same Knights Templar coin recovered from Ariston's withered body. "You can have it," he said. "I've figured out where Natira is."

"Is that a good thing? Or bad?"

"Good to know. Bad that he's back in the game."

"Is he here in the Northwest like you thought?"

"Nope. He vanished right after I went searching. Thankfully, the Unfallen picked up traces of his presence the next day in Frankfurt, Germany. Since then, our nineteenth revenant has hooked back up with Erota and the Collectors in Lipova. It's just what Erota's been waiting for: a chance to challenge Megiste for control of the cluster."

"Sounds like things are about to get ugly."

"As we speak, the House of Ariston is heading south to Israel."

"So let them fight it out, kill each other off. What do we care?"

"You really should read more Tolkien. Didn't we talk about this already—the principle of fellowship, sticking together, all that? It's not like it works any different for the Collectors. They're at each other's throats half the time, and believe me, that's our saving grace. But if two or three of them actually form a plan and stick to it? Uh-oh. I'd rather face off with a dozen Collectors fighting for themselves than a couple fighting for each other."

"Which brings us back to the cell phones. We need to stay in touch."

"Point taken. Got it."

"You up for a game of chess before my lunch break's completely gone?"

"I have a few more things," Nickel said, "that need to be said."

"Fire away."

"First, you need to know that Teodor is gone."

"Gone?"

Her father gave a grim nod, and Kate took it like a slap across the face.

Nickel said, "I don't know what possessed him to do it—or maybe I do—but he walked right onto the property at Totorcea Vineyards and never came back. No sign of his body. I gave an anonymous call to the regional authorities, but they've found nothing to prove a crime was committed."

"You know this as a fact? What if he got away?"

"He didn't, Kate."

"How do you know? Like you said, there's no sign of him."

"Because he was eaten."

The blood drained from her face. Her stomach lurched.

"My guess is that they buried his bones in the nearby foothills," Nickel continued. "Either way, he won't be coming back."

"No. Hold on. No, no, no. I thought Collectors tapped the veins, passed on a few thorns, and that was about it. Since when do they devour entire bodies?"

"Shabtai's the one responsible. He's been roaming through the Carpathians for the past year or two, making a habit of indwelling wolves. He's picked up their traits. He's gone vircolac."

Kate recognized the Romanian word. "That's not even funny."

"Teo didn't think so either."

"How do you know all this?"

"My travels are as much reconnaissance as recruitment. Plus, I have the help of the Unfallen. They're often hindered by our Power of Choice, but they still manage to pass on warnings and messages."

Kate thought of the white-haired woman who had revealed herself in this very park. She found a measure of comfort in that.

"Sorry," Nickel went on, "but the calm's over and it's time to wake up. While Erota, Natira, and Helene head for their confrontation at the haunt of jackals, Shabtai's on a flight west. Destination: PDX."

"He's coming here?"

"To tranquil J.C., if I had to make a guess."

CHAPTER FIFTY-ONE

Less than thirty hours later, darkness started along the coastal range, filling the vacuum left by the setting sun. As that sphere of burning gases descended into the Pacific's far edge amid sizzling bursts of orange and magenta, the darkness oozed down through the forests, over rolling foothills, and into the valley. It flanked Junction City and filled the gaps in between, dimming street lights and neon along the main thoroughfare, until inanimate buildings themselves seemed to hold their breath in fear of what was to come.

Kate said good-night prayers with Kenny, then closed the panel to his room with instructions for him to lock it down. She rolled out the throw rug and placed Gussy in a padded bed on top. A picture of domestic tranquility.

After watching the blackness complete its stranglehold on the city—was her imagination going schizoid here?—Kate closed the shades and backed away from the window.

And waited.

She heard Mr. Gustafson's car rumble down Oak Street and pull into his driveway. The clock in the kitchen *tick-tock*ed. Her stomach grumbled, wondering why she hadn't fed it dinner.

The truth was she couldn't eat. She felt sick. She'd lost two children under her watch, and lost a brother she didn't even remember.

Kenny too? Not if she could help it.

Her cell phone rang. "Dad," she said, recognizing the number.

"You got the doors locked?"

"Uh-huh."

"Kenny's in the basement?"

"I'm not dumb."

"Make sure you've got the MTPs and your dagger nearby. He's here."

She stepped back and dropped into her armchair. "Shabtai?"

"Just got the call from the arcade. I left before closing, but instructed the kids on duty to call if they spotted anything suspicious. I told them what to look for. Sounds like he came sniffing around right before ten— hunched over, looking cranky, an abnormal amount of facial hair. Yeah, I'm sure this is him."

"And I'm supposed to sit tight? Act like everything's normal?"

"For now, it'll have to work." Through the cell, Nickel's voice was steady, but Kate could imagine him patting his fingers against his cheek as he rummaged through his mind for an alternative. "Or," he said, "you could lock yourself down there with Kenny. I mean, that'd keep you both safe."

"While Shabtai breaks in and waits for us to come out? No, thanks. I'd rather do this face-to-face. *Mano a mano.*"

"Womano a werewolfo."

"Funny."

"I'm on my way over."

She closed the phone and took a sip from her necklace vial.

❧

Judean Desert, Israel

Erota's human habitation was exhausted and her head ached. Helene looked worn-out as well, yet she never complained and carried herself with quintessential grace. Natira, spearheading their march through the predawn desert, showed no signs of slowing, his stamina born from years of military discipline.

The trio of Collectors had arrived last evening on a flight into Tel Aviv. Erota did the talking at customs, turned savvy by her recent travels in Israel. From there, they hired a taxi minivan called a *sherut*—literally "chariot"—and paid the driver five hundred shekels to transport them to a drop-off spot near Susiya.

"*Todah*," Erota thanked him, handing over an extra hundred.

Money had a way muzzling suspicions and ethical concerns, as Collectors had proven countless times over the centuries. If it worked, why change it?

Now, hours later, they were crossing a corner of the Judean wilderness. This region had a venerable heritage upon which they could draw. Hadn't the Master Collector himself once used this terrain to test and tempt the Nazarene?

"If Megiste's as clever as she likes to portray, she'll be watching for us," Erota said. "This northern approach is different than the way I came last time."

"There are how many, you say?" As they forged onward, Natira slipped into battle mode. "I need particulars: numbers, locations, guard posts . . ."

"Five Collectors, that's all."

"Names."

"Barabbas, of course . . . Sizewise, he'll be your greatest threat, and I suspect he'll also be the one guarding the entrance into the cave system. Megiste . . . She's crafty. We can't let her out of our sights. Then there's Hermione, Dorotheus, and my sister, Domna."

"Geographical features?"

"Gentle slopes, if I remember correctly, my son," said Helene. "Old hillside dwellings. Ruins and eroding walls. It's an archaeological site, the town where the Man from Kerioth was born. It's sandy, with scattered rock, and little vegetation this time of year."

"Concealment will be a problem then."

"Which is the reason Erota's arranged for this nocturnal approach. It's a desolate area, so I don't believe we'll be running across any humans."

High-pitched yelps pierced the air, devolving into maniacal laughter.

"Jackals," Natira said. "I'll never forget that sound."

"Let's hope you haven't forgotten how to fight," Erota jibed. "We're counting on your leadership, Natira. You are the heir, the rightful ruler. If Megiste's conniving isn't brought to an end, your brother won't be the first victim of her renegade ways."

He muttered the name like a curse: "Megiste."

Erota was a partner in his enmity. This landscape, with its sense of biblical doom and malediction, would serve as the perfect place to empower and ensconce a new king. Yes, *"from the haunt of jackals."*

Junction City

A number of things occurred in a matter of minutes.

Kate was standing at the edge of the window, her eyes peering around the drawn curtain's hem. The yard was still swallowed by darkness, yet there was no mistaking the shock of white hair that flashed across the lawn and took up residence near the bushes along the fence.

The Unfallen? Could a lady that old really move that fast?

Kate had seen it with her own eyes, or with eyes now acclimating to things beyond the mortal sphere. Hadn't Nickel been explaining to her the effects of the Separation, as well as the possibilities that opened up when its dividing line was erased? Time and matter, volume and space, the physical senses—all dimensions to be expanded for a larger defining purpose.

When would he teach her to bridge, though?

There hadn't been enough time, he told her. He'd been waiting for her to choose the Blood from whence such power flowed.

Right now, Shabtai was coming, and Kenny—as a mortal—was still susceptible to the laws of this present reality. Kate found her old fears starting to surface, and she reminded herself of the Unfallen woman's vow: "*One day they'll be coming . . . trust me to keep watch.*"

She ventured another peek outside. No sign of the Chihuahua, which was probably a good thing, considering the foe now prowling their streets.

The next thing that happened caused her heart to stop.

A light footfall from within the house.

She hadn't heard anyone enter the premises. To do so would require the breaking of a window or door. Dagger in hand, she slipped across the living room's hardwood floor in her socks and poked her head into the lighted hall.

"Mom, I can't sleep." Kenny had scooped up a drowsy Gussy in his arms.

"What're you doing? You already took your potty run, and I told you to keep the panel closed and locked."

"Something's wrong."

"That's the point." She aimed a finger down the stairs. "Back in bed."

"Can we pray? The two of us?" He wore a forlorn look, and a faint blue glow emanated between the gaps in his dark hair. Though it faded in moments, there was no denying its significance or the gravity of her son's request.

She yielded. "Sure."

He moved into her arms and mumbled a few short sentences.

The third thing that happened was so haunting, so low and loud, that they grabbed onto each other until the howling ended. Kate nodded her head toward the basement and Kenny complied without another word. She checked that he had secured the lock, then scurried back to the front window.

"*Trust me to keep watch.*"

Kate craned her head, but the Unfallen was beyond her line of vision now. She looked the other way, and that's when she saw him.

The werewolf slunk through the shadows. He dropped to all fours, sniffed, then marked the ground with pheromones from the scent glands in his paws. Matted with silver-gray hair, he scanned the area with hungry eyes, their irises ringed in yellow.

From what Nickel had explained, this was Shabtai, a teenaged male who'd inhabited temporary lupine hosts until they began to dominate his own mammalian tendencies. As a mother, Kate found his appearance almost tragic.

Shabtai moved with the cautious confidence of his breed. Even as he skirted the moonlight on the sidewalk, a tree branch shifted overhead and allowed pale luminance to splash over his preternatural eyes. Hackles raised, he threw back his head and howled again. This time, when he lowered his chin, his hard stare locked onto Kate's position at the glass.

She jerked back, but he was already advancing on loping legs.

In the hall, Gussy snapped to attention with a low growl. The dog came rushing into the living room, pressed her nose to the door and barked.

Then, from the cover of a boxwood in the neighbor's yard, a ball of white fur shot into view. The Chihuahua was no match for the beast, yet it attacked as though twice the wolf's size, sinking tiny jaws into the hind leg. The werewolf whipped around, snarling at this nuisance. The Chihuahua tried to hang on and finally tore away a chunk of fur as it was tossed aside.

Rising into an upright position, baring his fangs, the man-child named Shabtai charged the Preston household. He rocketed into the front door, and the entire structure seemed to shift on its foundation.

Gussy went crazy, yapping at the invader.

Kate gripped her weapon. The vial was warm against her throat. She had never been so afraid or so angry, committed to protecting her child's life at all costs.

The werewolf thundered into the obstacle a second time. The force was too much, splintering the wooden frame at the lock and hinges, gouging the dead bolt inward through the wall. The entire panel crashed to the living room floor, with Gussy dashing under the sofa before it could flatten her for good.

"Get out!" Kate yelled. "You don't belong here!"

The creature dropped into a crouch, his tongue lolling as he eyed her. *"Out!"*

He showed little concern. He surveyed the room and the doorway leading into the hall, then lumbered with long strides that direction.

Kate hurled a table lamp into his path, saw the yanked cord whip across his nose, and followed it with the thrust of her body, the arching plunge of the blade. She was aware of her own strident scream, but it sounded alien and far removed. Her arm came down, the point of the dagger aimed at the wolf's chest.

He dodged back, instinct driving him into a low defensive position. Then, with teeth glimmering and nostrils flaring, he seemed to reevaluate. He rose onto two legs, his torso narrow beneath his ribbed and hairy chest, and bounded past her into the corridor. His man-claws ripped back the rug, began tearing at the seams around the floor panel.

Kate followed. She was still screaming. She swung her weapon.

He thrust her back with a paw that peeled skin in raw strips from her wrist, then returned to his chore with a vengeance. She swung again, slicing away a patch of silver hair that hovered in the hall's darkness like glowing needles. Each time she attacked, though, he held her off with clothes-tattering slashes of his claws and fangs.

The panel was coming loose.

A backspinning hind leg deflected Kate's next foray, and the dagger careened from her grasp into the wall. She darted beneath the werewolf's forearms, snatched up her weapon, then rolled clear. The creature turned her way, his weight shifting from the panel.

Behind him, the square glided open, a black mouth that retched up the small form of a child. Terror exploded through Kate's being. Her son—*no, not now, not here!*—was propped on the highest step, a metal tent peg in hand.

Before Shabtai could respond to this unexpected maneuver, Kenny plunged the MTP into the creature's planted right foot. Metal pierced fur and flesh, wood and flooring, anchoring the enemy in place. The wolf shrieked, swiveling his torso toward his assailant. Kenny left the spike to its task and dropped back beneath the closing panel even as curved claws tore the air above his head. One paw wedged into the opening, yet retreated as hydraulic compression threatened to sever it at the wrist.

In desperation, Kate retreated one step out of range of the creature's flailing arms and hauled back for an all-or-nothing launch of her dagger. If it struck home, it would incapacitate this foe in seconds, destroying the Collector within.

If not . . .

She could not consider that. For her protection, she trusted the Nazarene Blood flowing through her, yet she was too small, too weak, to confront the werewolf in close quarters. This was her only chance.

The wolf gave a rib-rattling growl and reached down to free himself, heaving on the spike in the center of his foot. Wood and metal screamed. Blood spurted from the wound. Kate took aim and waited, waited.

Shabtai rose back into full view, his yellow eyes angling her direction.

Please, God—give me accuracy, give me strength!

And that was the moment when the fourth and final thing occurred.

The sound of a shofar shook the night. Raw, throaty, and primal, it froze the werewolf in his tracks, its reverberation rattling windows and disturbing eardrums. It was a sound Kate recognized from her Jewish background—a call to war and to judgment. Rooted in the story of Abraham and Isaac, the horn was a symbol from the ram that had taken Isaac's place upon the sacrificial altar.

The shofar blew again.

Shabtai snapped at the air, eyes narrowing, ears flattening.

Kate knew now that her father was close by. Nickel had come, as he'd promised on the phone. The ram's horn was an instrument from his day-pack of tricks, small enough to tuck into a coat pocket if necessary.

The third blow erased all memory of the earlier howls.

The werewolf took two steps back on his hind legs, then made a hasty, four-legged retreat. As Kate turned, she noticed the white-haired Unfallen behind her.

"You were here?"

"The entire time, dear heart. That's my job."

Nickel came racing into the house, shofar dangling from one hand, an MTP from the other. He surveyed and interpreted the situation—the compromised front door, the shredded hall floor—then shot out into blackness, vanishing around the street corner as he gave chase.

"I'll keep an eye on Kenny," the Unfallen woman said.

Without a second thought, Kate sprang into action, following after her father and the vircolac.

Ruins of Kerioth-Hezron

From behind a boulder, Erota spotted two jackals on the opposing slope. The tawny animals were lean, with long narrow noses and black bristles along their winter pelts and tails. They glided on small paws, breezing like desert zephyrs down the slope into the forsaken town of the Betrayer.

One was dragging a carcass, or maybe only a limb. Were there any metatarsals attached?

She squinted from her downwind perch. The jackal dragged the appendage into the dusty dawn, revealing bones that protruded from torn trousers. Hmm. Looked like a two-legger had lost something.

Erota found this fitting. Hadn't the psalmist in the Hebrew Tanakh warned of a time when the wicked would be food for jackals? Now, she and the others witnessed that reality for themselves. She could guess where these body parts would end up—as added flair in Megiste's cave collage.

Beside Erota, Natira appeared unfazed. "Those jackals," he said in a gruff whisper, "are they from the House of Eros?"

"Let's watch and see," said Helene. "I have my suspicions."

Low stone walls blocked the pair of jackals from sight, then they reappeared on the other end of the ruins, where they ducked beneath a tangle of white broom bushes. A full minute passed before the heads of two women snapped up amidst the dry branches. The jackals trotted off, released from their temporary servitude to these Collectors.

"That's my sister, Domna," Erota said.

"And my sister," Helene pointed out. "Dorotheus."

"Let's see where they take the leg. It still has patches of skin on it, so the body couldn't have been all that long in the grave."

"It may've been lost in the desert," Natira said.

Domna and Dorotheus scrambled from the foliage, the lone leg held between them, and climbed to a cleft in the slope. Barabbas emerged before them, his wiry beard fuller than the last time Erota had seen him, his eyes alert beneath shaggy red brows.

Together, Domna and Dorotheus bowed before the husky man.

Together, they offered up their catch to his strong hairy arms.

"Barabbas," Natira muttered.

Serving under Megiste, the man was nothing but a rabble-rouser. He would've rotted in days of yore if it weren't for the people granting his freedom for a chance to watch the Nazarene's crucifixion.

Barabbas sniffed at the severed limb, then dismissed Domna and Dorotheus by heading back into the central cave. The women moved horizontally along the slope until they reached the entry to their own dwelling. It was possible Hermione shared the same space with them.

"I've been under that soil," Erota said. "There's a labyrinth of tunnels."

Helene raised an eyebrow. "No doubt it'll be dangerous, but I don't think they're expecting us. Vanquish Megiste, and I'm sure the rest will fall in line with us."

"Never underestimate a foe," Natira said.

"Good advice. And what was the size of the one who did this to you?" Erota's finger traced the wide scar from his collarbone to his stomach. The journey was one of ridges and valleys, ribs and compact muscle.

"Not one," he said. "Six brought me down. A seventh delivered the blow."

"Six, No, Seven . . . I sense a theme. Come along. This is your throne to claim. You are son of Ariston, offspring of Helene, our cluster's long-lost overlord. Once you've taken control, you can complete your search for the Nistarim, and we'll draw them here to serve as final artistic touches."

The keening of faraway jackals merged with the moaning wind. It was as though the wildlife and these environs were grieving the wrongs birthed in this valley.

"Final Vengeance shall be ours," Erota said. "Lead us on, my Black King."

CHAPTER
FIFTY-TWO

Junction City

This much seemed clear: the werewolf had come to find Kate and to verify Kenny's future significance. As Kate sprinted through shadowed alleys and turned onto Sixth Street, she figured that he must've isolated their location by harnessing Teodor's memories and then tracking his scent through J.C.

That scent led back to the Holly Street Apartments.

Up the stairs. To Teo's abandoned corner unit.

The beast careened along the second floor walkway with Nickel close on its tail. The MTP flew from Nickel's hand and missed by a hair, sailing off over the railing and clattering onto pavement below.

Kate churned up the steps, a few seconds behind. Her wrist bled, the claw wounds burning. Nevertheless, her bronze-handled, silver-bladed dagger was in hand, and at the base of her spine, angel wings were tattooed as a reminder of those Unfallen who had her back.

The werewolf exploded into the apartment, leaving the door cock-eyed on its hinges. Nickel weaved his way through the shower of splinters and pursued the enemy from room to room in a barrage of door slams and wall banging. Kate joined him as he cornered their enemy in the kitchen.

The beast crouched there, lips curled back to display his wicked teeth. The room smelled of urine, a wolf's form of territory-marking. Had he used this apartment for a lair last night?

A low snarl emitted from Shabtai's throat, then cracked for a second. Was that what it sounded like? A teenager whose voice was changing?

That mothering sympathy rose again in Kate's chest.

Nickel had an opposite reaction, zeroing in on the weakness. He tugged another MTP from his belt and stepped forward, his body angled sideways. The werewolf growled. He was trapped. The only way out was through one of them.

He chose Kate.

Even as Shabtai catapulted over the kitchen table at her, Nickel threw a sideswipe with his crude spike. The wolf yelped and landed on the table in a crouch. He took a retaliatory swipe at Nickel's head and nearly caught him.

This was a Collector, Kate reminded herself.

From the Field of Blood.

As those yellow eyes played to Nickel, she spun around the table and stabbed her dagger into Shabtai's throat. He shrieked in agony. She stabbed again, into the chest this time. And again. Her silver blade, bane of the vircolac, sent geysers of red shooting across the table and against the grease-spattered wall.

When she was done, she vomited once into the sink.

"Rinse that down for thirty seconds," her father said. "Then wipe your prints from the faucet handle."

"What?"

"Just do it, Kate. We've got to scram."

"Why? We can explain that we were defending ourselves."

"Come on—let's go, let's go. He's not traceable. He's Jerusalem's Undead. But try explaining that to any cop on this continent, and we'll be put in a white padded room with more than enough pills to keep us in our place."

She lost the rest of her stomach's contents. Then complied.

Sirens warbled in the distance. The banished Collector had left behind a young man's corpse, lean and sinewy, but with unkempt claws and wolfen characteristics. Using a shirt sleeve to cover his fingerprints, Nickel swiped an old steak knife from the kitchen counter and planted it in one of the werewolve's existing wounds. Even with FBI assistance, the local authorities would face an incomprehensible mess, considering there'd be no records on their John Doe.

"Atta girl," Nickel told her. "You did good. There's no reason at all you should feel guilty for killing the undead."

Ruins of Kerioth-Hezron

Barabbas was the first to see them coming. He squeezed into view and faced their encroachment, feet planted, arms hanging like stumps of wood at his sides. He was a murderer from long ago, a simpleminded man bent on performing the will of his master—whoever the master might be.

"What do you want?" he demanded. "Identify yourselves."

Erota grinned at his ignorance, but to his credit he recognized them once they drew a few strides closer.

The moment he did, he exploded forward. His arms churned and his knees pistoned him up the incline, on a collision course with Natira. His lips peeled back as though torn away by the passing wind, but in reality making way for fangs that had dropped down for attack. His eyes flared emerald green.

Natira maintained the superior elevated position. He filled his lungs with the brisk morning chill and lifted both arms with fingers curled to form huge mallets. His thick brown hair waved about his neck. His own teeth elongated in even rows, each one an ivory spike with razored edges. He was a vampiric entity as large as any Erota had seen, his size and strength a match for Hercules, Sisera, and the Collectors' offshoot called the *Nephilim*.

Erota was inspired. "*Traife*," she yelled out.

Her lord's eyes flicked her direction, slits of green with wisps of blue flame around the pupils.

"Traife!" she repeated.

He roared in understanding and accelerated toward Barabbas.

The word was Hebrew, referring to an animal that suffers pain before being killed and offered as sustenance for humans. That pain made it traife: ceremonially unclean, unkosher. And that was the favorite sort of food for Those Who Hunt.

Still advancing, Natira scooped a rock from the ground and wind-milled it at his foe. Barabbas dodged the missile, but slipped. His hands pawed at loose soil, trying to regain his offensive posture.

Natira spotted his advantage. He bellowed and vaulted over the rocks.

The two undead warriors collided in a brawling mass of fists and tear-ing teeth. Barabbas bear-hugged the bigger man and tried to contain him. They struggled, both buttressed on massive legs. The strain showed in mus-cles that snapped like ropes across their shoulders and through their arms.

With another bellow, Natira pulled his head back, then crushed it forward into the henchman's bearded face. Blood flew from the fractured nose.

They both yelled out, and Natira's right arm came loose. His gnarled pincers stabbed at his enemy's neck and grabbed hold of the Adam's apple. He squeezed and twisted.

Barabbas rocketed a knee into Natira's gut, but the giant held on.

Another knee.

Squeeze.

A knee.

Twist.

A raspy gurgle, followed by a wet, tearing sound.

Erota reveled in the sight of traife being served. The undead hench-man dropped to the earth, his throat bleeding away the last of his ingested sustenance. Standing over him, Natira held an Adam's apple between pin-kie and thumb. He let it splat onto the dirt beside Barabbas.

"Pull yourself back together when you find the strength," he told the fallen man. "The next time I see you, you'll bow your knee to me, henchman."

Erota skirted the carnage and joined Natira.

He wiped off his hands. "Where is my brother's killer?"

"Dear Megiste? Why, she's just through that opening."

"Show me."

"Come along."

The Collector Procedure Manual supported the action they were taking here, and Erota moved ahead in that knowledge. Let Megiste make threats all she wanted, her reign had been built on a foundation of deceit. Worthy material, sure, yet unable to stand before more skillful manipulations.

With Natira functioning as the Black King, Erota viewed herself as his queen, orchestrating this game. She strode across the slope to the cave opening.

"If you're here, Megiste, be warned. We're coming in."

With Natira following, she took a fearless step inside. He grunted and nearly stumbled as he squeezed his way through, skin lacerated by rough stone.

Erota swayed. Felt intoxicated.

Natira, too, showed the effects of this palatial setting. He gasped and fell to one knee with a hand across his chest.

That rich coppery scent flowed even stronger than before. It dripped from bowers of interlaced vines and sloshed through the cavern in a cloying wave. Myriad candles were lit, illuminating the pale walls of this chamber of thorns.

Megiste and the others had been busy. The Six, No, Seven scheme was larger than before, evident in every inch of the walls—a work of devious machination. The dealings so despised by the Pesky-Picky Almighty were featured in seven overlapping panels.

Severed feet, caught as they ran to evil.

Eyeballs full of arrogance and disdain.

Hands stained with blood.

And so on, and so on.

It was beauty beyond compare for Erota, a slap at the Almighty for the curse of the Separation. If they could not enjoy the physical senses in the way they'd done long ago, then why allow those same senses to be enjoyed with impunity by Earth's pitiful knuckle-draggers.

Brambles weaved in and out of the mass, a malignant infestation that bound the panels together and refused to let any go free. There was evidence of wasted lives, untapped potentials, polluted minds, and cankerous hearts.

Was any greater proof necessary? How much longer till Final Vengeance could be dealt out?

"Where is she?" Natira said at last.

There was no sign of Megiste. Fanning through the tunnels and caverns, they found resplendent lodgings and adornments, but the alabaster priestess had disappeared, perhaps alerted to their approach by desert creatures under her beck and call. It seemed she had left the House of Eros on its own.

"It doesn't matter," Erota told Natira. "By a mere whisper, you could banish her for such insolence. You are our lord now, and she can't deny your lineage."

He shook his head. "I don't want to banish her."

"What then? Is it not why we came?"

"We came," he said, "to take back the haunt of jackals. We came," he said, "to join as a cluster and advance in unified strength. From here, I will take dominion over the Concealed Ones and destroy all Those Who Resist."

"But your brother's killer?"

"And my stepson's," Helene said, entering on tapered legs.

Behind her, Domna, Dorotheus, and Hermione were a sullen yet relieved group. Haggard faces and bloodless lips hinted at a policy of self-sustaining greed on the part of Megiste the priestess.

"Have no doubt," Natira said. "I will avenge."

"Then do so now," Helene urged. "Please, son—speak the word."

He lifted his arms, hands outstretched for all five women to see. From the cave's fissure, another joined their midst. It was Barabbas, wobbling forward on hands and knees. His Adam's apple was lodged back in place, his breath producing pink bubbles from the ragged edges.

"We are Six, No, Seven," Natira proclaimed, kicking the henchman in the ribs. "We'll employ the same strategies and sup from the same souls, and the vengeance I seek will come, I assure you. I'll take it with this deformed hand. Our ultimate purpose is not so far off. With most of the Nistarim at my mercy already, we'll soon complete and drink freely from our vast Collection of Souls."

For the first time in years, the Akeldama Cluster smiled as one.

"Lord Natira," Erota said. "We'll trust and follow you as king."

"Lord Natira!" the others echoed.

Vines twisted at these words, contorting, running down along the far wall to form a tall crimson-tinged throne. Even as their ruler seated himself, a crown of jagged thorns also twined into position, coming to rest upon his undead skull.

Junction City

The following week, in her living room on Oak Street, Kate tried to take it all in. She'd survived. Her son was safe. The Unfallen had been there, guarding her comings and goings at the front door. Her father had galloped onto the scene, blowing a shofar like the cavalry in some kosher-spaghetti western.

And she'd been the one to put the creature down.

"How're you feeling?" Nickel asked.

She took a breath. "Kenny's still here, that's what matters. You should've seen how brave he was."

"You two have been compromised, though. Nah, I don't mean the cops. I'm talking about the Akeldama Collectors. They sent Shabtai to check on you, on your son, and eventually they'll realize something went wrong."

"You want us to move again? We've tried that before."

"What I want is for you to trust good ol' Dad. You may be looking at a few months of inactivity, but don't ever lower your guard. You got that?"

"Got it. So I just keep going through the motions."

"Work. School. Soccer games. Trips to Safeway. And I'd suggest you and Kenny keep poking your faces in at church."

"Church?" She shot him a look.

"It's those people you've been hanging out with, the ones you made friends with at the hardware store . . . That's church. The group of you getting together on a Thursday night. Or going to the coast for a weekend. Those Who Resist, just living out their lives together and dealing with their thorns—no masks, no pretense, none of that. All in honor of the Nazarene."

"You think Ms. N. K. Lazarescu would approve?"

"Nikki's not you. I thought you'd let go of all that."

"I still get phantom pains."

"The old root, you mean? Those thorns're dead, Kate, so don't let them sneak back. It's a decision you have to make."

"I know. Day by day by day."

"By day."

He grinned and wrapped an arm around her. She settled in against him, and they sat that way for a few minutes, detoxing from the recent events. Gussy wandered in and hopped into Nickel's lap.

Kate ruminated on her Chattanooga days, with little Jacob, and Nickel's promises that her infant son would be safe. Soon heading into 2004, she wanted assurance that a repeat disaster was not in store. "Who's going to be watching Kenny during the next few months? I need to know he's not going to be hunted down while I'm ringing up customers for caulking guns or two-by-fours."

"Don't worry," Nickel said. "Even when things look grim, he'll be safe. I'll be in the background, running Nickel's Arcade. And"—he lifted his cell—"always a phone call away. The Unfallen will be around, too, though mostly out of sight."

"Okay," she conceded. "I can live with that."

"Heck, you might even end up with a few mortals helping out."

"Regular Joe Blows, you mean."

"Men *and* women. Formed from the earth, from the clay."

"Clay? Great. Well, that sets my mind at ease."

"Hey, now, don't go mocking the lowly pawns. The best chess players will use even the little things to confound the wise." Nickel reached into his daypack and pulled out a board. "You ready for a rematch against your old man?"

With the game spread across the couch cushions, Kate opened with another Evans Gambit. The tremors in her fingers became less pronounced with each successive move. Honor . . . duty . . . combat. Like she'd been taught since she was a small girl.

"Kenny turns thirteen in March," she said, waiting for Nickel's next move. "Are you sure he'll be one of them——humble in spirit, a righteous soul?"

"Whether he gets the Letter or not, he should live like he *could* be."

"But you think he will?"

"Put it to you this way, Kate . . ." Nickel slid his queen across the board, then glanced up. "The moment you think you've reached your expiration date, think again. I have a feeling your real mothering's only just beginning."

CHAPTER
FIFTY-THREE

Early August 2004 — Junction City

Kenny Preston was thirteen and a half now. His brow bore the letter Tav.

This summer, he'd kept busy delivering newspapers, working on Gussy's doghouse, and playing games down at Nickel's Arcade. He rode his bike around town, explored the parks, the train tracks, and alleyways. Some weekends he spent out at Uncle Terry's on the McKenzie River, with water survival one of his latest acquired skills.

No big shocker, really. After six-year-old Reggie's death in the river, not to mention the white-water thrills with Dov Amit, Nickel was determined to never lose another in that manner.

Kate was proud of her son, of his hard work and teachable spirit. He was one of the Nistarim, commissioned to bear up the world's sorrow and sin.

Nevertheless, her parental worries reactivated each morning, and each night she thanked God again that Kenny was alive. She knew mortals, even regular Collectors, were blind to his translucent blue markings, yet that didn't erase her concerns that someday the undead would come hunting.

And if they did, if they saw his Letter, they'd target him for annihilation.

"That day's almost here," Nickel told her early one morning.

"What?" Kate handed him a cup of Stash tea, then joined him at the dining table. "Kenny can find enough mischief on his own."

"Sure, he's survived the more recent schemes of local Collectors—but that's a whole other story. Right now those ol' Akeldama bloodsuckers are shifting their attention back our way."

"What's that mean for us?"

"Means a new approach to the game. Erota and Natira have been gaining strength, and their haunt of jackals is becoming a pestilent nightmare."

"Oooh, fancy words. You've seen the place?"

"Just last week."

"And they let you waltz on through, no big deal?"

"Kate, really. You should know me better than that. Change of hair color, a beard, a pick, and a spade, not to mention some handy-dandy khakis and sandals . . . I showed up with a small group from the IAA, and the Collectors seemed to buy it all the way. They stayed hidden, hardly even interested."

"The IAA?"

"Israel Antiquities Authority. All in a day's work."

"You're unbelievable."

He scooted aside his mug to spread out a yellowed map on the table. Light blue lines formed a grid over rugged topography and stark Hebraic writing. Three dark-red stains smudged the map's corners, leaving one unmarred.

"What's this?"

"A bird's-eye view of the Kerioth-Hezron ruins. And these . . ." He tapped the stains. "These are drops of blood. From Erota, Megiste, and Ariston. I visited the cave near Sinaia, the depot parking lot, and, most recently, these ruins, and started bringing it all together. Try that one on the right."

Kate sneered at him. Realized he meant it. She grimaced, then dipped forward for a touch of the tongue. Moisture worked into the drop, activating scenes from within Erota's recollections. They were brutal and sensual, a barrage of images that Kate would rather skip past.

"That is disgusting." She tried to wipe the residue from her mouth, then gulped her tea in burning draughts.

"If you don't face the harsh realities, you'll never know how good the good news is. Anyway, those three drops are not the whole story. Before it's over, I'll be adding a drop of yours."

"My blood? For what?"

"To send a message," Nickel said. "To someone very special."

"Who?"

"We'll get to that later. For now, we've got to make sure you disappear off their radar completely. I figure you have that women's retreat you're coordinating for this weekend, up the McKenzie River. Not far from my place, actually."

"What about it?" Kate sipped again at her tea.

"Well, all the info's been printed. It looks good, official, nothing to question. So let's just say that you vanish for good while on your way there?"

"Seriously? That sounds ominous."

"A staged accident. Maybe a sharp curve on those mountain roads."

"Now you're scaring me."

"In the big picture, it's for your good. For all of ours."

"What if we just stop running from them, stop hiding?" She set down her mug. "I'm sick of letting Collectors dictate the way we live. Let's take the initiative and do this on our terms. Go for the jugular."

"Ahh, nice bit of irony."

"Well, why not?"

"Because there's more going on here, things we're still lining up. And this is much bigger than one kid—no disrespect to Kenny. The Nistarim, all thirty-six of them, are scattered across the globe. Five each in seven different regions, and in each region there's one who acts as a guardian, a messenger."

"Wait a sec, math whiz. Five times seven is thirty-five. Where's Number Thirty-Six?"

"I think you mean Number One. He's been here all along."

"The Nazarene?"

"First one out of the grave, and He's calling us to join him. Not just the Concealed Ones, but all Those Who Resist. What we're aiming at is the chance to help others rise from death back to life."

"Okay, you lost me again."

"Where two or three gather, that's where Yeshua's presence is strongest, right? A day is coming when bones will rise up and take on flesh. Don't you want to be a part of that, striking at the doubly dead by raising up an army of the doubly alive?"

"Uh, sure. If that's what it's going to take."

"That's the spirit. You and me, Kate—that makes two. Add Kenny to the mix—three. What if we throw in Dov, just for kicks?"

"Dov? Will I ever get to see him again?"

"Eventually. And he's not the only one."

She sat up. "Who else?"

Nickel pushed back from the table, his eyes twinkling. "You still have that postcard I gave you?"

"From Italy?" She nodded. "I've been using it as a bookmark."

"And you've never cheated? Not even a little taste to see what you'd find?"

"C'mon, Dad." She batted innocent eyes. "You know I'm a good girl."

"I know you are."

"I did think about it a few times, though."

"Well, now I'm giving you my permission. Just wait until our drive up into the mountains, and then you take another taste. I think you'll be surprised."

"In a good way, I hope."

He smiled. "Go thumbing back through the memories. I'm pretty sure you'll know what I'm talking about, once you get there."

"Okay, Mr. Cryptic."

"Sounds a little too close to *crypt*."

"Mr. Mysterious?"

"Better."

From the direction of the garage, Kate heard Kenny dragging in his bike. Done with his paper route, he'd be ready for a cup of hot chocolate to warm his hands. Even in the summer, mornings here could be chilly.

Nickel said: "Before he gets in . . . Are we on for your little accident?"

"Do I really have a choice?"

"We all have a choice, Kate. Even a toddler can decide whether to listen to Mom and Dad or to reach for that candle and get burned."

She swallowed. "I'll do it. Whatever you say, I'm with you."

Kenny popped in, waving a five-dollar bill. "Look, someone left me another tip under their doormat. Oh, hi, Uncle Terry. You're here early today."

"Yeah, your mom and I, we've got something we need to talk with you about. Grab your hot chocolate and take a seat. This is serious stuff."

CHAPTER
FIFTY-FOUR

Mid-August—Cascade Mountains

Kate Preston's car ascended the steep grade through a deluge of rain. Highway 126 followed the McKenzie River into the Cascades, a north to south bulwark of snowy peaks. All she could see were prickly blankets of evergreens that covered rugged terrain and clung to the sides of plunging chasms.

"I'm scared," she said. "I admit it."

She was alone in the Nissan's front seat, the wipers slapping back and forth in a feeble attempt to increase visibility. Maybe she didn't want to see what was coming. Maybe she'd be better off walking by faith, not by sight.

"You sure about this, Dad?" She angled the rearview mirror for a peek into the backseat. If it weren't for the gravity of this situation, she would've kidded Nickel about his scrunched position down on the floorboards.

"You want to get these Collectors off your back, don't you?"

"Of course," she said.

"We've tried identity changes, colored contacts, different names. None of those've done the trick. Well, how about letting them sift through the evidence of your death, huh?"

"How am I going to know when it's time? Can't you tell me beforehand?"

"If I did, you might turn back around."

"Ohh, that's a big encouragement."

"You still want to go through with it, don't you?"

She hesitated. Gave a slight nod.

"Then just trust and keep moving. There are other factors at work here, but I have a good idea what the Collectors are up to, and we're going to use that against them."

"Not the Akeldama Collectors, I hope."

"Nah, these ones aren't the undead sort. They're part of the Consortium, which means they won't be able to see all of what we're doing."

"And what about Kenny?" She threw a look at her father through the mirror. "You give me your word he'll be okay?"

"'You're in good hands with—'"

"Dad, enough with the old slogans. Please tell me you'll take care of him."

"I will. I'll guard him with my life."

She still had her doubts about this harebrained scheme.

"It'll work," he said, reading her expression. "Crazy as it sounds, this gives us a better chance of saving you, Kenny, and others caught up in this battle. It's time to put it all on the line. Just do it the way we practiced."

"I know I'm supposed to surrender. Let go. Let spirit and flesh work together. Whatever. This whole bridging thing, it feels awkward—like I'll spin off into a million pieces."

"Should get easier. Even with your link to the immortal realm at half-strength, you're the only one I've seen who could do this, aside from the original Nistarim. Of course, learning to go with the flow's half the fun. Remember Phillip in the Christian Bible, the way he was swept away to another town in an instant? Now *there's* some mega-bridging for you."

"What if I mess up?"

"Like you did while trying to get out of Kenny's basement?" He flashed a grin. "That doesn't count. I'd locked you in, and the moment Gussy got hold of your pant leg, she shook you out of your groove."

"Causing me to smash my head into the panel, thank you very much."

"You headbanger, you."

"As long as I'm not listening to some rocker whine about his life."

"Absolutely. We have too much to live for, huh?"

"And this, coming from the man who wants me to die." She spotted a white pickup ahead and eased on her brakes.

"I'll be right beside you," Nickel said. "Our own little fellowship."

"Thank you, Mr. Tolkien."

"And," he added in a somber tone, "if worse comes to worst, I'll have a seventy-two-hour window to revive you."

"With me having your genes and all."

"Levi's?" He smirked. "Didn't know you owned a pair."

"You, buddy boy, are so eighties. But I . . ." Her eyes misted over, or maybe that was the rain marching across the pavement and pelting the car. "I love you anyway. I want you to know that. No matter how this turns out, I'm just glad we're on the same side."

"I think your mother is too."

"Yeah? I'm beginning to believe that." Kate used her shoulder to brush a drop from her cheek. Both hands were on the Nissan's wheel, sweaty despite the chill of this summer storm.

"You have that postcard in your pocket?" Nickel double-checked.

She patted her black jacket. "Got it."

"Good. When this is all over, you do just exactly as I said."

On the right, a guardrail paralleled the cliff that fell away toward the river. The trees were dark green with moisture, the sky dark gray. A Dodge Duster was parked off the road and its driver stood outside, waving his arms.

Broken down? Out of gas? That had to stink in weather like this.

Ahead of Kate, the pickup's brake lights burned bright red before being washed out suddenly by twin stabs of white.

"Oh, no."

"Stay on your toes," Nickel told her. "This might be the opportunity I was hoping for, something dangerous and deadly looking."

A logging truck descended in the other lane, head beams slashing through the rain as it fishtailed under a load of felled trees. The weight of the Douglas firs wreaked havoc on the driver's ability to stay in his lane, and his eyes bulged at the windscreen.

Swerving to avoid a collision, the white pickup plowed into the back of the Duster at the road's edge. The waving man dove clear, while the pickup's momentum rammed the unoccupied vehicle over the rail into the gully below. Sliding to a stop, the pickup was left with one tire hanging off the edge.

"Not good," Kate mumbled. "Not good, this is not good at all."

"What now?"

She felt her father's hands pull against the headrest as he edged forward for another peek. Despite his breath tickling her hair, she was comforted by his nearness, his warmth.

But it was not over.

The logging truck jackknifed, grinding, twisting, until the cab flipped onto its side. At the same time, the trailer's chains gave way and released a rolling wave of monstrous evergreens.

"The Evergreen Game," Nickel whispered.

"What?"

"Sacrifice to win. This is it."

"Dad!" she shouted. "What am I supposed to do?"

"Trust and let go."

The logs bounded over the rain-slick pavement, a tumbling mass that would crush her car beyond recognition, then toss it down the ravine into the McKenzie. It would take days to identify the vehicle and registration, assuming the expenses would be approved for dredging it from the rapids.

She shoved on the brakes, buying one more second, maybe two.

"This is it," Nickel said. "Good-bye to the queen and the knight."

With the chopped end of a tree trunk spearing toward her wind-

shield, she did her best to relax, to let go. She closed her eyes and refused
to accept destruction, chose instead to bridge the Separation. She felt the
steering wheel lose substance beneath her grip, heard an air horn and
pounding rain and screeching metal and tinkling glass, felt a ruuussshhhhh
of cold air, then a hand brushing over hers, tasted water and ozone and
pure oxygen, watched the material r e a l m

    e-

       x-   p-

                  a-   n-

                                      d ,

        strrrr——ettttcccchhhhhhhh—— i—n—g

to its molecular limits in subservience to the passage of her head, her
body, her limbs. Spirit and flesh worked as one in this dimension, and
time was the servant here not the master.

Fully intact, Kate Preston rose from the Nissan.

Her time was not yet over.

Far from it.

Beneath her, the huge log that had speared through the front wind-
shield carried the vehicle over the cliff and hammered it down into the
ravine where both broke the river's surface in a cataclysmic baptism of
white water and froth.

Journal Entry

July 9—

Everything's changed, and I do mean everything.

Two days ago, I was sitting in that same diner by the dock, wondering what to do. I'd pulled up every memory I could from the droplets. I'd bled them dry—so to speak—and the questions still remained: Was Kate gone? Had she bridged safely? I had no way of knowing.

I ordered another refill and started thinking again about returning on the next ferry. Here it is, 2010, and all that I've seen in these bloodstains happened years ago. As for this map, maybe it's the one Cal Nichols had. Maybe not. He could've lost it or passed it on to someone else. Who knows?

Still numb, scared to move forward or back, I folded the papers into my journal and tucked them into my coat pocket. This coat's special to me, a Levi's jacket with lambskin lining, a reminder that someone's been watching out for me through the years, sending clothes, books, boxes of food. I've never been alone, not completely—that is, until I saw those logs come bouncing down the mountain into Kate's car.

I was still wrestling with emotion, refusing to believe the worst, when the bell above the diner door rang. I looked up from the booth, and there she was.

She had sunglasses on and her hair was dyed with pink through the front, but it was her. After everything she'd been through, and all I'd gone through with her in the memories, I had no doubt . . .

Gina Lazarescu.

She nodded at the cook behind the counter, then turned my way like she knew right where I was sitting. She wore a Seattle Pacific University sweatshirt with the sleeves scrunched at the elbows. The scars on her left arm were hard not to stare at. I saw others glance, then turn away. She was forty-five, I figured, but looked like a college girl. She was beautiful.

Easing into my booth, she said one word: "Jacob."

Everything changed in that moment. I've never been called that name before, but as soon as she spoke it, I knew it fit. Jacob. That was me. She touched my face, ran warm fingers over my pocked skin. I flinched, self-conscious of my own scars, but there was no revulsion in her touch. Only love.

"Mother?" My voice was hoarse.

"It's me," she said. She took my hand and set it on her arm, where gnarled skin looked translucent in places and shiny in others. "In all my imperfect glory."

"I thought you were gone."

"And I thought the same about you. Nickel says it was for our own protection, that we both had to die to really live. I'll explain how it all worked later, but right now none of that matters, Jacob. It's time."

My heart was racing. "Time for what?"

"Isn't your birthday just around the corner, little man? Thirteen years since that horrible day in Chattanooga, and here we are together again. You know what this means, don't you? It's time to go be who we were born to be."

To be continued . . .

April 2010

Book Three
Jerusalem's Undead Trilogy
Valley of Bones

ACKNOWLEDGMENTS

Amanda Bostic, Leslie Peterson, Jocelyn Bailey, and Allen Arnold (editors and publisher)— for keeping this dead dream alive by clearing its air passages and using a defibrillator when necessary.

Jennifer Deschler, Katie Bond, Micah Walker (marketing team)—for doing things I didn't think possible, getting these books into hands far and wide.

Kristen Vasgaard (cover art and design)—for working till we got it right, so that these covers would pop off the shelves.

James Holmes and Scott Phillips (friends)—for showing me that even sales-people have souls, and for prayer, food, and laughter to prove it.

Dave Robie and BigScore Productions (literary agent)—for standing by these ideas, even when others didn't believe.

Carolyn Rose Wilson (wife)—for striving to bless others through song, whether or not you receive the attention deserved . . . I am a man still in love!

Cassie and Jackie Wilson (daughters)—for game nights, movie nights, and lots of fun times together . . . Who says the Nistarim can only be boys?

Mark and DeeDee Wilson (father and wife)—for constant encouragement, online help, financial rescues, and listening ears.

Shaun and Heidi Wilson (brother and sister)—for e-mails, phone calls, and all the dreams we have of spending another week together in Puget Sound . . . Maybe we'll find out who's living on Lummi Island.

Silvia Krapiwko (researcher) and Zvi Greenhut (archaeologist) at the Israel Antiquities Authority—for that initial insight and encouragement, and for giving these wild ideas some incredible grounding.

Henk and Irene Wolthaus (friends in Germany)—for making the emergency phone calls, welcoming me into your home, praying for the sick, and feeding this hungry American . . . After thirty-five years, we're still family.

Emil Holder (shofar player)—for sharing with me the raw beauty of the ram's horn and sounding the alarm for what lies ahead.

Jake Chism, Cory Clubb, Karri Compton, CJ Darlington, Anne MacDonald, Mara McGuffy, Frank Redman, Jeremy McNabb, Calvin Moore, James Nichols, Michelle Pendergrass, Julie Porter, RelzReviewz, Susan Sleeman, Nora St. Laurent, Michelle Sutton, Brandon Vazquez, Meli Willis, and many more (bloggers/reviewers)—for words of encouragement, challenge, and grace . . . There were days I would have quit if it weren't for you!

The Council of Four, Sta Akra, Jeff Gerke at Marcher Lord Press, Tosca Lee, and my Nashville Nucleus (novelists)—for raising the bar, exploring the far reaches of creativity, and letting me tag along.

Sean "The Scandalizer" Savacool (friend and author)—for Olde World fun, plot ideas, and dreaming out loud . . . Congrats on finishing a book of your own!

Rick Moore (friend and author)—for getting the word out and for pressing forward in the pursuit of godly dreams and marriage.

Tom Hilpert (friend and author)—for reminding me, through word and deed, that fellowship is a glue to hold us all together.

As I Lay Dying, Brian "Head" Welch, Chevelle, Coldplay, Demon Hunter, Eastern Block, Killswitch Engage, Evanescence, Plumb, P.O.D., Poorly Built Parachute, Red, Resurrection Band, and Underoath (rock bands, young and old)—for helping me tune out distractions while drumming along on my keyboard.

Readers everywhere (young and old)—for taking this journey with me from the grave to new life . . . The Nazarene Blood will prevail!

And last, to the Nazarene (Savior and friend)—You alone bring healing, and Your mercies are new every day. Without You I am lost.

If you'd like to delve deeper into stories related to the Jerusalem's Undead Trilogy, read Eric Wilson's *Dark to Mortal Eyes* and *Expiration Date*. Although they are not Undead novels, supernatural elements do intersect the two series, with certain characters and settings trading places. Have fun discovering the secrets between the pages. There's more to come!

I welcome your feedback online:

www.JerusalemsUndead.com * JerusalemsUndead@hotmail.com
www.myspace.com/JerusalemsUndead
www.erics-undead-fans.webs.com

READING GROUP GUIDE

1. A new über-Collector is revealed in the prologue. What made his presence menacing? Was it believable? Did you remember that his father, Lord Ariston, had wondered about this missing son in the early chapters of *Field of Blood*?

2. Did you agree with Gina's early decision to lead the Collectors away from Cal and Dov? What did you think about her interaction with the abused Romanian wife? And later, her confrontation with the husband?

3. Cal tries to mentor Dov even as they are on the run. Which of their interactions did you enjoy? In what ways did you see Dov begin to wrestle with his own insecurities and past?

4. Castle Bran is a real place in Romania, as are all locations throughout this series. Was there any foreshadowing in the fact that Gina and Teo met in such a place? As Gina struggles with her feelings for men in her life, did you favor one more than the others?

5. As the story progresses, did you begin to suspect the identity of the anonymous journaler? Did you find this part of the plot a distraction, or did you find it worthwhile once the truth was revealed?

6. The Collectors have specific goals: to feed, breed, persuade, and pos-

sess. How did they pursue these goals at the Haunt of Jackals? What were your thoughts about the collage of Six, No Seven Things within the caverns?

7. Cal Nichols reveals his connections to Gina in a Bucharest cafe. Did you find Gina's reactions believable? Why do you think she still hesitated to drink the Nazarene Blood?

8. Natira traverses the globe, on the prowl for the Concealed Ones. Were the snippets of him doing so effective in raising the stakes? Did they make the story seem smaller or larger in scope?

9. Gina and her adopted son take on new names and live in relative safety for a time. Did you find the name change confusing? If you've read Eric's earlier book, *Expiration Date*, did you make the connections between the two stories and series?

10. A Rasputin prophecy begins drawing Erota and Natira together again. Did you enjoy this historical element? Did you like the additional explanation of the true-to-life D.B. Cooper mystery? Had you heard of it before reading this story?

11. Teo takes steps to be with Gina, but not all turns out as he plans. How did you feel about his final scene? Would you have liked it better if things turned out differently?

12. When Gina and Kenny face the werewolf, the vircolac, in what ways do they show us how they've changed? Did you think their joint acceptance of Nazarene Blood fit their characters?

If you started with *Haunt of Jackals*
. . . you only know part of the story.

FIELD OF BLOOD

JERUSALEM'S UNDEAD TRILOGY

ERIC WILSON

BOOK ONE IN THE
JERUSALEM'S UNDEAD TRILOGY

THOMAS NELSON
Since 1798